1906 – NOVEMBER

Eric R Davidson

Published by Edge60

Yet again I have tried my utmost to be historically accurate, both in the geography of Aberdeen and also the speech and conduct of my characters, during the writing of this book.

My thanks, therefore, to my wife, Heather and son, Andrew, for their patient reading of the manuscript, their correction of my mistakes and their suggestions for improving the speech and conduct of my characters on the occasions where I drifted back in to 2014. Having said that, however, should you as the reader now pick up on something that we have missed I would be obliged if you would simply accept that this is a work of fiction and was never meant to be a definitive history of Aberdeen.

My thanks also to my son, Adam, for providing the original idea for the covers of all three books.

I continue to be indebted to the content of *The Diced Cap*, which provided a detailed history of Aberdeen City Police and I would also like to thank Alan Rennie, the Archivist at His Majesty's Theatre, for his time and assistance in providing me with some of the detail regarding the opening of the theatre. I also found *One Hundred Years of Glorious Damnation* by *Edi Swan* invaluable in providing background information about His Majesty's Theatre.

Finally I also must acknowledge the background information, regarding the politics of Aberdeen, which I found in *ABERDEEN 1800 – 2000, A New History*

One final point that may be of help to anyone reading this book; £1 in 1906 is equivalent to £100 today.

**MYS
Pbk**

Eric R Davidson

Aberdeen – November 2014

About The Author

Eric R Davidson spent most of his working life in the Civil Service before having a second career with Grampian Police in Aberdeen. His role with Grampian Police came to an end in 2013, which allowed Eric to concentrate on his main passion, which was writing. The outcome of having more time to concentrate on his writing has led to the 1906 trilogy of books being written

Eric has also written two books about *Military Intelligence (London)*, or *MILO* for short. These are set in the 1970s and follow the actions of a fictional section of Military Intelligence, created essentially to monitor Germany and ensure that another Adolf Hitler does not rise from the ashes of World War Two.

Eric's other main passion is Crystal Palace Football Club. During the football season Saturday afternoons are a time of concern until the final results are known.

Other books by Eric R Davidson

1906 – September

1906 – October

1908 - Summer

MILO – The Varga File

MILO – The Assassin File

Inspector Fraser's First Case (A Short Story)

===

ONE

<u>Thursday 01 November – Morning through to mid afternoon</u>

Doctor Symon, Acting Police Surgeon for Aberdeen City Police, had been kept busy throughout the months of September and October and as November got underway it seemed that his skills would continue to be needed as his mortuary found space for two more bodies of men who had died at the hand of others.

The mortuary was set at the back of the parade ground, which was located to the rear of the police office in Lodge Walk. Currently in Doctor Symon's mortuary were the bodies of George Cathcart, who had been found dead in a close off of the Guestrow and Guy Le Fondre, who had been battered to death on the doorstep of his own house on the last day of October.

Guy Le Fondre was lying on the slab in front of Doctor Symon, his body naked apart from a towel draped across the lower half of his torso. Standing across from Doctor Symon were Inspector Sandy Wilson and Inspector Jake Fraser. Sandy had been given responsibility for the investigation in to Cathcart's death and Jake was the officer in charge of the Guy Le Fondre inquiry.

The two police officers were trying not to look down at the dead body too often for the condition of Le Fondre's head did not make pleasant viewing. One side of his skull had been depressed with the impact of a large stone, or some other heavy object and blood had firstly poured and then congealed from and around the wound. What had once been a handsome face was now a bloody mess.

"Your thoughts on what may have happened to Mr Le Fondre?" Jake then said to the Doctor.

Doctor Symon looked down at some notes he had in front of him. "As you would have expected from the visual signs, Mr Le Fondre was killed with two blows to the head. The first blow was to the left side of the head so I'm assuming it was delivered by a right-handed person. From the position of the wound it seems safe to say that Mr Le Fondre was facing his killer when the blow was struck. The second blow was to the back of the head, no doubt delivered after he had slumped to the ground. The second blow was the killer's way of ensuring the job was done properly as I'm sure Le Fondre would have been dead after the first blow. By the amount of blood lying around the corpse it is also safe to say that he died where he was found. He still had his wallet and contents so I'm guessing that robbery wasn't the motive."

Jake thought for a moment.

"So Le Fondre gets home late. He presumably took a cab so a little time has to elapse while he gets out of the cab and makes his way up to the front door. The killer must have been waiting for him. The killer says something, Le Fondre turns around and then the first deadly blow is delivered."

"Sounds perfectly plausible," added Sandy Wilson. "Does it mean that Le Fondre knew his killer or was he just responding to a noise he heard behind him?"

"Good question, Sandy and certainly it would be good to know the answer to that sooner rather than later." Jake then turned to Doctor Symon, "Do we have anything more on Cathcart?"

"He died from one knife wound to the chest. The knife had a long and wide blade and I have already suggested to Inspector Wilson that I believe Cathcart was killed somewhere other than where he was found on the Guestrow. The knife is more the shape of something you would find in a kitchen and there just wasn't enough blood at the location of the body for him to have been killed there."

"And then there's the button," added Sandy Wilson, producing a button from his pocket as he spoke.

Jake took the button and looked at it. "Where was this found?"

"Clutched in Mr Cathcart's tightly clenched fist."

Jake studied the button closer. It was definitely from a woman's garment and from the jagged threads attached it was also obvious that the button had been torn off of an item of clothing rather being knocked off by accident.

"It's clearly a woman's button," added Jake. "So are we to assume that he may well have been in the process of attacking some poor woman when he was killed?"

"That is the working theory," agreed Sandy. "I'm guessing he attacked this woman, perhaps in a house nearby and either her husband or her pimp came to her rescue."

"He was stabbed in the chest so it's conceivable it could have been the woman herself who killed him?" added Jake.

"I had already thought of that but it seemed strange that she would not simply report what had happened as it would clearly be seen as self-defence. There had to be some reason why she didn't do that and we came to the conclusion that she might have elected to remain silent were someone else involved."

"Someone else whose identity needed protecting?" added Jake.

"It makes sense," said Sandy.

"And there is also the little matter of no woman that I know being able to carry a man of the size of Cathcart for any distance," Symon added. "I'm assuming that the crime was not actually committed in the Guestrow or there seems no way that the body would have then been left there."

"That being the case," added Sandy, "someone had to have carried the body for at least the length of the Guestrow."

"Which ought not to have gone unnoticed," said Jake.

"And yet it did," added Sandy." We've had officers asking all over town for information concerning that night and apart from one or two, rather vague references, to two drunks we've heard nothing."

"I suppose the first question we need to ask ourselves Is are these murders linked, in other words did the same person commit both crimes, perhaps by way of clearing up some loose ends?"

"I think a woman committed the first crime," Doctor Symon said, "but from the severity of the blows I'd suggest a man killed Le Fondre."

"Or just a very angry woman," added Jake and Symon had to concede that that could well be the case.

"So what do we know about these two men?" Sandy Wilson then said.

"We know that Cathcart worked for Le Fondre and that both men seem to have had something to do with the murder of Constable Thomson. We also know, not surprisingly, that Le Fondre was a Member of the Business Club and that, no doubt, there are others at that Club who have been working with, or for, him."

"We always seem to end up back at the Business Club, don't we?" said Sandy Wilson.

"It certainly plays a prominent part in many of the cases we have on the go at the moment," agreed Jake.

The Business Club was situated in Bon Accord Square and was run, at least as November started, by Joe Tredwall and his brother Cecil. However, Cecil had recently been charged with double murder and was now awaiting trial and sentencing whilst his brother Joe had decided to sell the Club as he now felt it had been bought, in the first place, with tainted money.

Jake had been keen to speak to the Members of the Club for weeks but knew that they were protected by a wall of silence that seemed to surround the place like a comforting blanket. Breaking through that silence was never going to be easy especially as so many of the Members were prominent people in the local community with power and influence over others.

However, with the fact that he could now directly tie Guy Le Fondre to the Club Jake now hoped that he might get that access he so sorely wanted. There was much to be learned about Guy Le Fondre and George Cathcart and Jake was firmly of the belief that much of what he needed to know lay behind the heavy doors of the Business Club.

Jake thanked Sandy and Doctor Symon for their time and then made his way back to his office. There was much still to be done as the new month of November got underway and he was keen to get started.

***

As Jake sat in his office Constable Henry Davis was preparing to leave home. He, his wife Bella and their two sons were currently living in a flat on the Shiprow though they were due to move to another police house in Urquhart Road as soon as the present occupant moved out. However, moving house was not the thought uppermost in the mind of either Henry or Bella.

It had been here, some nine days ago, that Bella had killed George Cathcart as he had tried to attack her in the kitchen. She had grabbed a knife lying nearby and held it out just as Cathcart had lunged at her. Henry had cleared up both the mess of blood and the body, taking it round to the Guestrow. With every day that had passed since that fateful night the young couple began to think that they might just get away with the crime.

Henry had then used the death of Cathcart to move his way up the chain of command amongst those working for Guy Le Fondre. Henry had occasionally provided Le Fondre with items of interest from the police investigations in return for a healthy retainer. Davis had taken over from Constable Alexander Thomson who had been murdered earlier in the year after he had ceased to be of use to Le Fondre and his associates.

Everything had been going so well for Henry that he had found it hard to believe what his ears were hearing as his shift the evening before had been coming to an end.

Henry had heard colleagues talking about a murder in Kings Gate. At first he had thought nothing more about it until the name Le Fondre was mentioned. At that point he paid very close attention to what was said, even though there was little for anyone to discuss at such an early stage of an investigation. Henry knew there could be no other Le Fondre in Aberdeen but he also knew that Le Fondre's death would mean serious problems for a select group of people connected to Le Fondre and his money.

Unfortunately for Henry Davis he did not know anyone of importance connected to Le Fondre who might be of help to tell him what the future might hold. He desperately wanted to find out if the money he had been getting paid would still be forthcoming or whether he would have to return to receiving only his police pay.

As he kissed his pretty wife goodbye and made his way out of the house Henry hoped that there was some kind of back-up plan following Le Fondre's death and that someone would contact him in due course. He had grown accustomed, in a very short space of time, to the extra money and he so wanted to provide a good life for his wife and children which would go way beyond the income of a police officer.

***

Scott Thane had had a busy last day of October. He had been visited in the early afternoon by Mr Gladstone, Guy Le Fondre's butler who had brought both the news of his employer's death and the box he had been instructed to take to Thane in the event of that death occurring. Guy Le Fondre had always known he was not the most popular person in Aberdeen and had prepared for the eventuality of his death some time ago.

Le Fondre had kept papers of interest, details of his business interests and some spending money in that box, which he had kept in a wardrobe in his bedroom. He had always been aware of the fact that he had taken the lead in those business matters that were less savoury and that, if Scott Thane was to now have to take over, there would need to be some form of information transfer. Le Fondre trusted Mr Gladstone to carry out his instructions in the event of his death.

Mr Gladstone had not let him down, nor had he tried to open the box that had been locked using a giant blob of sealing wax.

Thane had sat down, after Mr Gladstone had left and started to look through the contents of the box. Amongst the information provided were brief details of what would be in Le Fondre's will. Thane was pleased to see that the will made no mention of matters non-domestic and that anything to do with the business existed nowhere other than in the box that Mr Gladstone had delivered.

Thane removed the money from the box but realised at once that it in no way covered the total money that he knew Le Fondre kept at home. Le Fondre had never made it a secret that he kept money in other places and Thane could only now assume that that cash would, in some way, find a route to Harriett. The will had made it clear that she would be the main beneficiary so all that time she had spent intimately washing Le Fondre had certainly paid off for that young woman though Thane did not grudge her the inheritance as clearly Guy Le Fondre had cared for her a great deal.

Thane now knew that he would have to fully takeover the running of the film company, which he and Le Fondre had set up to make films with an explicit sexual content. He also knew that it now fell to him to keep control of any other, slightly unsavoury activities that Le Fondre may have been involved in. He had now been provided with enough information to at least keep things running in the short term.

He set aside the details of Le Fondre's other money-making schemes with a view to looking at them later and deciding which of them, if any, he would continue to run. Thane assumed there would others in Aberdeen prepared to pay him some money to take over what Le Fondre had been doing.

It was certainly clear, from the contents of the box that Le Fondre was in to far more in the way of illegal activities than Scott Thane had ever known about. Given that the police were already likely to be showing an unhealthy interest in what Thane might be doing over the coming weeks it made no sense to be connected to other matters that might further interest the police.

If Scott Thane was honest with himself then he had not been entirely surprised to hear of his partner's demise; Le Fondre had always swam in murkier waters and it now appeared to Thane that things might actually be better with Le Fondre out of the picture. He would be able to shape and build the company his way and that would start by off-loading those less savoury activities that may have given Le Fondre some perverse sense of pleasure but which Thane saw as no more than a lengthier prison sentence were he ever caught.

Thane also felt some relief that Cathcart was not still alive as he would have been impossible to work with. The man had been nothing short of an animal and again, Thane felt the world was a better place without him. At least Ben Aspinall, who had effectively replaced Cathcart, was a man who treated Thane as the employer he was and did not seem to be seeking any personal gain for himself.

Thane had spent the rest of the day contacting people who needed to know that the chain of command had changed. Le Fondre had provided contact details for all the people he regularly worked with, though only a handful of them needed to be contacted with any urgency. By the end of the day the only person Thane had not contacted was Henry Davis; he would leave that little job for Aspinall, whom he had contacted first and met with in the Club Bar on Market Street.

It mattered little to Aspinall who paid him and provided him with his instructions. He had been employed recently by Le Fondre. Aspinall had had little time to make any impression on the business being run by Le Fondre and Thane but now looked forward to working with Thane alone as they continued to bring in more money than either man could ever spend in a normal lifetime.

Thane had also contacted Harriet. Le Fondre had provided her address within the information that had come with the will and Thane had gone there as soon as he had put out the word that he wanted to meet with Aspinall. Thane had told Harriet what had happened and she appeared suitably distraught at hearing the news of Le Fondre's death. However, her demeanour changed the moment that Thane informed her of her part in Le Fondre's will. She no longer hid behind her handkerchief and Thane had got the impression that he might not have been bringing her news after all.

Perhaps Guy had already told her that he intended leaving her a wealthy woman were he to die? Either way, Thane was not interested in Harriet Cruickshank or the future she might now carve out for herself. Scott Thane had more pressing matters to deal with so he had bade Harriet farewell and left her to grieve.

The last thing Thane felt he needed to do was to contact Willie Ifield. He decided he would do that in person and that it would wait until the first day of November. Thus, as the clouds gathered overhead and the first of the day's rain started to fall, Scott Thane made his way in to the building on Poynernook Road from where Willie Ifield ran his business.

There had been a piece in the morning paper about Le Fondre's murder so Thane now knew that he could talk openly about Le Fondre's death, as it was in the public domain.

Thane told the man at the reception point who he was and that he was there on a matter of business concerning Guy Le Fondre. The man recognised the name so he asked Thane to have a seat while he went upstairs to check with Miss Sangster if Mr Ifield was free to see visitors.

Miss Sangster thought it rather strange that Scott Thane should be there to see Mr Ifield. He had said that it was *about* Guy Le Fondre. She wondered, for a moment, what that might mean. Had Le Fondre finally done something that might put his partnership with Mr Ifield in jeopardy? She went through and told Mr Ifield that Thane was in reception and was he happy to see him. Willie Ifield said that he was and Miss Sangster went downstairs. She found Scott Thane sitting by the reception point.

"This is a surprise, Mr Thane," Miss Sangster said.

Thane stood up and smiled at the extremely attractive Miss Sangster. "I have some news for Mr Ifield concerning Guy."

"In that case you had better come this way," Miss Sangster then said and led the way upstairs.

Moments later Thane was sitting in Willie Ifield's office. Ifield was a small, balding man with a well-groomed moustache and beard that seemed to emphasise the pointed nature of his chin. Due to his lack of height, Willie Ifield was in the habit of wearing especially made, built up shoes to try and add a few much needed inches, however those shoes did not help him in the slightest as he sat behind his desk. There was something strangely comical about this little man sitting behind such a huge desk.

Thane did not waste any time in getting to the point.

"Have you read this morning's paper?"

"If you mean by that, do I know that Le Fondre is dead?" Ifield said, "Then the answer is yes."

Thane could instantly tell that the news of Le Fondre's demise had obviously not bothered Ifield in the slightest. He sat at his desk looking unconcerned by anything. He was a man accustomed to adapting to any circumstances; a man who went in whatever direction the wind might take him.

Thane spoke again. "Guy's death has meant a little restructuring of the business, but I believe that I have taken over the reins without the horse realising there has been a change of rider."

Willie Ifield sat forward. "I'm very pleased to hear that, Mr Thane. To be honest I do not believe that the demise of Mr Le Fondre is entirely bad news; he was something of a loose cannon, not to mention one of the most obnoxious men that I have met in a very long time."

Thane reacted with some horror. "The man was murdered, Mr Ifield and nothing in his character, however black, should have led to that."

"I did not mean to sound cold-hearted about what has happened," Ifield then said, "my comment about it not being entirely bad news was meant to be at a business level only. I firmly believe that with your financial acumen and my ability to get the best out of every business I have ever become involved with, that we will enjoy a very successful partnership and one, I might add, that might be able to function without the law being on our backs every five minutes. I do not believe that Mr Le Fondre would have been quite as careful as you and I will be."

"I agree that Guy cared little for the consequences of his actions but he still had a great mind when it came to making money. We may yet come to miss that."

"Perhaps," Ifield added.

Scott Thane then paused for a moment, his eyes studying Willie Ifield that little bit closer. He eventually spoke again.

"Not that you'd be likely to tell me but did you have something to do with Guy's death?"

The question was delivered in a flat, unemotional tone and for a moment Ifield was so taken aback by it that he took a few seconds to respond.

"Why ever would you think that?"

"I really don't know, but you do have a reputation, Mr Ifield."

Willie Ifield laughed. "Ah, yes, the dreaded reputation. Mr Thane I do not, as you seem to think, go around killing people, especially people who might turn out to be of some use to me. Surely, however, even you would admit that Mr Le Fondre would not have been short of enemies, he was a thoroughly unpleasant man who created a new enemy practically every time he opened his mouth. He seemed to revel in upsetting other people and I feel sure that there was an ever growing list of people who would cheerfully have murdered him and not been too concerned about the consequences."

"Well, irrespective of who actually killed him; he's dead now and we have to move forward," Thane then said.

"And move forward we shall," Ifield agreed," only, perhaps, not in the same way as had been planned."

Ifield sat back in his chair, mildly amused by the look of concern that had now crossed Scott Thane's face.

"You're not pulling out of our partnership are you?"

Ifield smiled. "Of course I'm not pulling out but I am, however, going to take a step back from things, starting with the fact that I shall not be at the launch tomorrow; you will have to deal with that entirely on your own."

"I had already thought of that, "Thane then said, "and decided that a big launch of the business would seem imprudent now that Guy is no longer here to deal with the more unpleasant questions that might come our way from the police. I have decided, instead, to start the business operating and to have some kind of Press event once we have proved ourselves to be the success that I know we will be."

"A very wise decision, Mr Thane. Certainly for the moment I would ask that you keep my name out of any conversations that you may eventually have with the police. They have the same low opinion of me that you obviously have and it would only complicate matters."

"Does that mean you'd rather I didn't contact you again after today until the police have concluded their investigation in to Guy's death?"

"I would certainly maintain a sensible distance for a week or so until we see in which direction that particular investigation goes," Ifield agreed.

"Am I correct in thinking that Daniel has an interest in buying the Business Club?" Thane then enquired.

"He does indeed have notions of taking over the Business Club and I may see fit to invest in that as well in due course. Unfortunately my son also appears to have his head full of some rather hopeful ideas concerning my assistant, Miss Sangster."

"She is a very beautiful woman; he could do a lot worse," Thane added.

"Oh, indeed she is a very beautiful woman, but far too good for my son. Daniel sees every woman he meets as being his wife one day. He doesn't seem to be able to differentiate between likely and unlikely candidates when deciding on who might make a good wife for him."

Thane noted a hint of jealousy in Ifield's tone. No doubt he was regretting his age and the fact he was already married, both of which would have stood in the way of him making any impression on Miss Sangster himself.

"So we are agreed that we start work on the films next week, as planned and basically wait and see what happens with the police investigation in to Guy's death?" Thane now said.

"That would seem to be the best approach. What happened out at that farm with the kidnapped women was nothing short of sickening, Mr Thane and the more we can distance ourselves from that the better."

Thane sat forward with a look of concern etched on his face. "I knew nothing about that until it had been stopped. That was all Guy's doing."

"But he is no longer here to admit to his part in the kidnap and killing of innocent women and I do not believe that the police will necessarily accept your word when you say you knew nothing about it. After all, Mr Thane, you will have an awful lot of lies tied up in any answers you may one day give the police."

"Guy assured me that all traces of those women will be long gone by now, so hopefully nothing will ever give us away. None of the film employees would have been aware of what was happening; the women simply came and went as far as they were concerned. Cathcart is dead and any hired muscle whom he might have used would have been well paid to keep their mouths shut."

"Maybe so, but there is still potential for all that to come back to haunt us someday," Ifield added.

Thane briefly gave some thought to his dead partner. It had taken Le Fondre long enough to tell him about the need to kidnap and kill women so that they could be used in the sex films; what other unsavoury activities might he and his cohort, Cathcart, have been involved in and would any of that come back to haunt them as well?

Thane eventually spoke again. "We have to hope, Mr Ifield that neither of us gets drawn in to the mire created by Guy Le Fondre. Somehow, if anything regarding the murders of those women does come to light, then I will just have to deal with it and of course I will make it abundantly clear that you had nothing to do with anything that may have occurred before you agreed to be our partner."

Ifield smiled. "You can tell the police anything you like, Mr Thane, but if the police believe that they can link me to a multiple murder then I feel sure they will do just that. They have been trying to blame me for every major crime carried out in Aberdeen over the last twenty years. Somehow, I can't see them stopping now."

Thane stood up.

"Well. Mr Ifield, I won't keep you away from more pressing matters. If your son does buy the Business Club I look forward to seeing him there on a regular basis. Perhaps he could become a go-between should we have any relevant information to pass to each other?"

"That would be a sensible idea," Ifield agreed. He stood up and offered a hand to Thane. "Here's hoping that by the next time that we meet properly we will both be making a lot of money from the films that you will start making next week."

"One thing," Thane said as he paused just short of leaving the room. "You had said when you visited the farm that you might be able to arrange for us to show our films at the Palace Theatre. Would that still be the case?"

"I shouldn't think I'll have any problems persuading the people there to include your films in their programmes. That is assuming that your films are of a good enough quality."

"Mr Ifield there is little point in launching a film-making business if we are to make films of a sub-standard content. I have put a lot of money in to employing the right people and I do not intend messing it up now."

"Excellent. Well, good luck again, Scott. Could you ask Miss Sangster to come in once she has seen you out of the building?"

By the time Scott Thane reached the door of Ifield's office the man himself was already busy reading some papers that had been lying on his desk. It seemed that nothing was ever allowed to get in the way of Willie Ifield and his business.

***

Five minutes later Miss Sangster was sitting across from Willie Ifield with her notebook perched on her lap and her pencil ready to start taking dictated letters. They were just about to begin when the door opened and Daniel came in. He was carrying a copy of the morning paper.

"Have you seen the piece in the paper about Le Fondre?" he said.

"I've just had Thane in my office discussing how best to proceed now that Le Fondre is no longer with us."

"Has something happened to Mr Le Fondre?" Miss Sangster then asked.

"He's been murdered," Daniel said, sitting down on the chair beside Miss Sangster.

"How awful," said Miss Sangster.

"It was just Tuesday evening that I saw him last as well," Daniel said with a tone of disbelief.

Willie Ifield looked surprised. "Where were you on Tuesday that led to you seeing Le Fondre?"

Daniel paused for a moment as if deciding how best to answer the question. The silence was clearly annoying his father and he even managed to make matters worse by glancing across at Miss Sangster in what was nothing short of a conspiratorial look. Willie Ifield picked up on it immediately.

"Is there something you want to tell me, Daniel?"

Daniel Ifield gave himself another few seconds before responding. He eventually turned to Miss Sangster and asked her to leave the room for a little while. She did so immediately. Daniel took a few seconds more before eventually providing his father with an explanation of what he had been doing on Tuesday evening.

"Joe Tredwall invited me to go to the Club on Tuesday evening and enjoy some of the facilities there. As I was to be having an early evening dinner I asked Miss Sangster if she would like to join me and to my extreme delight she said yes."

"So you were both at the Business Club on Tuesday evening?" Willie Ifield then said.

"We were."

"And you met Le Fondre?"

"Well we didn't exactly meet him. We all left the dining room at the same time and he seemed upset and annoyed with something. Anyway, he said some rather unnecessary and unpleasant things to me and then went off with his lady friend to another part of the building."

"I wish you hadn't been there, Daniel."

"But why, father, we were only having dinner."

"You may have been there for a perfectly innocent reason but in being there you will have invited the police to come asking us questions about the Club and God knows what else."

"But there is no connection, at least nothing sinister," Daniel insisted.

"The local police don't need much to come knocking at our doors. You saw what that Jake Fraser was like when he was here trying to link us to the sex films and the missing women. They see us as the answer to everything."

"But if the police do come asking questions I have no problem with telling them that I intend buying the Business Club and that was why I was there; simply seeing for myself the kind of services provided. I'm sure Joe will be happy to speak to the police as well."

"But if you were seen having words with Le Fondre then that clearly implies some connection between you, doesn't it?" Willie said, his face set in an expression of extreme annoyance.

"I hadn't thought of that," added Daniel.

"That's your problem, Daniel, you never stop to think about anything, unless it is dressed in a skirt."

"That's a bit harsh, father."

"Is it? Good God Daniel, do you even begin to realise how disappointing it is to have a son who seems lacking in the brain department?"

"Sorry," was all that Daniel could say.

"Honestly, Daniel, I think you had better be prepared for a visit from the police sooner rather than later. I feel sure that someone is bound to tell them that you were seen having words with Le Fondre on the night he was killed. You know yourself how those Members like to stir the dirt on others whilst all the time enjoying the fact they live behind a wall of silence when it comes to the police."

"I'll get something prepared in my mind," Daniel agreed, then changed the subject in the hope that it might at least slightly diminish his father's wrath. "Can we now talk about the purchase of the Business Club?"

"When are you next meeting with Tredwall?" Willie asked.

"On Saturday. We're to discuss business over dinner."

"And will Miss Sangster be invited to that as well?" Ifield asked rather sarcastically.

"Of course not. Saturday is about business not pleasure."

"Very well, you have your meeting and hear what Tredwall has to say by way of the price he is expecting for the sale. I am happy to let you buy the place as long as the price is right and as long as you agree to clean up that particular establishment's image. I believe that the Tredwall brothers really didn't care what went on behind that front door. However, I won't have the Ifield name attached to anything that is so obviously underhand and potentially illegal. I've said it before, Daniel, I will not give the police any excuse to camp out at my front door pestering me with questions that I'd rather not have to answer."

"Don't worry, father, I will make sure that the Membership is only made up of gentlemen whom we can trust to maintain a solid and upstanding public image. The less acceptable kind, like the Le Fondre's of this world, will find that their application for continuing membership will flounder on the rocks."

"Excellent. You can see me on Monday and let me know what Tredwall wants for the sale of his business, but before you deal with any of that there is the little matter of putting a stop to the flow of women coming from Scandinavia to be in the sex films. It will be some time before Thane can start making those type of films again so there will be no need for the women. Get in touch with all relevant parties and put a stop on everything until we feel it's safe to start up again."

"I'll deal with that right away," added Daniel.

"And good luck with your meeting on Saturday. I doubt if I will see you tomorrow as I intend taking your mother out for the day and won't be in the office."

"Very good, I'll see you on Monday," Daniel said and hurried out of the room before he said, or did, anything further to annoy his father. Before returning to his own office he stopped off at Miss Sangster's desk.

"What did your father say about Tuesday evening?" she asked.

"He wasn't very happy that we were there are at all even though he knows it was for business reasons only. I can see his point, however, as the police will be delighted to find out that an Ifield could, in anyway, be connected to Guy Le Fondre."

"Are you still going ahead with the purchase of the Business Club?" Miss Sangster then asked.

"As long as I can get it at the right price," Daniel said.

"I'm sure you will," Miss Sangster concluded with a smile and then returned her attention to the work that was lying on her desk.

Daniel looked down at Miss Sangster and he wondered if he might not already have fallen in love with her. Perhaps a day might come when he would allow himself to make his feelings known to her but, for the moment, there were other plans to be made and other roads to go down. For the moment Miss Sangster would have to remain out of reach and for the moment he had other matters to attend to.

Daniel moved away from Miss Sangster's desk and walked along the corridor to his own office. For the first time in a long, long time he was actually beginning to feel happy with life and he was slowly filling with a new found confidence for the future. A future that would allow Daniel Ifield to show the world that he was not the idiot that his father seemed to think that he was.

***

At a little after one o'clock Jake got off the tram at Queen's Cross and made his way down to Stanley Street where he intended visiting Johnnie Gordon and Alice Mitchell. Johnnie had become known to Jake when he had reported the murder of another Business Club Member. Johnnie had then agreed to pass on to Jake any snippets of information that he may have heard at the Club. To assist Johnnie in this matter Jake's friend, Alice, had suggested that her presence might detract attention away from them effectively spying on the Members of the Business Club. Jake had not liked the idea but he had gone along with it in the absence of any other plan.

Jake was now hoping that Johnnie could tell him something about Guy Le Fondre that would help with the investigation. He was also keen to see Alice again. Alice had once been a prostitute but Jake had made it possible for her to walk away from that life and she was now trying to create a proper life for herself. As Johnnie was now supposed to be the man in her life she had moved in with him in his Stanley Street property. It had all been above board and was purely part of their cover story whilst they attended the Club.

Jake arrived at the front door of Johnnie's home. He knocked on the door and stood back to await someone coming to open the door for him. It was not long before the door opened and a young maid allowed Jake to enter. She then led Jake through to a back room where Johnnie Gordon and Alice were sitting eating a light lunch.

Johnnie stood up. "Inspector?" he said with a quizzical tone to his voice.

"Jake," announced Alice as she leapt from her chair and hurried over to embrace the man she would never forget for all the good he had done for her, "it's so good to see you again."

"Always good to see you, Alice," Jake said as they broke their embrace. Alice hooked her arm around Jake's and led him over to the table.

"Sorry if I'm interrupting, "Jake then said, "but I didn't want to bother you at work and I was hoping you might be home for lunch."

"I'm actually doing some work from home," Johnnie explained. "There are times when being one of the partners makes it a little easier to plan work in a way that suits me better."

Johnnie was a partner in one of the more established legal firms in Aberdeen. He was accustomed to spending a lot of time away from the office, though usually that meant being in court rather than staying at home.

"Anyway," Johnnie then said as he stood up and offered Jake a handshake," it's good to see you again, Inspector. I assume this visit had something to do with the death of Guy Le Fondre?"

"Le Fondre's dead?" Alice asked with some surprise.

"It was in the paper this morning," Johnnie then explained. "Someone murdered Guy Le Fondre on Tuesday."

"How terrible," Alice responded.

"And I wondered, with the Business Club connection, if you might have known the gentleman?" Jake then added as he turned to face Johnnie.

"Have a seat, Inspector," Johnnie said first. He and Alice then sat back at the table. "As with so many of the Members at the Business Club I didn't know Le Fondre that well though we did cross paths on occasions."

"He made some rather crude comments about me that first night we were at the Business Club," Alice said. "I didn't like the man."

"Not many people did," added Johnnie. "There was a dark side to the man that kept others at arms-length. I know he was having a relationship with a young woman called Harriet. Everyone assumed she was a prostitute though I firmly believe that Le Fondre was trying to do for Harriet what you did for Alice."

"Do you know anyone called Harriet?" Jake then asked Alice.

"I don't think so," came the rather uncertain reply. "Having said that some of the girls use different names for different clients; some men like a particular name over others."

Jake then turned back to Johnnie. "Did Le Fondre have any close acquaintances at the Club?"

"He used to dine a lot with a fellow called Scott Thane. There was word around the Club of them possibly being in business together but I never heard anything definite on that front. Le Fondre also dealt a lot with a horrible man called Cathcart who was given pretty much free rein around the Club because Le Fondre vouched for him."

"We know about the connection between Le Fondre and Cathcart. We even have reason to believe that they may have some connection to my friend Tommy's death."

"You finally have a lead in Tommy's murder?" Alice asked.

"I believe we have," Jake replied. He then turned back to Johnnie. "Do you know where Scott Thane lives?"

"I'm afraid not. Obviously you will get him at the Club."

"He may be at the Club," Jake agreed, "but whether we get to see him, or not, is a different matter. Is there anything you can tell me about Scott Thane?"

"Used to be in the banking business but now seems to work for himself. He's another one who keeps himself very much to himself and there have been no occasions on which we have needed to socialise."

Jake seemed quite happy, for the moment, to accept that that was all he was likely to learn from Johnnie. He could still sense that Johnnie and Alice were very happy together and he now turned the conversation to more personal matters.

"Anyway, how are you both doing?"

"Fine," replied Johnnie glancing across at Alice.

"We're doing very well," Alice added.

"I'm happy for you," Jake then said.

Alice moved a little closer to Jake as she spoke next.

"Would I be right to assume that you won't be needing any more inside information from the Business Club?"

Johnnie's expression was one of horror. Jake noticed it immediately and deduced that Johnnie needed an excuse to keep Alice near him for a little while longer. Jake held back a smile.

"It might be necessary for you both to keep your ears open at the Club just a little longer."

Johnnie's expression changed again. He visibly relaxed.

"I'm glad we can still be of help to you, Inspector," he then said. "Is there anything in particular you would like to know?"

"I'd be interested in anything to do with Le Fondre or this Scott Thane. Don't be too obvious, I don't want you getting in to any trouble with your fellow Members."

"I think we can both gather information without being too obvious," Johnnie added, a smile forming on his face.

Alice was also smiling and Jake felt that there might be more to their relationship than simply a business arrangement whilst they visited the Business Club. In his heart he hoped that Alice might be finding someone who could look after her for the rest of her life. She certainly deserved that.

Jake stood up. "I'll let you get back to your lunch and sorry for interrupting you at this time of day."

"Not a problem," said Johnnie standing up.

Alice also got to her feet and hurried over to Jake. "I'll see you out," she said and once more hooked her arm through Jake's as she did so.

"Until the next time, Mr Gordon."

"Please, call me Johnnie."

"I'll do that the next time we meet," Jake concluded and led the way out of the door with Alice close by his side.

When they reached the front door Jake turned to face Alice. "Are you happy?"

Alice grinned. "Very. He's a lovely man, Jake."

"Do I detect a budding romance here?"

Alice suddenly looked embarrassed. "Oh I don't know about that."

"He clearly thinks the world of you," Jake added.

"We are getting on well together so let's just leave it at that for the moment. Talking of getting on well together how are things with you and Margaret?"

"Things are going well," Jake said as a smile seemed to automatically appear on his face.

Alice could tell from Jake's expression that he thought a lot of Margaret and that perhaps there was a budding relationship there as well. She hoped the same happiness for Jake that he hoped for her.

"I wish you every happiness together," Alice then said as she threw her arms around Jake's neck and planted a kiss on his lips.

"If you hear anything useful about Le Fondre or Thane......."Jake then said.

"We'll let you know," concluded Alice as Jake turned to leave. Alice then went back to finish her lunch.

***

The side door to the theatre was open as usual. Workmen came and went from various doors around the building and he had come to know which doors were safer than others to enter and leave. The man made his way inside, making sure as he did that no one saw him. He took his time. He wandered through the main auditorium and marvelled at the work that had been done. There were still some men, high up on either side of the stage working on the paintwork.

No one seemed to pay any attention to him as he walked around the auditorium. He kept close to the wall until he could make his way through one of the doors and out in to the main foyer. From there he made his way up a flight of stairs and in the corridor was delighted to find some tools and also a few other items that seemed relevant to electric lighting that was going in. He stooped down and put some of the items in to a bag that he had brought with him. He smiled at the thought of the workmen searching for these items and how, no doubt, they would all be blaming each other for losing them.

He made his way back downstairs and re-traced his steps to the side door. Just before he left he glanced, once more, back in to the main auditorium. His anger rose at the sight of such opulence. Why would anyone want to spend so much money on something as trivial as theatre? He turned and went outside again, turning right and walking down to the street that ran behind this new building.

He walked for a little while until he found himself across the road from the Grammar School. He was on Esslemont Avenue and to his right was a considerable drop to the burn that flowed below. He checked that no one was watching him and then threw the bag, containing the tools, down in to the burn. It landed with a resounding clatter and then settled in the water. The bag was still visible but from street level it was unlikely that anyone would ever identify the contents.

He then strolled back home where he made himself a cup of tea before sitting down and pondering on what he might do next.

TWO

Thursday 01 November – early evening onwards

Jake sat at his desk and looked down on the sea of paper that was threatening to engulf him. For what seemed like an age he had been involved in a murder inquiry and now, here he was, having to identify the murderers of the very people he felt had been involved in murder themselves. Would this procession of death never end?

Jake had completed the last of the paperwork regarding Cecil Tredwall and everything was now ready to be sent off to the courts. Jake knew that the trial would not last long as Cecil had already pleaded guilty to the murders of both his father and Vernon MacKenzie. All the court would be required to do was pass sentence and that would probably mean the noose for Cecil.

In another pile of paper Jake had placed the notes he had made concerning Guy Le Fondre and there was also a list of people whom he would need to interview. On the face of it there seemed no obvious reason for Le Fondre being murdered on his own doorstep but it was quite possible that the man had hidden secrets that would lead to his killer.

Jake thought for a moment about what Johnnie Gordon had said about Le Fondre and his lady-friend, Harriet. Had Le Fondre been trying to release Harriet from the life of a prostitute and if so, had it really been with the same intention that Jake had had with Alice?

He then thought about Alice and how happy she seemed to be in the company of Johnnie Gordon. Almost out of the blue Jake's mind was filled with thoughts of Margaret. Yet again in thinking about Alice, Jake found himself now thinking about Margaret. It was beginning to look as if he would need at least one of them in his life to make it wholly complete.

Jake took his pocket-watch from the pocket of his waistcoat and noted the time. There seemed little point in trying to do anything further so he decided to head for home, or at least what passed for home at present, but first he would visit Margaret as he had what he hoped would be good news for her.

Jake's domestic situation was rather complicated. He was living in the home that had been owned by his friend and colleague, Alexander Thomson. Tommy, as he had been known to just about everyone, had been taking money from the criminal fraternity for years. He had bought his flat on Esslemont Avenue with the money and had then, by way of hiding everything from his wife, charged himself a rental payment each month.

After his death Tommy's wife had left Aberdeen and was now living in Edinburgh. It had been arranged that Jake, should he wish to do so, could take over the rental costs of Esslemont Avenue but, of course, he had now found out that the house was not actually legally owned by anyone having been bought with illegal earnings by a man who didn't exist. As things stood there was no one to legally receive the rental payments but Jake had agreed to stay where he was until everything was sorted out.

Two groups of lawyers were pouring over previous legal decisions to see if they could find a solution to the problem. Obviously had Jake been able to buy the property then it would have solved everything but he was never going to be able to do that on a Police Inspector's salary. It seemed that the only possible solution was to sell the property and have the money raised from that sale returned to the Treasury.

Jake did not know, therefore, how much longer he would be able to live in the Esslemont Avenue property.

In the meantime he had his own property in the Guestrow, which was lying unused. Jake did not want to return to living in the Guestrow and had pretty much decided to find a long-term tenant for that property and at least make a little extra money in the process. He knew that he would have to get permission from the Chief Constable as it was frowned upon for police officers to make money from a source other than their day job. That was a bridge to be crossed some other day.

Jake put on his jacket and left the building. He made his way along Broad Street and then onwards in to Rosemount. The decision to visit Margaret had been somewhat last minute and he now hoped that it wasn't too late an hour to be doing so. He had met Margaret when he had interviewed her regarding a murder that had occurred in the city in September. They had become close friends since then and Jake always valued the time he spent with her.

He entered the tenement block on Rosemount Viaduct, where Margaret had her flat and climbed up to her door. He knocked and waited for a response. It did not seem very long before the door was opening and Margaret's face lit up at the sight of Jake standing in the stairway.

"Jake, how lovely," she said and stepped forward to accept a kiss from Jake.

They then went inside the flat and Margaret closed to door. She then led the way in to the front room where she invited Jake to have a seat.

"Tea?" Margaret then asked.

"It's not too late to call is it?" Jake replied.

"Of course not. Now do you want a cup of tea or would you prefer a bottle of beer, I'm sure I have a couple in the cupboard."

"Tea would be lovely."

"Then make yourself comfortable and I will be back in a minute."

Jake looked around a room for which he was become ever more acquaint. It looked almost gloomy in the gaslight and he looked forward to the return of better days when the sunshine could once more stream in the large, corner window and flood the room with a natural and warming light.

Margaret returned a few moments later carrying a tray on which she had placed a teapot, two cups on saucers and a plate of biscuits. She laid that on the small table that lay in front of Jake and then returned to the kitchen for the milk and sugar. Soon they were both sitting on the settee sipping at their cups of tea.

"How are things at work?" Jake then asked.

"Busy. We are hoping to run classes at the Institute to provide ambulance instruction for seamen and what turned out to be a simple, little idea has actually turned in to a lot of work, particularly for me. A meeting has been arranged for the sixteenth at which, hopefully, some major decisions can be taken. Of course, I'll do all the arranging and then the local Councillor will take all the credit; I am, after all, merely a woman."

"Would you like me to have a word with him?" Jake quipped.

Margaret smiled and her beautiful face lit up. "It might be better if you didn't," she replied.

"Anyway, I should think that ambulance instruction would be essential knowledge for seamen," added Jake.

"Indeed it is. You can hardly run to the doctor's surgery when you are many miles out to sea. The more these seamen can do for themselves the better."

"Was it your idea to provide this instruction?"

"Yes it was, which is why is it quite galling that other's will get the credit assuming the idea is a success. Of course, if it fails miserably then I will be given full credit for making the suggestion in the first place," Margaret said with some annoyance in her tone.

"You need to ensure that you get all the credit that is due to you. You are always thinking of others, Margaret Gifford and it is high time that others started thinking of you."

"An honourable thought, Jake, but unfortunately that's just not how it is," Margaret added. "Women are nothing more than an adornment around an office or other place of work. We need to know our place, it's as simple as that."

"Then someone needs to change all that," Jake added.

"Indeed they do. Men need to realise that there is really no reason why women could not do most of the jobs that men do," Margaret insisted.

"You are not suggesting that women could do the job that I do, are you?" Jake then asked.

"Perhaps we are not ready for the more physical side of being a police officer," Margaret conceded," but there must be jobs, within the police, which a woman might actually be quite good at doing."

"I'm sure there are," agreed Jake, "and one day those jobs will be identified. In the meantime, however, the reality is that women have to accept that employment, often as not, is not a necessity in her life. That is what husbands are here for."

"I have always sought my own way in life, Jake," Margaret then said, "and I have found it slightly galling at times to be treated as some kind of second-class citizen just because I am a woman. I do my job as well as any man."

Jake took Margaret's hand. "I'm sure that you do your job better than any man because you care about what you do. I have worked with few men who ever truly cared about the job they were doing. A man is under pressure to earn money for both himself and his family so he has little time to ponder on where that income may come from. It is often the case that you simply follow in your father's footsteps."

"The day will come when we women are better accepted in the workplace," Margaret then said.

Jake did not disagree.

"If I may lighten the topic of conversation," Jake then said," I would like to ask you to accompany me to the Palace Theatre on the seventeenth of this month as I have been rather fortunate in acquiring these from a colleague who can no longer attend himself."

Jake produced two tickets from his pocket and let Margaret look at one of them.

"Harry Lauder," Margaret announced with some glee. "I never thought that I would get a chance to see the great man."

Margaret threw her arms around Jake's neck and they kissed. They enjoyed the first kiss so much that they kissed again and when they parted Margaret was still smiling broadly.

"You've nothing else planned for that night?" Jake then said.

"I never have anything planned and more importantly, it's the day after the event at the Institute I referred to earlier, so I welcome the chance to relax knowing that that will all be finished by that time."

"To Harry Lauder then," Jake announced, by way of a toast. They clinked tea cups together and laughed.

***

Henry Davis was at the end of a lane that ran off from Regents Quay. He had just lit a cigarette and was taking a moment before continuing on his beat. He only had an hour more to work and had little intention of doing very much in that time. He was exhaling smoke thoughtfully when he noticed a man coming towards him.

Davis had expected the man to pass by but instead he stopped and turned to face the young Constable.

"I'm told you're Henry Davis."

"Who told you that?"

"That doesn't really matter, does it? Now, are you Henry Davis or not?"

"Who might you be?" Davis added.

"I might be someone who has good news for Henry Davis, if I ever find him," the man replied, getting slightly annoyed at his questions being answered with questions all the time.

Davis took another drag on his cigarette and blew out the smoke with extra force. He looked at the other man with some suspicion, but he was intrigued to know what this visit was all about.

"I'm Henry Davis, now what's this good news you bring me?"

"My name is Ben Aspinall and I, like you, briefly worked for Mr Le Fondre. I'm here to tell you that we both now work for Mr Thane and that I will be responsible for contacting you from now on. Mr Thane wishes to retain your services and to continue paying you for any relevant information that you can provide for him. The first little job he has for you is to try and find out how well the investigation in to the death of George Cathcart is going."

"I would have thought Mr Thane would be more interested in who killed Guy Le Fondre?" Davis suggested.

"Okay, the need to know Cathcart's killer is perhaps more personal to me. Cathcart was a friend of mine and I want to know who killed him, hopefully before your police colleagues get around to arresting the person."

"I may not know who it is until my colleagues arrest someone," Davis then said.

"That may well be the case, but I'd still like to know who it is as soon as possible. Would that be okay?"

"As long as I get paid I don't mind what I do," Davis then said.

"Good man. Now, how best can I contact you? I can't spend half my life wandering around the harbour every time I want to speak to you."

"I showed Winston MacDonald where to leave messages for me?" Davis then said.

"You'd better show me as well," Aspinall added. "I'm not convinced that MacDonald can be trusted to do anything other than the most basic tasks. It may be necessary for me to do things myself at times."

Henry Davis took Aspinall to the lane where there was a series of loose bricks in one of the walls. By removing two of the bricks a small hole was unveiled, which was big enough for leaving messages or small packages.

"Just don't leave money in here," Davis said quickly. "I'm pretty sure no one else knows about this place but I wouldn't trust leaving money."

"I'll make sure that you are spoken to personally when it comes to any payments," Aspinall said. "Any other information we will arrange to leave in this hiding place. If you have any information for us then leave it in the same hiding place. I'll arrange for MacDonald to check it each day and he can then bring anything to me. Are you happy with that arrangement?"

"It makes sense," agreed Henry Davis.

"Excellent," Aspinall concluded and went on his way.

Henry Davis stood at the end of the lane and lit a cigarette. As he smoked it he pondered on what he would do with regard to the Cathcart investigation. Clearly there was no way that this man, Aspinall, could ever be told the identity of Cathcart's killer though there might be a need to provide him with some information simply to illicit a payment if nothing else. It was a problem that would require some thought.

Davis eventually finished the cigarette and crushed the discarded butt under his foot before continuing on his way.

***

Johnnie Gordon had gone to the Business Club himself that evening. He had explained to Alice that without her being with him he might be able to talk to more people and it would also allow him to go to the Smoking Room where, of course, guests were not allowed.

Johnnie had arrived at a little after eight and he had found all the talk in the main bar seemed to be about Guy Le Fondre. Some seemed surprised by what had happened and others reckoned that the man deserved everything that had come his way. There seemed no middle ground, it was clearly either one opinion or the other.

Much to Johnnie's annoyance Courtenay Troup, father of Johnnie's last lady friend, Daisy, was in the main bar with a group of friends. He came across as soon as he noticed where Johnnie was standing.

"Finally come to your senses with regard to that Alice?" Troup said.

Troup was bitter about the fact that Johnnie had not continued with his courting of Daisy. Troup was keen to have his daughter married as quickly as possible so that someone else could take responsibility for her. He had thought that Johnnie would have made a suitable husband and Daisy certainly seemed interested. However, things did not last that long and Johnnie was now being seen around the Club in the company of some ex-prostitute called Alice.

Johnnie had never taken Daisy to the Club, something that Courtenay had found unacceptable.

"Alice couldn't come tonight, but we'll make a point of finding you the next time we are here seeing as you seem to be missing her tonight," Johnnie finally replied.

Troup looked suitably offended and went off to join his friends again. Johnnie took a drink to the Smoking Room and got himself in to a conversation with two Members who seemed to have very strong views about Guy Le Fondre.

Reggie Baxter and Maitland Middleton had been Members of the Business Club since the day it had opened and prior to that they had been Members of various Gentlemen's Clubs so they had personal standards that they felt should be observed at all times. Both felt that Guy Le Fondre did not live up to the standards of others. Without realising Johnnie's relationship with Alice both men talked of their disapproval that Le Fondre brought Harriet to the Club and almost flaunted the fact that she had been a prostitute.

Both men were of the opinion that men like Le Fondre lowered the tone of any establishment. Baxter then went on to say more on the subject of the Business Club and its membership.

"Take Daniel Ifield for example. If it wasn't for the fact that he hopes to buy the place and his father has money, then that man would not be allowed through the doors of an establishment such as this"

"Why are you talking about Daniel Ifield?" Johnnie then asked.

"Oh, I thought you knew," Reggie then said. "Daniel Ifield was in the Club the night that Le Fondre was killed. Now talk about lowering the tone; I mean Willie Ifield is nothing more than a common man who has been lucky to make some money. Just being rich does not change your breeding," Baxter added with some disgust.

Johnnie sat forward in his chair and tapped the ash off of the end of his cigar in to an ashtray that was sitting on the table in front of him.

"Are you sure that Daniel Ifield was here the night Le Fondre was killed?"

"Positive," Baxter added. "He was in the dining room at the same time as Le Fondre. I was just finishing my own meal when they both got up to leave. I heard them having words as they stood in the doorway."

"Are you sure they were speaking to each other?" Johnnie asked in some surprise.

"Words were exchanged certainly. Le Fondre said something that I didn't quite hear and then Ifield blew up at him, or it might have been the other way round," Baxter said. Johnnie got the impression that Baxter's mind perhaps was no longer as sharp as it may have once been. "They weren't exactly shouting at each other but the conversation was certainly quite heated."

"But you don't know what they were talking about?" Johnnie asked.

"Didn't hear much of what was said," Baxter replied," but it seemed to have something to do with the young lady who was with Ifield. Pretty as a picture she was. Anyway, knowing Le Fondre he probably passed some inappropriate comment and Ifield had reacted accordingly. You know better than most how twisted Le Fondre could sound when talking to others."

Baxter's comment referred back to the things that Le Fondre had said in the presence of Alice.

"Did the two men give you the impression that they might have known each other already?" Johnnie then enquired.

"Hard to say," said Baxter. "Their conversation didn't last that long so it might simply have been a case of Le Fondre's big mouth landing him in trouble again."

"Were you aware of anything else happening between the two men that evening?"

Baxter thought for a moment and then said that he didn't see either of them after their altercation outside the dining room.

"Thoroughly bad lot that Le Fondre, so I for one am not sorry to know that he won't be around ever again," Middleton added downing the last of his whisky and holding the glass aloft to indicate to the waiter that he would like a re-fill.

Johnnie did not join them in another drink. He made his way back do the bar and had one more there before heading off in to the night.

***

As that first day of November drew to a close there were a number of people, connected in some way to Guy Le Fondre, who would be expecting a visit from the police over the coming days and weeks. Some would need to hide certain facts simply to protect themselves whilst others would be able to answer questions with a degree of honesty.

Somewhere in the sea of information that would bubble to the surface as the inquiry progressed Jake Fraser would have to isolate fact from fiction. As he lay in his bed that night, finding sleep hard to come by, his mind was awash with thoughts connected to Le Fondre's death; to Alice; to Margaret and to simply making some sense of his own life in terms of his surroundings and his relationships.

Jake had a feeling that the month of November was going to be a very important one for him personally though, in truth, he had no idea how that importance might manifest itself.

Eventually the thoughts subsided and eventually Jake slipped in to a long and welcoming sleep.

THREE

Friday 02 November – mid-morning through to mid-afternoon

Jake paid a visit to the offices of Ledley, Ward and Delaney, which were situated across Bon Accord Square from the Business Club. Jake was greeted at the reception area by a pretty looking young woman, immaculately dressed in what passed for the latest fashion.

"Could I speak with Mr Delaney, please?" Jake announced as he showed the woman his identity.

"I'll see if he is free," the young woman replied with a smile. "Please have a seat."

Jake sat down and watched the woman disappear through a door to her left. The reception area was quite small with only three chairs and a small table on which lay the morning newspaper and some old magazines. Some time passed before the young woman returned and asked Jake to follow her.

He was soon being shown in to a small office filled with cabinets and bookcases. There was a window looking down on the back of the building and a well-dressed young man sitting behind a desk that was strewn with papers. He looked as if he was drowning in work and when he stood up to welcome Jake in to the room he was barely visible over the piles of paper and files.

"Thank you, Miss Weston," the man said to the young woman who left the room. "Inspector Fraser, I believe?"

"And you must be Mr Delaney?" Jake added as they shook hands.

"Francis Delaney, Inspector."

Both men sat down.

"I am here about the last will and testament of Guy Le Fondre," Jake then began. "I found a copy of the will at Mr Le Fondre's house but there were no contact details for the benefactors and I wondered if you could provide me with an address for Miss Harriet……," Jake broke off to check his notebook, "….Cruickshank."

"I'm sure that won't be a problem," Delaney then said and started to shuffle papers and files around on his desk. He was clearly looking for one particular file but there seemed little organisation in the manner in which he conducted his search. "It was a terrible business with Mr Le Fondre. There seems to have been so many murders in this city recently."

"I had noticed," Jake added with a slight smile.

Delaney missed the humour initially but eventually registered what Jake had just said.

"Of course you'd know about such things," he then said and continued moving paper around.

"Did you know Mr Le Fondre well?" Jake asked as a means of making good use of the time it was going to take Delaney to find Harriet Cruickshank's details.

"I met him on perhaps three occasions. He seemed a nice enough gentleman and not the sort you would expect to be murdered."

"Oh, what sort gets himself murdered, Mr Delaney?

Delaney stopped his search and seemed even more flustered by Jake's question. "Criminal elements," he eventually said.

"And you would say that Mr Le Fondre was not a criminal?"

"Oh, definitely not."

"Based on three meetings?" Jake added, taking some fun out of making Francis Delaney look and feel very uncomfortable indeed.

"He just seemed a nice man, that's all," Delaney concluded as he finally pulled a file from the middle of a bundle placed to the right corner of his desk. "Ah, this is it."

Delaney pulled the file in front of him and opened it. He moved some papers off the top of the pile within and then started to read through the sheet he had now uncovered.

"Mr Le Fondre owned the property that was occupied by Miss Cruickshank. She was living there at no cost it seems. I presume that once all the legal issues have been completed, there will be no reason for Miss Cruickshank to continue living at King Street as she will, by then, be the proud owner of Mr Le Fondre's house on King's Gate."

"Am I correct in thinking that only Miss Cruickshank and Mr and Mrs Gladstone benefit in any way from Mr Le Fondre's will?"

"Yes, that is the case. Miss Cruickshank basically gets everything in terms of the house and the majority of the money from Mr Le Fondre's bank account. Mr and Mrs Gladstone get the remainder of the money and I believe the expectation would be that they would continue to live and work in the house even though Miss Cruickshank would be moving in. At least I am assuming Miss Cruickshank will move in, she may well decide to remain where she is and ask us to sell King's Gate, in which case Mr and Mrs Gladstone would require another solution to their domestic situation."

"Could you please write down Miss Cruickshank's full address for me?" Jake then asked.

Delaney did so at once. As he did so, Jake asked another question.

"Has Mr Le Fondre ever required any other business issues to be dealt with by you or anyone else at your firm?"

"Not that I am aware of," Delaney replied. "I am sure that Mr Le Fondre would not have put business the way on any of my colleagues. He always seemed more than satisfied by the service I provided."

"Thank you, Mr Delaney," Jake concluded as he put the paper in his jacket pocket after checking the address noted on it.

Both men then stood up again and shook hands.

"Have you any idea when the will is to be read?"

"As it only really involves three people I would be aiming to clear this as quickly as possible. I should imagine we will send the letters out on Monday and invite Miss Cruickshank and Mr and Mrs Gladstone to come here on Thursday."

"I would be obliged if you would let me know on Friday of next week that all beneficiaries had been informed of the content of the will," Jake then said.

"I will send a note to Lodge Walk as soon as I have had my meeting," Delaney answered.

"Thank you, I'll find my own way out."

Jake made his way downstairs and passed the lovely Miss Weston. He stepped out on to the pavement and stood for a moment looking across the grassy central area at the Business Club on the other side. As he did so he couldn't help thinking that Delaney had described Le Fondre as being a nice man. No one else had said that about him, even on one meeting, so it seemed interesting that he should come across so well to a lawyer.

Perhaps Le Fondre had been one of those men who got pleasure from annoying those around him. He had only met Delaney to discuss the financial arrangements that ought to be in place in the event of his death. There would be no need for games with Delaney as there was nothing to be gained.

Guy Le Fondre was a typical Member of the Business Club. There always seemed to be secrets to be kept behind the doors of that building. No one was ever what they appeared to be and if anyone, outside of the Club, asked any awkward questions then a veil of silence descended.

Jake wondered if the answers to whom Guy Le Fondre really was still lay behind the front door of that building, or had the veil of silence already descended, meaning that he would never know?

***

As Jake made his way out of Bon Accord Square, Scott Thane was enjoying a whisky in the main bar of the Business Club. He was interrupted by someone with a message from the front door. There was a Ben Aspinall asking to see him. Thane cursed to himself but asked for Aspinall to be shown through.

Aspinall was soon seated across from Thane.

"May I buy you a drink," Thane said to Aspinall who was looking around with a degree of discomfort. Unlike Cathcart, Aspinall did not enjoy his time in the Business Club. He had never been one for rubbing shoulders with people outside of his own perceived position in the class pecking order. Aspinall wanted to make as much money as he could in life but he never wanted to be a member of the upper classes and to him, the Business Club was an advert for the type of man that he simply didn't like.

Once both men had their drinks Aspinall began his update of all that he had done over the previous twenty-four hours. As a conclusion to his report he informed Thane that he had spoken to Henry Davis and also sent someone to see Yule. Aspinall was fairly confident that everything was now continuing as normal and that all those people who needed to know that it was business as usual had now been contacted.

"My thanks, Mr Aspinall," Thane then said reaching in to his pocket and taking out a roll of banknotes. He counted out five pounds and slid them across the table. "A little extra for your efforts."

Aspinall picked up the money and pushed it in to his pocket. "Thank you, Mr Thane."

"Since we last spoke, Mr Aspinall, I have had a chance to read through all the material left to me by Guy Le Fondre and I have come to the conclusion that I really cannot be expected to run everything that he has left behind. I now know that apart from the film-making business, of which I know just about everything now, Guy also had a finger in two other pies. These other pies were even more illegal than some of the activities that were going on within the film-making business and quite frankly, I have no stomach for taking on such areas of work."

"I wasn't aware that there was much outside of the film-making," Aspinall added.

"Nothing else was making the regular money that the films did, but there is scope to expand in to prostitution and robbery. Guy ran small teams that operated in both areas and he appears to have had some return from both. Apparently Guy arranged for Harriet's pimp, Walter Bailey, to be murdered and with Bailey out of the way Guy decided to move in. I have no doubt that Harriet knew nothing about any of that. However, the prostitution side of the business was now being run by a man called Raymond Stiles and I'll tell you how to contact him when you get the paperwork tomorrow."

"You also mentioned a team in to robbery," added Aspinall.

"Yes. There is a small team of thieves in Aberdeen who are stealing at the request of clients who then pay reasonable sums of money for the stolen items. For example if you wanted a particular painting then you would set up a deal with a man called Flood, I have no first name and he would do the rest; for a price."

"So you need someone to run these other areas of business?" Aspinall said.

"I do."

"What percentage would then be paid back to you?"

Thane thought for a moment. "I'd be happy with twenty per cent; after all I'd not be doing any of the work so it would be unfair to ask for too much in return."

Aspinall thought for a moment. "Would you be happy if I took over both elements of the business?"

"Mr Aspinall, if you feel that you can control Stiles and Flood then go right ahead. I don't know how close Guy was to both men for, in all honesty, I never heard him mention their names at any time. Of course, they were probably accustomed to working with Cathcart and as you are now the new Cathcart that pretty much makes you their boss anyway, doesn't it?"

Aspinall smiled. "In that case, Mr Thane, I will take over both areas of business and see to it that you get your payment at the end of each month. I will come back tomorrow and we can discuss matters further."

Both men shook hands. Aspinall left and Thane ordered another drink. He was happy that money would still come in from Guy's highly illegal pastimes, but at least Thane no longer had any direct link and that ought to mean the police would never be battering down his door, no matter what might come to light in the future.

***

Jake stopped off at Lodge Walk to find Mathieson, then both made their way around to King Street where they climbed to the first floor flat address that had been supplied for Harriet Cruickshank. Jake knocked on the door and waited for someone to open the door.

A little time passed before the door did open. Harriet Cruickshank certainly did not look like a prostitute as she stood before Jake and Mathieson dressed in expensive clothing and with her hair tied up in the latest fashion. What Jake did notice, however, was the fact that everything Harriet Cruickshank wore was black.

"Miss Cruickshank?" Jake asked.

"Yes."

Jake and Mathieson then showed Harriet their identification and Jake asked if they might come in for a moment. Harriet paused, as if she was contemplating saying no, before eventually stepping back and inviting them in.

Inside, the flat was every bit as immaculate as Harriet was herself. Everything was in its place and most items on show were worth more money than Harriet Cruickshank had ever been likely to earn in her previous employment. It was quite obvious that Guy Le Fondre had been lavish in the money he had spent on Harriet.

Harriet led the way in to the front room and they all sat down.

"I expect this is about poor Guy," Harriet then said as she produced a handkerchief, apparently from nowhere and started dabbing at her nose.

"How did you find out about Mr Le Fondre's death?" Jake then asked.

"I read about it in the paper."

"When did you last see him?"

"On the day he was killed. We had dinner together that evening."

"Was this at the Business Club?" Jake said.

"It was. We had a lovely time so you can imagine how I felt when I read the paper….." Harriet began, but appeared to break down in mid-sentence.

"What was the nature of your relationship with Mr Le Fondre?"

Harriet composed herself again.

"I'm sure you already know that, Inspector."

"If you would just answer the question please, Miss Cruickshank," Jake added.

"We were very good friends."

"Lovers perhaps?" suggested Jake.

Harriet smiled. "I don't think we could be described as lovers though some of our moments together were quite intimate."

"I'm sorry but I don't understand what you're saying. You were intimate but you were not lovers?"

"When Guy and I first met he asked me to do something for him that might seem rather strange to others," Harriet then explained. "He wanted me to wash him. I was not required to do anything else, just wash his entire body with warm water."

Jake glanced at Mathieson who had the same quizzical look on his face as Jake no doubt had himself.

"You never had sex with Mr Le Fondre?"

"Never. Guy thought that the sexual act was filthy and degrading. He could never have brought himself to putting a part of his own body inside someone else's."

"So all you ever did was wash Mr Le Fondre?" Jake asked again, still with an air of disbelief.

"That was all."

Jake now thought of all the money and property that Harriet Cruickshank was about to inherit. Such a fortune for providing no further service than a flannel and water. It seemed beyond belief that someone should value such a simple act so highly.

"How long had you known Mr Le Fondre?"

"Around a year, I don't remember exactly when we started seeing each other."

"And how long have you been living here?"

"Six months. It was Guy's first step to changing my life...."Harriet replied and disappeared behind her handkerchief again.

It was certainly an apparent sign of emotion and yet Jake felt it was more like a piece of rather uninspiring acting than any true show of emotion for a lost loved one.

"Were you aware that Mr Le Fondre intended to include you in his will?"

Harriet tried to look surprised but, yet again, that lack of acting skill let her down. Feeling the surprise hadn't looked as authentic as she might have hoped she once more lost herself behind the handkerchief.

"I can't believe he thought enough of me as to leave me something in his will," she eventually said.

"So you didn't know?" Jake asked again, by way of clarifying a point.

Harriet took a moment to respond. "I can assure you, Inspector, that I know nothing of any inheritance but I would be very pleased to receive anything from Guy as I felt our relationship was developing in to something a little more permanent and that may be a small sign that he thought so too."

Jake could sense that, at least for the moment, he was unlikely to get anything very meaningful out of Harriet Cruickshank. It was fairly obvious that she knew a lot more than she would ever say so he decided to keep his questions on a general level until he gathered some real evidence to use against her.

"Mr Le Fondre obviously had a lot of money, Miss Cruickshank, do you know how he made that money?"

Harriet smiled again. "He inherited family money, I think. I don't think Guy ever did what most people would describe as normal work. He had money of his own and he enjoyed the freedom of doing what he liked when he liked. He was not the type to ever be tied to conventional employment."

"Was there anyone, perhaps at the Business Club, who Mr Le Fondre might have been closer to than the others?"

"I believe that Guy was thinking about going in to business with Scott Thane though I have no idea what that business might have been."

"And Mr Thane is also a Member at the Business Club?" Jake then said.

"Yes he is."

"Do you know where he lives?"

"No I do not, I'm afraid."

"Was there anyone else close to Mr Le Fondre?"

Harriet pondered for a moment. "No, I don't think so."

"No one else at the Business Club was a close friend of Mr Le Fondre's?" Jake asked, sounding as if he found that hard to believe.

Harriet again gave the question some thought. "I can't remember ever seeing him in anyone else's company, apart from Mr Thane. Guy was a very private person, Inspector and did not make friends easily."

"Did you ever know a man by the name of George Cathcart?" Jake then said.

"He did some work for Guy, I believe, though I never actually met him."

"And how about a Donald Yule?"

Harriet did some more thinking. "No, that name means nothing to me."

"Very well, Miss Cruickshank, we'll not take up any more of your time for the moment. However, I suggest that you do not have any thoughts about leaving Aberdeen as there is every likelihood that we will need to speak to you again."

"I have no intention of going anywhere, Inspector."

Jake and Mathieson left the flat and made their way down to the street. As they began walking back toward Lodge Walk the rain started to get heavier, whipped up by a stiff breeze.

"Well, what did you make of that?" Jake asked Mathieson as they both turned their collars up and pulled their hats tighter on to their heads.

"She knows more than she was saying," Mathieson replied.

"Yes, she would be well advised to put her stage career on hold if that were to be the level of performance."

Mathieson smiled as they both hurried to get back to base and out of the rain.

***

Harriet watched from her window as the two police officers left the building and started to walk back in the direction of Lodge Walk. She hoped that the interview had gone well. She had obviously been expecting a visit from the police as they would see her as being a suspect; after all she was going to be a very rich woman as a result of Guy Le Fondre's death.

She had liked Le Fondre, there was no doubt about that, but she was going to enjoy spending his money even more. She would move to King's Gate at the first opportunity and start living the life a lady. What a step up for someone who had, until very recently, made her living from having sex with strangers in return for money.

From now on she would only have sex with men of her choosing. In fact she had already chosen one. Yes, there was a new man in Harriet's life. They had made plans together and she was already looking forward to those plans coming to fruition.

***

Wolfgang Schwieger had got back to the farm in time for lunch. It had been quite a journey from Aberdeen, involving a train to Ellon and then a horse and cart a few miles out the Auchnagatt road. Its location had obviously been chosen for its privacy, but many of the people working there had often wished it had been a little closer to civilisation.

He had been pleased to find Maisie Strachan still there as he knew she was due to leave that day. Maisie had been sent to the farm by way of paying back a debt to Willie Ifield. Her punishment had been to star in as many of the sex films as possible. As a consequence she had been filmed having sex with more men than she might have preferred. However, it had been worth it, if only for the fact that she was now clear of that debt to Willie Ifield.

In fact she was now completely clear of Ifield in every respect and for that she would have done almost anything.

Wolfgang had been the man running most of the filming sessions. It would have been too grand to call him a director as he rarely worked to any script or adopted anything like a structured approach to his work. The new people coming in would work in that way but then they would be making proper films, unlike Wolfgang who basically wanted to get the leading lady's clothes off as fast as possible and then close in on the action that followed.

Wolfgang knew that his time at the farm was almost up. There would be no job for him under this new regime and probably little need for the sex films at all if the general films proved popular. Wolfgang had decided not to wait until he was shown the door; he was going to head back to Germany and see if he could run a film-making business of his own.

But first he needed to see Maisie. He had grown to love her in the relatively short time she had been at the farm. He didn't think she felt the same way about him but he was still going to try and persuade her to come to Germany with him.

He found Maisie in her room. She was packing a bag and looked a little surprised to see Wolfgang enter the room without waiting to be invited.

"Maisie, I'm so pleased I caught you," Wolfgang said.

"You might have knocked first," Maisie said.

"My apologies," replied Wolfgang, "but I wasn't entirely sure that you were still here."

"Even so, you should still have knocked first," Maisie added and Wolfgang nodded his head slightly by way of conceding his error. "So where have you been since Tuesday?"

"In Aberdeen."

"What were you doing there?"

"Business. I had some money to collect and now that I have that money it is time for me to leave."

"Money? What money?" said Maisie.

"As I said, just a little business that I needed to bring to an end. It doesn't matter where the money came from, Maisie, the fact is that I now have enough money to get away from here and start afresh."

Maisie turned to face Wolfgang with a look of surprise on her face. "Where are you going?"

"Back to Germany. There is no way that I will be needed around here once they start making proper films. I think I can start my own business back home, so now seems the right time to go. However, before I leave, I needed to ask you a question."

"And what might that be?" asked Maisie, pausing in her packing for a moment.

Maisie had a feeling that she knew what Wolfgang was about to say next. She had sensed that he had been falling in love with her and she now felt sure that he might even propose.

"I want you to come to Germany with me?" Wolfgang actually said.

Maisie was slightly taken aback. She was prepared to knock back any proposal of marriage for she had no intention of marrying any man, let alone Wolfgang Schwieger, just at the moment. She took a few seconds to allow his question to fully sink in.

"Why would I want to go to Germany with you?" Maisie eventually said.

It had not been the response Wolfgang had been seeking but he had prepared himself for Maisie being difficult to persuade; after all he was asking her to give up everything and take a giant step in to the unknown.

"I know you don't love me, Maisie, but you must know that I love you; I love you very much. You may not love me, but I know that you care for me or you would never have taken me in to your bed in the way that you did."

"Wolfgang, I was a prostitute," Maisie said, "I made a living out of having sex with men so it rarely means anything to me."

Wolfgang shook his head. "I just don't believe that. We have some feelings passing between us and I know that we can build on that. If you come to Germany with me then I can offer you a better life than you might have here. I can offer you a new life, Maisie, as no one would know who you were or what you might have been. It would be a chance to be the Maisie Strachan that you've always wanted to be and perhaps, one day, you might then agree to become my wife?"

With the proposal coming after his request to take her to Germany, Maisie's response was slightly different from the one she had prepared.

"Marriage?" she said. "Can't I have a moment to decide whether, or not, I wish to go to Germany before I then have to consider whether, or not, I would ever wish to become your wife?"

"I just thought your decision about going to Germany might be that little bit easier if you knew how deep my feelings for you run," Wolfgang said.

Maisie though for a moment. She had nothing planned for her life in Aberdeen beyond rejoicing in the fact that Willie Ifield would no longer play a part in it. It did seem a tempting offer for her to go somewhere where no one would know her; where no one would know what kind of past she had had. There was something exciting in being able to start again; maybe even re-invent herself and as Wolfgang had said, be the Maisie Strachan she had always wanted to be.

Then there was the little matter of marriage. She didn't love Wolfgang, but then she had never loved any man. Wolfgang was the first man in her life to offer her a chance to better herself. Maybe the prospect of being his wife wasn't as bad after all, though she had no intention of telling Wolfgang that just yet.

"When are you leaving for Germany?" Maisie then asked.

"Immediately. I'm going to pack and catch the next train to Aberdeen. I'll then get the first train to London and spend a little time there before making plans for how exactly I get back to Germany."

"So my decision has to be made here and now?"

"Sorry," Wolfgang said, taking Maisie's hand in his own. "Sometimes the quick decisions turn out to be the best."

Maisie thought for a few moments. "Okay, let's do it."

Wolfgang put his arms around her and held her tight. "You won't regret this, Maisie. I'll make sure that you don't regret it."

"I'm just talking about going to Germany for the moment," Maisie then said quickly as she broke their embrace. "We can talk about marriage once we see how living together in Germany works out."

Wolfgang grinned. He swept Maisie in to his arms again and kissed her with as much passion as he could muster. As they parted once more Wolfgang spoke again.

"You have made me the happiest man in the world, Maisie and I promise that you will not regret your decision."

"I hope not," concluded Maisie returning her attention to the last of her packing. Wolfgang went away to collect his own things from the room that he had been using. He had some money that he needed to pack safely and at least for the moment, keep out of Maisie's sight.

An hour later they were on the train to Aberdeen. Maisie asked Wolfgang if he knew that Le Fondre was dead. Wolfgang said he had read something in the paper. He then went on to say that it was partly because of Le Fondre's death that he had decided to move on.

"I don't believe that Mr Thane has a business head, "Wolfgang then went on to say, "and as a result I believe the business will fail. On the other hand the idea of making films is a good one and there will definitely be money to be made. I prefer to make that money for myself."

"We'll need to stop off at my flat in Aberdeen so that I can collect a few more things," Maisie had then said.

"Don't collect too much, my love, "Wolfgang added. " We will never be able to carry it all and remember we do have shops in Germany as well."

Maisie smiled. She was sure that she was warming all the more to Wolfgang and for a brief moment she had the notion that perhaps their relationship might just have a chance after all.

***

Jake was getting accustomed to being interrupted by Sergeant Bill Turnbull sticking his head around the door.

"Sorry to bother you sir, but there is a Mister Johnnie Gordon at the front desk asking to see you."

Jake immediately thought that something might have happened to Alice though there was, of course, a variety of other reasons that may have brought Johnnie Gordon to Lodge Walk.

"I'll be through in a moment," Jake replied and finished the paragraph on which he had been working. He then went to the front door.

"Johnnie, what can I do for you?" Jake said with a cheeriness to his tone that probably did not accurately reflect the day he was having.

"Could we have a word in private somewhere?" Johnnie replied.

"Of course," added Jake and he led the way through to the interview room. Jake closed the door and both men sat down.

Johnnie told Jake what he had discovered at the Business Club with regard to Daniel Ifield having words with Guy Le Fondre on the night that Le Fondre had been killed. Jake immediately thought about Miss Sangster when he was informed that there had been a woman with Ifield and that she may have been the reason for the men having words.

"I didn't speak to anyone who saw anything else happen between the two men after that," Johnnie concluded.

"That's very helpful, Johnnie," Jake said. "Is there anything you can tell me about Scott Thane?"

"Not a lot. Thane is a much quieter character than Le Fondre ever was. He keeps himself pretty much to himself and apart from seeing him with Le Fondre at times I don't believe I ever saw Thane talking to anyone else in the Club."

Jake considered what Johnnie had just said before he spoke again.

"Very well, Johnnie, my thanks for this information. How is Alice by the way?"

"The same as she was yesterday; very well," Johnnie replied with a smile. "You really have no need to worry, Inspector, I will take care of Alice for as long as she will allow me to."

"You are very serious about her, aren't you Johnnie?"

"This will sound daft, Inspector, but I feel that I have loved her since that first moment I saw her when you visited my house to ask for my help in gathering information at the Business Club. Alice has that little girl lost look that makes you want to put your arms around her and never let go."

"I know what you mean. Anyway," Jake then said, "I wish you well and hope that you both find happiness together."

"You don't know how happy those words make me feel, Inspector."

"Please, call me Jake."

Johnnie Gordon stood up and offered his hand. Jake stood up and they shook hands.

"When I feel that the time is right, I am planning to ask Alice to marry me. If Alice does me the honour of accepting my proposal of marriage would you be good enough as to give her away at the wedding, seeing as you are the closest thing to family that she has?"

"I would be honoured to give Alice away," Jake added and the smile on Johnnie Gordon's face could have illuminated the room, "just don't leave it too long before asking Alice to marry you."

"I need some courage first," Johnnie conceded. "I am so afraid that she will turn me down."

"I hope she sees the sense in your proposal," Jake concluded and Johnnie Gordon turned and left the room, greatly heartened by Jake's comments.

Jake sat down for a moment and pondered on the possibility of Alice getting married. He had mixed feelings about it, if he were truthful to himself, but deep down he recognised that she had a life to live for herself and if being Mrs Johnnie Gordon was to better that life then who was he to stand in her way.

Jake focussed once more on the job in hand. He went to find Sergeant Mathieson before the pair of them set off to visit Daniel Ifield.

***

Miss Sangster had come to the front door to take Jake and Mathieson up to Daniel Ifield's office. Jake had wanted to ask Miss Sangster some questions about her night at the Business Club but decided that it might be better to speak to Daniel Ifield first. Looking at Miss Sangster's obvious beauty Jake was clearly of the opinion that she was certainly the type of woman that men would fight over. It made perfect sense that someone like Le Fondre would see Miss Sangster as a challenge and at the same time see Daniel Ifield as an opponent.

Jake and Mathieson were led in to Daniel's office and then Miss Sangster left, closing the door behind her.

Daniel Ifield was immaculately dressed as usual in a dark coloured suit with a white shirt and blue tie. He stood up as the policemen arrived in the room and politely shook hands with them both.

Once they were all seated again, Daniel asked how he could be of help.

"Did you know a man called Guy Le Fondre?" Jake began.

"I did not know him as such but, as I am sure you already know, I did have words with him at the Business Club last Tuesday evening."

"And why would you be having words with a man you didn't know?" Jake then asked.

"Quite simply he felt it necessary to pass a rather uncomplimentary comment about my right to be there with someone as beautiful as Miss Sangster. Mr Le Fondre seemed to be suggesting that he would be a better candidate to be seen in the company of Miss Sangster, which seemed strange seeing as he was already at the Club in the company of an attractive, young woman."

"How did the young woman with Le Fondre react?"

"She seemed accustomed to Le Fondre's actions so I was left to assume that the man must have carried on like that on numerous occasions."

"What exactly was said, Mr Ifield?" Jake enquired.

Ifield thought for a moment. "I had noticed the man that I now know is Guy Le Fondre looking across at us throughout our meal. It was patently clear to me that he was looking at Miss Sangster and I have to say that I found it a gross intrusion in to what was meant to be a quiet dinner. Anyway, we all left the dining room at around the same time and I suggested to Le Fondre that he should mind his manners and not stare at other men's companions. It was then that he passed some comment about me not being suitable for someone as beautiful as my companion. He seemed to know who my father was and felt that we Ifields were too rough to be seen with ladies of class. He found the whole scene mildly amusing and went off along the corridor with his lady friend."

"And you didn't see him again?" Jake prompted.

"No, I did not. I was at the Club to view the surroundings as a prelude to a meeting that I have with Joe Tredwall tomorrow. If all goes well I intend buying the Club. Anyway, after those words with Le Fondre I went to find Joe and ask him who the man who had just been so offensive to me, was. He seemed to know Le Fondre pretty well and gave me his name almost at once."

"Had you ever met Guy Le Fondre before?" Jake then asked.

"I believe I have already told you that I did not know Mr Le Fondre until that night," Ifield answered.

"What did you do after you had words with Mr Le Fondre?"

"Miss Sangster and I went to the main bar and had another drink. I then arranged for a carriage to take Miss Sangster home. I went back to the bar for another drink and then left around half an hour later."

"Can anyone vouch for the time you left?" Jake asked.

"I'm sure the doorman will remember as I tipped him rather well for organising my carriage."

"And you went straight home?" Jake then enquired.

"Well of course I went straight home, Inspector."

"Can anyone confirm the time that you got home?"

"I live alone, Inspector, so no, there is no one to confirm what time I got home."

Jake thought for a moment. "That should be all for the moment, Mr Ifield. However, would there be somewhere that we could have a quiet word with Miss Sangster?"

Ifield looked a little nervous at that moment.

"Why would you want to speak to Miss Sangster?" Ifield asked, almost without thinking.

"Miss Sangster was present at the Business Club on Tuesday evening and will be able to corroborate what you have just said. Surely you would *want* us to speak to her?" Jake explained.

"Of course," Ifield eventually said. "I will vacate this office. Feel free to use it for as long as you want."

Jake turned to Mathieson. "Would you bring Miss Sangster in, please?"

"I was going to……" Ifield started to say.

"That's all right, Mr Ifield, Sergeant Mathieson will find Miss Sangster. I'll let you know when we are finished."

Ifield left the room and made his way along to where Miss Sangster had her desk. He arrived just as Sergeant Mathieson was escorting Miss Sangster back along the corridor. They exchanged a glance in the passing but nothing was actually said. Daniel sat down at Miss Sangster's desk and waited patiently for her to return.

Along the corridor Miss Sangster had arrived in Daniel's office and had been offered a seat, which she had accepted. Jake explained that he wanted to ask some questions about Tuesday evening and the time that she had spent at the Business Club with Daniel Ifield.

"Firstly, Miss Sangster, might I ask how well you know Daniel Ifield?" Jake then said.

"He is my employer's son, Inspector and beyond that I don't know him at all."

"But you did accompany him to the Business Club on Tuesday evening for dinner?"

"Yes I did."

"Why did you do that?" Jake then asked.

"Because I was asked. There didn't seem to be any reason for saying no."

"I believe there was an incident as you left the dining room?" Jake enquired.

"We met a rather objectionable man who was somewhat abusive towards Mr Ifield. For some reason he seemed to have taken a liking for me and felt that he might be better suited to be seen in my company."

"Had you met this man before?"

"No."

"Had you, perhaps, seen the man before, perhaps here?"

Miss Sangster gave the questions some thought. "If I had then I don't remember. However, there are many men who visit these premises to see either Mr Ifield Senior of Mr Ifield Junior and it is perfectly possible that I could be seen without being aware of it."

"Do you not come down and show visitors up to the offices above?" Jake asked.

"On many occasions I do, "Miss Sangster replied, "but not always."

"Then, as far as you know, you had never met Guy Le Fondre before Tuesday evening?" Jake asked by way of clarification.

"That is correct."

"Do you know why Mr Ifield was at the Business Club in the first place?"

"I believe he has some hopes of buying the Club and he was there to enjoy some of the services of the Club prior to making a decision. As he was to be having dinner he asked if I might like to accompany him. As I said, I saw no reason to say no."

"What did you do after Mr Ifield and Mr Le Fondre had words?"

"We had a drink in the main bar and then I went home. Mr Ifield stayed on to have another drink."

"So you won't know what time Mr Ifield would have left the Club?"

"No, I would not."

"How did you find out that the man who had had words outside the dining room was Guy Le Fondre?" Jake asked.

"Mr Ifield told me."

"And how did he find out?"

"I really don't know. He left me for a few moments in the main bar and when he came back he seemed to know about Le Fondre and the man that he was. I can only assume that Mr Ifield had spoken to someone in the interim."

"And Mr Le Fondre never bothered you again?"

"No."

"Did you get the impression that Mr Ifield might be annoyed with Mr Le Fondre for showing an interest in you?"

Miss Sangster smiled and when she did she looked even more beautiful. "I am aware that Mr Ifield may have feelings towards me and that he does not take kindly to anyone else showing an interest in me, as you put it. It goes without saying, therefore, that Mr Ifield was extremely unhappy with Le Fondre."

"Did Mr Ifield say anything?" Jake prompted.

"Only about how rude Le Fondre had been and how, in days of old, such words might have led to a duel as both men sought honour in the presence of a lady."

"Was Ifield saying that he would have liked to kill Le Fondre?" Jake said.

"Not at all," Miss Sangster responded. "He was merely referring to the fact that duels had been fought for less. I do not believe for one moment that Mr Ifield actually meant that he wanted to kill Mr Le Fondre. Goodness me, Inspector, you cannot be thinking that Mr Ifield might be a murderer, that would be too horrific a thought."

"At this moment in time, Miss Sangster, I have no idea who murdered Mr Le Fondre," Jake said. "All I can do is continue to gather information and hope that when it is all added up I will have a suspect at the end. How long have you worked for the Ifields?"

"I have worked for Mr Ifield Senior for the last four years. I only do the occasional bit of work for Mr Ifield Junior."

"Do you like Daniel Ifield?"

"He is a very courteous gentleman, Inspector, so I am sure it would be difficult for any woman not to like him."

"Would you lie for him?" Jake then asked. It was a blunt question and one that he probably shouldn't have asked, yet there was something about this woman's demeanour and the manner in which she was answering his questions that made him think there might have been an element of pre-planning.

Miss Sangster responded as he assumed she would. She was offended to be asked such a question and of course she would not lie on Daniel Ifield's behalf. In fact, she had added, she would not lie to the police on anyone's behalf.

Jake decided not to ask any more questions and allowed Miss Sangster to return to her desk. Daniel Ifield came back in to his office a few moments later.

"When are you due to meet Joe Tredwall tomorrow?" Jake then asked as Ifield sat down again behind his desk.

"We are having dinner tomorrow evening at the Business Club. I get the impression that after the arrest of his brother, Joe Tredwall does not want to continue as owner of the Club so I am sure we will be able to come to some arrangement with regard to the price."

"I presume, although you say you are buying the Business Club that you really mean your father, or at least your father's money will actually be buying it?"

Daniel Ifield shifted in his seat again. Jake noticed that Daniel always looked uncomfortable any time his father was mentioned.

"My father is funding the purchase but I will be paying him back from any profits made after I take over the ownership."

"Tell me, Mr Ifield, if you had been owner of the Business Club already would you have allowed someone like Guy Le Fondre to be a Member?"

"I most certainly would not." The reply was emphatic.

"Are you in love with Miss Sangster?" Jake then said.

The change of topic threw Ifield completely. He took a moment to think about how best to answer but he did eventually speak.

"Miss Sangster is a very beautiful woman, Inspector, but I do not allow myself to fall in love with our employees. We have a very good working relationship, which I enjoy and certainly for the moment I seek no more than that from Miss Sangster."

"Very well, sir," Jake added though he was still not wholly convinced that Daniel Ifield's feelings for Miss Sangster did not run deeper than he was admitting. "Well I think that is everything for the moment," he then added as he stood up.

Ifield stood up as well. "I'll get......." he started to say.

"We'll find our own way out," Jake interrupted.

Ifield watched Jake and Mathieson leave his office then sank back in to his chair. The door had only been closed what seemed like a second or two when it opened again and his father came storming in to the room.

"I said the police would be here to see you but even I didn't expect it to be that quick."

Willie Ifield crossed the room and sat in the chair vacated by Jake. Daniel Ifield was still looking a little shocked by the line of questioning that had just been fired in his direction. On top of all that he now had his father's rage to contend with.

"I think it went quite well," he said.

Willie Ifield laughed out loud. "Daniel you have no idea how it went. That Jake Fraser is a devious so and so. I've heard even his own colleagues don't fully understand how his mind works when he is on a case. What I can tell you is that everything you said today will be filed away in the man's brain and should he see or hear anything that even remotely contradicts what you said then he will be back seeking an explanation. I don't like the man, Daniel, but even I have to admit that he is a bloody good police officer."

Daniel knew all this already and it made it all the more imperative that he chose his words well when in Fraser's company. "I think he accepted that Le Fondre's words with me were simply over Miss Sangster and that there was no other connection between us."

"And if he finds that connection?" Willie Ifield then said.

"If he finds the connection then he involves you as well, father," Daniel replied.

"Then let us hope that he never does connect us to Le Fondre," Willie added.

He then stood up and left the room. On his way back to his office he asked Miss Sangster to come in to his office. He asked her how it had gone with the police and she told him what she had been asked and the answers she had given. It all sounded perfectly acceptable to Willie Ifield; he could only now hope that it all sounded as acceptable to Inspector Jake Fraser.

FOUR

Saturday 03 November – afternoon onwards

Mathieson came in to Jake's office in a high state of excitement. He had been doing some door to door enquiries around Guy Le Fondre's house working on the theory that some people might have been at work when the police officers would have called during the week. He had appeared to have struck gold.

"I spoke to Mr Stanley Zanre, who lives across the road from Guy Le Fondre's house. He runs a small shop in Rosemount and is rarely at home. However, he was at home this morning and also late on Tuesday night when he happened to notice a man hanging around outside Mr Le Fondre's home. Mr Zanre told me that this man was there from around eleven o'clock and all he appeared to be doing was walking up and down the pavement, even though the rain was quite heavy at that time."

"Did he see Le Fondre arrive home?"

"Unfortunately he didn't but he did give me a description of the mystery man," Mathieson said with growing excitement. "I've written down what he said."

Mathieson handed a piece of paper to Jake who read it with increasing interest.

Small, thin looking man. Groomed moustache and beard. Pointed nose. Dark, possibly brownish hair. Wearing a light brown coat.

"This could be a description of a lot of men but it could also be a description of Willie Ifield," Jake then said.

"Exactly what I was thinking," added Mathieson.

Jake sat back in his chair and read the description again. It could certainly be Willie Ifield who was being described but why would Willie choose to be outside Guy Le

Fondre's house? Jake still thought it would have made a lot more sense had the description fitted Daniel; at least he had some kind of motive.

"If it was Willie Ifield, why would he want to kill Guy Le Fondre?" Jake then said. "I mean, as far as we know there was no connection between the two men."

"None that we know," added Mathieson." However, that does not mean to say there was no connection. Maybe they did know one another and Willie simply went there that night to talk to Le Fondre and things got out of hand?"

"The evidence seems to point towards Le Fondre being struck with a blow as he turned around," Jake then said. "I don't think he had time to discuss anything with anyone. I think he turned in reaction perhaps to someone speaking and as he turned he was hit on the head with the rock. No, whoever went there that night to see Le Fondre went with the intent to kill."

"Which brings us back to the need for a motive," Mathieson added and Jake nodded his head in agreement.

"And whatever it is, we need to find it fast. I also want you to try and find out what you can about Miss Sangster. There was something about that woman that was too calm and collected yesterday. Also find out when Daniel left the Business Club and try to find the carriage driver as he might be able to confirm that he at least took Daniel home."

"What do we do about this description?" Mathieson then asked.

"For the moment we sit on it," Jake replied. "We need a lot more than this before we pay Ifield Senior a visit. You know what a slippery character he is at the best of times and if we go throwing unsubstantiated accusations around he'll come back at us with all legal guns firing. Get that other information for me, meantime and we'll then decide how best to proceed after that."

"I'll get on to it right away," Mathieson added as he left the room.

Jake looked at the piece of paper once again and hoped against all hope that it did turn out to be Willie Ifield. How nice it would feel to finally lock him up for something.

***

Daniel Ifield made his way to the Business Club at a little after five o'clock. The day had been wet and cold but the darkness of evening was bringing a dry spell so Daniel decided to walk from his house on Mid Stocket Road. As he walked along he felt a contentment that he hoped would last forever. Life was beginning to sort itself out and the future, at least as far as Daniel Ifield was concerned, had never looked brighter.

When Daniel arrived at the Business Club he knocked on the door and stood back to wait for someone to open it. There was only a slight delay between the two actions and he was soon inside taking off his hat and coat and awaiting the arrival of Joe Tredwall. The wait had not been long before Joe Tredwall came down the stairs and advanced towards Daniel.

48

"Shall we have a drink first or do you want to go straight up for dinner?" Joe said after the two men had shaken hands and exchanged pleasantries.

"Might I suggest dinner as I am really hungry?" Daniel replied.

"Dinner it is then," Tredwall added with a smile and led the way up to their table in the dining room.

The room was already quite busy with most of the tables already occupied. One or two tables were still free and it was to one of them that Joe led Daniel Ifield. The table they were to occupy was in the far corner of the room by the window, which overlooked Bon Accord Square. The two men sat down and Daniel looked around at their fellow diners. He noted that many of the Members chose to have dinner with attractive lady companions and he immediately wondered how many of them might actually be their wives.

Drinks were ordered and the two men sat back to look at the menu. Joe already knew it by heart and did not need to read its contents before deciding what he would be having to eat. Daniel noticed that many of the dishes on offer had also been on the menu on the Tuesday he had been there.

"How often does the menu change?" he asked.

"We make minor changes each day and produce a brand new menu every Monday, which then runs for a week. The chef deals with all that, you won't have to bother yourself with what goes on the menu."

"I might choose to get a little more involved?" Daniel suggested.

"In that case you will be looking for a new Chef," replied Tredwall," as the current Chef will not stand for any interference in his work."

"Duly noted," added Ifield with a smile.

By the time the waiter came back with the drinks the order was ready for him. Daniel had vegetable soup and the steak; Joe went for the prawn cocktail and the salmon.

"What *was* your impression of the place after Tuesday?" Joe then asked.

"Very good, though that idiot Le Fondre nearly spoiled it all by being so damned rude to me at the door there."

"Terrible that he should meet such a violent death that very night. Even if he was a bit of a loudmouth he hardly deserved that," Joe then said.

"Terrible indeed. Joe, on that subject, could I ask a small favour of you?" Ifield then said.

"What might that be?"

"If the police ever ask you if I came to you seeking identification of Le Fondre would you be good enough as to say I did. You can even add a little to the price of the Club if it will ease your conscience to bend the truth on my behalf."

"I didn't know that you knew Le Fondre before Tuesday?" Tredwall added.

"I didn't really know him," Ifield explained. "My father and I were considering doing some business with Le Fondre but nothing had happened as yet. Anyway, I don't want my father being dragged in to this business as he inevitably would be if the police were ever to find out that we did know Le Fondre before our confrontation on Tuesday."

Tredwall looked rather warily at Ifield. "You didn't have anything to do with the poor man's death did you?"

"Good Lord, no," Ifield responded.

Joe Tredwall considered that response for a moment and then decided to give Daniel Ifield the benefit of any doubt. He also decided to add five per cent to the sale price of the Business Club.

"Are you happy to go ahead with the purchase of the Club?" Tredwall asked.

"What price are you hoping to make?" Ifield replied.

Tredwall named his price. Ifield tried not to look too happy as the figure was considerably lower than the price he would have been prepared to pay. Ifield held back from saying anything too quickly, as if he were mulling over the figure that had just been quoted. He finally felt the time was right to answer.

"I think we can meet that figure. Would you be happy to get your solicitor to draw up the necessary papers and I'll let my father have a quick look over them before we reach a final decision?"

"I'm happy with that," agreed Tredwall and the two men shook on the deal just as the waiter arrived with the starter course.

"When do you think you will have things ready?"

Tredwall thought for a moment. "We'll have lunch on Wednesday; I'll have everything in place by then."

"Are you sure?" Daniel asked, feeling slightly as if he was being rushed.

"Ever since Cecil was arrested I've thought of nothing other than selling this place and getting the hell out of Aberdeen," Tredwall replied. "The quicker you can take this Club off my hands the better as far as I am concerned. I used to think that this was all that I wanted in life, but I don't feel that way anymore."

Glasses were clinked together. "To Wednesday and the deal, hopefully, being concluded," said Daniel Ifield.

***

Half an hour after Joe Tredwall and Daniel Ifield had started their meal Jake and Margaret were leaving her property on Rosemount Viaduct and heading off for their own meal that night.

Jake had finished earlier than he might have expected and had stopped off at Margaret's on the way home to invite her out for some food and to give her some time to change.

Jake and Margaret went back to the Queen's Restaurant on Union Street and were shown to a table in a restaurant that was already starting to get very busy. A pretty waitress took their coats away and Jake and Margaret sat down. Margaret was looking as attractive as ever with her hair tied up. Her dress was a deep purple colour and followed her every curve.

"This is a lovely way to spend a Saturday evening, thank you for asking me out," Margaret said as she looked around the other diners.

A waiter came over with the menus and placed them on the table. He also took an order for drinks though that only amounted to two glasses of water.

"Off alcohol tonight?" Margaret asked with a smile.

"I might have a glass of wine with my main course," Jake replied, "but, for just now, water will be fine."

They started to look at the menu. The waiter delivered the glasses of water to the table and then left Jake and Margaret for a few moments longer to continue their perusal of the menu. It was eventually the pretty waitress who returned to take their order.

They both went for the Longchamp Soup although Jake was left wondering why they hadn't just called it pea and ham in the first place. Margaret then ordered Sole in a White Wine Sauce and Jake ordered Roast Beef. To accompany their main course there was cabbage and potatoes. The waitress finished writing everything down and then, with a sweet smile, turned and made her way to the kitchen.

Margaret looked around again and noticed someone she recognised sitting at another table. She waved and received a wave back.

"Someone from work?" Jake asked looking round at the other woman.

"She used to work with me," Margaret replied, "but decided a working life surrounded by men was not for her. I don't suppose I can really blame her, she has a husband who never approved."

Jake looked around at the man sitting opposite the waving woman. He looked of military bearing and had a face that looked as if it disapproved of everything.

"Didn't he trust his wife in the company of all those seamen?" Jake asked with a light hearted tone.

Margaret smiled. "Just look at her Jake. Does she look the type to be interested in the men of the sea?"

Jake smiled. "Perhaps not."

When the soup was brought Jake ordered his glass of wine but Margaret decided to keep drinking glasses of water. The soup was excellent and the waitress was soon taking away their empty soup plates. A waiter came over with their drinks and they then chatted for a few moments before the main course was delivered to their table. It proved to be every bit as good as the starter.

"That was excellent," Jake announced as he finished chewing his last mouthful and put his cutlery on to his plate.

Margaret was still enjoying the last of her fish and was not going to be rushed. Jake finished his wine and pondered on whether, or not, he would find space for the bread and butter pudding, which was one of the sweets on offer.

Margaret eventually finished her main course and sat back in her chair with a satisfied sigh. They both agreed that the food had been of the highest standard and it was further agreed that they would both try the bread and butter pudding but that they would like a few moments to digest what they had already eaten first.

"Are you likely to get any time off at Christmas?" Margaret then asked.

Jake was slightly taken by surprise by the question. Christmas wasn't that far off but he hadn't really given any thought as to what he might do.

"I may have to work part of the day but I'm sure I can be free in the evening," he replied.

"Then you must visit me and I will cook us a nice, Christmas meal," Margaret added.

"That would be lovely," Jake said.

A few minutes later the bread and butter pudding was placed before them and little more was said until it had all been eaten.

***

Henry Davis finished packing the last of the boxes he had acquired for their move to Urquhart Road. He had heard that day that the flat would be vacant on Monday and that he and his family could move in on Tuesday. Henry and Bella were excited to be finally moving to a flat that would allow some space for them and the children.

With everything packed in to boxes the flat looked very bare. Henry's attention was drawn to the stain on the floor by the sink. He had tried, on numerous occasions, to remove the stain altogether but there was still a dark mark on the floor that clearly did not look healthy.

Henry decided to acquire a piece of linoleum on Monday and to have it in place over the stain before they left the property on Tuesday.

"I think linoleum would be the best plan," Henry said as Bella stood beside him looking down at the stain on the floor.

"Somebody is going to find this someday," Bella said.

Henry put his arm around her and pulled her closer. "That may well be the case, but hopefully that will not be for a few years by which time people will have forgotten all about the death of George Cathcart, or anybody else for that matter."

Bella put her head on her husband's shoulder. "I wish I could believe that."

Henry took his arm down and turned his wife to face him. Even with her hair dishevelled and her face covered in the dust of cleaning the flat Bella Davis looked beautiful. She had a natural, radiant beauty. It had been that natural beauty that had drawn Cathcart to her, eventually leading to the incident with the knife that fateful night.

"No one is ever going to link us to the death of Cathcart. Even if they find the blood stain it doesn't prove we had anything to do with Cathcart. However, if that link were ever to be made then please understand, my love that I will take the blame for any crime that may be identified."

Bella started to cry. "Henry, you can't do that."

"Yes I can. The boys need their mother."

"They need their father as well," Bella insisted.

"Not as much. There will be no discussion on this; if the police can prove that we had something to do with Cathcart's death then I will confess to the crime and you will say nothing beyond agreeing with anything that I might say. Do you understand?"

Bella continued crying and looking at her husband in silence.

"Do you understand?" Henry asked again.

Bella still said nothing but eventually there was the merest hint of movement from her head that indicated a nod of agreement.

Henry took his wife in his arms and kissed her passionately on the lips. "I love you, Bella Davis and I will never let anyone or anything harm you."

They kissed again and Henry let his hand slide up and over the mound of Bella's left breast. The boys were both sleeping in the other room so Bella knew that the love-making that was about to follow would have to be done outside of the comfort of a bed.

***

By the end of the day everyone who had been recently employed by Scott Thane had arrived at the farm. The housekeeper had been there since Friday evening and had already tidied the place up a lot. All evidence of the previous film-making activities had been removed and all personnel involved in the making of those films had now moved on, just in case the police ever decided to pay a visit.

It was imperative that those now working at the farm knew nothing of any importance and that, at least to them, this was indeed a new venture.

FIVE

Monday 05 November – all day

What was to become the wettest day of the month started as it meant to continue with the rain falling from the sky as if it was never going to stop again. People made their way to work with hats pulled over faces and umbrellas held high wherever possible. The gutters ran with water and the sky was the darkest grey. It was a day that made it clear to the people of Aberdeen that the winter months now lay ahead and certainly as far as the weather was concerned, things were only likely to get worse.

The Number One Circular Route tram, which left Castle Street then made its way around a large part of the city centre before returning to Castle Street was arriving at the stop at the end of Union Terrace. A number of people got off including a dapper looking gentleman wearing a bowler hat and bow tie as well as long coat that pretty much covered everything that he wore beneath. The gentleman did not carry an umbrella but instead held an ornate cane in his right hand, which he leaned upon casually as he set off along the pavement, his expensive looking boots kicking through the small puddles that lay in the various dips in the paving.

A little way up from the large and inspiring statue of William Wallace the gentleman crossed the road and entered through the central door of many that ran the length of the front of the new building that was to become His Majesty's Theatre. The gentleman then made his way up to the Upper Circle. In the corridor before he was required to enter the theatre area itself, he opened a door and entered a large room that was his office. He took off his rain covered coat and hung it on a peg that had been attached to the wall behind his desk.

He placed his bowler hat on the small ledge above the peg, checked that the carnation in his buttonhole was still in place and then sat down behind a desk that was spotlessly clean. He took a small key from his right, jacket pocket and unlocked the top left-hand drawer. He took out a pile of papers from that drawer and then opened the drawer on the other side of his desk. From that he took paper and pens and then arranged everything on his desk ready for the day.

He was proud of his office. It was a large space with room for two cabinets, his desk, four chairs and a small settee. In front of the settee he had placed a coffee table, which he tended to use when guests visited his office. On the wall was a picture of the King and lying on the corner of his desk was a picture of his wife.

He had just finished putting everything in its place when there was a knock at his door.

"Come in," the gentleman announced.

The door opened and a rather nervous looking young man walked in to the room. This was Peter Grant, assistant manager and someone who still had not got accustomed to working with someone so well respected as Mister Harry Adair Nelson. Nelson was a man with a proven theatrical background. He had been especially chosen by Robert Arthur, the money behind the new theatre, because of his background in theatre ownership and everyone had a confidence in the success of the new theatre because they had Nelson at the helm.

However, there was already a strictness to the discipline within the building and it was already clear to the staff who were there through those final days of the building work that things would only get worse in terms of what Mr Nelson would expect from his team. Although he never showed emotion in front of his staff Mr Nelson made it clear from his posture that he did not like hearing bad news and he certainly did not want to hear about anything that might delay the opening of the theatre.

Unfortunately for Peter Grant he had arrived that morning with some news that he knew would not be met with much joy from Mr Nelson.

"What is it, Peter?" Nelson said looking up from his desk.

"There has been another incident, Mr Nelson."

"What do you mean, there has been another incident?"

Grant moved a little closer to Mr Nelson's desk. "The workmen's foreman has reported that tools have gone missing again, which will delay the finishing of some of the jobs."

Nelson looked away from Grant and thought over what he had just been told. There had been a number of incidents over the last few weeks. At first it had been put down to careless workmen but it soon became clear that the incidents were being created rather than just happening. It was as if someone was trying to prevent the theatre from opening.

"Should we involve the police yet, Mr Nelson?" Grant asked.

Nelson's eyes flicked up to look through his assistant manager. "There will be no police inside this theatre before we open. These are only minor, annoying incidents and nothing to bother the police with. We are having enough trouble pleasing the council inspectors without having the police involved."

"Very good, Mr Nelson," Peter Grant said.

"Have a word with the foreman," Nelson then added. "Whatever happens we must be ready for opening on the third of December."

"There is still quite a lot to do, Mr Nelson," Grant suggested.

Nelson sighed. "There is indeed a lot to be done, which is why it is all the more imperative that the workmen do not become distracted by these minor incidents but that they, instead, work all the harder to have this place ready on the night."

"I will speak to him, Mr Nelson."

He then placed the post for that morning on Nelson's desk and turned to leave the office.

***

Sunday had been a pleasant day for Jake. He and Margaret had walked through the Union Terrace Gardens and then had high tea in the Palace Hotel before Jake walked Margaret home and then carried on to his own flat on Esslemont Avenue.

Jake had felt in good spirits as he had left home that morning. Having seen a lot of Margaret over the weekend he was happier than he had been for a few days. His happiness, however, was somewhat washed away as he walked to work through the pouring rain. By the time he reached Lodge Walk his coat and hat were soaked through and his boots had leaked some water through to his socks.

Jake looked so bedraggled when he arrived at Sergeant Turnbull's front desk that the good Sergeant made him a cup of tea and suggested that the Inspector dry out a little before he did much that morning. Jake did not need much persuasion and he was in his office, drinking his tea, when Mathieson came in.

"What a day, sir," Mathieson commented.

"Not very nice, Mathieson," agreed Jake, "and we have no option but to go back out in it as soon as I've dried from the first soaking."

"Who are we going to see today?" Mathieson asked.

"Harriet Cruickshank for a start. She never mentioned anything about Le Fondre having words with Daniel Ifield and she also never mentioned that those words were over another woman. Talking of that other woman did you find out much about the lovely Miss Sangster?"

Mathieson took out his notebook. "Not very much, I'm afraid. Helen Sangster is twenty-six and lives with her mother in a house on Albert Terrace. She has worked for the Ifields for the last four years. She was initially employed as a clerkess but was quickly chosen to be Willie Ifield's personal assistant. She may be very efficient but I'm sure her beauty made her stand out more than anything else. I spoke to another member of staff and they confirmed what we already suspected and that is that Daniel Ifield certainly gives the impression that he would like Miss Sangster to be more than an employee. Interestingly the same member of staff reckoned that Willie Ifield had deeper feelings for Miss Sangster than he would ever make public. Apparently it's a bit of a joke around the company as to whether it will be the father or the son who will make the first move with Miss Sangster."

"I'm sure Ada Ifield would have something to say if Willie tried to do anything that might put their marriage in danger," commented Jake.

"Perhaps, but it is interesting, none the less, that both men seem caught under the spell of Helen Sangster," added Mathieson.

"And if both Willie and Daniel thought that Guy Le Fondre might be trying to take the lovely Miss Sangster away from them they might be inclined to do something about it," Jake added.

"Jealousy; it's one of the oldest motives for murder," added Mathieson.

"Are you happy that this man Zanre is a reliable witness to the fact that someone answering to Willie Ifield's description was standing outside Le Fondre's house on Tuesday night?"

"I have no reason to doubt the man at the moment," Mathieson answered. "I've checked him out and he is the owner of a shop on Rosemount Place that seems to stock pretty much everything and is open nearly all the hours of the day. I confirmed with his one employee that Mr Zanre finished early on a Tuesday. He apparently does that quite often for some reason. He would, therefore, have been at home at the time he said he was."

Jake smiled. "Which is highly inconvenient for Willie Ifield if he really was the man hanging about outside Le Fondre's house."

"Indeed it would be, sir," agreed Mathieson.

"Okay we will add Ada Ifield to our list of calls today. Let us find out if Willie was at home on Tuesday."

"I also found the carriage driver who took Daniel home on Tuesday. He confirms that he dropped Daniel off at his home at a little after ten o'clock. He didn't actually see Daniel go in to his house."

"Even if he did, Daniel is less than a ten minute walk from Le Fondre's house so he would have plenty time to go in to his house and then come out again later. If no one can actually put him in his house that night then he still has no alibi."

"It still seems hard to believe that Le Fondre would have had words with Daniel Ifield about Miss Sangster simply having seen her in the dining room of the Business Club. He would surely have had to have met her before to have formed any kind of emotional bond?"

"I agree," said Jake, "but at the moment we have no proof that they did meet before. It is possible, however, that Le Fondre visited Willie Ifield at his place of work and had seen Miss Sangster from a distance. She is a striking woman and even from a distance would have made an impression on someone like Le Fondre."

"There's nothing to connect Willie Ifield and Le Fondre," added Mathieson.

"I know," agreed Jake, sounding somewhat downbeat. "Anyway, come back and see me in an hour and we'll go out and conduct some interviews."

"Very good, sir," concluded Mathieson as he left the room.

***

Harriet Cruickshank could not wait for the moment that Guy Le Fondre's will was read out and she could finally go public on the fact that she was a very rich woman indeed. However, until that moment she had to continue living her life to the best possible standards. It had been a few days since she had last received money from Le Fondre but, of course, there was already another man in her life and he had taken over the burden of meeting Harriet's expenses in the meantime. They both knew that once the inheritance was cleared, Harriet would no longer need the financial support of anyone.

Harriet felt that she was finally get some return for the life she had been forced to live. It had been a life that had never offered much and in turn, Harriet had little to offer back beyond her looks. As a fifteen year old she had wound her uncle around her little finger and he had given her money to stop her telling the rest of the family what he was doing to her in the dead of night. By the time she was twenty she had been thrown out of the family home for being free with her favours with too many men.

Now effectively on the street Harriet had turned to the only source of income available to her and it was at that time that she had fallen under the cruel control of Bailey. She had remained under the terror of that man until Guy Le Fondre had set her free. For three years she had made money for Bailey by having sex with as many men as she could meet in the course of what passed for a working day. Now that Le Fondre was no longer around to protect her, Harriet wondered why she had never heard from Bailey again. It would have been just like the man to try and claim her back.

Harriet's rejoicing at the new man in her life was not just with a concern for money. Her relationship with Le Fondre had never involved sex beyond her washing him and him fondling her breasts at times. Harriet had needs, which she had sometimes dealt with by returning to her old profession. However, whilst Le Fondre had been alive she had always ensured that she was spotlessly clean after one of her sessions, before she met him.

Now that he was dead she didn't need to do that anymore; her body was her own again and she had every intention of satisfying her most basic needs as much as she possibly could. Those needs had been met during Sunday when she had met her new man and they had gone to a hotel room for what turned out to be six hours of uncontrolled passion. By the time she had returned home late in the evening she was sore in places that she had forgotten even existed.

Harriet had wakened on the Monday morning and washed. She still tingled at the thought of what she had done the day before and as her wet hands travelled across her body she thought about Le Fondre and could now have some understanding of why he felt so sexually charged by being washed.

Harriet dressed and had some breakfast. She was just at the point of thinking that she might go out for the day, even though the rain was pouring down, when there was a knock at her door.

When Harriet opened the door she was mildly annoyed to find Inspector Jake Fraser and Sergeant Mathieson standing in the hallway.

"May we come in, Miss Cruickshank?" Jake enquired.

"Of course," Harriet replied and stepped back to allow the police officers to enter her property.

"My apologies for our condition," Jake then said, "but it is absolutely pouring down out there."

Harriet noted how wet the two police officers were and suggested that they sit in the kitchen. She offered to make them a cup of tea but they declined. They sat at the kitchen table and Jake began his line of questioning.

"The last time we spoke, Miss Cruickshank, you omitted to tell us that Guy Le Fondre had words with another gentleman after your meal. Would you like to tell us about that now?"

"My apologies, Inspector, I didn't think that that had anything to do with Guy's death."

"Two men have heated words with each other only a few hours before one of them is murdered and you didn't think it was relevant?" Jake said not even trying to hide his disbelief.

"My mistake, Inspector."

Did you know who that other gentleman was?" Jake then asked.

"I believe it was Daniel Ifield."

"What prompted their verbal exchange?"

"I really don't know, Inspector, you know what men are like, they get so upset about nothing at all half the time."

"Was it not the case that they were having words about another woman, Miss Cruickshank? Another woman who was there with Mr Ifield?"

Harriet paused for a little while. She really wanted these police officers to go away and leave her alone but she knew that they would not do that until she had answered all their questions. Throughout her entire life Harriet had never been good at answering questions. She sighed.

"There did seem to be some posturing over her, yes."

"And did you get the feeling that that was not the first time that Mr Le Fondre had seen that other woman?"

"They were just being silly men, Inspector. Perhaps Guy had seen the other woman before, I really don't know, but the fact seemed obvious that he found her extremely attractive and it moved him to pass the odd comment in the direction of Ifield."

 "How did that make you feel?"

"How do you think it made me feel, Inspector? It made me feel small and unwanted for a few moments but then Guy and I went off to one of the rooms and everything was back to normal again. I knew that Guy had eyes for other women but he always came back to me because I was the only one to fully appreciate what gave him sexual satisfaction. Anyway, I could tell from the other woman's expression that she would never have cared to have someone like Guy in her life. She just looked at him with disgust on her face."

"Are you telling me that you weren't annoyed with Mr Le Fondre for openly showing an unhealthy interest in another woman?" Jake then asked sounding as if he would find such a notion hard to believe.

"Guy was not showing an interest in that woman," countered Harriet. "The main reason for him saying what he did was to annoy Daniel Ifield. Guy got pleasure out of annoying people and the more he disliked the person worse he was."

"But why would he want to upset someone that as far as we know, had never met Mr Le Fondre prior to that night?" Jake then asked.

"Oh, sorry Inspector, I got the impression that the two men *did* know each other. They were certainly quick enough to square up to each other."

"And you still insist that that kind of behaviour from Mr Le Fondre did not upset you?"

"As I said, I did find it all rather annoying and upsetting but only for a short period of time. Guy did these things to upset other people; but he never knowingly did anything to upset me."

"But why would Guy Le Fondre have any desire to annoy Daniel Ifield?"

"It was probably because Guy would have seen him as being common and certainly not worthy of owning an establishment like the Business Club. Guy might even have seen himself as being the owner of the Club ahead of someone like Ifield. He would, therefore, have seen Ifield as being the perfect target for verbal abuse. However, the quickest way to get under Ifield's skin was clearly to attack him on a level that suggested he was a bit of failure with women. To be honest the woman standing beside Daniel Ifield was way outside of his league."

"Do you happen to know if Guy Le Fondre had ever had any business dealings with Willie Ifield, Daniel's father?"

"I never had anything to do with Guy's business arrangements, Inspector. I was in his life purely to bring him sexual pleasure and absolutely nothing else. He never mentioned anything of that kind to me and I most certainly would never have been asking. The one thing about our relationship was that I knew my place and I would never have done anything to jeopardise my position in Guy's life."

Jake considered what had been said for a moment. He eventually spoke again.

"Very well, Miss Cruickshank, I don't think there is anything else that I wish to ask you at the moment. Good day to you."

Jake and Mathieson left the flat and made their way down to street level. The rain had eased slightly and was not quite as heavy as they made their way back to Lodge Walk.

***

Scott Thane got off the train in Ellon and walked to the carriage that had been arranged for him. The carriage had been sitting outside the Station Hotel and there were a number of people coming and going as he climbed in to the carriage and indicated to the driver that he was ready to go.

As he made his way out to the farm the rain continued to fall, showing little sign of letting up. Overhead the sky was a dark and dirty grey and there was a mist in the air that affected visibility and seemed to reduce the world to little more than a field's width. There was very little traffic on the road and the journey did not take that long.

By the time they reached the farm the rain had eased slightly but Thane had to be careful as he climbed down from the carriage as the farmyard was little more than a sea of mud. He picked his way through the puddles, trying to ensure that he did not get the bottom of his trousers too dirty. With some sense of relief he found his way to the front door where he grabbed the door knocker and rapped twice.

The door was opened by the new housekeeper and she showed Thane through to the front room where a number of people had gathered. Thane took off his coat as he looked around the faces, mentally trying to put names to some of the people whom he had briefly met before. He quickly realised that Wolfgang was not among them. He also noticed that Maisie was not there but then remembered that she had been due to leave anyway.

Thane was quite relieved to see that Wolfgang and Maisie were not there as it was probably best that anyone with so much knowledge of the obscene films should now be as far away from the farm as possible. The last thing he would have wanted was for someone to start talking about what had been going on at the farm prior to the arrival of the new, professional, staff.

Thane was pleased to see that all the major players were in the room and that he now had a professional crew who could make professional films for a wider market. After he had spoken with many of the people gathered in the room he then went, along with Giles Hampton, who would be the main director of their productions and Tony McRobb, who would be the senior cameraman, over to the converted barn where the bulk of the action would be filmed.

"Quite a set-up you have here," Hampton said as they arrived in the new studio. "What were you using it as before?"

Thane paused for a few seconds before answering with a blatant lie. "There was nothing film related here before, your films will be the first action this studio has seen."

Hampton seemed a little surprised by that response but let it pass. McRobb started to wax lyrical about the equipment he would have at his disposal and both men seemed confident that they could make films of the highest quality.

"I take it you don't have a script to work with at the moment?" Thane then asked.

"We have the start of one and I would propose as everyone is now here that we just get started. We can worry about the end of the film once we know what it is," Hampton replied.

"That seems to be a good idea to me," Thane then said. "If we are not working then we are not making money and after what I have poured in to this venture I would like to be enjoying some return sooner rather than later."

"I am sure the return will be manifold, Mr Thane. I believe that the film business will only get bigger as time passes and that we are at the beginning of a great journey, which I am sure will make us all wealthier than we are at present."

"I hope that you are right, Mr Hampton," Thane then said. "I have a partner who is in the process of arranging for us to show our films in a local theatre. However, I am keen to get as wide an audience as possible so I will be making contact with like-minded people across the country so that we have as many outlets as possible for showing our films."

"Excellent, Mr Thane," Hampton added.

Thane satisfied himself that there was no evidence of the previous filming that had gone on in the studio and hoped that there was also no evidence of the women who had been fed to the pigs at some point of the last year.

They returned to the farmhouse and Thane went back in to the front room where those who were still there were sitting enjoying a cup of tea and some baking, which had been done by the housekeeper. Everyone looked very much at home but to Thane each face that he saw was nothing more than an additional cost. With the making of the new sex films closed down for what could be some time, he now had a limited return coming back from the showing and sale of the films already made.

If the studio did not start making money soon Thane knew that he would have to eat much further in to the savings that he and Le Fondre had amassed than he had ever intended. However, matters were eased slightly by the money that Le Fondre had passed to him in the box brought over by Mr Gladstone. Thane wondered if Gladstone had taken any of it before bringing the rest over. He finally decided that if he had then he should only be praised for having such an enterprising thought.

Thane sat down and a young woman brought him a cup of tea and a piece of cake. She was strikingly beautiful with long, dark hair and blue eyes that positively sparkled in his direction. She then went back for another cup of tea for herself before coming back and sitting beside Thane.

"I am so pleased to finally meet you, Mr Thane," the woman said in a soft voice that seemed to wash over Scott Thane and make him feel very comfortable in her presence. "My name is Sarah Elder. I am an actress and I've worked with Giles before so I know the finished product is going to be excellent."

"I am very pleased to hear you say that, Miss Elder."

"Oh, please, call me Sarah."

"In that case I am very pleased to meet you, Sarah," Thane then added and shook her hand. He took a little longer than might have been absolutely necessary to let it go again as he lost himself, for a few seconds, in the deep pools of her eyes.

Tea and cake was finished and Scott Thane took a minute with Giles Hampton, before he left, to make sure that filming would be underway before the end of the week. Hampton was happy to provide Thane with the assurance that there would be a film to promote by the end of December.

"I'm telling you, Mr Thane, "Hampton then added, "nineteen hundred and seven is going to be quite a year for all of us."

"Excellent," Thane concluded, shaking Hampton's hand, casting one last glance in the direction of Sarah Elder and then making his way out to the carriage again. The rain was back on and the mud gathering all the more in the farmyard.

Scott Thane thought about Sarah Elder and the warmth of that thought accompanied him all the way back to Aberdeen.

***

In the middle of the afternoon Jake and Mathieson caught the tram out to the Ifield's house on Queen's Road. The door was opened by a rather portly looking woman who had the look of someone who had just been interrupted and would rather be getting back to what she had been doing.

"Is Mrs Ifield at home?" Jake asked showing his identification.

"She is," replied the woman who then ushered the police officers in to the house and showed them through to a room at the back of the house. The woman asked Jake and Mathieson to take a seat and then said she would go for Mrs Ifield.

A few moments later Ada Ifield walked in to the room. She wasn't the most beautiful woman in the world but she had a certain attraction to her that had not disappeared over the years. At forty-three she was ten years younger than her husband and she clearly enjoyed the life of being the wife of a very wealthy man.

"What can I do for you, Inspector?" Ada said as she almost floated across the floor towards them. Her blue dress had a white design on it and the pearls around her neck had not been cheap when purchased.

"I have a few questions about your husband," Jake replied.

"Please, sit down," Ada then said and waved an arm in the direction of the settee. Once they were all seated it was Ada who spoke again first. "Would you not be better speaking to my husband?"

"We will be speaking to your husband, Mrs Ifield, but it would be helpful if you could answer some questions first."

Ada Ifield looked unsure of herself. "I'm not sure I should be answering any questions without my husband being here."

"Basically all we need to know is whether, or not, your husband was at home last Tuesday evening up until around midnight?" Jake then said.

Ada thought for a moment. "He was out with a friend on Tuesday."

"What time did he get home?"

"I have no idea, Inspector. I have not been sleeping so well recently and have taken to using the spare room. As a result I not only have been sleeping better but I also cannot hear any movement in the house."

"What time did you go to your bed that night?" Jake asked.

"At my usual time," Ada replied.

Jake glanced at Mathieson who had paused in the middle of taking his notes. It was clear from the silence that Ada Ifield had no intention of elaborating on her reply without a prompt of some kind. Jake offered that prompt.

"And what is your usual time, Mrs Ifield?"

"Just before eleven. I always do some sewing and then a hot drink is brought to me, which I drink before retiring."

"Thank you very much, Mrs Ifield," Jake then said. "That is really all we needed to know."

Ada Ifield brightened and stood up. "That didn't hurt after all," she commented and Jake smiled.

Once out of the house Jake turned to Mathieson. "We might as well go and speak to Willie Ifield now before he has time to speak to his wife and come up with some kind of a story, should he feel that he needs one."

Two tram rides later and Jake and Mathieson were entering Willie Ifield's place of business. Jake did not wait at the door to be introduced; he showed his identification and kept on walking. Once up the stairs he knew exactly where to go to find Willie Ifield.

Ifield was less than pleased when his office door opened and two police officers walked in. He had been in the middle of giving some thought to the price, proposed by Joe Tredwall, for the sale of the Business Club. On the face of it all seemed well and Willie was looking forward to Daniel formalising the deal on Wednesday. Now his thoughts had been shattered by this intrusion.

He leapt to his feet with outrage etched on his face.

"Inspector Fraser, what is the meaning of this?"

"A few questions, Mr Ifield that is all."

Ifield looked down at the papers on his desk. "I really am extremely busy, Inspector and this is not a good time."

"It's a good time for me," Jake responded and sat down on the chair opposite Ifield, Mathieson sat in the corner with his notebook poised and ready.

Ifield remained standing for a moment longer, his face still showing how annoyed he was. Miss Sangster had by then appeared in the doorway.

"Is there anything you want me to do, Mr Ifield?" she asked.

Ifield stood a few seconds longer and then slowly sank in to his chair. "Just close the door, please Miss Sangster," he eventually said.

The door closed and Willie Ifield now sat back in his chair and looked from one police officer to the other. Jake began speaking.

"I'm sure you will already know, Mr Ifield that we were here on Friday talking to your son, Daniel. We were particularly interested in his actions on Tuesday evening of last week?"

"I was aware that you had spoken to him but, surely that can have nothing to do with me."

"Perhaps not, though it would now help our enquiries if you were to tell us what *you* were doing that night?" Jake added.

Ifield sat forward with a look of perceived understanding crossing his face. "Oh I see, Inspector, if you can't pin something on one Ifield it's time to try another, is that really your philosophy?"

Jake smiled. "Aberdeen City Police are not in the habit of pinning anything on anyone, Mr Ifield. We are here to gather further evidence in our enquiry in to the murder of Guy Le Fondre."

Ifield sat back again, a look of surprise now on his face. "The murder of Guy Le Fondre; why would you think that I was connected with that in any way?"

"Mr Ifield, we have a witness who places someone of your description at the scene of the crime. To allow us to count you out of our enquiries we are, therefore, required to ask you what you were doing that night."

Ifield looked horrified. "Someone thinks that I killed Le Fondre?"

"I didn't say that, Mr Ifield, I merely said that someone of your description was seen outside Mr Le Fondre's house around the time that he was killed. If you can give me a satisfactory answer as to what you were doing that night then we'll be on our way."

Ifield sat back in his chair again. For a moment he seemed lost, his face going an obvious shade of white. Jake noted his response.

"I really don't think I should be saying anything else until I have my solicitor present," Ifield then said.

"Very well, Mr Ifield, could I ask you to attend Lodge Walk in one hour, with your solicitor? I should also add that Sergeant Mathieson will remain with you, during that time, so that you do not have any opportunity to affect any evidence that you may seek to give us."

"I don't need to be baby-sat, Inspector. You have my word that I will be at Lodge Walk in an hour and that I will answer any questions that you may have in front of my solicitor."

"I'm sure that you will answer my questions, Mr Ifield, but I will still leave my Sergeant with you, just in case you have any notions of doing something daft."

Willie Ifield seethed silently for a moment. His fists clenched on the table as if he wanted to hit someone. Jake felt that that someone was probably him, but he was not going to give Ifield any opportunity to create an alibi for himself for that night.

"Very well, Inspector, have it your way," Ifield eventually said.

Jake stood up with a smile. "I'll see you in an hour then."

And with that Jake left the office and Mathieson remained in the corner with Willie Ifield's beady eyes staring right through him.

***

As agreed, Willie Ifield arrived at Lodge Walk an hour later. Accompanying him was Sergeant Mathieson and a tall, grey-haired man, wearing a pin-stripe suit and a bowler hat. Even though the three men had only walked from a carriage to the door of the building they were all showing signs of being quite wet. It was obvious that the heavy rain had returned.

Mathieson took Ifield and his solicitor through to the interview room and then went to find Jake, leaving a young Constable in the room. Jake and Mathieson came in to the interview room ten minutes later and the young Constable was asked to wait outside as he might be needed again later. Once in the room Jake and Mathieson sat down opposite the other two.

Ifield introduced his solicitor as being Nigel Porteous. Porteous looked every bit the solicitor with every square inch of his attire screaming wealth at the world around it. Ifield then sat back in his chair to await Jake's questions.

Jake was not convinced that the interview would be very productive as Willie Ifield would not be someone who could be easily intimidated. However, there was enough evidence to make an interview necessary and Jake could only hope that there might be a chink in Ifield's armour as he presented his story of the night on which Le Fondre was murdered.

"Were you at home on Tuesday night of last week?" Jake asked first.

"I was not."

"Where were you?"

"Visiting a friend. We played cards and had a few drinks."

"Could we please have the name of this friend?"

"Bob Lawson."

"Address?"

Willie Ifield gave Jake an address on Fountainhall Road. Mathieson wrote it down.

"What time did you leave Mr Lawson's?" Jake then asked.

"Around midnight, I should think. I was certainly home by half past."

"Apart from Mr Lawson, can anyone else confirm what you are telling me?"

Ifield glanced at his solicitor. "I shouldn't think so. I walked home and I don't remember seeing anyone."

"We believe that Mr Le Fondre was murdered around half past midnight so it is highly convenient that you should be telling us that you were home by then," Jake then said.

Porteous now puffed up at that point. "Are you accusing my client of lying, Inspector?"

"Not at all, I am merely saying it is strange that Mr Ifield should seek to prove that he was home by half past midnight, which just happens to be the time that Mr Le Fondre was killed."

"Mere coincidence, that is all, "added Porteous.

"Is it also mere coincidence that the description we received of a man waiting outside Le Fondre's house happens to fit Mr Ifield very closely?"

"As my client wasn't there, Inspector, it rather proves that it is mere coincidence, doesn't it?" Porteous responded.

"Your client *says* he wasn't there, Mr Porteous, there is no proof that he is actually telling you the truth."

"And there is no proof that he may be lying, Inspector."

"Perhaps not, Mr Porteous, but if you would just excuse me for a moment," Jake said and he stood up and made his way to the door. Mathieson remained behind.

Jake arranged for two uniformed police officers to go to the Fountainhall Road address and to bring Mr Lawson back to Lodge Walk. They were then to place him in the second interview room and to notify Jake when they got back. Jake then returned to the interview room where Ifield and his solicitor were chatting casually as he entered the room.

"Did you know Mr Le Fondre?" Jake asked as he returned to his seat opposite Ifield and Porteous.

"No."

"You'd never met him?"

"No."

"Do you know if your son, Daniel, had ever met Mr Le Fondre?"

Ifield was starting to look bored. "No."

"Why then do you think Le Fondre felt it necessary to have words with your son at the Business Club last Tuesday?" Jake enquired.

"I have no idea. Were he alive you would really have needed to have asked Mr Le Fondre that question."

"Do you know a man by the name of Scott Thane?" Jake then asked.

"No."

"You have never met Scott Thane?" Jake added.

"I believe I've already told you that I don't know anyone by the name of Scott Thane," Ifield replied.

"Are you happy that your son is buying the Business Club?"

Ifield looked surprised at the change of subject. "He hasn't bought it yet, we still have to discuss the asking price."

"Are you happy that he *wants* to buy it?" Jake then enquired.

"It's high time my son stood on his own two feet and if it takes the purchase of the Business Club to achieve that then so be it."

Jake asked a few more questions which, quite frankly, were taking him further away from the matter in hand but the questions were being asked as a stalling tactic rather from any need to have them answered. He was waiting for Lawson to be brought to the police office and he did not want to let Ifield leave meantime.

As it was there was half an hour of meaningless questions and further excuses for leaving the room before Jake got the message that Lawson was in the other interview room. He once more excused himself and went through to see him. Jake asked Mathieson to come with him and then asked a young constable to keep an eye on Ifield and Porteous.

Bob Lawson was a small man with beady eyes and a balding head. He had a slight twitch, which seemed to throw his head to the right every now and again. He was not at all happy at being dragged down to the police office and demanded an explanation.

"My apologies, Mr Lawson," Jake said, sitting down," but we are having a little chat with Mr Willie Ifield and he has told us that he was in your company on Tuesday evening. I did not want Mr Ifield to leave before I had a chance to speak to you so that was why I asked a couple of officers to collect you and bring you here. I do not intend to keep you long and then we will arrange for a carriage to take you home."

Lawson sat down and appeared to relax a little as a result of what he had just heard.

"I was with Willie on Tuesday," he then said.

"What time did Mr Ifield arrive at your house?"

Lawson paused for a moment. "I should think it was around seven."

"And what time did he leave?"

Lawson again paused, as if pondering on what answer he might give. Eventually he gave his reply.

"Late."

"How late?" Jake pressed.

"Very late."

Jake was getting a little annoyed. "Can you be somewhat more precise, Mr Lawson?"

Lawson went quiet again. "Around midnight I suppose; I didn't feel any need to check my watch."

"What did you do?" Jake then asked.

"What did we do?" repeated Lawson, looking slightly confused.

"Yes, Mr Lawson," added Jake, the annoyance evident in his tone," what did you and Mr Ifield do all evening?"

"Oh, sorry. We played cards."

"Which particular game?" Jake said.

The silence returned as Lawson gave that question far more thought than might have been necessary. He did eventually answer.

"We played Cribbage."

"And who won?"

"We played more than one game and honours were even by the end of the night."

"Do you often meet for evenings of cards?" Jake then asked.

"Occasionally."

"Was anyone else there on Tuesday to confirm what you are telling me?" Jake then asked.

"No, it was just the two of us."

"What was Mr Ifield wearing?"

The question hit Lawson like a punch to the stomach. The look of almost panic that crossed his face was evident to both Jake and Mathieson and he slumped back in his chair for a few seconds. He quickly recovered and sat up again, his head slightly tilted away as he gave some thought to an answer. The twitch was worse, however, with his head flicking to the right on a more regular basis.

The silence continued. "Is the question too difficult?" Jake added.

"No, I'm just trying to remember, that is all. I don't usually make a point of noticing what my friends are wearing."

"Unless it is a lady?" suggested Jake.

Lawson acknowledged that that might be true and then said that Ifield had been wearing his work suit, dark blue he thought.

"If you would excuse us for a moment, Mr Lawson," Jake then said and made his way back to the other interview room. Jake and Mathieson exchanged rooms with the constable.

Jake sat down and began asking Ifield the same questions he had asked Lawson. The two men agreed on the fact that they had played Cribbage though Ifield offered a score of 2-2 when pressed on the result. However, when it came to the topic of clothing the responses parted company rather dramatically.

"I had changed for the evening so I wore a casual jacket and trousers."

"And you left around midnight?" Jake said.

"About then, yes."

"Excuse me a moment," Jake then said and got up to leave again.

"Honestly, Inspector," Porteous rather erupted, "how much longer is this little charade going to last?"

Jake paused in the doorway. "Oh, this is no charade, Mr Porteous and we'll be finished when I return. Mathieson, stay here I'll be right back."

Jake went to the other room and asked the constable to take a statement from Mr Lawson. Once that had been written and signed Jake sat down again and asked a few more questions.

"So you say that Mr Ifield was wearing his work suit and that suit was probably dark blue?"

Lawson did not answer for what seemed like an eternity. By the very fact that the question was being asked it seemed logical for Lawson to assume that the Inspector now did know what Ifield had been wearing that night and it had clearly not been his work suit. It was a major lesson for him; if you are going to be part of someone else's alibi at least make sure you've agreed on all the details. Lawson began to wonder how much longer he could keep up the pretence.

"I may have got the clothing wrong, Inspector. As I said earlier, I am not in the habit of paying much attention to what my male friends might be wearing."

"So you often mistake a work suit for a casual jacket and trousers?"

Lawson regained the look of someone whose options were narrowing by the minute. He thought about sticking with the story that he had loosely agreed with Willie Ifield but then he began to think about *why* Willie had asked him to lie. Why had Willie needed the alibi in the first place and in agreeing to provide him with that alibi was he now putting himself in danger of being charged with something serious? Lawson could not afford to get in to any real trouble with the police. He decided to tell the truth.

"Very well, Inspector, Mr Ifield was not with me on Tuesday. He does sometimes come to me on a Tuesday evening and we do play cards, only this week was not one of those sessions."

Jake smiled. "Excellent, Mr Lawson. Now if you would amend your statement accordingly and sign the paper I'd be much obliged."

Jake left a Constable to oversee the writing of the new statement and to then organise a carriage to take Mr Lawson home. Just before he left the room, however, Jake informed Lawson that he may yet face charges for lying to the police. The sweat that broke out on Lawson's brow indicated that man was suffering greatly for getting himself unnecessarily involved in other people's issues.

Jake then went back to face Ifield. This time, on his return, there was no dialogue between solicitor and client and Willie Ifield had a look on his face that betrayed his concern for not knowing what Jake had been doing every time he had left the room. He was about to find out.

"I've been speaking to Bob Lawson, Mr Ifield," Jake began.

"Excellent," Ifield responded, "now we can get this whole matter cleared up."

"The only way we will get this whole matter cleared up will be if you start telling me the truth, Mr Ifield," Jake added and Ifield's expression changed to one of concern again.

It was Porteous who reacted first however. "Whatever do you mean by that, Inspector?"

"Very simple, Mr Porteous, your client is not telling me the truth at the moment. It may even be the case that your client has not been telling *you* the truth and if so we'll find that out in a moment. You see, Mr Ifield, you almost got your story agreed with Mr Lawson only you forgot to mention clothes to him. I'm sorry to say that he said you were wearing your work suit and of course you didn't say that at all. I have just put it to Mr Lawson that the story about the clothes didn't match and he is now signing a statement to the effect that you were *not* with him last Tuesday evening. Now, as we have proof that you were not with Mr Lawson that night, maybe we can now move on to where you *really* were that night?"

Ifield sat back in his chair and Porteous gave him a rather stern look of annoyance. It seemed that he hadn't been as truthful as he should have been with his solicitor either.

"May I speak with my client alone for a moment, Inspector?" Porteous then said.

"Only if you can talk some sense in to him telling us the truth," Jake replied and then said they could have ten minutes.

Jake and Mathieson left the room and went to have a quick cup of tea. By the time they returned Willie Ifield was not looking so confident.

"Are we ready to talk now, Mr Ifield?" Jake said.

"Firstly I do not want Bob Lawson to be dragged in to this anymore than he has been already. I used Bob as an excuse occasionally and made the mistake of doing so again regarding this matter. Bob is not involved beyond providing a cover story for me so I do not want any action taken against him."

"Very well, Mr Ifield, assuming that I am happy with what you tell me I give you my word that we will take no action against Mr Lawson," Jake replied.

Ifield glanced at Porteous, who still looked anything but happy. Ifield then began to speak.

"I also do not want my wife Ada to ever hear a word of what I am about to say. On Tuesday evening, through until after midnight, I was in the company of a young woman. This is a young woman whom I meet with quite often and yes, before you ask, I do pay her for her services. Her name is Mathilde Dupont, she is French and I have been visiting her for the past year or so, usually on a Tuesday."

Ifield took a piece of paper from his pocket on which he had written an address. He slid it across the table.

"This is where Mathilde lives and I am sure she will verify everything that I have said."

Jake looked at Ifield and then at Porteous. His gaze then returned to Ifield.

"Why didn't you just tell me this in the first place?"

"Because I do not want Ada to know anything about it and I also feel an element of shame at having to admit to seeing a prostitute. A man has needs, however and those needs are no longer met at home."

"Very well, Mr Ifield, you may go for the moment. Depending on what we hear from Miss Dupont we may need to speak with you again."

"I understand," Willie Ifield said.

Ifield and Porteous then left the building and Jake and Mathieson returned to Jake's office.

"Do you believe him?" Mathieson asked.

"I believe that he may have bought the support of Miss Dupont," Jake replied, "but that does not necessarily mean that he is now telling us the truth."

"When do we pay the young lady a visit?"

Jake took his pocket watch from the right pocket of his waistcoat and checked the time. It had been a long day so he decided to get some sleep first and tackle Miss Dupont with a clearer mind the following day.

"We've done enough for today, Sergeant, so let us both get cleared up and go home. I don't know about you but I could certainly be doing with some food and a good night's sleep."

Mathieson did not need to be told twice to go home and by the time their watches had moved on a further thirty minutes both men were well on their way home, cursing the fact that it was still raining and feeling some sympathy for anyone who had made arrangements to hold a party in celebration of the fact that it was Guy Fawkes's Night.

SIX

Tuesday 06 November – mid-morning until mid-evening

Jake left his flat and set off to work with a thick haze hanging over the city. The rain of the day before had moved on and now it seemed as if the thick, grey cloud had come down to touch the earth. It made visibility difficult and Jake expected to hear, as the day progressed, of an increased number of road incidents mainly due to pedestrians walking out in front of carts or trams that had appeared, unexpectedly, out of the mist.

Jake arrived at the office and found Mathieson writing up the notes he had taken from the interviews the day before. Mathieson was looking a little annoyed and without saying anything he picked up the morning paper and opened it in front of Jake.

"I've no idea how MacBride got this story unless it came from Ifield's solicitor."

Jake scanned the front page story. It stated that Willie Ifield, *that well-known local, business-man,* had been interviewed by the police in connection with the murder of Guy Le Fondre. It then went on to say that the police had little by way of evidence and that there had been a hint, in the past, of the police harassing Mr Ifield over his potential involvement in previous cases.

"I'll speak to MacBride," Jake said and threw the paper down. This was the kind of thing that did little to help an inquiry. It was typical of the Press; they get half a story and they twist it in to a full story. Jake was even more annoyed by the fact that he thought that he and Alan MacBride had a good working arrangement and that MacBride would have spoken to Jake before printing anything.

Jake left the building and made his way round to the Daily Journal offices on Broad Street. He introduced himself at the door and insisted that he see Alan MacBride at once. The little man on reception was suitably intimidated by this irate police officer and he led Jake up to the second floor and in to a small room furnished with a table and four chairs. Jake sat down and waited.

Two or three minutes later and the door opened. Alan MacBride walked in and his hands were already held up in defence.

"I know you're annoyed, Inspector, but don't take your anger out on me; I was told to print what I had even though I knew it was only half the story."

"Do you realise the damage you may have done to our case, Alan?" Jake said as MacBride sat down opposite.

"I know it won't have helped," MacBride acknowledged, "but, like I said, I was told to print what I had."

"How did you get the information?"

"Now you know, Inspector, that I can't tell you that."

"It had to be from either Nigel Porteous or Daniel Ifield," Jake added. "No one else knew that we had interviewed Willie Ifield and no one else would have wanted to undermine our case at such an early stage. I mean you practically said that we were trying to pin something on Willie Ifield without any real evidence."

"The wording did get changed a little from my initial version," MacBride added. "Look, Jake, Willie Ifield is a very powerful man in this city with a lot of friends in places that can be helpful at times."

"And one of his friends just happens to be your editor?" Jake added.

MacBride said nothing but his silence spoke volumes. Eventually MacBride did speak, but it was ask a question.

"Why don't you tell me your side of the story and I'll see that it gets printed?"

"There is no side to the story from my perspective at the moment," Jake replied. "As I have always said, Alan, when I have something that you can print you continue to be the first person I speak to. As soon as I have something concrete in this case I will let you know, but I won't be dragged in to some kind of debate through the Press about whether or not Willie Ifield really is the fine upstanding gentleman that he would like to portray in this city."

"All I ask, Jake, is that you don't see my name on the page and assume that I am doing this through some personal desire to see the local police and their work undermined. My name goes against the stories for which I have acquired the information. How that story is ultimately worded, however, is down to the editor and I can't help it that that man is a personal friend of Willie Ifield's."

Jake had calmed down considerably and had realised that this was not a situation of Alan MacBride's making.

"I hadn't wanted this investigation to be public knowledge quite yet," Jake then said. "I needed more time to build my case and now I'll have to do so against a backdrop of Willie Ifield's friends, family and solicitor doing all that they can to slur the work that we are doing."

"I'm truly sorry, Jake. Please don't let this affect our personal arrangement."

"Quite the reverse, Alan, this strengthens our arrangement for as soon as I have enough with which to charge Willie Ifield then you will have your story. However I will demand that your story occupies the same front page space as the nonsense which was printed today.

Jake then stood up and left. Alan MacBride had no doubt he had just annoyed a man whom he wished to call friend. He did not like being put in such a position and knew that he had just moved one step closer to telling his editor what he really thought of him.

However, for the moment, MacBride decided to play the game and see what developed. He had a feeling that Willie Ifield might regret what he had started as it would only make Jake Fraser all the more driven to get the evidence he needed to put Willie Ifield away for a very long time.

***

Henry Davis had been given the day off so that he could move himself and his family from their rather small abode in the Shiprow to a much larger, two-bedroomed flat on Urquhart Road.

He had enjoyed the fact that he could stay in bed a little longer. He had been disturbed by Bella getting up around an hour earlier to feed Sidney but the baby had gone to sleep again and Bella had come back to bed. Ronnie, their eldest son, was sleeping in the other room.

Henry and Bella took the opportunity to make love in the comfort of their bed. It would be the last fit of passion in their current address and they took their time enjoying each other's body.

It was nearer ten, therefore, before they got out of bed and dressed. Henry had arranged for a colleague, who owned a horse and cart, to call at midday to help move what little possessions they had. There would be no furniture as both properties were owned by the police and as such, they came furnished.

Henry had spent the previous evening laying a nice, new piece of linoleum over the stain on the floor that betrayed the location of Cathcart's death. It all looked nice and tidy now and Henry felt sure that no one would feel the need to replace or remove the linoleum for some time to come.

Henry and Bella had breakfast and Ronnie ran around expressing his excitement at the fact he would have a new home by the end of the day. Sidney did not have any other thought in his head other than to sleep his way around to his next feed.

***

Mathilde Dupont's address was on Park Street so Jake and Mathieson had been able to walk there from Lodge Walk. It was mid-morning and the mist was showing signs of clearing though it still looked bad out towards the sea.

They let themselves in to the tenement block and climbed the stairs to the first level where Jake rapped on one of the doors. They stood back to await a response but nothing happened. Jake knocked on the door again. This time the door to his right opened and a small, rather wizened looking woman popped her head around the door and enquired if they were there to see Mathilde.

"Yes we are," replied Jake, showing the woman his identification.

The woman then stepped out in to the hallway. "I'm a bit worried about Mathilde. I haven't seen her since last Wednesday and it's not like her not be out and about each day."

"Maybe she's out already?" Jake suggested.

"Mathilde helped me out a lot. She gets my shopping for me when she can and she makes a point of checking on me at least every second day. I know what she has to do for a living, Inspector, but she's a good and thoughtful girl at heart."

"Thank you for the information."

The woman took a little while to realise that she was no longer needed and she turned and went back in to her property and closed the door. Jake then tried Mathilde's door; it was locked. However, he felt he had sufficient cause to check the inside of the flat so he and Mathieson applied some joint shoulder pressure to the door until it gave and opened with a crash.

The smell inside the flat was strong and to both Jake and Mathieson it was obvious that what they were about to find would not be a pleasant sight.

What they assumed would be the body of Mathilde Dupont was lying on the bed. She was on her back and the body was already discoloured and beginning to decompose. The two officers hurried back out of the room. Mathieson could not prevent the inevitable as he raced down to the toilet on the lower level, threw open the door and vomited violently in to the toilet bowl.

Jake held his handkerchief over his face as he closed the front door to stop the sickly sweet smell of decay from permeating through the rest of the building. He then waited for Mathieson to come out of the toilet before telling him to return to Lodge Walk and get the Doctor and a team of men to take the corpse back to the mortuary.

Jake then sat down on the staircase and waited for everyone else to arrive.

***

Jake had not felt much like having lunch. His nostrils were still filled with the smell from Mathilde's flat. He made his way across to the mortuary and found Doctor Symon working over the remains of the dead prostitute. Doctor Symon's face was covered with a white mask and he seemed to be poking at the body rather than carrying out a close examination. Clearly even a medical stomach wasn't always that strong.

"Bit of a mess, eh Doctor?" Jake announced, trying to sound as cheery as possible.

"She's been dead at least a week and the maggots have had their fill of her so it might be difficult for me to tell you very much about the actual cause of death. I think there might be bruising around her neck but the discolouration of the skin makes even that difficult to say with any certainty."

"Is it possible that she could have been killed last Tuesday evening?" Jake then asked.

"It would fit my very loose timescale," Doctor Symon replied. "To be honest, Jake, I may not manage to narrow it down any further than sometime between the evening of last Tuesday and the evening of last Wednesday. She would have looked even worse if this had been the summer and the air temperature had been higher."

"She looks bad enough, Doctor," Jake said and turned to leave. He paused in the doorway. "If you do discover anything that might be of interest you will let me know?"

"Don't I always?" Doctor Symon replied and returned his attention rather grudgingly to the body that lay before him.

Jake went back to his office. Willie Ifield's alibi was no longer of any use to him, which meant Jake was back at stage one with regard to the statement made by Mr Zanre. Jake had sent some officers around to the area again to ask other neighbours in the hope that they might uncover someone else who witnessed the strange man hovering outside Le Fondre's house.

Jake still needed to find a definite connection between Guy Le Fondre and the Ifields, but for the moment he still felt that Daniel Ifield was a better candidate for murdering Le Fondre than his father. A connection between the two men would, therefore, be extremely helpful.

Thinking about a possible connection brought Jake back to Scott Thane. He had rather placed that name at the back of his mind after Johnnie Gordon had mentioned it, but the fact that Thane might have been in business with Le Fondre would put him in a position of knowing whether, or not, there had been any involvement from the Ifields. It was also possible, though highly unlikely that he would admit it, that Thane had had something to do with the making of the obscene films.

Either way, Jake felt the time was right to find Thane and have a word with him. The only place that Jake knew for sure he would find Thane was the Business Club and much as Joe Tredwall did not like his Members being disturbed at the Club Jake felt he had no other option but to call there. He collected Mathieson and they made their way up to Bon Accord Square.

***

Henry and Bella Davis stood in their new flat and grinned. They could never have imagined, in their wildest dreams, that they would have such a spacious property so early in their marriage. They could now put both boys in to one bedroom, they could have the other and that still left a kitchen and front room. Compared to the squashed, damp property they had just left they were now occupying a palace.

Ronnie ran from room to room and squealed with delight. Sidney gurgled happily in his cot and Bella wandered about with a duster wiping away imaginary dust as the place was already spotless. Whoever had been there before had cleaned it from top to bottom before leaving.

"We need to celebrate this properly," Henry then said as he grabbed his coat and put it on. "I'll be back in a minute."

Henry hurried off to the shop on the corner where he hoped to buy a couple of bottles of beer. Bella continued to clean the flat and Ronnie continued to run around. The new surroundings were already causing Bella's humour to improve. She had come to live with herself over the death of Cathcart but she would never forget what happened that night nor would she ever stop thinking that one day a knock would come at the door and this would be Henry's colleagues armed with the evidence they needed to prove who had killed Cathcart.

***

Jake and Mathieson arrived at the door of the Business Club. Jake knocked and almost immediately the door opened. Jake showed the doorman his identification and asked if they could come in. Once inside he then asked if they could see Joe Tredwall. It transpired, however, that he was not at the Club that day. Jake then asked if Scott Thane was there.

The doorman seemed unaware of Joe Tredwall's desire not to involve any of their Members with the police for he went to inform Thane that there were two police officers wanting to see him.

To Jake's complete surprise the doorman came back and said he had been asked to show them up to one of the upstairs rooms. The doorman further said that Mr Thane would be up in a moment.

True to his word Scott Thane came in to the room about three minutes after Jake and Mathieson had sat down. Thane was carrying a whisky and looked as if he may have had one or two already. He made his way over to the only remaining spare seat and sat down.

Jake took a few seconds to study the young man. He was, as were all the Members of the Business Club, dressed immaculately and it was clear that he took a great pride in his own personal grooming. However, his face was set in an expression of concern and he sipped, rather nervously, at his drink. Those few seconds of silence proved too much for Thane who felt the need to say something first.

"I believe you wanted to see me."

"Yes, Mr Thane, my thanks for giving up your time. I don't intend being too long about this but your name has arisen in our investigation in to the death of Guy Le Fondre and we were hoping that you might be able to help us gather a little more background information regarding Mr Le Fondre."

Thane sipped at his drink again. "I'll do what I can, Inspector, though I can't imagine I can be of much help."

"You did know Mr Le Fondre?" Jake then asked.

"Not as a friend, but I did know him as a prospective business partner."

"You had discussed going in to business together?"

"Yes we had."

"What type of business was that to have been?"

"The business is up and running, Inspector. We had arranged to launch a film-making business at the weekend. The timing may not have been perfect, but I decided to launch it any way as I believe Guy would have wanted me to continue without him."

Jake glanced at Mathieson. "A film-making business?"

"Yes, that's right Inspector.

"And you are telling me that this business only started at the weekend, is that correct Mr Thane?" Jake then asked.

"Yes, that's right. Originally I was just going to look after the finances but with Guy's death I find myself doing everything."

"Do you know that there already is a film-making business running in this area?"

"No I did not, Inspector. I do hope that won't affect my projected profits."

Jake studied Thane for a moment. He was trying to read this man's reactions to the questions and it was not proving very easy.

"Are you telling me that you have launched your business without seeing if there might be any competition in the area already?" Jake asked with some disbelief.

"I suppose I always thought there would be room for more than one if indeed there was competition. I must admit I hadn't heard of anyone else when I was setting up my team and to be honest, I really don't think that anyone else would provide the level of film-making that I will."

"Where did you get your team?"

"From all over the country. I placed advertisements in newspapers and we received a number of replies from some well qualified individuals. They then travelled to Aberdeen where Guy and I interviewed them. I don't know much about film-making, Inspector, but I do have an eye for employing the right people."

"And where is this team to be based, Mr Thane?" Jake then enquired.

"Guy and I had bought a farm out beyond Ellon with the intention of using that as our base. We spent rather a lot of money building a studio and equipping it with all the necessary items that would be needed to make a high standard production. We now need to get these films made and released as quickly as possible so that we might stand some small chance of recouping at least some of our investment. I expect you will have noticed that any films shown in Aberdeen are always well attended so there is definitely money to be made. Anyway, in answer to your question, the team are all now located at the farm and the filming of our first story is due to start this week, all being well."

"It does seem to be true, Mr Thane, that people turn up in large numbers to view these moving pictures but it perhaps depends on what type of film is being shown," Jake added, all the time watching Thane for a change in expression or some other sign that he knew more than he was saying.

"Whatever do you mean by that, Inspector?" Thane replied.

"The other company, to whom I referred earlier, are known for making a certain kind of film; one which seems to be proving very popular with the men in particular."

Thane's expression did not change. He sipped at his drink and continued to look at Jake with a calmness that seemed to indicate he had nothing, whatsoever, to be concerned about.

"I'm sorry, Inspector, I still have no idea what you are talking about. If there is indeed another film-making company in this area then it cannot be manned with the same high quality employees as our company or I feel sure that the people we interviewed would have already been contacted by our rivals."

"Very well, Mr Thane," Jake then conceded," perhaps we should move on. How well did you know Guy Le Fondre?"

"Not that well at all," Thane lied. "As I said we had agreed to enter in to business together but beyond that we weren't really friends."

"I have been told that you dined quite a lot with Mr Le Fondre," Jake added.

"I suppose we did. It was the only time when we could sit and discuss where we hoped our business might take us. We did have a lot to discuss by way of buying the farm and then how best we might attract the right calibre of employee to our little business."

"Did you know a George Cathcart, Mr Thane?"

"No I certainly did not," Thane replied with a venom that betrayed the fact he did actually know of him in some way. "That odious man was an employee of Guy's and although I did meet him a couple of times, I never actually *knew* him. Thankfully someone did us all a favour by killing the nasty little man."

"How about a Donald Yule?" Jake then asked.

Thane thought for a moment. "Not a name I recognise though again he may have had something to do with Le Fondre."

"I'm a little confused, Mr Thane," Jake said and he let that comment hang in the air for a few seconds before explaining exactly why he was confused. He wanted to knock Thane off guard a little and see what response he got. He eventually spoke again.

"We know that Donald Yule was in the Business Club during the month of October accompanying some obscene films that were being shown at a party. We also know that Cathcart was connected to Yule and now you have admitted that Cathcart was in turn connected to Guy Le Fondre. That being the case I find it almost impossible to believe that Guy Le Fondre did not, therefore, know that there were films being made in this area already. I mean his men were showing them."

Thane sat in silence for what seemed like a long time.

"He never mentioned anything to me, Inspector," Thane eventually said. "However, the showing of films does not, in itself, indicate that the films were being made locally."

"I agree, Mr Thane. However, one of the films shown had, in its starring role, the sister of one of the men who had been invited to the party. A sister, I might add, who had been on the missing persons' list since earlier in the year. A sister I might further add who has still never been seen again. As she went missing in this area I have to assume that any film in which she was appearing must have been made in this area as well. Do you still tell me that you know nothing about the making of these obscene films?"

"I can assure you, Inspector, that I have no knowledge of the films to which you refer, nor would I have expected Guy to have been involved with them either beyond, perhaps, agreeing to show them at the Business Club for a small fee."

"Had Mr Le Fondre been involved in the making of these films, would he necessarily have told you?" Jake then asked.

"Of course he would," Thane replied. "Why would he have pretended to set up a film-making business with me if he already had one running somewhere else in the area?"

"When you say that you bought the farm with Mr Le Fondre does that mean that you both visited it and decided to buy it or did one buy on behalf of the other?"

"Guy found the property; I simply dealt with the purchase of it."

"So it was possible that Mr Le Fondre was already using the property before he told you about it?" Jake then asked.

Thane looked a little surprised by the question and gave it some thought before answering.

"I suppose he could have been using the property," Thane eventually conceded. "Suffice to say, however, that there was no indication of anyone having been there when I first visited the place some week or so after we bought it. I have also supervised the installation of the equipment since we purchased the farm and again, as I have already said, there was never any evidence, to my knowledge, of the place having been anything other than a farm prior to my first viewing it."

"Perhaps, Mr Thane, but I'd be obliged if you gave us the address of the farm anyway," Jake added.

"Why would you need that, Inspector?" Thane asked looking a little worried in the process.

"As I said earlier, Mr Thane, we are investigating the disappearance of a number of women from this area. Now it is just possible that Mr Le Fondre, or his associates, may have had something to do with that and it seems to me that a farm would be the ideal place in which to hide evidence."

Thane looked outraged. "My God, Inspector, you can't seriously think that Guy Le Fondre had anything to do with missing women? He may have been a bit strange as a person but I feel sure that he was no killer."

"I never mentioned that anyone had been killed, Mr Thane, I merely said that we were searching for missing women. Is there something that you know and would now like to share with us?"

"You said that the woman in the obscene film had never been seen again so I assumed, from that, that you meant she was dead. If my assumption was incorrect then I am sorry and no I do not know anything about these women or what might have happened to them."

"That may well be the case, Mr Thane, but I feel it will still be necessary for us to visit the farm. If nothing else we need to rule it out of our enquiries. Now may I have the address?"

Thane felt trapped in a corner. The very thing he was trying to hide was the very thing that made most sense to Inspector Fraser. A farm was the ideal place to hide any trace of those women. Thane knew that he had no option other than to provide the address and hope that, if the police did visit, there would be nothing left to find.

"What other income did Mr Le Fondre have?" Jake then asked as Thane wrote down the address of the farm and handed it to him.

"He had money inherited from his father but beyond that I wasn't aware of him having another income. He certainly didn't work for anyone else."

"And yourself, Mr Thane, where does your money come from?" Jake then asked.

"I used to work for a bank, Inspector and was able to set aside enough money for me to finance myself in setting up a small business in which I offered financial advice to clients as well as checking their accounts. Although I am not a fully trained accountant I have enough knowledge of accounts to get by. After Guy and I started talking about the new film business then obviously I turned my entire attention to bringing that to fruition. I put a little money in to the venture myself but I have to say that the lion's share of the finance came from Guy and he would obviously have got the lion's share back had he lived."

"So his death does wonders for your own finances, Mr Thane?"

"Obviously, as the sole owner of the new business all profits generated will now come to me, but please don't think for one moment that I would have killed Guy simply to feather my own nest."

"And you still say, Mr Thane that you and Mr Le Fondre were not in business before?" Jake said again.

"I do, Inspector."

Jake simply did not believe what he was being told but in the absence of anything tangible by way of evidence he had no other option than, at least for now, to accept what Thane was telling him.

"Do you know a Miss Harriet Cruickshank?" Jake now enquired.

"As with Cathcart, I do not *know* her on a personal level, Inspector, but I do know that she was the most recent lady friend that Guy had. I believe he cared a lot for Harriet."

"Have you spoken to Miss Cruickshank since Mr Le Fondre's death?"

"I wouldn't know how to contact her, Inspector," Thane replied. "As I said, I didn't know the woman."

"I'm getting the picture, Mr Thane," Jake then said after a long sigh, "there seems to be a lot of people that you don't know."

"I'm sorry that I cannot be of more help, Inspector," Thane then added.

"I'm sure the day will come, Mr Thane, when you *will* be a lot more helpful," Jake concluded and he and Mathieson then made their way to the door. "Until the next time we meet....." Jake added and the two police officers left the room.

Thane sat for a little while longer. He had just spent the last few, uncomfortable moments lying to the police. He dare not admit how well he knew Le Fondre and to cover that basic fact he had basically been required to lie about everything else.

He finished the last of his drink. He was a worried man as he felt sure that the police would quickly find evidence that would link him far closer to Le Fondre than he had just suggested.

He started to think about how best he could deal with the second wave of questioning especially if those questions followed a police visit to the farm.

Meanwhile Jake and Mathieson were back down at the front door. As the stepped down on to the pavement Jake turned and looked back at the closing door.

"Well, what did you think of that?" he said.

"Thane is a very cool character indeed, sir," Mathieson added.

"Yes, Sergeant, he would like us to think that he is a cool character, but I am not so sure he would remain quite so cool under pressure. I certainly did not believe much of what he said. However, until we uncover some more evidence there is little I can do by way of challenging him."

And with that the two men returned to Lodge Walk.

***

Wolfgang and Maisie had made their way down to Southampton where they were waiting for the first chance to sail to Hamburg. Maisie had noticed that Wolfgang seemed to be in possession of quite a lot of money but she did not want to ask where it might have come from. He seemed so upbeat and elated about the fact he was going home and the fact that Maisie was going with him that she did not want to do anything to upset the moment.

They were travelling as Mr and Mrs Schwieger and had booked in to a small hotel close to the docks. Wolfgang had given Maisie a ring, which he said had belonged to his mother. Maisie did not mind the fact that they weren't legally married. Having spent most of her life being paid to have sex with men it made a pleasant change that she only had to wear a ring now.

As she lay in bed that night, Maisie was giving some thought to the day they would sail and the life that lay ahead. Wolfgang was sleeping, his arm tenderly around her and his breathing low and relaxed. They had only been in Southampton a few hours and yet Maisie already felt that Aberdeen was a million miles away.

She felt safe and secure with Wolfgang. She no longer had to worry about pimps or Willie Ifield. She was free to make a life for herself and she was looking forward to having the opportunity.

The fact that Wolfgang had money did concern her a little, but on the other hand it at least meant they would not have financial worries in the first few months that they were in Germany. She was also sure that Wolfgang had the skills to find work and to make a success of that work, especially if he could ultimately work for himself. She snuggled closer to him.

Yes, everything was looking good for them. Apart from the one serious concern that Maisie had. There was one thing uppermost in her mind as she lay close to Wolfgang in bed that night.

Were they really simply heading off to a new life in Germany or were they running away from something far more sinister, something left back in Aberdeen?

SEVEN

Wednesday 07 November – mid morning until early evening

Around ten o'clock in the morning a major incident occurred on Union Street that occupied the majority of uniformed police officers, who were already in the area, as well as Inspector Jake Fraser, who just happened to be passing.

Fifty feet of overhead, electric wires fell to the street. The wires were live but fortunately no one was underneath and no one was close enough to be affected by the lines lying on the ground. It transpired, however, that as soon as the wires came in to contact with the rails they were rendered dead.

However, the street around the area of the fallen wires had to be kept clear and all passing public were required to keep moving or they, in turn, would cause another blockage point on what was always a very busy thoroughfare. It had never ceased to amaze Jake that the higher the risk of death or injury the higher the number of people who wanted to gather and watch. Jake had long thought that people seemed to have a natural interest in the suffering of others.

It took the police a little while to keep the area clear so that the electricians could begin the job of repairing the wires. Once Jake had finished lending a hand he made his way back to the office where he spent a little while telling Sergeant Turnbull what had just happened before going through to his office and actually getting on with some work.

***

Police Constable Phillip Marshall and his wife, Anna, were in a high state of excitement. They had been married for six months and spent all of that time living with Anna's parents. Now, through the fact that Phillip was a police officer, they had been provided with a property of their own.

It wasn't much. It was in the Shiprow, not the best of areas and the space was limited, though at least it was *their* space, something they had not had with Anna's parents. They now stood in the larger of the two rooms and looked around with an eye that sought ways of improving their surroundings.

Phillip put a protective arm around his wife and Anna moved closer. She was a small, attractive looking woman with a bright smile and a bustling approach to life. Her husband was a man who approached everything that he did in a very slow and measured manner. He rarely got upset about anything and Anna had still to witness her husband's temper, even though they had now known each other for two years.

The room was in need of a little decoration. It was clean in terms of dust and dirt but there was a tiredness to the paintwork and there seemed no doubt to Phillip and Anna that they could bring new life to the place. They went through to the other room and looked around what, to them, would be the bedroom. Again, beyond a lick of paint here and there it wasn't that bad.

Phillip didn't know Henry Davis all that well but he knew that it had been Henry who had lived in this flat before him. Obviously Henry had cared little for painting for it appeared that many years had passed since the flat had last seen a coat of paint.

"Our own place," Anna said with a grin, "I can hardly believe it."

"At least that was one advantage to being a police officer," Phillip added.

They went back through to the other room. "I'd better start taking the boxes up from the cart," Phillip then said.

They had borrowed a horse and cart from Anna's father but only had it for a short while. Phillip had managed, however, to get everything they possessed on to the cart and now only needed to bring it all up to the flat before being able to return the cart to his father-in-law's place of work.

Anna took some dusters from her bag and started to give the place another wipe over. She sang to herself as she worked, feeling happier than she had ever felt before. This really was the start of proper married life and she couldn't wait to get some food cooking and make herself feel like a proper wife.

Phillip meantime brought all their boxes up to the flat and then set off to return the cart. He did not have far to go as his father-in-law's place of work was just off the Green. Phillip walked back and found his wife in the bedroom dusting around the windows. He walked up behind her and slipped his arms around her waist, bringing his hands up over her breasts and kissing her on the back of the neck.

Anna giggled. "Phillip, what are you doing?"

"What we can do anytime, now that we have our own place," her husband replied.

Anna spun in his arms and faced Phillip who was grinning broadly. "But not just now, surely?" Anna said.

Phillip started to undo the buttons on his wife's blouse. "Why not, we have all day to unpack the boxes?" he added as he began to steer his wife towards the bed.

***

Daniel had enjoyed his lunch with Joe Tredwall. The two men got on well together and Daniel soon realised that Joe had no intentions of causing any unnecessary problems over the sale of the Business Club. The price agreed was fair and the paperwork had been drawn up as quickly as Joe had intimated. Lunch had, therefore, been more of a chat involving two friends than a business venture.

Before he left the Business Club, Daniel was accosted by Scott Thane, eager to get some information to Willie Ifield. Daniel listened with interest and agreed to pass on the information to his father.

Daniel made his way back to work and went straight to his father's office. Daniel had noticed how worried his father had looked ever since his session with Jake Fraser. It was the first time in his life that he had ever seen his father look so worried but perhaps this had been the first time, in the business life of Willie Ifield, where the police had got closer to him than he would have preferred.

Miss Sangster was already in the room taking notes. She asked if they wanted her to leave but both men seemed happy to have their brief conversation with her still present.

Daniel laid the paperwork on his father's desk. "I don't know if you'd like old Porteous to have a look over the paperwork as well?"

"If it is all as straightforward as I believe it will be then I don't think we need to waste any more time by having Porteous look at it," Willie added. "I'll finish replying to the mail and then read through the documents later today."

"Good. By the way, Thane spoke to me before I left the Club. He seems a worried man."

"What's been happening?"

"The police interviewed him and Fraser now knows about the farm. Thane reckons the police will be paying a visit to the farm sooner rather than later as he is pretty sure that Fraser sees a link between the farm and the sex films."

"Well of course Fraser will see a link between the farm and the making of the sex films because that is what any sane-minded individual would do. I knew as soon as Thane went public with his film-making business that the police would assume he had something to do with the making of those films. They are not stupid."

"I doubt if Fraser will waste any time in arranging a police search of the farm," suggested Daniel.

"We'll just have to hope that Le Fondre didn't leave any evidence then, won't we?" Willie added. "Any way, we'll talk more about that later."

"Very well," concluded Daniel as he left the room.

***

Phillip and Anna got out of bed. They had made love twice and then slept for a little while in the aftermath of their passion. In the time they had spent with Anna's parents they had often felt embarrassed to make love and their sex life had been limited to those occasions when they had been left alone in the property.

Now there were no barriers to what they did. They could enjoy each other's body any time they choose and they would bother no one else in the process.

Phillip went out on to the landing and visited the toilet. Anna washed using the bowl that she unpacked from one of their boxes. Half an hour later they were both unpacking items and clothing and finding a home for everything in the various drawers and cupboards throughout the property.

"What do you think of this new piece of linoleum?" Phillip had then asked as he stood in the room holding a lamp and trying to decide the best place to put it.

"It's all right," replied Anna, "though perhaps it looks a little too new and somewhat out of place."

"That's what I was thinking," agreed Phillip, "and perhaps the floorboards underneath might look better. When I get a chance I'll lift the linoleum and see what's underneath."

***

Scott Thane met with Aspinall. For once he had arranged to meet with Aspinall somewhere other than the Business Club. They met in the Empire Café at 101, Union Street and over a pot of tea discussed where their business ventures might go as a result of the current police interest.

"I dare not do anything at the moment," Thane said, "as long as the police are effectively watching me."

"Do we put everything on hold?" asked Aspinall.

"Inspector Fraser will not stop until he has turned over every stone surrounding my business and seen for himself what might be lying beneath. I wish to God I'd known what Guy was up to long before I did for I would have had nothing to do with most of what he had got himself involved with. However, we cannot afford to put a hold on everything. There are too many people who need to be paid and too many people who, in turn, pay us. I dare not do anything myself so, for the moment, I would like you to take over the responsibility of logging what money we make and what money we pay out."

Aspinall looked surprised. "You are a very trusting man, Mr Thane."

"I have to be, "Thane replied. "I don't feel I have any other option giving the fact that, as I say, we cannot afford to simply stop everything. Good grief, I'm not at all sure that we could just stop everything; there are too many people depending on us."

"Very well, Mr Thane, though you have to realise that I am no accountant and that counting was never my strongest ability at school."

"Do your best and remember I'll be checking the books when I finally get the chance," Thane added with an element of threat in his voice.

"Don't you worry, Mr Thane," Aspinall then said, "I won't do anything to upset you or anyone else connected to your business. I also promise to protect your money until you are ready to move it somewhere else."

"Thank you, Mr Aspinall," added Thane. "It may be some time before business can return to normality for if the police visit the farm where the films were made then who knows what they might find. I only had Guy's word that he covered his tracks out there. If they do find anything truly damning then I'm the only one left to suffer the consequences."

"So, you made some dirty pictures," Aspinall said, "that's hardly the end of the world."

Thane sat forward in his chair. "In the making of those films Guy Le Fondre arranged for women to be abducted and then murdered. In between they were forced to participate in the making of our films. Now, if that is discovered it most certainly will be the end of the world, at least as far as I am concerned."

Aspinall sat back in his chair. "Ah, that is slightly different."

"If you come back tomorrow I will give you a letter of authority that can be shown to anyone who might question your right to deal with the finances of my company."

"Very well. I won't let you down, Mr Thane," added Aspinall.

"I'm sure you won't, Mr Aspinall," said Thane, "though just remember that if I do find anything amiss with the finances I will not take it lightly."

Aspinall smiled. "I may not be the best at counting, Mr Thane, but I am trustworthy and I am loyal to my employer. I may make the odd mistake through ignorance but I would never do anything through malice or by way of seeking some form of personal gain."

"I hope so. Look, one person who can be of use to me at this time is young Davis. He is a bloody policeman after all so he needs to keep me informed of what is happening, particularly when it comes to Jake Fraser."

"I'll speak to Davis later and arrange for him to keep us in the know," added Aspinall as another cup of tea was poured.

***

Aspinall walked around the harbour area later that evening but did not find Henry Davis. He did see two other police officers and was left to assume that Davis was not, for some reason, on duty that day.

Their little chat would have to wait until another day.

EIGHT

Thursday 08 November – early morning until late afternoon

There were a few envelopes passed through to Jake around half an hour after he had arrived in the office. There was always the odd nutcase who liked to write to the police and offer their opinions on something that was of intense interest to them. Jake was well known around the city and his name, more than others, tended to be put on these letters.

Jake sifted through the envelopes and one caught his eye amongst the others. The writing on the front was quite neat and there was no postmark. Presumably this envelope had been hand delivered.

Jake picked up his silver-plated letter opener and slit the top of the envelope. He put the letter opener back down on his desk and took a single sheet of paper from the envelope.

He sat back and read the short, neatly written message.

Guy Le Fondre and Scott Thane were the men behind the making of the sex films that were shown in the Business Club. The farm where they made the films needs to be visited. You are looking for missing women. Look at the farm, especially where they kept the pigs.

Obviously the note was not signed. Jake took the envelope and its contents and made his way through to the front desk. Sergeant Bill Turnbull was checking over a list of items that had been given to him but he looked up immediately when Jake appeared in front of him.

"Yes, sir, what can I do for you?"

"Where did this envelope come from, Bill?" Jake asked.

Turnbull looked at the envelope. "Delivered by a scruffy wee lad this morning. He said he had been given a three-penny piece by a gentleman to deliver the envelope to Lodge Walk. I don't think the wee lad knew anything more."

"Thanks, Bill," Jake concluded and went back to his office.

This was the break he had been seeking. Someone clearly knew that there was a link between Thane, Le Fondre and the sex films. If nothing else it proved that Thane was lying through his teeth when he claimed to not know Le Fondre or anything about the man's business ventures. It also gave Jake the reason he needed to organise a search of the farm. The only problem for Jake was that the farm was outside his jurisdiction and he would need to get the Chief Constable on board before anything could be organised.

Jake decided there was no time like the present, so he left his office and made his way up to the Chief's room on the floor above.

***

A small group of people gathered in Francis Delaney's office at a little after half past nine that morning. Harriet Cruickshank had gone through the pretence of mourning by wearing a black dress. However, the rather low cut bodice and abundance of cleavage seemed to harken back to her days as a prostitute rather than her somewhat misguided attempt to play the grieving 'widow.'

The Gladstones sat in the other chairs provided. Mr Gladstone looked as severe as ever although it was evident that his eyes were drawn more to Harriet's cleavage than to anything else in the room. Mrs Gladstone had a look of boredom about her though she perhaps felt overshadowed by the young woman sitting beside her and showing her breasts to the world. Mrs Gladstone would never, at any age, have shown her breasts to the world in such a common fashion.

Delaney also had difficulty keeping his eyes from straying towards Harriet Cruickshank's cleavage as he read through the will. The content was short but Delaney could not help thinking, as he read it, that this was not the first time these people had been made aware of what it would say.

Five minutes later Harriet knew, publically, that she was a very wealthy woman and the Gladstones knew that they at least still had a roof over their head as well as a little money for their old age. Delaney then handed Harriet a sealed envelope, which he said he had been instructed to give her in the event of Mr Le Fondre's death.

Harriet opened the envelope and took out the single piece of paper that had been neatly folded and placed inside. She read through the contents and fought to keep the smile from forming on her face. The piece of paper, which she currently held in her hand, had just informed her that there was even more money for her to spend and it was lying concealed in the house.

Harriet had known that she would be rich but she had never realised just *how* rich.

"Not bad news I hope?" Delaney had then asked.

"No," Harriet replied, taking a handkerchief from her bag and holding it to her face," it is just a final message from Guy. He really loved me."

"I'm sure that he did," added Delaney though he still could not lose the feeling that Harriet Cruickshank was playing a part rather than coming across as genuinely grieving for a lost one.

Harriet stated that she would move in to the house and made sure that the Gladstones were still happy to work for her. They said that they would. Harriet then asked Delaney to arrange for the sale of the flat in which she was currently living and for the proceeds of that to be split between herself and the Gladstones. Mr Gladstone had actually managed a smile at that moment and both he and his wife thanked Harriet for her generosity.

Bank details were provided so that Delaney could arrange for any money due to be paid as quickly as possible. Everyone then left and Delaney turned his attention to other matters.

***

Peter Grant was doing his mid-morning tour of the building accompanied by two men from the Council who both wore stern expressions and looked as if neither of them had smiled in years.

The theatre was now less than a month away from opening and Grant knew that they could not afford to provide the Council with any reason for complaint at this late stage. Although still officially a building site, the theatre was already beginning to look like a place where ordinary Aberdonians would come and lose themselves in its splendour. There was a feeling that they were most certainly on the last lap now and that all the work that was still to be done was by way of finishing things off rather than starting anything new.

The decoration was ornate and everything was of the highest quality. For someone whose life was rarely lifted above the mundane, the theatre would be seen as a place of true luxury. It wasn't just the entertainment being provided it was the whole experience of visiting the theatre and being able to lose oneself in a different world.

Before permission would be given to open the theatre to the public they still had to prove to the men from the Council that the property met all the criteria that had been set for them, particularly when it came to the health and safety of the paying public.

The small group made its way down the central aisle and up on to the stage. The men from the Council looked at everything with an intensity that on occasions caused Grant to move from merely being concerned in to the realms of actually being scared of these men.

One of the men had the plans for the building in a folder that he carried around with him. At various points in time he would suddenly stop, flick his folder open and read some of its contents. He would then study a completed item before him before moving on. It seemed to Grant that these men were intent on finding a reason to keep them closed when, in actual fact, they ought to have been doing all that they could to get the place opened on time. With Her Majesty's Theatre, on Guild Street, closing at the end of the month it was imperative that the new theatre opened without delay.

As they stood on the stage one of the men from the Council suddenly made his way off to the left. Grant hurried to catch up with him for it was obvious that the man had seen something to attract his attention.

"What is this?" the man asked as Grant arrived beside him.

Grant looked down at the body of a dead cat. At first he didn't know what to say; the cat had not been there half an hour ago when Grant had first gone to meet the men from the Council.

What was going on?

"I will have it removed at once," Grant said. "I don't know how it got here but I'll certainly make it my business to find out."

"Obviously we cannot have the public coming in to a building where there are dead cats lying around," the Council official said with a face that looked even more stern.

"Well obviously," Grant agreed, already looking around for some obvious explanation for the appearance of a dead cat. The fact it was dead did rather imply that someone must have put it there. But, again, why?

Grant arranged for the cat to be removed and then after the Council men had left he went up to Mr Nelson's office.

"What is it, Peter?" Nelson said as Grant arrived in his office.

"Another incident, Mr Nelson. We found a dead cat at the side of the stage."

Nelson looked very worried indeed. "We?"

"I was doing the rounds with the men from the Council."

"Oh," was all that Nelson could say. He sat back in his chair and thought things through for a moment. "It does seem as if someone is trying to sabotage the completion of this building, doesn't it?"

"I have felt that way for a while, Mr Nelson and I strongly advise that we get the police involved. I fear that if we don't this person may yet do something that really will succeed in keeping us closed beyond the beginning of December."

Nelson thought some more. "Very well, Peter, take a walk down to Lodge Walk and report the problems we have been having."

***

Jake was sitting with the Chief Constable. William Anderson was well liked by the men of Aberdeen City Police for he was a man who cared for his men and did all that he could to make their lives as bearable as possible. He had high standards and as long as those standards were met he would have backed his men at all costs.

He was dapper looking gentleman who looked almost military when dressed in his uniform. He had listened to what Jake had to say about the films and the possibility that the farm may hold vital evidence. The Chief agreed to talk to his counterpart in the Aberdeenshire area and for a search to be arranged. The Chief would send some men out from Aberdeen but suggested that Jake leave the part of leading investigating officer to one of the Aberdeenshire based Inspectors. Jake had no problem with that.

Jake then said that he wanted to hold Scott Thane in custody for a couple of days while the search was undertaken. He did not want Thane to be in a position where he might influence the outcome of the search by removing evidence first. However, Jake had to admit that beyond his anonymous letter he had no other evidence to use against Thane.

"Perhaps you need to speak with Thane again," the Chief suggested, "only this time you need to make him *think* that you have more evidence than you actually have. You never know what you might uncover."

Jake smiled. He had been thinking of taking that course of action anyway, but it made him feel better to hear the Chief suggest the same. The Chief usually did things by the book but he had been known to slightly bend the rules when it perhaps suited.

Jake left the Chief to arrange the search of the farm and went looking for Mathieson. He found his Sergeant at the front desk talking to Sergeant Turnbull. They were talking about possibly going down to Dundee the following Saturday as Aberdeen were due to play there. The Sergeants rarely attended football matches as they were nearly always working, but on this occasion they were both due to be off on the Saturday and it seemed a good opportunity for them to go and see their team.

"I believe there will be a special train running," Mathieson was saying as Jake arrived beside them, "and the cost will be three and six."

"Then we should go," Turnbull concluded and then both Sergeants turned to face Jake.

"Mathieson would you do me a favour and go and collect Scott Thane from the Business Club and bring him here. If he wants his solicitor then tell him to arrange for everyone to meet here. Do not let Thane phone anyone other than his solicitor."

"Very good, sir," said Mathieson and made his way out the door.

Jake was about to leave the front desk area when the door opened and a smart looking young man came in.

"Can I help you, sir?" Turnbull enquired with his usual, polite efficiency.

"I would like to speak to someone about incidents that have been occurring at the new theatre building," the man said.

Jake stopped in his tracks and came back. "What incidents?" he asked.

"Various, rather strange, things have been happening," the young man added, "and Mr Nelson and I are of the opinion that someone is trying to prevent the theatre from opening."

"Why would anyone want to do that?" Jake asked.

"I have no idea," the young man replied, "I was rather hoping that you might be able to tell me that after some kind of investigation."

Jake smiled. "Very well, Mr.......eh?

"Grant. Peter Grant. I'm the assistant manager at the theatre."

"Okay, Mr Grant, Sergeant Turnbull here will show you through to the interview room and I will arrange for someone to take a statement from you."

"Thank you."

Jake went away to find someone suitable to take Grant's statement and then went through to his office to prepare for Scott Thane being brought in.

It was Constable McGill who spoke to Peter Grant. McGill had been given the short-term role of helping the non-uniformed officers wade through the sea of paper that had amassed due to all the enquiries that had been necessary over the last three months or so. Jake thought it might do the young, police officer some good to escape from the paperwork for a little while and to be able to concentrate on a case of his own.

McGill was a fresh-faced young man with fair hair and piercing, blue eyes. He would be seen, by most women, to be a handsome gentleman though the thinness of his frame did make him look rather underfed and not at all robust. Some women, however, may have seen this as an excuse to mother the young man so he would still attract feminine attention.

"Now then, Mr Grant," McGill said after getting the personal details written in to his little, black book," tell me about these incidents at the theatre."

Grant started to talk. He told McGill of at least six incidents, which could not be explained, culminating in the story of the dead cat. McGill had to admit that none of the incidents could be properly explained if it were not accepted that someone was deliberately making them happen.

"Why do you think someone would want to stop the theatre from opening?" McGill then asked.

"Your colleague asked me that," Grant replied, "and I'll tell you what I told him. I don't know and I'm hoping that you might now find that out."

"But you must have some idea as to why someone would try to sabotage the opening of the theatre?" McGill pressed.

"Someone with a grievance, obviously, but beyond that I really have no idea," Grant insisted.

"Have you many employees at the moment?" McGill then enquired.

"We have almost recruited our full quota of staff but until the theatre actually opens they will not be needed beyond a little training that Mr Nelson has organised. We don't have any staff at the theatre at the moment if that is what you are asking."

"How many workmen are still to be found in the theatre?"

"I don't know the actual amount as it varies from day to day, depending on what jobs need to be done. I should guess that it is somewhere in the region of fifty."

"How well do you know the new staff who have been employed?" McGill then asked.

"Not that well. As I said, they have been told that they have a job but until the third of December that job does not formally exist."

"And you obviously won't know the workmen who are in your building?" McGill then said.

"Well of course not," replied Grant in a tone that conveyed how stupid he thought the question had been in the first place.

McGill remain unperturbed by how good or bad his questions sounded. He was busy gathering evidence and if that required the odd silly question to be asked then so be it.

"So it is possible that one of the new staff, or one of the workmen, could be intent on delaying any work being done as you move towards opening night?"

"Even I could have come to that conclusion, Constable," Grant then said. "However, neither I, nor Mr Nelson, are in the habit of employing criminals and only a criminal would have thoughts on sabotaging the work being done at the theatre."

"I'm sure you would never knowingly employ someone intent on sabotage, Mr Grant," McGill conceded, "but, in truth, you really have little idea as to whom you have employed, either by way of employees of the theatre or workmen attending under contract."

"I suppose," Grant then said, rather grudgingly, "though I doubt very much if this is the work of anyone already connected to the theatre."

"One of the workman may be trying to extend the time taken to finish the theatre so as to receive payment for longer?" McGill then suggested.

"I am sure there are plenty other jobs waiting in Aberdeen for these workmen, Constable, so I doubt if they need to make our job last any longer than it needs to."

"You may well be right, Mr Grant," McGill concluded. "Beyond the workmen are there any other people currently in the theatre on a daily basis?"

"Not at the moment. Until the work in an around the stage has been completed to the satisfaction of the Council we are unable to let anyone in to the building."

"At least that will make it a little easier to interview those people who are in the building," conceded McGill.

Once he had written down everything that seemed relevant, McGill then asked if he could accompany Grant back to the theatre so that he could have a look around for himself. Peter Grant was delighted that the young Constable was showing so much interest in the situation and felt sure that a solution would soon be close to hand.

***

By the time Peter Grant and Constable McGill left the building the other interview room was occupied. Scott Thane had arrived at Lodge Walk with Mathieson but without a solicitor. He said nothing on the journey down and remained silent as they seated him in the room and then left him to sit on his own for a little while.

They noticed McGill leaving. "What have you given young McGill?" Mathieson asked.

"Incidents at the new theatre in Rosemount. Thought it might do him some good to have an inquiry of his own and anyway, it'll give us a chance to better assess the lad as a detective."

"What about Thane then, sir, do we have any reason to have him in here?"

Jake let Mathieson read the anonymous letter. "There's nothing to say that any of that is true, of course," Jake then said, "but I'm hoping that I can persuade Thane to think that we have more than simply the word of an anonymous writer."

And with that the two police officers went in to interview Scott Thane once again.

Thane was sitting with his fingers intertwined and his thumbs rubbing together. He looked like a man with problems. Jake and Mathieson sat down and Jake checked, one final time, that Thane did not want a solicitor present.

"I have no need for one, Inspector, "was all that Thane said.

"Very well, Mr Thane, as long as you are aware of your rights, "Jake continued.

"I am, Inspector. Now what is this all about?"

"When we last spoke you told me a number of things that I now believe not to be true."

Thane tried to look confidently at Jake but there was a nervousness to him that simply would not go away.

"What might those things have been?" Thane then said.

"You said you did not really know Guy Le Fondre and yet you *were* in business together and probably had been for some time. You said you knew nothing about the sex films that were being made when in fact you and Mr Le Fondre were the money behind the making of those films. You said you know nothing about women going missing and yet I now have reason to believe that those women probably went missing on the farm where you made your films; the same farm where you now tell me you have launched a new film-making business."

Thane looked even more worried. It was obvious that Jake Fraser appeared to know quite a lot, but exactly how much might that be? Thane wanted to bluff his way out of this but knew that, in doing so, he might be doing nothing other than digging a deeper hole for himself.

"Well, Mr Thane, what do you have to say to my assessment that you have been lying to me on practically every front?"

"You can have nothing connecting me to Le Fondre and therefore, nothing connecting me to the films or the missing women."

There was little conviction in Thane's voice. Jake let him sit for a moment before continuing.

"My Chief Constable is, at this very moment, organising a police search of the farm where your films were shot, Mr Thane. Now you might choose to continue with these lies hoping that we find nothing when we search the farm. However, I am of the firm belief that we *will* find something and that when we do the fact you chose to lie about it will be held against you in a court of law. If, on the other hand, you choose to co-operate with us then that, in turn, would be reflected in any sentence the judge would see fit to impose."

Thane sat silently and thought over what had just been said. He could try simply blaming Le Fondre but he doubted if Fraser would believe that now that he had told so many lies already. It might actually be the truth but it wouldn't be seen that way by others.

Thane found it difficult to decide how much Inspector Fraser was likely to know. It hadn't been that long since the last meeting and yet, here he was being questioned by a police officer conveying greater confidence in the evidence he now held. But where could that evidence have come from as Fraser had already admitted the police had not, as yet, been at the farm?

Jake could see that Thane was giving his situation a great deal of thought and that he was unlikely to say anything that might incriminate himself. It was unlikely that Thane would say very much at all, for the moment, so Jake decided to go over it all again, only in a slightly different manner and see if Thane would show any sign of opening up.

"Mr Thane, we have a witness," Jake began. Thane looked briefly horrified and then quickly regained his composure. "We have someone who categorically states that you and Le Fondre made those sex films and made them at the farm that you have already admitted buying. This witness also states that there will be evidence of the missing women at the farm. All we need to find, Mr Thane, is evidence of human remains. If we do then you will face a conviction for murder."

There was sweat on Thane's brow and his eyes were darting around as if seeking a solution to his predicament somewhere in the room. He eventually spoke.

"There is no evidence directly linking me to anything, Inspector, in what you have told me."

"Perhaps we haven't a nice photograph of you at the farm, Mr Thane, but then maybe we don't need that to get a conviction. I can link you to the films. I can link the missing women to the films through the appearance of Irene MacKenzie in one of them. If I can, therefore, provide the jury with evidence of human remains on the farm then I feel confident that they will put all the pieces together and the completed jigsaw will be more than enough to convict you not only of making obscene films but also being an accomplice in the murder of those poor women. However, until we have the evidence of those women being at the farm you will remain here as our guest, Mr Thane. Sergeant Mathieson, would you please find Mr Thane a comfortable cell to sit in for the next forty-eight hours or so."

Thane jumped to his feet. "You can't keep me……..," he began to say.

Jake stood up slowly and smiled. "Oh, but I can, Mr Thane."

"In which case I want to see a solicitor," Thane then added.

"The moment I have my evidence and can charge you with the crimes I have already mentioned will be the moment when I will gladly allow a solicitor to speak with you. However, I look upon you as currently doing no more than helping us with our enquiries, so unless you want to change what you have already told me there seems no need for a solicitor to see you. Good day."

And with that Jake left the room.

***

Constable McGill was enjoying his walk round the new theatre. It was certainly quite a place with ornate designs everywhere and everything finished to the highest standard. Peter Grant came across more as an expectant father, rather than an assistant manager at the venue. Everything he said about the place was said with a pride and an almost puffing of the chest. Grant clearly saw this theatre as being somewhere that would not only make an impression on Aberdeen but on the country as a whole.

"Who designed the building?" McGill asked.

"Frank Matcham. Mr Matcham is a genius when it comes to the design of theatres and I feel that he has surpassed himself with our venue. It truly is a beautiful building and might I add, the only granite theatre in the country."

They were standing in the Stalls Bar. This would be a bar for the lower end of the social spectrum; there were other bars for a better class of person elsewhere in the building. One of the main elements of the seating arrangements, which was already perfectly clear to McGill, was there seemed no way that the social classes would ever be allowed to mix. The area for the cheaper tickets was fenced off and had its own entrances.

"Has anyone been paid off recently, Mr Grant?" McGill then asked as they made their way in to the main auditorium.

"As I believe I have already said, Constable, we have employees in name only. No one has actually started their employment as of this moment so there is no chance of anyone needing be paid off."

"Any workmen who have lost their job as a result of a management decision here?"

Grant thought. "I can't think of anyone though you may want to check with the foreman, Alf Douglas. Anyway, why all these questions about people losing their jobs?"

"Looking for motive, Mr Grant. Just trying to find someone who might have a grievance against either someone working here or the building itself."

"I just can't imagine anyone wanting to harm this building in any way whatsoever," Grant added looking around with that glazed, paternal expression on his face.

"I ask you again, Mr Grant," McGill then said, "can you think of anyone who might have something to lose with the opening of this building?"

Grant gave the question some thought. "Some of the staff at Her Majesty's on Guild Street will be losing their jobs when our theatre opens. The decision was taken to close Her Majesty's so that there would not be a clash of interests in the city. We have all of their backstage staff coming here but amongst the front of stage staff there could be a few who will have to find employment elsewhere. I suppose it is just possible that put in that position someone might see us in a rather bad light. However, Her Majesty's will close whether we open on the third, or not, so delaying work here would not really benefit an aggrieved employee of Her Majesty's."

"Perhaps not, Mr Grant," McGill said and made a note in his book. "However, it would at least provide someone with a motive for sabotaging this building."

"Oh don't go accusing anyone at Her Majesty's as it may have nothing to do with them at all," Grant then said.

"I won't be accusing anyone, Mr Grant, but it might just be a place to start should there be no other obvious direction to my inquiry."

McGill made the last of his notes and they then set off towards another area of the building.

***

The Chief spoke to Jake later that day to confirm that a search of the farm would take place the following day. Men would be sent out from Aberdeen to help and the Aberdeenshire police would coordinate the work that needed to be carried out. The Chief further said that he would update Jake as soon as he had some more information. It was agreed that Scott Thane should remain in the cell until the search had been concluded.

Jake thanked the Chief and then sought his permission to go home. He had put in a lot of hours and was feeling generally weary. The Chief told Jake to pack up and go.

However, Jake did not go straight home. He stopped off at Margaret's and put a note through her letterbox inviting her out for a meal that night. He may have felt weary but that would never stop him from wanting to see Margaret.

As he made his way through Rosemount to Esslemont Avenue he could only hope that Margaret had nothing else organised for that night. He was not to be disappointed as it turned out.

NINE

Friday 09 November – afternoon until late evening

The police descended on the farm at a little after lunchtime. The occupants of both the farmhouse and the film area were shocked by their arrival and obviously could do little to help the police with the questions that were asked of them.

What they were able to say, however, was that they all knew Scott Thane but only a handful knew Guy Le Fondre. They knew nothing about films being made before but Tony McRobb did express surprise, once more, that Scott Thane had claimed that the equipment had not been used. Giles Hampton also thought that everything at the farm had 'the feel of a place that had been used before.'

Everyone had been able to say that there was no one at the farm, apart from the housekeeper, when they arrived. Many of them spoke about Scott Thane's short visit and of course, they were all outraged that, in some way, they may have found themselves involved in a police inquiry.

With everyone being kept in the farmhouse the large number of police officers were then allocated to different parts of the farm. Along with the police were a couple of experts in identifying human bones and two senior officers who were to share responsibility for the search and any ultimate findings.

The weather had been kind to them. The sky was an overcast, light grey and the air was chilly, but there was no immediate sign of rain as the army of police officers began to search the buildings and the grounds.

***

Constable McGill knocked on the door of Inspector Fraser's office and awaited some form of permission to enter. He heard a voice from within and though not entirely sure of what had actually been said, assumed that permission had been given. Constable McGill now opened the door and went in.

"Ah, Hector, have a seat."

"Thank you, sir," McGill said as he sat down.

"Now, tell me how the inquiry at His Majesty's Theatre is going?"

"I wanted to speak to you about that, sir," McGill then said. "There have been a number of unexplained incidents at the theatre each of which on its own would mean little, but taken altogether it rather implies that someone is doing all that they can to either delay or prevent the opening of the theatre next month. It seems strange that anyone would want to do such a thing but the evidence is there none the less. I have to say, sir that I am struggling to find a motive for these crimes. One possibility might be the fact that Her Majesty's Theatre is closing as direct result of His Majesty's opening. I thought that one of their staff, who may have lost his or her job due to the closure, would then have a grievance that might have led to them taking this action. I was aware that you spoke to some of the staff at Her Majesty's with regard to the Mabel Lassiter investigation and I wondered if you would either suggest who I might speak with or, perhaps, you might wish to carry out the next part of this investigation yourself?"

"I am involved in trying to find three murderers, Constable and have little time to get involved in what may be nothing more than a petty dispute at the theatre. I assume there are a number of workmen involved in the final preparations for the opening?"

"Yes, there are, sir."

"And have you spoken to any of them yet?"

"Mr Grant, the assistant manager, did suggest I speak to the foreman but I haven't done that as yet."

"I agree with Mr Grant, "Jake then said. "You need to speak to everyone at His Majesty's before you go anywhere else. The chances are that this is an internal job of some kind and probably has nothing to do with Her Majesty's or anywhere else for that matter. Should the staff at Her Majesty's have any cause for grievance over the opening of His Majesty's then the last thing they would want was some young copper almost accusing them of committing crimes that, in all honesty, they will know nothing about."

"Of course, sir, I seem to have been getting a bit ahead of myself."

Jake smiled. "It may well be that Her Majesty's will require a visit at some point as, I agree, losing your job might be a motive for carrying out these malicious acts. However, there is a time and a place for everything and for the moment, the only place you need to concentrate on is His Majesty's."

McGill stood up. "Thank you, sir, for the advice. I'll get back to His Majesty's and speak to the workmen."

Jake smiled to himself as the door closed behind McGill. He had been there himself at one time; the keen desire to solve that first case often clouded the judgement along the way and it needed that older, more experienced mind, just to make sense of things at times. McGill was a good policeman and Jake had no doubt that he would make a good detective as well, once he had learned his trade.

Jake then returned his mind to the cases in which he was currently involved. There was still nothing that might lead to the killer of George Cathcart and Jake was fairly confident that Thane would be no help there. As for the killing of Guy Le Fondre; there still seemed much to be uncovered and Jake had no leads at all regarding the death of Mathilde Dupont. All in all things continued to go rather badly in terms of Jake ever being able to solve any of those three cases.

Jake had received a note from Francis Delaney informing him that Harriet Cruickshank and the Gladstones were now formally aware of the content of Guy Le Fondre's will. Delaney also offered the opinion that the will had not come as a surprise to any of the parties. This, in turn, did not come as surprise to Jake.

Then there was the possibility that Willie Ifield could be involved in some way. It all seemed highly improbable to Jake and he decided to have a word with Stanley Zanre just to see for himself whether there might be some possibility that Zanre was lying.

***

At the farm some of the police officers were getting more and more annoyed as their lovely uniforms became covered in mud and possibly a lot worse. Those who were in the buildings felt very lucky.

Outside, where the pigs used to roam free, were fifteen officers, armed with sticks, who were poking and prodding around with no clear idea of what they might be looking for. None of them had ever seen bones before, at least nothing beyond a chicken or the occasional pork chop. At the moment this was nothing more than a wallow in the mud. It was over their boots and clinging to their clothes.

Back in the farmhouse two Constables were searching the bedrooms. They checked in all the drawers and wardrobes and under beds. They then moved the beds to check that nothing had fallen down the back of them. Both men stopped dead in their tracks as their eyes fell on words that had been scratched on to the wall.

One of the men ran to get an Inspector.

Five minutes later Inspector Edwin Howe was standing looking down at the writing. The message was simple:

They brought me here. Men have sex with me. They film me. I think I am going to die. Do not forget me. Betty Ewart.

Howe wrote the message in to his book and turned to the two Constables. "Did you find anything else in the room?"

"No, sir."

"Very good. Close off this room meantime, I don't want anyone wandering around in here until we have had a chance to check out the name at the end of this message."

At that moment there was a shout from another room. Howe hurried through to find one of the Constables standing beside a large wardrobe that had been moved away from the wall. The Constable had a dress in his hand.

"Found this behind here," the Constable said holding out the dress.

Howe took hold of it and looked more closely at the material and the possibility of there being a clue concealed about it. There was nothing obvious but he found a bag and put the dress inside it. They searched behind the bed in that room and found another, simpler, message scratched in to the surface of the wall.

Help.

There was little doubt to Howe and his men that they had uncovered rooms where someone had been kept against their will. Howe hurried downstairs to the front room and sat down at the table to make some notes. As he worked he paused briefly to fill and light his pipe. He was in the middle of enjoying his smoke when the door opened and Inspector Ernie Taylor walked in.

"We've found something," he said.

"So have we," Howe added.

Taylor's men had found bones; lots of them. It seemed that the pigs weren't totally efficient in getting rid of evidence. They had managed to eat their way through most of the bodies presented to them but the smaller bones and the chewed parts of the bigger bones had dropped to the ground and become pressed in to the mud so that the pigs could no longer get at them.

The police officers bagged more bones than they would have preferred. It clearly indicated that many bodies had been disposed of at that site. The experts were able to confirm that at least some of the bones were human. Along with the messages left in the farmhouse bedrooms there was no doubt in either Howe or Taylor's minds that they had found the site on which the Aberdeen missing women had met their deaths.

Howe left Taylor to gather all the evidence together and to bring it to the office in Ellon as soon as he was ready. Howe went straight to Ellon where he had the rare treat of using the telephone to contact Aberdeen.

***

Two hours later Jake and Sergeant Mathieson were back in the interview room with Scott Thane. By that time they had been updated on the telephone by Edwin Howe and the bags of evidence had been transported in to Aberdeen and were now being studied by Doctor Symon and two scientists from Aberdeen University.

Jake had sent a message to Grace Lord asking her to call at Lodge Walk as soon as possible. Grace had been the first person to suggest to Jake that women had been going missing in the city. She had provided names for Jake.

By the time Jake took Thane in to the interview room Grace had been to Lodge Walk and had identified the dress, found behind the wardrobe at the farm, as having belonged to Martha Skinner, another of the women known to have gone missing in Aberdeen.

Jake already knew that Betty Ewart was yet another of those women named by Grace on the day that she had reported the missing women. Jake now knew that his case against Thane was watertight and although he could not prove, categorically, that Thane had anything to do with the murders, he could prove Thane's involvement in everything else.

"You can have that solicitor now, if you want, Mr Thane," Jake said as all three men sat in the room.

Thane looked like a beaten man. He knew that Inspector Fraser would not be offering him legal assistance if there was no need for it. That meant they had found something at the farm and that meant that he had little chance of getting out of this now.

"I'm happy to hear what you have to say first," Thane then said.

Jake smiled. "Oh and you seemed in such a hurry to speak to one the last time we met," Jake said, rather sarcastically.

Thane did not rise to the bait. He sat, silently awaiting his fate it seemed.

Jake then opened a folder he had taken in to the room with him. He had a note of the two messages left in the bedrooms at the farm and in a bag at his feet he had the dress. He also had a few of the bones that had been found and a statement from the scientists that the bones were most certainly human.

"This was found scratched on to the wall in one of the bedrooms in the farmhouse," Jake began and he slid a sheet of paper across to Thane that he had prepared a few moments earlier.

Thane ran an eye over the writing but said nothing.

Jake then slid another piece of paper across; this time only the word 'Help' was written on it. Again Thane looked at it but said nothing.

"Behind the wardrobe in another room we found this," Jake then said and he produced the dress from the bag at his feet. "We have had someone already confirm that this dress belonged to a woman who went missing in Aberdeen some months back and has never been seen again. It was in this same bedroom that word 'help' had been written on the wall. Now, Mr Thane, are you finally prepared to drop any pretence of not knowing what was happening at that farm and to start telling me the truth?"

Thane thought for a moment longer. He knew he was beaten. There was no way that he could explain himself out of this mess. He slumped in to his chair.

"Okay, Inspector, I'll tell you everything, however I don't expect you are going to believe me now, even when I am telling you the truth."

"I will assume, for the moment, that what you are now about to tell me is the truth. Perhaps in telling me the truth you will, in some small way, help yourself when it comes to your court case."

Thane went silent again for a moment as he got everything sorted out in his mind before starting to speak.

"As I said, you have to believe me when I say that I did not know about the missing women and what happened to them until after the deed was done. It was a decision made by Le Fondre alone to use those women, I swear I was not involved with any of that."

"Very well, Mr Thane, I accept that you knew nothing about these women. Now would you please tell me everything regarding your relationship with Mr Le Fondre and the business arrangements that you had with him?"

Thane started to tell Jake everything. He covered his business arrangements with Le Fondre and confessed to the fact that they had made the sex films. He stressed again, however, that he played no part in the abduction and murder of the women.

"I should have told you that from the very beginning," Thane insisted, "but I couldn't say anything about the women without implicating myself in the making of the films. However, now that I have told you everything I must continue to stress that Le Fondre only told me about the missing women when Cathcart reported that the lack of women was slowing production of the films."

Thane did not mention Willie Ifield sensing that that would be unwise just at the moment.

"Tell me about the murder of Constable Thomson?" Jake then said.

Thane again thought for a moment before saying anything.

"That, again, had nothing to do with me," he eventually said. "I knew we were employing a police officer to keep us abreast of any police investigation that may have touched on our business arrangements. I dealt with the payments so obviously knew the person existed. However, I had nothing to do with the decision to have the man killed. Guy decided that Thomson was no longer of any use to us and that there was a chance that he might even talk to his colleagues about us. Guy decided that we could not take the risk of simply ceasing to employ Thomson; after all, he knew too much. Unknown to me Guy arranged for George Cathcart to take care of Thomson. You can talk to Marian Lawrence, if you like; she was the young lady whom I believe kept you busy that night while Cathcart killed your friend."

The memory of the night Tommy had been killed came flooding back to Jake and he could clearly see, in his mind's eye, the grieving, young woman standing at the door of the tenement block. She had rather expertly prevented him from immediately following his friend in to the building. Jake had often wondered why she had played a part in the events of that night and now, it seemed, he would finally have an opportunity to speak to her.

"Where can I find her?"

"She's back in Aberdeen again," said Thane and provided Jake with an address in Crown Street.

"Okay, Mr Thane, who is the new police officer on your pay list?" Jake then enquired.

"There isn't one," Thane lied. "After all the trouble we had with Thomson we decided to take our chances and leave any direct contact with the police out of it."

"Now I thought we were doing so well, Mr Thane," Jake added. "Up until that last statement I was prepared to believe all that you have said. However, I just cannot believe that you did not replace Constable Thomson, probably before he was killed. I need the name of the police officer that you have been paying for information?"

"There isn't one," Thane insisted.

Jake looked at Thane for a moment trying to read, from the man's expression, whether, or not, he should believe him. He felt sure that Thane was lying and yet he had no way of knowing for sure.

"Did you speak to Harriet Cruickshank about the contents of Le Fondre's will?"

"Yes I did. I didn't want her to think that Guy had forgotten about her."

"So you knew what Mr Le Fondre intended doing with his money?" Jake then asked.

"I didn't have all the details but I certainly knew that Harriet was going to be a very rich woman indeed and I felt she should know that as soon as possible."

"And the Gladstones?"

"No, I didn't speak to them."

"You keep telling me that you knew nothing about the abducted women and their eventual murder; how then did you think Le Fondre was getting his actresses?"

"I presumed we were paying prostitutes to do the job for us. I even, rather naively thought that we might actually be employing real actresses."

"You said you dealt with all the financial elements of the business?" Jake then said.

"Yes, that's right."

"Then surely you were well aware that women were not being paid to participate in the movies you made?"

"I assumed they were being paid from the cash that was kept at the farm," Thane replied.

"But you would have had to supply that cash, Mr Thane," Jake added. "It seems to me, Mr Thane that you may not have known exactly what was going on at the farm but as long as the profits kept rolling in you were more than prepared to turn a blind eye."

Thane sat in silence for a moment. "Perhaps you are right, Inspector," he eventually said. "I didn't know what was going on at the farm but I should have done. I should have paid more attention to what we were producing and asked more questions. I will have to live with that for the rest of my days."

"Though depending on the outcome of your trial, those days may be numbered," Jake added rather coldly.

Thane looked at Jake with horror in his eyes. "I didn't know that those women were being murdered and I will not be branded along with Guy Le Fondre and George Cathcart as being a killer."

"Then here's hoping the judge and jury come to see things your way, Mr Thane. Until then I'm going to leave Sergeant Mathieson to formally charge you and those charges will include my belief that you may not have actually had those women killed but that you most certainly had more idea that something might have been amiss than you have ever said. You will have your moment in court to try and persuade a jury that you are innocent of the more serious charges."

"You have to believe me, Inspector, "Thane pleaded, "I had nothing to do with anyone's death. Look, if you can find Wolfgang Schwieger then I feel sure that he will support what I am saying. He wouldn't have known anything about the women being killed but he will be able to tell you that they were there because of Le Fondre and Cathcart and that I had nothing to do with it."

"Who is Wolfgang Schwieger?" Jake then asked.

"Wolfgang was the man who made our films. I believe he left the farm on Friday, probably in the company of Maisie Strachan, though I have no idea where they were going."

"Who is Maisie Strachan?"

"She was our last 'actress,'" Thane replied.

"And where did Maisie come from?" Jake then asked.

"She was a prostitute and we paid her well for her services," Thane replied, once more returning to what was little more than a half-truth.

"Why are they travelling together?"

"Wolfgang fell in love with Maisie, it's as simple as that."

"But you have no idea where they might be now?"

"I imagine that Wolfgang will have tried to get back to Germany. He often spoke about running his own film-business back home. The funny thing is that Wolfgang came in to Aberdeen with me the night that Guy was killed. I never did find out why he was going in to Aberdeen; the man was never usually in the habit of going anywhere."

Jake wrote down the names. Perhaps, in this Wolfgang Schwieger he had another suspect for killing Le Fondre.

"Did Wolfgang Schwieger have any problems with Mr Le Fondre?" Jake then asked.

"No more than anyone else. I suppose there were times when Wolfgang felt belittled by Guy's attitude towards him. Wolfgang saw himself as being better than the films he was making."

"And was he?"

"Sorry?"

"Was he better than the films he made?"

"Not really. I can't imagine Wolfgang making a proper film," Thane said.

"Was Wolfgang sacked or did he just leave?"

"That's just it, Wolfgang's position at the farm was never in any danger. We had always wanted him to work with the new people. After all, we intended going back to making the sex films and would have needed Wolfgang then."

"So why did he leave?" Jake enquired.

"I don't know. The fact he left with Maisie, however, may be your answer. As I said, Wolfgang rather fell for Maisie's charms and the fact she was prepared to go with him may have prompted him to leave now rather than wait."

"Perhaps," agreed Jake, "but there is still the matter of why Wolfgang went in to Aberdeen that night. Is there anyone who might know where Wolfgang might have gone?"

"I shouldn't think so. Wolfgang was a loner and no one ever knew what was going on in that Germanic head of his. As far as I know he did not know anyone in Aberdeen but with him being a man who kept himself to himself he may just have kept that from me as well."

"Can you provide us with a description of Wolfgang and Maisie?" Jake asked.

Thane provided a very sketchy description of both Wolfgang and Maisie, which Jake wrote down. He read it back.

"How well did you know these people?" Jake then said.

"Not that well. I only saw Maisie Strachan a couple of times and Wolfgang was hardly a close friend even though he had been at the farm quite a while now."

"And yet he travelled with you to Aberdeen on the Tuesday, Mr Thane. Surely, during the journey from Ellon to Aberdeen you had ample time to formulate an opinion as to how Mr Schwieger looked."

"Sorry, Inspector, I suppose I've never been that observant."

"Very well, Mr Thane, we'll leave it at that. Sergeant Mathieson I'll leave you to charge Mr Thane formally."

Jake left the room and hurried back to his office where he put on his jacket and left the building. He was keen to visit the address in Crown Street and find out what Marian Lawrence would have to say about the night that Tommy had been murdered.

It had been a long journey to get to this point but he was now almost there with regard to knowing exactly what had happened. It was late afternoon and darkness had already descended across Aberdeen. The street lights were lit but in many places they made little difference. The air was cold and most people that Jake passed were now hurrying home from work, keen to shut the doors and curtains to the world and snuggle down in front of a nice, warming fire.

Jake turned in to Crown Street and covered the short distance to the address he had been given. He entered the door and climbed the flight of stairs to the door on which the name 'Harris' was pinned. Jake looked at the details provided by Thane and hoped that the 'Harris' residence was also the place where Marian Lawrence was currently staying.

Jake knocked on the door. A few seconds passed before the door was finally opened. The young woman standing before Jake could easily have been the distressed woman he had dealt with outside the tenement while Tommy was being knifed to death inside. The main problem for Jake was that he had never really got a look at the woman's face that night. She had carefully kept a handkerchief up to her face most the time.

No, Jake could not be sure about the woman's face but her height and hair colouring matched his memory of what she looked like.

"Yes?" she said.

Jake showed her his identification and introduced himself.

"What can I do for you, Inspector?" the woman then said.

"Might we talk inside, Miss Lawrence?" Jake then said.

The woman looked surprised that this police officer knew her name. She stepped back and allowed Jake to enter the property. They were soon sitting through in the front room. Jake explained why he was there and then told her that Scott Thane had provided her name.

"I'm not here to arrest you, Miss Lawrence, though there are many reasons why I probably should. However, I just want to know exactly what happened the night that Constable Thomson was murdered. I also want you to tell me what part Scott Thane played in it all."

"If I may take the second question first," Marian Lawrence said in a soft, sensual voice," I can tell you that Scott Thane had nothing to do with it, as far as I was aware. The deed was organised by George Cathcart at the behest of someone called Guy Le Fondre. Cathcart was an odious man who knew me through the fact I had done some acting at Her Majesty's and he used to hang around the exit when we came out. He liked looking at us for some reason and always tried to be in our company. Anyway, he asked me to do a job for him one night. I was to act the part of a distressed woman. He took some pleasure in ripping the clothing that I was wearing just to make things look that little bit more authentic. Cathcart told me that when he gave the signal I was to scream and make as much noise as I could. If Constable Thomson arrived alone then I was to direct him straight in to the building. If there was anyone with Constable Thomson then I was to prevent them from entering at the same time as Constable Thomson. Cathcart was inside waiting to do the deed. Once you went inside I just walked away. Cathcart got out the back."

"And Thane played no part in it?" Jake asked again.

"I never met Thane. I knew of his existence because he was the one who paid us all."

"Do you know that George Cathcart and Guy Le Fondre are both now dead?"

"Yes. I only came back to Aberdeen after I was told that Cathcart was dead. As I said, he was a horrible man who liked to hang around you. He had a strange opinion of women; I'm pretty sure he never really liked us and that any chance to inflict pain on us was gratefully accepted."

Jake thought of Grace Lord immediately. Cathcart had paid her a visit and from what Jake now knew she had been very lucky not to have been hurt by the man who seemed to be nothing short of a sadist.

"Has anyone said anything to you about how either of those gentlemen may have died?" Jake enquired.

"I only know what I have read in the papers concerning Le Fondre and as for Cathcart, everyone just seem delighted that the man is dead. How he was killed seems so immaterial."

"We think a woman may have killed him," Jake then said. "Would you have killed him, given the chance, Miss Lawrence?"

"George Cathcart was a violent and vicious man who looked at you as if he meant to rape you, Inspector. Given half a chance his hands would be on your body and there would be a leer in his face that brought terror to your heart. Had he got too close to me then yes I would have gladly killed the man rather than be subjected to some kind of sexual attack. If another woman got that chance then I feel sorry for what she may have gone through but I commend her for having the guts to kill the man. If you ever find her don't charge her with murder, Inspector, thank her for ridding the planet of a thoroughly horrible and nasty man."

For a moment Jake pondered on not bothering to find Cathcart's killer. After all, Jake now knew for certain that Cathcart had killed Tommy. He also knew for certain that Cathcart had terrified Grace during his visit to her flat. No doubt the man had terrified many other women and for that his death probably was a blessed release to many. Yes, just for a moment he thought about walking away from all this and leaving Cathcart's killer free to enjoy the rest of his or her life.

The only problem with that was that Cathcart's death could still be connected to Le Fondre's death and Jake did want to get that killer, especially if it turned out to be Willie Ifield.

Jake thanked Marian Lawrence for her time and then got up to leave.

"Thank you, Inspector," Marian said as he opened the front door for Jake.

"Not at all, Miss Lawrence," concluded Jake and he left the flat to make his way back down to ground level.

Jake then caught the tram all the way around to Rosemount. He got off the tram and made his way in to Stanley Zanre's shop where he was soon talking to the man himself. Zanre told Jake the same as he had told Mathieson and he further said that he would be happy to appear in court, if necessary and talk about the mystery man whom he had seen the night that Le Fondre was killed.

Jake came away having no reason to doubt what he had just been told. Now all he had to do was to find a formal connection between Willie Ifield and Guy Le Fondre. That process would start with the death of Mathilde Dupont. She was to be Willie Ifield's alibi so it seemed highly unlikely that he would have had anything to do with her death.

Jake would speak with Doctor Symon and find out if there was anything further known about how the poor woman had died.

***

Stanley Zanre had not liked the fact that the police had called again to question him about his evidence for the night of Guy Le Fondre's death. Stanley Zanre had never liked telling lies and yet here he was lying to the police. Zanre knew how much trouble he would be in should the police ever find out that he was not telling the truth. However, for the moment his fear of what might happen to his family was driving him to continue with the same story.

He only hoped he had remembered everything that he had been told to say.

TEN

Saturday 10 November – most of the day

Jake was informed at nine o'clock that his investigative skills were once more required after a dead body had been found in one of the rooms of the Bon Accord Hotel. As Mathieson was away hopefully enjoying the football trip to Dundee, Jake collected Constable McGill and they made their way round to Market Street where they were met by one of the assistant managers. He was a tall, rather spindly looking young man with a long neck and a very prominent Adam's apple. He seemed keen to hide the presence of the police from the hotel customers as he led Jake and McGill upstairs to the first floor.

The door was opened and Jake and McGill were allowed to enter the room. The assistant manager then left them alone and went back downstairs. Jake stood by the bed and looked down at the body of a young man. He looked to be in his twenties; handsome and muscular. His eyes were open and his face was slightly contorted. Some people looked almost serene in death; this was most certainly not one of those occasions.

The man lay on his back with his right arm outstretched so that his hand actually hung over the edge of the bed. There was an empty glass lying on the floor. Jake looked around the room and there was no apparent sign of a bag or anything else that might accommodate an overnight stay.

McGill checked the man's pockets. He found a piece of paper in the man's jacket pocket and there was also a small wallet in the inside pocket of his jacket. McGill looked at the paper and then moved across to where Jake was now standing.

"This appears to be a name and address, sir," he said handing the paper to Jake.

The name and address written on the paper was that of Mathilde Dupont.

"This ties in nicely with the note left here on the bedside table," Jake added.

McGill glanced down at the roughly written note:

I am sorry for what I did to Mathilde. It should never have happened.

"Who is Mathilde Dupont, sir?" added McGill.

"A woman who was murdered last week but who features in the investigation in to the death of Guy Le Fondre. She was given as Willie Ifield's alibi but, of course, she is no longer around to confirm or deny his story."

"So are we to assume that this man is the killer of Mathilde Dupont?" McGill then asked.

"So it would seem," replied Jake, taking the wallet from McGill," though it may be of more than passing interest that the note is not signed."

"You mean anyone could have written it?" McGill asked.

"That is exactly what I mean," Jake confirmed as he turned his attention to the wallet.

He opened the wallet and looked through it for any means of identification. There was nothing inside with a name on it and Jake also noted that there was no money in the wallet either. Unless this man had paid for the room in advance then the absence of money rather suggested he had no intention of ever paying for the room; unless he expected someone else to meet the cost of course.

"Anything else in the pockets?" Jake then asked.

"Nothing else, sir."

Jake wandered around the room though he did not really know what he might be looking for. McGill checked around the bed and in the drawers of the bedside cabinets. Apart from the Bible there was nothing.

Jake was still looking around the room when the door opened and Doctor Symon came in.

"Morning, Jake, yet again we meet over a dead body."

"I don't do this on purpose, Doctor," Jake replied and Symon smiled.

He moved closer to the body and studied it for a moment.

"Not much thought required for this one, Jake," Doctor Symon then said. "Poison I'd guess and no doubt contained in the glass lying on the floor."

"It may be poison, Doctor, but is it murder or suicide?" Jake then said.

"That is a very good question, Inspector Fraser," Symon said. "On first glance I'd say suicide though I'll check for any marks on his body that might convey he was held down in some way, when I get him back to the mortuary. However, looking at him as he lies here it certainly looks like he's taken his own life."

"We have a note that seems to support what you are saying, Doctor, although it isn't signed. This man appears to have killed Mathilde Dupont and then, perhaps in a fit of remorse, came here to end his own life. He has no money on him so I'm assuming he did not come here expecting to have to pay for the room."

"There you go, then, suicide. I'll leave it at that until I have a proper look at him later," Doctor Symon concluded and left again.

"Constable, arrange for a photograph to be taken of this man and once it is in your possession, go round to Mathilde Dupont's accommodation and ask the neighbours if they recognise him. Also get me a copy of the photograph that is taken as I want to put it in to the papers and see if anyone can identify him. Could you also arrange for the body to be taken back to the mortuary, I don't think there's much more it can tell us here."

"At once, sir," McGill said with undue enthusiasm.

McGill left the room to organise a photographer. Jake had one last look around and then made his way out of the door. There was a uniformed police officer already standing there and Jake asked him to remain on duty until the body was removed.

Jake went back downstairs and found the assistant manager in his office. When Jake entered there was another man already sitting in the room who was looking rather worried, as if he had done something wrong and it had just been discovered. He was drinking a cup of tea and looked up at Jake with some suspicion.

"This is Edgar Harvey, he was on the reception when the dead man and his lady friend arrived," the assistant manager said. "I'll leave you alone to talk. Would you like a cup of tea or coffee, Inspector?"

"There's a pot here so I'll just have tea," Jake replied.

The assistant manager produced a cup from one of the cupboards in his office and then left the room. Jake poured some tea in to the cup then added milk and sugar. He then sat down. All the time Harvey had been watching him but saying nothing.

"The assistant manager said something about the dead gentleman and his lady friend arriving? What happened to the lady?"

Harvey sipped some more of his tea and then looked up at Jake. His face set in an even more worried expression and Jake guessed that the missing woman was probably the problem. With the man dead and the woman missing it was obvious to anyone that there would be no payment for the room now.

"I don't know. I saw them go up together but I never saw her come down again. I had to go to one or two of the other rooms, in the course of the evening, so it is perfectly possible that she left whilst I was otherwise engaged."

"When did the man and woman arrive?"

"They registered at a quarter to nine yesterday evening."

"What name did they give?"

"He signed the book as Mr and Mrs Smith."

"Not very imaginative," Jake added.

"Names just wash over me, I'm afraid" Harvey then said. "I never stop to think if there might be some chance that any couple signing the register might not actually be married."

"Though being this close to the harbour it must happen quite a lot?" Jake suggested.

"I suppose so," added Harvey, though he seemed slightly detached from the conversation as if his mind were on other things.

"Can you describe the woman?"

Harvey didn't need to think about the answer. He responded almost at once.

"That's just it, I can't. It was as if she was making sure that I wouldn't remember her by holding back and never getting too close to me. She was halfway up the stairs before I had even organised the key for the room. I just assumed that they were eager to enjoy each other's company, if you know what I mean?"

"You said names wash over you, Mr Harvey, but from their demeanour would you have believed that they might have been a married couple?" Jake then asked.

"Thinking back it ought to have been obvious to me what their arrangement was. The woman was more than likely a local prostitute but, like I said, I never got a proper look at her so I may be doing her a great disservice in suggesting that."

"So she may not have been a prostitute?" Jake asked.

"She could have been anything, Inspector, but surely a proper lady would not be randomly seeing a gentleman in a hotel bedroom?" replied Harvey.

"So you *do* think she was a prostitute?" added Jake.

"I only suggest that given the manner of their liaison, Inspector, it seems more like the actions of a man paying for a prostitute than anything else."

"Did they have any luggage with them?"

"Not that I noticed."

"I presume that no one paid for the room?"

"The man paid the deposit on the room. We don't take the final payment until departure as not all the guests have food while they are here."

"Did he take the cash from a wallet?" Jake then asked.

"Oh yes, it was a very fancy wallet and he made quite a show of waving it around beneath my nose as if I ought to be envious."

"Did you notice if there was a lot of money in the man's wallet?"

Harvey thought for a few seconds. "As I said he did wave it around quite a lot but I didn't really notice what might be inside. No, wait a minute, now that I really think about it he did offer me money from a small bundle of notes. Considering the small amount that is required, by way of deposit, I thought it rather an unnecessary show of wealth."

"Might he have been trying to impress the young woman?" Jake suggested.

"I wouldn't have thought so," Harvey replied. "As I said, the young woman was already heading up the stairs by the time the man was showing me his wallet."

"How many other guests were in the hotel last night?" Jake enquired.

"We were not too busy; I believe six of our rooms were occupied."

"And is everyone still here?" Jake asked.

"We kept everyone here until the police arrived. Your officers are interviewing all relevant parties in the dining room."

"Thank you, Mr Harvey, that will be all for the moment."

Jake took another drink from his teacup and then left the room. He went through to the dining room where he found a small group of people being spoken to by uniformed police officers. Jake decided not to get involved meantime and went back up to the room where the body was lying.

Moments later McGill arrived with the photographer. He had also brought the ambulance to take the body back to the morgue. Pictures were taken and then the body was removed. The photographer was asked to develop the pictures immediately and to get them to Constable McGill at Lodge Walk.

With the room now empty Jake and McGill stood looking down at the bed again. Jake started to speak.

"A man and a woman arrive at a hotel and book a room as a married couple. The man on the reception tells me that they looked like a couple keen to enjoy each other's company. All that information leads you to think that as soon as they got inside this room they would be on that bed making love before you could switch the light out. However, we find the man fully clothed and there are no obvious signs on this bed that he had sex with anyone. Why was the woman here if it wasn't for sex?"

"Maybe they came here to talk about something?" McGill suggested.

"And having spoken to each other he then commits suicide and she empties his wallet of all its money and then casually leaves. Doesn't really add up, does it?"

"But there seems to be no denying that he did commit suicide," added McGill, "so maybe he came here to have sex and then changed his mind. Knowing that he was going to kill himself he gives all his money to the prostitute and tells her to leave. Once on his own he takes a poison that he had brought with him and ends his life as he had always planned to."

"Indeed it must have been planned, Constable, as there is no sign of a pencil with which to write the note, nor is there a bottle in which he brought the poison. Now we know that a note was written and it seems fairly obvious that poison was ingested so, that being the case, we can only come to one conclusion; now what do you think that might be?"

McGill thought for a moment, then his expression brightened as he thought of an answer.

"The woman must have taken the pencil and bottle away with her."

"Exactly," added Jake.

"But why?" McGill then enquired.

"That is the very question that we need to answer, Constable. Why would a woman stand back and watch a man commit suicide, then casually clear up all the evidence, empty the man's wallet and then leave?"

"It's a bit of a puzzle then, sir?" McGill said, feeling quite glad that he would not be the one to sort out the puzzle.

"Indeed it is, Constable, indeed it is," Jake muttered as he continued to look around the room in case he had missed something of importance.

***

The hiding place worked well for Henry Davis and Aspinall. Through leaving messages they had been able to arrange a meeting after Davis had told Aspinall about Scott Thane now being in custody. As far as Davis was concerned the business had lost its leadership and he could now see no financial future other than living solely off his police income.

They met at the end of the lane, which lay at the back of the Post Office at the bottom of Market Street. Both men lit a cigarette and stood, looking across the road at the harbour beyond.

"What happens now?" Davis then asked.

"Nothing changes in the short term," Aspinall said. "Mr Thane has given me enough information to allow me to run things at least for a little while. Assuming they don't hang him then Mr Thane could always still run the business from prison. I could visit him for instructions."

"He has been charged with being involved in the murder of various women, Mr Aspinall, so there may be every chance that Mr Thane will hang. That being the case I ask the question again, what happens now?"

Aspinall drew on his cigarette and exhaled a cloud of smoke. "As long as Mr Thane is in a position to provide me with instructions then we carry on as normal. Should that change then we will have to re-assess won't we?"

"Just when things were looking so good," Davis muttered.

"How are the police investigations in to the deaths of Le Fondre and George Cathcart going?" Aspinall then asked.

"Nothing much has happened with regard to Cathcart," Henry Davis replied. "To be honest I haven't heard anything that makes me think there's been much progress in either case. I'm hearing that there might be a possible suspect for the Le Fondre murder but no names are being mentioned."

"What do they reckon happened to Cathcart?"

"Someone knifed him to death and left him in the Guestrow. From what I'm hearing Inspector Fraser is of the opinion that Cathcart may have been a bit rough with a whore and got it from her pimp. Let's face it the man was warped when it came to women."

Aspinall finished his cigarette. "George never did know how to be nice to the ladies," he eventually agreed and Davis got the impression that Aspinall might be happy to accept the idea that a pimp had killed Cathcart.

Davis now finished his cigarette and squashed the stub underfoot. "Until I hear otherwise I'll keep leaving little updates for you in the usual place."

"Very good."

And with that both men went their separate ways.

.   ***

McGill got the photographs back around the middle of the afternoon. He had held on to the address and now made his way to the flat where Mathilde Dupont had lived and died. He did not need to go in to that flat, of course, he merely wanted to show the neighbours the rather unpleasant photograph of an, as yet, unnamed man, who looked clearly dead and ask them if they might have seen him before.

McGill knocked on six doors altogether and spoke to ten people in total. Amazingly no one passed out at looking at the photograph of a dead man and equally amazingly three people reported seeing the man enter Mathilde Dupont's flat. Their sightings were spread across a period of three weeks and the last was on the night that she was believed to have died.

Armed with this information McGill returned to Lodge Walk and sought out Jake Fraser.

"So our dead man did know Mathilde Dupont. That being the case it looks ever more likely that he was the one who killed her," Jake said after he had listened to what McGill had to say.

"That has to be good news, isn't it, sir?" added McGill.

Jake gave the whole matter some thought. Nothing made much sense to him. Why did Mathilde Dupont have to die and was her death connected, in some way, to the fact that she knew Willie Ifield? Why then did the mystery man take a mystery woman to the Bon Accord Hotel so that the mystery man could commit suicide and the mystery woman could run off with his money?

Absolutely nothing made any sense.

"How does the photograph of our mystery man look?" Jake then asked.

McGill handed him a copy and Jake looked at it. He decided that the photograph was a little too macabre to be given to the Press. He hoped that Doctor Symon might manage to make the face look a little more presentable in the mortuary and that another photograph might be used for the papers.

"What now, sir?" McGill then asked.

"What we do now, Constable, is forget about our mystery man for the moment and spend some time with you telling me what you've found out at the theatre regarding the other case on which you have been working."

McGill took out his notebook and looked positively excited to be discussing a case, his case, with the Inspector.

"I've spoken to all the workmen and their foreman. Quite honestly, sir, they told me nothing of any importance and I got the impression that they neither knew anything of any consequence nor cared for that matter that these little incidents had been occurring. The idea that the disappearing tools were in any way connected seemed beyond them."

"So what are you left with?" Jake then said.

"A series of unexplained incidents that may, or may not, be connected. If they are connected then someone is quite clearly trying to delay the work that must be done to get the theatre ready for opening. If they are not connected then I'm wasting my time."

"If we assume they are connected then there seems to be no obvious suspect?" added Jake.

"Not within His Majesty's at any rate. There is the staff of Her Majesty's, whom I referred to the other day. Some of them will lose their jobs over the new theatre opening and weak though it may sound, it is still the best motive I can come up with at the moment."

"But we know for a fact that Her Majesty's would close now whatever happened to His Majesty's," Jake said, "so there would be little to be gained by delaying matters for a few days or even weeks. It's not as if the decision to close Her Majesty's would be reversed."

McGill thought for a moment. "Is it worth proceeding with my enquiries, sir?" he then asked.

"Hold on a day or two and see if there is another incident then we can discuss matters again," suggested Jake.

"Very good, sir and thank you for the advice."

"Not at all, Constable and thank you for the work you have done today," Jake concluded and McGill made his way out of the room.

Jake turned his attention back to Scott Thane and the events at the farm. He checked his notes again and came across the names of Wolfgang Schwieger and Maisie Strachan. Wolfgang had gone to Aberdeen on the Tuesday evening on which Le Fondre had been killed. He had then returned to the farm on the Friday, met up with Maisie Strachan and then they had both left the farm and made off somewhere. But where? Had they gone to Germany, as suggested and if so, why decide to go now?

What had made Wolfgang decide to leave the farm now? Had it anything to do with the fact that he had gone to Aberdeen the night that Le Fondre was killed? Was it possible that Wolfgang Schwieger could have been the one to kill Guy Le Fondre and if so, why then were people telling him that someone looking like Willie Ifield was more likely to be the killer?

As with the mystery man in the hotel room nothing much was making sense to Jake in the Guy Le Fondre murder either.

Jake went through to the Desk Sergeant and arranged for him to send out a message to all Forces throughout the country asking them to be on the look-out for a German man in the company of a young woman. He provided Thane's descriptions even though he knew they were far too general to really help anyone with identification.

Having cleared everything for the day Jake then made his way up to Margaret's where they had a light evening meal followed by two beers for Jake and a glass of wine for Margaret. They chatted until nearly midnight when Jake got up to leave.

"See you tomorrow?" he said as they walked to the door.

"Come for lunch," Margaret added.

"I'll be here around midday then," concluded Jake.

They kissed at the door and then Jake left.

ELEVEN

Monday 12 November – early morning through to early evening

Sergeant Mathieson arrived at work just before seven in the morning. The air was cold and yet again there was rain in the air. Mathieson felt the same depression that many felt as they went in to the winter months. He hated the darkness and he hated the prospect of snow. He often felt that he had been born of reptilian stock and needed the heat of the sun to give him energy to face the day.

Mathieson went through to see Jake just in case he had missed anything of importance over the weekend. However, before he could say anything Jake had a question of his own.

"How was the match?"

"No goals I'm afraid but as a game it was all right. Couldn't get over the size of the crowd, though," Mathieson added, "the journalists reckon there were as many as twelve thousand at Dens Park."

"Twelve thousand, just to watch Aberdeen?" Jake responded with some surprise.

"And all for no goals being scored," Mathieson then said with a sigh. "Ah well, that is the joy of football, you can never be sure what you are going to get."

"More money than sense," was Jake's assessment of the situation.

"You may well be right, sir," agreed Mathieson with a smile.

"How was the journey down?" Jake then asked.

"Very good. The coaches on the train were very modern and very comfortable. I thought that it being a football train we would have been given the poorer end of their rolling stock, but no, it was well worth the three and six."

Jake updated Mathieson on the body being found in the Bon Accord Hotel and how that body connected to Mathilde Dupont. He also told him about the mystery woman and how they were no closer to identifying her.

"I might also want you to keep an eye on young McGill," Jake then said. "He is still investigating those strange occurrences at His Majesty's Theatre, which may or may not be deliberate and I feel he just needs a bit of guidance here and there. I've told him to wait until something else is reported but I get the feeling that the young lad wants to run before he has learned to walk."

Mathieson grinned. "We were all there at one time, sir."

"Indeed we were," agreed Jake turning his attention to the work he had planned for the day.

After he had cleared up some paperwork Jake then made his way over to see Doctor Symon. Yet again his mortuary was filling up with dead bodies and yet again their deaths seemed to be linked in some way.

Doctor Symon was confident that the man had died from poisoning and that that poison had been taken orally. He was still, therefore, pretty confident to say that the man had committed suicide as there was no evidence whatsoever that someone else had been involved.

"And what about Mathilde?" Jake then said.

"Pretty much as I had said before. She was strangled but beyond that I can't really tell you much more."

"And we now know that our mystery man was a caller at Mathilde's flat, including around the time we suspect she was killed."

"So that's all nice and tidy, isn't it?" Doctor Symon commented.

Jake thought for a moment. "That's probably what's upsetting me the most," he then said. "Everything is just a bit too tidy. It is as if someone is laying out the evidence in front of us and almost leading us by the nose to follow the clues."

"Or maybe it is what it is, Jake," added Symon. "Crime doesn't always need to be complicated."

Jake smiled. "Perhaps you are right, Doctor. Maybe I've been too long at this game and I now seek problems when there are none. I'd be a lot happier were it not for that unknown woman who was seen at the Bon Accord Hotel. I hate loose ends in an investigation."

"However, with nothing much to go on, you may never find out who that woman was," Doctor Symon added.

"Probably not," Jake then added with a sigh. "Okay, we'll put this down to our mystery man killing Mathilde Dupont, for reason or reasons unknown and then committing suicide as he could no longer live with himself. I'll write up my report to that effect and let the Chief know."

"Very good," Symon added, "and at least it will let me get a couple of bodies out of my mortuary."

"One last thing, Doctor," Jake then said. "Would you be able to make our mystery man look presentable enough for a photograph to be taken of him so that I could give it to the newspapers? I'd really like to identify him and that might be my only way."

"I'll see what I can do, Jake, but I'm not promising that the face of a dead man will ever really look good enough to grace the morning paper."

"I appreciate the idea may not be a good one," Jake conceded, "but if you can get me a photograph then it would greatly assist this inquiry."

"As I said," Doctor Symon responded," I will do what I can."

Jake went back to his desk and started work on the paperwork that would remove the murder of Mathilde Dupont and the apparent suicide of the mystery man from his current workload.

***

Phillip Marshall was due to work nightshift for the week and decided, as he would be at home during the day that he would get some jobs done around the house. Anna left him to it and went shopping for groceries.

Phillip had bought some paint and brushes. He had thought about removing the linoleum first but decided instead to leave it where it was as he would not be too upset with it getting splashed with paint. He still found it strange that the rest of the floor had been left bare and only the relatively small area at the sink had been covered. He presumed it had been done that way to deal with any water splashed from the sink area or, perhaps, money had just been short.

As he started the painting his mind wandered to the people who might have occupied the flat before them. Obviously it had to have been other police officers and he wondered if they had always been as young and excited when they had moved in. He then began to think of the couple who had immediately preceded them in the flat. He didn't really know Henry Davis and apart from knowing that his wife's name was Bella, he knew nothing else about the couple. He did start to wonder what, if anything, they had done to improve the flat. Had it been Henry who had laid the linoleum?

Phillip knew that Henry had Bella had been offered a bigger flat somewhere else in Aberdeen but he didn't know where. He wondered if he might get something a bit bigger someday. Perhaps they would need to have children first?

Phillip smiled at the thought of all the sex that might be needed before children began to arrive. He didn't know if it was something that ran in families but he did know that Anna's mother had not found it easy to get pregnant and Anna had eventually been an only child.

Phillip decided not to get too uptight about wanting children. After all it was the sex that he enjoyed not the desire to make babies as a result of their actions. Anna had never voiced an opinion on whether, or not, she might have wanted children. Given the dangers of childbirth he doubted if Anna would be in any hurry to bear children. Phillip had also been told that there was great deal of pain involved in the process of giving birth. He briefly thought of what lay between his lovely wife's legs and he caused himself to shudder at the thought of a fully developed baby passing through a relatively small space such as that.

Yes, having children, would need to be a discussion for another day in the Marshall household.

***

Joe Tredwall was sitting in Willie Ifield's office with Daniel and Miss Sangster present as well. All the paperwork had been signed and the money was already in Tredwall's bank account. The keys to the Business Club had been handed over and the small group were sitting with a glass of white wine in hand and a will to celebrate.

"Of late the Business Club has been nothing but bad news," Joe said. "I hope the change of ownership will change the luck of the place. You'd think it had been cursed given what has happened these last few weeks."

"You should never have allowed the likes of Thane and Le Fondre to be members of the Club," Willie said. "They were always going to bring you trouble."

"It's a Club, Mr Ifield and as such you can only control the membership to a certain degree. Perhaps I was guilty of not monitoring the actions of the members and I was certainly guilty of letting too many dubious things happen within its walls. However, I was always of the opinion that the members paid for the right to have their privacy protected and I suppose in doing that I rather left the door open for them to pretty much do as they pleased."

"Times will change under Ifield control," Daniel then said. "As membership comes up for renewal we will take a close look at each person and decide whether, or not, they will be allowed to continue as members of the Club. I certainly do not want the police knocking on the door every five minutes."

Tredwall smiled. "Funnily enough the police haven't been near us until very recently. I'm telling you that most of our troubles with the police stemmed from Guy Le Fondre and I, for one, am not sorry that man is no longer with us."

"I'll drink to that," Willie said and raised his glass. There were smiles all round as everyone else took a sip of their wine.

"Do you need me for anything else, Mr Ifield?" Miss Sangster then asked.

"You were not invited in to my office to work, Miss Sangster," Willie Ifield replied. "You are here as my guest to help celebrate Daniel's purchase of the Business Club. It may be necessary for you to deal with work generated by the Business Club on top of what you are already doing for here so we will need to discuss a small pay rise as compensation for you."

"That is very kind of you, Mr Ifield, "Miss Sangster said.

Daniel did not fully understand what his father had meant by Miss Sangster doing some work for the Business Club. "You cannot expect Miss Sangster to work at the Business Club, not with some of the men there being less that chivalrous in their approach to women."

"Daniel, I did not say that Miss Sangster needed to work *at* the Club. I merely said there will be Club related work that she may have to do but, of course, we would ensure that that work was brought here."

Daniel felt a little better after hearing what his father had just said. The thought of any woman being asked to work in a Gentlemen's Club was beyond Daniel's comprehension.

"Very well," Daniel eventually said," that make's sense and I wholeheartedly agree that Miss Sangster should get a pay rise."

Miss Sangster smiled at the prospect of being paid more. Tredwall noted the look on both Willie and Daniel's faces as they seemed to bathe in the warmth of that smile. There was no doubt that this woman had both men in the palm of her hand. Tredwall knew that he too would have been happy to do anything for a woman as beautiful as Miss Sangster, although he knew that he would never stoop as low as the Ifields had done in their push to make money.

Tredwall drank up and left. Miss Sangster took that as her hint to leave the room as well and Daniel sat across from his father. He held the keys of the Business Club in his hand as if he never meant to give them up again.

"Daniel, I may have a problem," Willie Ifield said.

"What kind of problem?"

"The police have a statement from someone that they saw a man, resembling my description, walking about outside Le Fondre's house on the night he died and before you ask, no it wasn't actually me. However, I have since found out that my alibi for that night is no longer as watertight as I had thought it would be. I won't say any more than that for the moment but I don't expect it will be long before Inspector Jake Fraser is back here asking me some more questions about that night. Depending on how things turn out I may not be able to spend quite so much time in the office as I would like to and it will, therefore, mean that you will have to split your time between the Business Club and here. Might I suggest that you employ someone to run the day to day management issues at the Club and that you spend more of your time here, just until the police interest passes."

Daniel looked disappointed. "I had wanted to get involved at the Club."

"Of course you do," agreed Willie, "and you shall, only not immediately."

"Okay, father, I will, of course, do what is best for the family business."

"Excellent," concluded Willie. "Now let's finish that bottle of wine."

***

Jake went for a walk. It wasn't the best of days but at least it was now dry if not still overcast and quite chilly. He made his way up through Rosemount until he arrived at Guy Le Fondre's home. He stood outside and looked around.

Zanre's home was across the road and there did indeed appear to be a clear view of anyone standing outside Le Fondre's house. Jake looked at the other houses. He felt sure that everyone would already have been interviewed but decided to go round the doors again anyway.

He knocked on the door next to the Zanre household and eventually the door was opened by an attractive, well dressed woman. Jake showed his identification and was invited in to the house.

"Sorry to trouble you again," Jake began, "but we are still trying to gather information regarding what may have happened the night that Mr Le Fondre, who lived across the road from you, died."

"I have already spoken to a police officer and told him that I neither saw, nor heard anything that night. I sleep at the back of the house and usually go to bed early."

"Is there anyone else in the house?" Jake then asked.

"My husband is away on business in England. He goes away quite a lot."

"Have you any children?"

"Just the one; a boy."

"How old is your son, Mrs eh.......?"

"Oh sorry, Mrs Leith, Hilda Leith."

"How old is your son, Mrs Leith?"

"He will be fourteen on his next birthday. He attends the Grammar School and we have high hopes that he will be a solicitor one day."

"Is that what your husband does?" Jake enquired.

"Oh, no," Mrs Leith replied. "Benjamin works in finance."

"I see. Does your son sleep at the front of the house?"

"Yes he does, but he couldn't be of any help to you, Inspector, as he goes straight to sleep whenever he goes to his bed."

Jake thought back to his own childhood and seriously doubted that Mrs Leith's son ever did anything that his parents thought he did.

"When will your son be home from school?" Jake then asked.

"He's actually at home today," came the reply. "He has not been at all well these last few days."

"Would it be possible for me to speak to him?"

"I don't see why not," Mrs Leith said. "Do you want me to bring him down?"

"I can easily see him in his bedroom if you tell me where it is."

Hilda Leith provided directions and also the name of her son. Armed with both, Jake set off to have a word with Master Maurice Leith.

Maurice Leith was lying in bed. He was reading a book and did not look all that ill to an investigative eye. He sat up with some suspicion as this strange man walked in to his room. Jake introduced himself and the lad brightened at the fact he was being interviewed by a Police Inspector.

Before he sat down Jake went over to the window and looked out. There was a perfect view across to Le Fondre's house. Jake then sat down on the edge of the bed.

"Do you spend much time looking out of your window, Maurice?"

"Sometimes."

"Do you look out of your window at night when you should really be sleeping?"

Maurice looked a bit uncertain but finally muttered the word 'sometimes' again.

"Were you looking out your window two weeks ago on the Tuesday?"

Maurice brightened at that point. "The night the man across the road was murdered?"

"Yes."

"I was at my window that night but you mustn't tell my mother and father. They will just get annoyed with me and banish me to my room for days on end."

"Did you see anything?"

"I saw a man. He was there for ages. That was why I kept going to the window as it seemed strange that someone should be out there for as long as he was on such a night of rain."

"Can you describe this man?" Jake asked next.

Maurice gave a description that matched what Stanley Zanre had said. Jake wrote everything down.

"Why didn't you mention this to anyone before?" Jake then asked.

"No one ever asked me before and I certainly wasn't going to admit to my mother or father that I was looking out my window at a time when I should have been sleeping."

"And you definitely saw this man?" Jake asked again for clarification.

"Oh yes, he was out there all right."

"Well thank you, Maurice, you've been very helpful."

Maurice grinned widely. It felt good to be helping the police with their enquiries.

Jake went back downstairs, thanked Mrs Leith for allowing him to speak to Maurice and then started to make his way to the front door.

"Waste of time with Maurice, I suppose?" Mrs Leith said.

Jake chose not to answer as he went out through the door. On the contrary he now felt that his case against Willie Ifield was beginning to strengthen.

Maurice was at his window as Jake walked down the front path and began his journey back to Lodge Walk. Maurice waited until the police officer was out of sight before going back to his bed. He lay back on the crisp, white sheets and stared up at the ceiling. He hoped he had remembered everything as his mind floated back to the day before Mr Le Fondre was murdered.

Maurice had been coming home from school when the carriage had pulled up beside him. The door had opened and a woman had put her head out far enough to attract Maurice's attention. She had a thick, blue cloak pulled around her body and a veil pulled over her face. Her voice was soft and alluring. Maurice did not need to be asked twice to get in to the carriage.

"Are you going to take me home?" Maurice had asked.

"I'll take you close to your home," the woman had answered, "and in return for that I wish you to do me a small favour."

"What might that be?" Maurice had then said.

The young woman had then undone the clasp at the top of her cloak and let it fall from her body. Maurice noticed immediately that the woman had a large amount of cleavage spilling over the top of her dress. Before she said anything further the woman leaned forward to be closer to him and the amount of cleavage seemed to grow before his very eyes.

"Firstly, Maurice," she said in a tone that brought a tingle to Maurice's young body," I need to be sure that you are happy to do me a small favour."

Maurice looked down on the woman's breasts and in that split second of joy he would have agreed to do anything for her.

"I would be very happy to do you a small favour," he then said.

"Excellent," the woman had then said as she had sat back in her seat a little further.

The woman had then explained that she had some information, which Maurice was to tell the police should they ever come asking him questions. Maurice had thought it awfully exciting to have the police come and speak to him and he sought assurances from the woman that there was every likelihood that he would get a visit. The woman felt sure that the time would come when the police would arrive at his door.

Maurice had been delighted to hear that. As the carriage rattled its way towards home his mind had been in two places. Firstly there was the joy of having such an ample bosom on show for him as, beyond his mother, he had never been this close to a woman's bosom before. Secondly he had already started to think about what he would say when the police came calling. The thought of being an essential witness in a case made him feel very excited, even if the evidence he was bringing to that case was all built on a lie.

Maurice had always thought of himself as being a good liar. He reckoned that all children were expert liars and that there was no difference telling a lie to a policeman than telling one to your parents.

As the carriage drew to a halt beside Maurice's home the woman had sought confirmation from him that he would tell the police exactly what she had asked.

"Of course I will," Maurice had replied cheerfully.

And that is what he did. He now lay back on his bed and allowed his memory to recall the sight of that ample bosom. Maurice now wondered how long it would be before another opportunity might come along for him to enjoy the sight of a young lady's bosom.

***

Jake arrived back at Lodge Walk and went straight to see the Chief. He wanted the Chief to organise a warrant so that Jake could search both Willie Ifield's home and his office. Jake had no idea what he might be looking for but basically anything that might further link Willie to the murder of Guy Le Fondre would do.

"Do you think you finally have him?" the Chief said.

"I have two witnesses who can place a man matching Willie Ifield's description outside Guy Le Fondre's house around the time that we reckon he was killed. I would like to get Willie Ifield in front of an identity parade so that our witnesses can categorically state that he is our man but before I can do that I would like to have something a little more concrete to link him to the crime."

"Very well, I'll see what I can do," the Chief finally said. "I do wonder, however, what you are likely to find two weeks after the crime. We all know that Willie Ifield has kept himself one step ahead of us for years so I hardly think he'd be the type to leave evidence lying around were he to be involved in this crime."

"Perhaps not, sir, but I need to start somewhere."

"Okay, Jake, leave it with me for the moment."

Jake left the Chief Constable's office and returned to his own. He had to agree with what the Chief had just said about Willie Ifield covering his tracks. He had indeed done it for years but maybe this time he wouldn't be able to wriggle away from the case that Jake was building.

TWELVE

Tuesday 13 November – all day

Jake got his warrant at nine o'clock and by half past nine he had a team of police officers going through Willie Ifield's office whilst he led another team out to the house.

Willie Ifield was still at home when they arrived and was suitably outraged at the intrusion, so much so that he kept saying as much as police officers checked in drawers, cupboards and various other areas around his house. Willie even went as far as using his house phone to contact Nigel Porteous and ask him to come over at once. Some of the police officers had wondered what it must be like to have a telephone in the house. Most of them, however, could not see the point of having one and saw it as being nothing more than a fad for the rich.

Porteous arrived half an hour later and sat with Willie and Ada while the police buzzed around the house like bees seeking pollen. Just when it looked as if they were going to draw a blank one of the Constables called Jake out to the back garden where he had been searching in a small shed

The shed had been organised quite tidily but one or two boxes had been disturbed and the Constable had noticed material of some kind in one of the boxes. The material looked stained by something and the Constable had thought it best that the Inspector looked closer at the contents.

Jake opened the box and noticed at once that there was what appeared to be a coat crumpled inside. He also noticed the same stains as the Constable. He took the coat out of the box and laid it out on top of the box. All down the front was stained with a dark coloured substance, which Jake felt sure was blood.

"Well done, Constable," he then said and picking up the coat he made his way back in to the house and through to the sitting room where Willie Ifield was sitting next to his wife and Porteous was in the chair opposite. All three looked at the item in Jake's hand with suspicion.

"What do you have there, Inspector?" Nigel Porteous asked.

"I was hoping that Mr Ifield might be able to answer that question, Mr Porteous" Jake replied.

"I really have no idea......," Willie Ifield began to say.

"Do you recognise this coat?" Jake interrupted.

Jake opened out the coat and looked at the maker's label. It was certainly expensive enough as to belong to someone with the tastes and money of Willie Ifield. He could tell at once, from Ifield's expression that he *did* recognise the coat, the only question now was to whom had the coat belonged?

"Very well, the coat is mine," Ifield then said.

"Do you normally leave your coats out in the shed?"

"I don't normally leave *anything* in the shed, Inspector, it must be weeks since I was out there."

"The shed is for the gardener to use, Inspector," Ada Ifield added, taking her husband's hand and squeezing it gently," my husband would have no need to go near it."

"But this coat is yours?" Jake insisted, his gaze never leaving Willie Ifield.

"It is mine, Inspector, but it should be hanging in my wardrobe upstairs as that is where I normally keep my coats."

"How might you then explain the fact the coat was in your shed and it appears to have been covered in blood?"

Willie Ifield looked at the coat and then back at Jake. None of this was appearing to make sense to him and he was desperately trying to remember when he might have last seen the coat.

"That coat is quite old, Inspector and I doubt if I've worn it this year. As to why it should be in the shed; I really have no idea."

"There was that day that you thought someone had been in the house, dear," Ada Ifield then said.

"No one would break in to our house and steal a coat, Ada, especially when you have jewellery lying around and none of that has gone missing, has it?" Willie said to his wife.

"You believe that someone was in your house?" Jake then added. "When would that have been?"

"Three weeks ago maybe," suggested Ifield.

"But you never reported anything?"

"Inspector, there was probably nothing to report. I found the back door unlocked and I had a sense that someone may have been in the house. However, beyond that there was no sign that anyone had been here and I came to the conclusion that I had left the door unlocked myself. Anyway, as I have just said, why would anyone break in and steal a coat only to cover it in what looks like blood and leave it in my shed. The whole thing is too preposterous for words."

"Yes, it does sound rather preposterous," Jake agreed but he was referring to Ifield's entire response and not just the bit about the stolen coat. Ifield picked up on the intonation.

"I know this is all sounding crazy, Inspector, but I have no logical explanation for the coat moving from my wardrobe to the shed let alone then explain how it came to be covered in blood."

"Unless you were wearing it the night you killed Guy Le Fondre?" Jake then suggested.

"Inspector, you have circumstantial evidence at best. Even if the coat did belong to Mr Ifield and it is covered in blood you have no proof that the blood got on to the coat whilst in the possession of Mr Ifield."

"Mr Porteous, we know that someone matching your client's description was seen outside of Guy Le Fondre's home on the night he was killed. Part of that description mentioned a light brown coat and as you can see, this just happens to be a light brown coat. We also know that Mr Le Fondre would have bled severely from a result of the blows inflicted upon him. It seems logical to then surmise that this blood covered, light brown coat came from the murder scene."

Willie Ifield leapt to his feet. "This is outrageous, Inspector. I have never been anywhere near Guy Le Fondre's home either wearing that coat or not."

"And as I say, Inspector, there is no evidence to suggest that that coat had been worn by Mr Ifield in a very long time. If someone was in the house a few weeks ago then it was clearly with the purpose of stealing an item of clothing so as to suggest that Mr Ifield killed Guy Le Fondre."

"And then they came back and hid the evidence in the shed, is that what you are suggesting Mr Porteous?"

"That is exactly what I am suggesting, Inspector. My client has no motive for killing Guy Le Fondre and even if he had I rather think Mr Ifield has more sense than to leave incriminating evidence lying around for you to find."

"He may not have had time to get rid of the evidence," Jake added.

Porteous smiled. "Leaving a bloodied coat around the shed is terribly amateurish, Inspector and you could never accuse my client of being an amateur in any shape or form. In fact I do believe that even you had previously suggested that my client, were he ever to be involved in criminal activities, would be good at covering his tracks. You've been trying to have him charged with something for years and yet you have never managed to get any useful evidence to use against him. Now, all of a sudden, my client makes the most basic error and hangs on to incriminating evidence when it would have so much easier to get rid of it. Does that really sound like the Willie Ifield you have been chasing for years?"

Deep down Jake would have conceded that Porteous had a point, but the evidence was pretty overpowering at the moment and Jake felt that he had no other option than to take things to the next level.

"The best criminals eventually make mistakes, Mr Porteous," Jake said.

"But not my client, not that I am saying for one moment that he is a criminal."

"Of course not," added Jake before he turned to face Willie Ifield again. "Anyway, Mr Ifield, I feel I have enough evidence for the moment to ask you to accompany us to Lodge Walk where you shall remain until we have a chance to perhaps make more sense of what we know."

Ada Ifield looked up at her husband, tears forming in her eyes. "Oh, Willie, what does all this mean?"

Willie Ifield held his hand up. "Don't worry, my love, there seems to have been some kind of mistake being made here. I'm sure it will sort itself out. Would it be in order for Mr Porteous to accompany me to Lodge Walk?"

"Of course."

Jake led Willie Ifield, walking alongside Nigel Porteous, out of the house whilst the other police officers continued to search the premises for any other clues that might be found. They made their way out to the carriage waiting at the end of the path. They all climbed aboard and then the carriage set off for Lodge Walk.

***

Wolfgang Schwieger and Maisie Strachan had found themselves rental accommodation in Hamburg. They had arrived the previous weekend and were intent on moving on as soon as possible. However, Wolfgang wanted to contact a few people in Hamburg first as he felt sure they would be able to help him set up his film-making business.

Maisie felt like a fish out of water, having no understanding of what anyone was saying to her. As long as Wolfgang was around to translate she was fine, but if he left her for any reason she felt so utterly useless.

Wolfgang had gone out earlier in the morning and Maisie was pretty much confined to the house. She had tidied up a little and one of the last jobs she did was to make sure that the crates they had used to transport their personal items were empty and that everything they had taken with them was now either hung up or put away in a drawer somewhere.

She finished with her own crate and then turned to deal with Wolfgang's. She opened it and checked that it was empty and found a brown paper parcel inside. She took out the parcel and opened it. There was a significant sum of money inside; it was all Scottish so not of any good to them in Germany, at least until some form of exchange could be organised.

Maisie looked at the money and immediately wondered where it might have come from. There was little chance that Wolfgang could have saved the money from his earnings at the farm. At the back of Maisie's mind was Le Fondre's murder. Wolfgang had certainly been in Aberdeen at the time of the murder and it was common knowledge that Wolfgang did not like Le Fondre. However, it was also common knowledge that he did not like Cathcart and Thane either, but he had clearly had nothing to do with anything that might have happened to them.

Maisie was still tidying up when Wolfgang came in. He was excited and happy though his mood seemed to change immediately when he saw that Maisie had found the money.

"You shouldn't have been looking in there," he said.

"I was just tidying up. I needed something to do."

"I suppose you'll want to know where the money came from?" Wolfgang then said.

"All I want to know," replied Maisie, "is whether, or not, this money had anything whatsoever to do with Le Fondre's murder?"

Wolfgang made his way quickly over to Maisie and put his hands either side of her waist.

"Of course the money has nothing to do with Le Fondre's death," he said. "I was nowhere near Le Fondre when I went to Aberdeen. In fact the only reason I went to Aberdeen was to collect the money."

"So where did it come from?" Maisie then asked with some relief in her tone.

"I was a little bit naughty," Wolfgang began, "when it came to printing the films we made. I always made a copy and I used to pass that copy to a contact who operated out of Aberdeen. The contact collected the copies from the milkman who came to the farm. We then set up our own business for showing the films. We made a tidy little sum but of course when Thane said that everything was going to stop for a while then we took that as a signal for us to stop as well. I went to Aberdeen to collect my cut and that is what is in my case."

"But why didn't you just tell me?" Maisie added.

"I didn't tell you because I wanted you to come to Germany with me and I have no idea whether or not I will be able to convert this money to German money. Obviously if I cannot then it will all be worthless and I didn't want you assuming we might be well off only to find out that we were not."

Maisie smiled and moved closer to Wolfgang. "I've never really had money of my own so being well off is not a position I have ever experienced before. If this money can be of use to us then that will be a bonus. If not, then we work for our money the same as anyone else."

"Oh Maisie, I do love you," concluded Wolfgang and they kissed passionately before embracing for what seemed like forever.

***

Jake went back to see the Chief Constable and update him on the progress being made in the investigation in to Guy Le Fondre's death.

"We have two independent witnesses who claim that they saw a man answering Willie Ifield's description outside Guy Le Fondre's home on the night he was killed. Those witnesses now need to see Ifield in an identity parade," Jake was explaining, "so that we can categorically prove that the man they saw didn't just *look* like Willie Ifield but indeed *was* Willie Ifield. Now that we also have Ifield's coat and it appears to be soaked in blood we are finally putting a case together that clearly points at Ifield as being our killer. Ifield cannot explain what happened to his coat but the fact it had been hidden away in a box would seem to imply that he did not want it to be found."

"Do we have enough to charge him?" the Chief asked.

"If our witnesses can pick him out at an identity parade then we'll have enough, sir, "replied Jake. "However, without that we have little more than circumstantial evidence, which may not be quite enough to please a jury."

"Very good, organise the identity parade to happen as quickly as possible and we just have to hope that your witnesses have good memories."

***

Two hours later and Jake had his identity parade complete in terms of having found other men to stand in it along with Willie Ifield. Jake also had both Stanley Zanre and Maurice Leith at Lodge Walk. Neither seemed very keen to participate in the identification process though both did accept how important their evidence would be if and when the case got to court. Maurice, in particular, looked excited at the prospect of being asked questions in a court of law, though he was less than impressed with the fact that his mother had to be there at all times.

Willie Ifield was brought from the cells and placed in a row of men who had been chosen for the fact that they also resembled the description provided by the witnesses. Stanley Zanre was the first person to walk along the line. He passed Ifield and continued to the end. He then came back and checked everyone again but he was unable to confirm which, if any, of the men, had been the one he had seen outside of Guy Le Fondre's house.

"I'm sorry, Inspector, but I can't be sure about any of these men" he said and walked away.

Maurice Leith, with his mother beside him, was then brought in. He walked up and down the line as well but eventually declared that he could not be certain. He thought that it might be Number Three but wouldn't swear to it. Jake knew for a fact that it was definitely not Number Three. He pressed Maurice to have another look at the line of men but his mother suggested that the boy had been put through enough and the parade was brought to a rather unsatisfactory conclusion.

Ifield was taken back to the cells and Jake went back to his office after arranging for a carriage to take the witnesses home. It was while he was in his office that a Constable came in with something else that had been found at the house. It was a pair of shoes, both covered in mud and both concealed in another box in the shed.

Jake despatched the Constable to collect some ground samples from around the doorway of Le Fondre's house. He then wanted those samples checked against the soil attached to the shoes. He hoped that it might be the final piece of the jigsaw and prove, once and for all, that Willie Ifield was indeed standing outside Le Fondre's home and at the very least, was a witness to the event if not actually the killer himself.

***

Phillip Marshall rolled off of his wife and lay on his back in the bed. They had been making love practically any time they were together and enjoying the fact that they could now close a door on the world outside. Anna Marshall lay beside him, her small breasts heaving with the effects of their exertions. Anna still felt some kind of guilty pleasure that they could go to bed at any time they pleased. Even though she enjoyed having sex with her husband she still felt that there was something wrong in making love during the day. She had always been educated to believe that sex was a night-time exercise; something which should always be done with the light off.

As it was they had just made love for the second time that day and Anna's body was aglow from the lovely sensations emanating from her pubic area. Phillip looked at his watch and decided it was time that he got ready for work. He was not due out of the house for an hour yet but he knew that if he did not get out of bed and start washing then he would most likely want to have sex again.

He got out of bed and looked back at his wife. Anna was a lovely girl who was certainly showing signs of enjoying sex as much as her husband did. She had been a quiet girl when he had met her and their first fumbling on getting married had not been a success. Anna had not liked the idea of being naked in front of Phillip and he had had to work on her for months before she eventually began to relax.

As she relaxed, however, so her pleasure during sex was heightened and as her pleasure grew her desire to perform the act grew. However, for Anna it was not just about having sex. In the back of her mind was the desire to have children and now that they had their own property that seemed a stronger possibility than ever.

Phillip washed and pulled on his uniform. Anna got out of bed and washed herself as well before putting on some clothes and going out to the toilet on the landing. By the time she returned Phillip was pulling up the linoleum in the kitchen whilst muttering to himself about never liking it.

Once he had lifted the linoleum both Phillip and Anna stood in silent shock as they looked down at the badly stained floorboards. Phillip was no expert but even to his novice eye it seemed certain that the stain on the floor could be blood.

In fact, it could be a lot of blood.

***

The soil samples had been retrieved from Guy Le Fondre's front door and to Jake's eye it looked the same as the soil attached to the shoes found in Willie Ifield's shed. There was a slight redness to the soil on the shoes that matched the sample gathered by the Constable. Jake had not had time to check if there might have been a similar soil in Willie Ifield's garden but he still felt he had more than enough with which to interview Willie Ifield again.

He was taken back to the interview room where he sat beside Porteous. Jake and Mathieson sat opposite.

"Well, Mr Ifield, you have had some time to reflect on your current predicament. Have you anything further you wish to tell me" Jake said.

"Yes, Inspector, I would like to tell you that someone is trying very hard to make me look like a murderer."

"So you are saying that all the evidence we have against you is nothing more than some fabrication created by an unknown third party?"

"I am saying that I had no idea my coat had gone missing from the wardrobe at home and I am also saying that I have never been near Le Fondre's home let alone be there on the night that anyone may have claimed to see someone looking like me."

Jake took the shoes from a bag had had brought in to the room. He placed them on the table in front of Ifield.

"Do you recognise these?" he then said.

Willie Ifield sighed heavily. "Yes, Inspector, they are mine."

"And they are covered in the same soil as was found outside Mr Le Fondre's house. Are we still talking about mere coincidence?"

"If we assume, for one moment, that there is some unknown party who is trying to provide you with enough evidence to allow you to charge my client with a crime that he did not commit, then it follows that it would be this same individual who would have broken in to my client's home and stolen these items with the sole intention of laying false evidence before you. Again this does not prove that my client was actually wearing these items at the time that Mr Le Fondre was killed."

"You may well be right, Mr Porteous," Jake then said, " and if we do accept that your client did not commit this crime, then perhaps your client can tell me who might want us to believe that he did?"

As Jake asked the final question his eyes flicked from Porteous on to Willie Ifield. Ifield did not take any time to consider the question before providing an answer.

"That I don't know," he conceded. "Ever since you shut me away in that damned cell I have been trying to think of who might hate me enough to do this. I accept that I have made many enemies over the years but I can't believe that any of them would stoop to this."

"You did know Guy Le Fondre though, didn't you?" Jake then enquired.

"He came to inform me of his sordid little film-making business. I have a certain status in this city, Inspector and most new businesses that are set up like to keep me informed so that our business interests did not clash in any way. I listened to what the man had to say and decided that there could have been some benefit to be gained in going in to partnership with him, but only after he had created a legitimate film-making company and moved away from making those horrible dirty pictures. Mr Le Fondre seemed amenable to that idea and we spoke some more about how our partnership might be best organised. I visited the farm to have a look for myself and felt that everything was certainly in place for us to run a proper company."

"So you did know that they were making sex films?"

Willie paused for a moment. He could see, by the look on his solicitor's face that he had probably said too much. However, he now only wanted to clear his name and he felt that lying about anything was unlikely to do him many favours.

"Yes, I knew he had been making films of that type but I assure you that I played no part in the making of any of those sex films and would never have considered the continuation of making such films after we had gone in to business together."

"You may not have wanted to make such films, Mr Ifield, but Guy Le Fondre was intent on making more, wasn't he?" Jake then asked.

Willie Ifield paused for a moment before eventually answering the question.

"Yes, I do believe that Mr Le Fondre felt there was too much money to be made from making films about sex for him to even consider stopping making them. I had made it quite clear to him that my money was not to be used for those purposes."

"When did all these business discussions take place?"

"Just last month. I promise that I did not know Guy Le Fondre before that."

"Did your son know Guy Le Fondre?" Jake said.

"He did, but for the same reason that I did. It was purely business."

"But it wasn't business that caused them to have words at the Business Club, was it?"

"You'd have to ask Daniel that."

"I already have and I suspect that you know why the two men were disagreeing. Was it not the case that both men had feelings for Miss Sangster and that it was Le Fondre's unwanted comments, addressed in her company that annoyed your son so much?" Jake suggested.

"Le Fondre may have shown an interest in Miss Sangster but it never went further than that. I know that Daniel did not like Le Fondre but whether it had anything to do with Miss Sangster's affections I wouldn't know. However, even if it had been, I hardly think they would have come to blows over it."

"So if your only contacts with Le Fondre had been business how did he come to have such feelings for Miss Sangster?" Jake then said.

"He noticed her the very first time he came to my office and made a point of having her around him if possible. I played along with it at first as I always thought I might have needed Miss Sangster to help me maintain the upper hand with Le Fondre. He did not strike me as a man who could be intimidated but I did think he was a man who might be persuaded to do things for a woman that he would not necessarily do for a man."

"And did Miss Sangster give Le Fondre reason to believe that there might be something between them?"

Willie Ifield was outraged. "Good heavens no. Miss Sangster didn't like Le Fondre and what little she did do was done because I asked her to and not through any desire of her own to be any closer to Le Fondre than was necessary."

"What did you ask her do?" Jake asked.

"I asked her to be with me when we went out to the farm. We all travelled in my car and I believe that Le Fondre got a sexual thrill from rubbing legs with Miss Sangster. She, in turn, put up with his attentions out of nothing more than loyalty to the company that employs her."

"Did she do anything more for Le Fondre?"

Ifield's anger rose to the surface again.

"No she did not, Inspector. The poor woman simply put up with the man leering at her all the time," he then replied with venom in his tone that convinced Jake even more that Willie Ifield had feelings for Miss Sangster as well.

Jake thought for a moment. It was possible that both Willie and Daniel had strong feelings for Miss Sangster and that Willie was, in some way, jealous of his son's youth perhaps. That would mean that both Ifields would have found Le Fondre's interest in Miss Sangster as deeply upsetting, if not exactly threatening. That may have been the motive for one of them to kill Le Fondre. The evidence pointed towards Willie and yet it was Daniel who seemed to be having the disagreement with Le Fondre.

However, Willie's motive for wanting Le Fondre dead may well have been to do with the making of the sex films. Willie saw the film-making business as being a potential source of profit and perhaps did not want to threaten that in any way by making illegal films of any kind. Willie had kept himself free of the police for years and it made sense that he would wish to continue in that way.

"You said that you had visited the farm where the films were made?" Jake then said.

"Yes."

"Did you know that women were taken to the farm and forced to participate in the making of the films before being murdered?"

Willie Ifield again paused before answering.

"Le Fondre did tell me that women had been forced to participate but I knew nothing of the murders."

"And what about Scott Thane, did you get the impression that he played a part in the darker side of his business partnership with Le Fondre?"

Willie Ifield did hesitate a second before answering.

"Quite the opposite, Inspector. Thane has no head for business and was quite clearly nothing more than the money man. I would not be at all surprised to hear that Thane had no idea of what Le Fondre was actually doing with regard to the making of those sex films."

Jake made a mental note of what Ifield had just said. If that were indeed the case and Jake was tempted to agree with Ifield, then Thane's prison sentence would be considerably lower than might have at first been expected.

"Yet knowing what Le Fondre had done, you were still prepared to go in to partnership with the man?" added Jake.

"Purely business, Inspector. I told him straight that if there had been any hint of him returning to his bad old ways then our partnership would end. I've said this to you so many times, Inspector, but I'm going to say it once more, in the hope that you will finally believe me. I have been involved in many business ventures and not all of them have been strictly to the liking of the police. However, I have never been involved in the death of anyone and have made sure that anyone else working for me followed that same philosophy. I am no murderer, Inspector, you have to believe me."

"I say again, Inspector," Porteous then added," does this sound like a man who would leave incriminating evidence lying around his shed for the police to find two weeks later?"

"At least for the moment, Mr Porteous, I am prepared to accept that I may need a little more in the way of hard evidence before I can charge your client. However, I am not prepared to let him back on to the street until I have had some time to get that evidence."

Jake then turned to look at Willie Ifield again. "You will spend at least the next forty-eight hours in the cells and then we will talk again."

"Someone is trying to make Le Fondre's death look as if I had something to do with it. You have to find that someone, Inspector." Willie Ifield then said.

"For the next forty-eight hours I will at least keep an open mind, Mr Ifield, but as soon as further evidence turns up I will be back and you will be charged. Of course if that evidence were to point to another suspect then that would clearly change my opinion of you."

Mathieson then took Ifield to the cells and Porteous made his feelings known to Jake about keeping his client locked up for two days more.

"I don't want Mr Ifield leaving town," Jake said as he left Porteous alone at the front door of Lodge Walk.

***

Constable Phillip Marshall arrived at work that evening and immediately went to see Sergeant Bill Turnbull. Bill was a well-respected officer around Lodge Walk and although he was not Marshall's immediate superior officer he was the one whom Phillip thought he might get the best advice.

Turnbull took the young Constable in to the room at the back of the front counter and sat him down. Marshall explained how he and his wife had moved in to their new home and that he had found what appeared to be a major blood stain on the floor underneath some linoleum.

"The stain is pretty big, Sergeant," Marshall then said. "I'm guessing someone was bleeding very badly while they were lying on that floor."

"You're sure the stain is blood?" Turnbull asked.

"I'm obviously no expert, sir, but it certainly looks like blood to me," Marshall replied.

"Very good. Give me a note of the address and if you don't mind I'll have a wander round and have a look for myself when I finish in an hour."

"That would be okay, Sergeant. Anna isn't someone who goes to bed early."

"And don't mention this to anyone, there's a good lad," Turnbull concluded and Marshall went back to his normal duties.

Turnbull went back to the front counter and took a large ledger from underneath the counter. He opened the book and turned a few more pages until he came to a list of names, each one of which had an address against it. He ran his finger down the list until he came to the address which Marshall had just given him. Clearly noted, in the Sergeant's own handwriting was the name of Phillip Marshall. Turnbull ran his finger along the line until he came to the box market 'Previous Occupant.'

He wrote the name Henry Davis in to his notebook then closed the ledger and put it back under the counter.

An hour and a quarter later he was waiting outside the door of the Marshall's new home waiting for someone to answer his knock. The door eventually opened and a pretty, young woman stood before him. Turnbull introduced himself and apologised for the late hour.

"Your husband said it would be okay if I called."

"Of course, Sergeant Turnbull, please come in."

Anna Marshall led the way through to the back room and they both stood over the stain on the floor. Turnbull bent down and looked even closer at the mark. There was no doubt in his mind that it was blood and it was not the kind of stain that came from cutting yourself shaving.

"Your husband said that the stain had been covered by a piece of linoleum," Turnbull then said. "Would you happen to still have that linoleum?"

"Yes."

Anna Marshall found the linoleum rolled up by the door. She gave it to Turnbull who opened it up on the floor and looked at the back of it. There was no sign of any stains on the linoleum, which led Turnbull to deduce that the linoleum had not been laid until sometime after the stain had been created. It had been, therefore, a deliberate attempt to cover something that would have looked suspicious to anyone who may have seen it.

"I'll hang on to this," Turnbull then said to Anna.

He then thanked Anna Marshall once again for letting him in to the house so late in the day and then told her that he would speak to her husband the following day. Meantime, Anna was to say nothing to anyone about the stain on their floor.

Turnbull then sat off for home.

***

Just before Jake left the office he was handed a photograph that had been taken of the mystery man in the mortuary. Doctor Symon had managed to do enough to the man's face to at least disguise the fact that he was dead. No doubt the readers of the morning papers would deduce for themselves that the man was probably dead but at least it was not as obvious as to put them off their breakfast.

Jake put the photograph in his pocket and set off for home. It was late and Jake was feeling more tired than ever. The working day was getting longer and he sat in the back room of the flat, drinking a bottle of beer and giving his body a few moments to totally relax. He knew that he would never sleep unless he managed to get some of the working day thoughts out of his head.

Half of him was elated to finally have Willie Ifield in the cells and the other half kept telling him that something wasn't right. He knew that he needed more evidence even though what he had already was pretty damning. Thoughts continued to roll around in his mind and Jake was finding it harder than ever to totally switch off from the turmoil of his job. To help him relax a little he thought about Margaret and the night they would have watching Harry Lauder. Whatever happened at work that day he was not going to be at the office beyond six o'clock.

Whatever happened at work he was not going to let it spoil his relationship with Margaret in any way. She was the only good thing in his life now that Alice had Johnnie Gordon and he was not going to lose that over some silly case. The more he thought about Margaret the better he felt. He suddenly had an urge to hold her and a burning desire to feel her lips on his own.

He knew that he would probably have to wait until Saturday for such pleasures. However, just thinking about them made him feel so much better; made his body and mind relax to a level where he now felt that he could go to bed and possibly sleep.

Jake finished his beer, undressed and went bed. It was to be a night of dreams. A night in which Margaret featured heavily in those dreams. A night in which he and Margaret did things in those dreams that allowed him to wake up next morning with a smile on his face.

THIRTEEN

<u>Wednesday 14 November – mid morning onwards</u>

Sergeant Turnbull came to see Jake after he had cleared all the paperwork that had been waiting for him when he had arrived at work that morning. Jake was still reading through reports relevant to Willie Ifield but he looked up as Turnbull came in to the room.

"Might I have a word, sir?" he said.

"Of course, Bill, sit yourself down."

"Thank you, sir."

Turnbull then went on to tell Jake about the apparent blood stain in the Marshall's home. Jake listened with interest.

"Who was there before the Marshalls?" Jake then asked.

"Henry Davis, his wife Bella and their two children."

Jake wrote the name down. "And you say there was a lot of blood?"

"I've seen enough crime scenes to know that someone bled severely in that room. I doubt if anyone could have bled as much as that and still survived."

"Is Henry Davis on duty at the moment?" Jake then asked.

"He is, sir. He'll be working at the harbour at the moment but he's due back for lunch at one."

"Okay, Bill, leave it with me."

"Very good, sir. I've told young Marshall not to say anything to anyone."

"Good."

Turnbull left the room and Jake sat looking at the name of Henry Davis and wondering if this might be the rotten apple they had been looking for. He took his pocket watch from the pocket of his waistcoat and checked the time. If he was to be ready to interview Henry Davis at one o'clock then he had much to do and little time in which to do it. He went to find Mathieson.

Ten minutes later both men were standing in the kitchen beside Phillip and Anna Marshall. All four were looking down at the stain on the floor but Jake was also looking around the location of the stain. It was close to the sink and certainly within reach of knives that may have been lying on the work surface beside the sink. To Jake this seemed the perfect location for Cathcart's death. The only problem for Jake was finding that connection between Davis and Cathcart.

Satisfied that they had just viewed the site of George Cathcart's demise, Jake and Mathieson made their way down to Guild Street where they caught the tram that would take them across to Craiginches Prison. Fifteen minutes after they arrived at the prison they were sitting in a room with Scott Thane.

Thane was already looking a shadow of the man that he used to be. His skin was grey and his shoulders seemed permanently slumped in a gesture of defeat. He was a beaten man with no future.

"What can I do for you, Inspector?" Thane said.

"I have something that I would like to discuss with you, Mr Thane," Jake began," but before I turn to that I thought you might like to know that Willie Ifield has now admitted to being a part of your business venture with Guy Le Fondre. He has also offered the opinion that he did not think that you were ever aware of much of what Mr Le Fondre was doing, particularly when it came to the making of the sex films. I may not like Mr Ifield but I do respect his view of business and I am prepared to accept that you probably did not have a major part to play in the less savoury aspects of what Guy Le Fondre was doing."

Thane visibly relaxed a little. "Thank you for telling me that, Inspector. I hope you also understand why I chose not to mention Mr Ifield's involvement in our business. I find the man quite terrifying and I was not of a mind to upset him if I could help that. I am glad that he has spoken to you, though I would have to add that I am surprised at the same time."

"Let us just say that Mr Ifield was happy to help us with our enquiries," Jake added and Thane thought it best to leave it at that.

"What else did you want to speak to me about?" Thane then asked.

"We are here to talk to you about Henry Davis," Jake said and the reaction from Thane instantly betrayed that the name did mean something to him. Thane chose to say nothing for the moment. Jake continued.

"We now know that Constable Henry Davis was working for George Cathcart who, in turn, was working for Guy Le Fondre. One possibility is that Constable Davis murdered George Cathcart whilst Cathcart was in the process of trying to rape his wife. Would you be of the opinion that a scenario such as that could well have taken place?"

Thane did not need to give the question much thought.

"It is perfectly possible. George Cathcart was the type of man who would have tried to force himself on any woman such was the man's animal instincts when it came to the fairer sex."

"Were you aware of his infatuation with Constable Davis's wife?" Jake then asked.

"George Cathcart had an infatuation with any woman who happened to be breathing, Inspector. In fact, I wouldn't have been surprised if the lack of life would actually have made much difference to him. The man was vile."

"Was Henry Davis employed by you in the immediate aftermath of Constable Thomson's murder?"

"Constable Davis was never employed by me," Thane responded. "As I've said to you before, Inspector, Guy dealt with matters of that kind. I have no idea when Henry Davis was employed, as you put it."

"But he did work for you?" Jake pressed.

"You said you already knew that," Thane replied," so I didn't feel any need to tell you again."

"And if he was employed he must have been receiving payment?" Jake added.

"Any payments to employees were always made through George Cathcart. I would arrange for Cathcart to get money and he would do the rest. To that end, I state again that I have no idea as to when, exactly, Henry Davis started working for Guy."

"So Cathcart would definitely have had a reason for being in contact with Henry Davis?" Jake then asked by way of clarifying a point.

"Oh, there's no doubt about that. George Cathcart would have been the only contact with Henry Davis."

"And it is therefore, perfectly possible that George Cathcart could have met with Bella Davis at some point?"

"I suppose so, though it would not have been common practice for Cathcart to be anywhere near Davis's home, or his wife."

"Perhaps not, but it is still possible that that is exactly what happened," Jake concluded.

He glanced at Mathieson. Both men were more than satisfied that they had enough evidence with which to face Henry Davis. Jake thanked Thane for his time and then he and Mathieson made their way back to Lodge Walk.

***

Henry Davis looked very nervous indeed as he sat at the table in the interview room when Jake walked in. He obviously had no idea how much, or how little, the Inspector knew about him or about what may have happened. He did, however, presume that it had something to do with that stain he had been forced to leave in the old property. That being the case he was about to face some rather unpleasant questions.

Whatever he may eventually answer to those questions he had already decided that at all costs, however, he was going to try and keep Bella out of it.

Jake sat down and laid a folder on the table in front of him. He noted Henry Davis glancing down at the folder and he could imagine the young man was now desperately trying to work out what this could all be about. Jake intended giving him as little to work on as possible. He needed this young police officer off guard for if he was what Jake suspected then he was going to prison for what might be a very long time indeed.

"We have been talking to man by the name of Scott Thane," Jake began. "Do you happen to know him?"

"I know he had some connection to Guy Le Fondre but beyond that, no I don't know him."

"How about George Cathcart, did you know him?"

Davis started to worry. It seemed clear, even this early in the interview, that Inspector Fraser had a clear line of inquiry. Davis spent a moment thinking over his limited options. Eventually he decided to answer truthfully, at least until he could gauge how much the Inspector actually knew.

"I know George Cathcart worked for Guy Le Fondre."

"So you are telling me that you didn't *know* George Cathcart?" added Jake.

Henry Davis thought for a moment. He knew that the more he lied the more chance there was of him forgetting what he had said and being caught out later. He decided to remain within an element of the truth.

"Okay, I knew George Cathcart?" he finally said.

"Wouldn't it be more accurate to say that you *worked* for George Cathcart?"

"No, sir, it would not be more accurate to say that. I did not work for George Cathcart though I did speak to him on occasions."

"Ah, so you actually worked for Guy Le Fondre?" said Jake, by way of clarifying a point.

"I received payments from Mr Le Fondre but whether, or not, I actually worked for him might be a moot point."

"Why were you receiving money from Le Fondre?"

"I was approached and asked to provide information as and when police activities might have touched on their business ventures."

"So you are admitting that you took money from Le Fondre in return for telling him information that only a police officer would know?" Jake then said.

"I did get money in return for information but, quite frankly, sir, the information I provided was never anything of any consequence. I was playing a game with them, sir, no more than that."

"How did you come to work for Guy Le Fondre?"

"As I said I was approached by Cathcart one night when I was on my beat. He explained what they were wanting and he asked if I could provide the kind of information he was requesting. As I needed the money and it seemed an easy way to make it, I agreed at once."

"You had no sense of loyalty to your uniform, Constable?"

Henry Davis smiled. "A sense of loyalty, with all due respect sir, does not pay the bills or put food in front of your family."

"Perhaps not, Constable, but it does keep you out of jail."

Henry Davis's face drained of blood and he looked as if he might vomit at any moment. Jake let the thought of jail hang in the air for a moment or two longer before he moved on to the next question.

"Were you aware that Constable Thomson had been working for them before you?" Jake enquired.

"Not at first. By the time I put two and two together I was already in too deep to tell anyone. Anyway, as I said, I needed the money."

Jake's temper rose briefly. "So because you needed the money you were prepared to pass information about police activities to criminals and yet you couldn't quite bring yourself to helping your colleagues solve the murder of a police officer?"

"I know he was a friend of yours, sir, but I truly believed that it was better that you, nor anyone else, became aware of the fact that Constable Thomson had been as rotten as he was. In a misguided way I was trying to protect Constable Thomson's perceived good name."

"A noble sentiment, Constable, but your duty is to this Force and the need for every member of that Force to uphold the law at all times. Your duty was to inform someone of what you knew about Constable Thomson's death."

"And have to admit in the process that I was just as bad as he had been? There was no way that I could say anything," Davis insisted.

Deep down even Jake could understand that.

"Very well, tell me what you can about Guy Le Fondre?"

"There's nothing to tell. I never got that close to him as I always dealt with Cathcart. Just before Le Fondre died I did try to make contact with him but with little success. I think he liked to keep himself above rubbish like me."

"Would you have any idea who might have killed Le Fondre?" Jake then asked.

Davis thought for a moment. "I'm guessing he had made a lot of enemies. He wasn't a particularly nice man who surrounded himself with other, not particularly nice men, which seems to me a recipe for trouble. Having said that, however, I can't think of any one person who might bear a greater grudge than others."

"Which brings me to George Cathcart," Jake then said and Davis visibly shuffled nervously in his chair. "What do you know about George Cathcart's death?"

"Nothing."

The answer was too quick for Jake's liking and the fact that Davis looked away as he said it added to Jake's overall disbelief of the response.

"Did George Cathcart ever have cause to visit your home?"

"I wouldn't have thought so," Davis replied. "Any contact was always made outside."

"So George Cathcart was never at your home?"

"I believe I have just answered that question, sir."

"And therefore, George Cathcart never had any reason to meet with your wife?"

Henry Davis's eyes flashed momentarily with an anger that seemed to come from deep within him.

"My wife had nothing to do with George Cathcart," he then said, somewhat emphatically.

"So, if we asked your wife, Constable Davis, if she had ever met with George Cathcart she'd be able to support your assertion that their paths had never crossed?"

Davis leapt to his feet and slammed his fists on the table. "With the greatest of respect, sir, will you please leave my wife out of this as she has nothing to do with anything. Nothing at all."

Mathieson stood up and motioned to move towards the Constable but Jake simply held up a calming hand.

"Sit down, son," he then said to Davis. After a moment Davis did sit down.

"Bella has nothing to do with this," Davis said again, only this time in a slighter calmer tone.

"Okay, Constable Davis, let us accept for the moment that George Cathcart had not been to your home, nor had he ever met your wife. Let us, however, re-visit your last home and perhaps I can ask you to explain why there is a large stain on the floor of those premises, close to the sink?"

Davis looked momentarily at a loss but an answer soon came to him.

"It's pig's blood. I got a lump of meat from my father and made a bit of a mess cutting it up."

"Pig's blood?" Jake repeated. "When did this mishap with a pig occur?"

"A few weeks ago, I can't remember exactly."

"And when did you decide to cover the mess with a nice piece of linoleum?" Jake then asked.

"Only a few days before we left the property. We had lived with it but I didn't expect that anyone else would have the same view. I thought it best to cover it."

"Is your father in the habit of giving you a whole pig?"

"No, it was a one-off."

"And you are telling me that you cut up an entire pig in your kitchen?" Jake then said with some disbelief in his tone.

"It wasn't a whole pig, just a large piece."

"From the size of the stain on your kitchen floor it would have needed to have been a very large piece of pig," suggested Jake.

"It was reasonably large, yes," Davis insisted, though he could tell that the Inspector was not believing him for a moment.

Jake paused for a moment. He then began to speak again in slow and measured tones.

"I'm going to tell you a story, Constable Davis and I do not want you to say, or do, anything until I have finished. Contrary to what you have said to me today, I believe that George Cathcart had called at your house, at least once, whilst you were away at work. I believe that, in some way, he forced himself in to your house and began to attack your wife. I have no idea where his fascination for your wife came from, but it was strong enough as to drive him to violent assault. Your wife was at the kitchen sink when the attack occurred and she, in a fit of fear and panic, grabbed the nearest weapon that she could find. This weapon was a kitchen knife, which she now held out in front of her. I now believe that as Cathcart lunged at her he forced himself on to the knife that your wife was holding. He died at her feet in a pool of blood. You then came home and found both the body and the blood and decided to cover everything up because you knew that if your wife confessed to the crime that you would have to explain the connection between yourself and Cathcart; something that you did not want to do. In the making of one very poor decision you branded your wife as an accomplice to the cover-up and you also possibly prevented your wife from now being looked at favourably by a judge and jury at her trial."

"I'm telling you, this has nothing to do with Bella beyond the fact that she was the victim of an attempted rape. I came home to find Cathcart attacking her. He had ripped her blouse and was about to lunge at her again when I grabbed the knife and killed him."

"I understand why you are now telling me that, Constable, but the problem is that your description of events doesn't really fit. The geography of the crime meant that both your wife and Cathcart would have been between you and the kitchen sink where I believe the knife had been lying. Add to that the fact that you would not have allowed Cathcart to lunge at your wife again; you would have pulled him away and probably hit him in the process. Perhaps then you might have reached for a knife and killed him. Another problem with that scenario is there was no bruising on Cathcart's face; no sign of a struggle with someone else at all in fact. However, even with all that the most damning evidence against you claiming that you killed Cathcart is this."

Jake opened the folder and took out the button that had been clenched in Cathcart's fist. He held it out on his palm and Henry Davis looked down on it with horror. Jake continued.

"The only solution truly believable, therefore, is that your wife grabbed the knife and used it whilst she was being attacked. Had she simply come forward at the time with her torn blouse then the fact that this was in Cathcart's fist would have cleared her immediately of any charge of murder. No one would have questioned her right to defend herself in those horrifying moments in which a man was trying to force himself upon her. However, now she is part of an attempt to prevent justice taking its course. Now she will stand in a court of law and perhaps not be seen purely as the victim."

Henry Davis began to weep. "What have I done?" he eventually said.

"Made an unholy mess of things, that's what you have done. It will be a long time before your children see their father free again and it may even be some time before their mother is released, depending on the view taken by the judge. I promise that I will do all that I can to try and get the court to be as lenient on your wife as possible but there is still no denying that she has played a part in a very serious crime and must suffer the consequences to some degree."

Davis wept some more. "I love Bella so much and now I have allowed my greed and my stupidity to spoil everything."

"Was my story accurate?" Jake then asked.

"Yes. I actually came in to the room after Bella had stabbed him but she was still standing with her blouse ripped and a look of shock and horror on her face. I knew that I couldn't say anything about Cathcart so I decided to leave the body somewhere and hope that we were never connected to it. I laid some linoleum over the stain and hoped that it would be many years before anyone chose to change it. Just my luck that the new occupants sought to change things at once."

"Sergeant Mathieson will take your statement, Constable Davis, whilst I go and collect your wife. I will make sure that you see her a little later."

"Thank you, sir," added Davis.

Jake went on his way and Mathieson settled down to witness yet another formal statement.

An hour later both Henry and Bella Davis were in the cells. Their children were with Bella's parents. Henry and Bella had both made statements and they had been allowed to see each other for five minutes before being led to separate cells.

Jake had returned to his office feeling satisfied that another case had been solved and the guilty parties arrested. However he felt no satisfaction in charging a police officer and his wife for having committed the crime. He sat at his desk and reflected on his slowly decreasing workload.

For once nearly everything had been cleared. All that was left was the need to find the murderer of Guy Le Fondre, though it was looking likely that he already had Willie Ifield for that.

Jake still felt slightly uncomfortable about the evidence that was piling up against Willie Ifield. Much as it was nice to have a case that seemed to be unfolding in a more manageable manner, it still seemed, to Jake at any rate, as if it was all, in some way, just a little too easy. The anonymous letter; the blood-stained coat; the dead woman who might have confirmed Willie's story and then the convenient suicide of her murderer. All a bit too tidy perhaps.

Then again, maybe this was just going to be a case that would be easily solved. Rather than someone trying to get Willie Ifield wrongly convicted of a crime he didn't commit it could well be that someone was actually helping the police to find the evidence they needed because the evidence was actually there and not being fabricated.

Before he did anything else Jake decided to go upstairs and inform the Chief Constable that he had not only solved the George Cathcart murder but had also uncovered the bad apple police officer in the process. The Chief was delighted to hear the news though Jake had the distinct feeling that the Chief was somewhat distracted during the time that Jake was updating him on the outcome of his cases.

Once Jake had finished speaking and the Chief had expressed his delight at the success he then turned his attention to the things that had been causing his distraction.

"I received a letter today," he began saying, "from someone who clearly wished to remain anonymous. In it this unknown person informs me that if Robert Wallace, the local businessman and political activist, attends the opening night of His Majesty's Theatre then he is going to be killed. The letter further states that it is bad enough that the theatre should be opening in the first place without making matters worse by inviting unworthy citizens such as Wallace. Are you aware of any issues with Robert Wallace?"

"No, sir, but I am aware of issues at the theatre. Constable McGill has been investigating a number of strange occurrences that have happened at the theatre over the last few weeks. So far they have all been relatively minor and probably no more than mischief making."

"I see this death threat as being more than mischief making, Jake," the Chief added.

"Agreed, sir, but it could still be part of the same case."

"What do you know about this man Wallace?" the Chief then asked.

"Not a lot," answered Jake. "I do know that he has created a lot of enemies in the city because he holds political views that rather clash with the liberal old school of Aberdeen and the North East."

"He's not that far short of being an anarchist, Jake. From what I've read the man wants to do away with any form of class system. My God, this country has been built on the class system; where would we be without it?"

Jake chose not to answer, but changed the subject instead. "Mr Wallace certainly has political beliefs that may be in direct conflict with others but I would hardly think that that should merit death threats. It isn't as if Mr Wallace is in a position to instigate any of his beliefs."

"You may well be right, Jake, but none the less I would like you to have a word with Mr Wallace and try to dissuade him from attending the theatre on its opening night. I can't take the risk that either Mr Wallace, or someone else, might get injured or worse by some lunatic on the loose."

"I can speak to Mr Wallace, sir, but if he chooses to attend the opening night of the theatre there is very little that I can do to prevent him."

"I appreciate that, Jake, but I would still like you to try," the Chief insisted. "You are very much the diplomat amongst my team of officers and I feel sure that you can manage to make Mr Wallace see sense."

"I'll do what I can," Jake rather reluctantly agreed and then stood up to leave the room.

Jake went back to his office and wrote up some more notes. He then decided that, even though it was late in the afternoon, he should pay a visit to Daniel Ifield. Jake still felt that Daniel was a better suspect than his father and that it could well be him who was pointing the police in other directions. Jake put on his coat and set off out in to the heavy drizzle that was falling outside.

***

Daniel was sitting in his office signing some papers when Miss Sangster showed Jake in to the room. Daniel looked up and there was an expression of disgust on his face.

"What do you want now?" he said in a tone that echoed that disgust.

"Just some more questions, Mr Ifield, if you don't mind?"

Miss Sangster closed the door behind Jake and he sat down opposite Daniel, even though he had not been formally invited to do so. Daniel finished signing another couple of papers and then put his pen down and sat back in his chair.

"Very well, Inspector, ask your questions."

"It appears that you did know Guy Le Fondre a little better than you stated on our previous meetings. Perhaps you would now like to tell me what you *really* thought of the man?"

"Very well, Inspector, I had met the man a couple of times for purely business purposes and always in the company of my father. That night in the Business Club was the first time I crossed paths with Le Fondre outside of these offices. As a consequence I really didn't know him at all, beyond the fact that he was a thoroughly obnoxious individual. It seemed to me that he believed he was better than anyone else when, in fact, he clearly wasn't."

"So you didn't like him?"

"Of course I didn't like him. Were it not for the fact that my father had agreed to do business with the man I would have never had anything to do with him after that first time he came here to discuss the possibility of a partnership."

"Did you get the impression that your father probably didn't like Le Fondre either?" Jake then asked.

"No one could have liked Le Fondre, Inspector and whoever did kill him did the world a favour in the process."

"And could that have been your father?" Jake asked.

"It *could* have been anyone, Inspector," Daniel Ifield answered.

"Including yourself?"

Daniel Ifield smiled. "Yes, it *could* have been me, but it wasn't. As I have already told you I was at home at the time Mr Le Fondre met his fate."

"At home with no one to confirm the fact," Jake added quickly. "You see that's my problem, Mr Ifield; neither you, nor your father, has anyone to confirm what you are telling me."

"But equally, Inspector, neither my father nor I has any motive for wanting Le Fondre dead. Good grief, we have come across many obnoxious characters in our business dealings but we haven't gone around killing them all."

"But did those other obnoxious characters ever cross the line with Miss Sangster?" Jake then asked.

Daniel Ifield's mood changed immediately. It was that same defensive swagger that had appeared in Henry Davis when his wife's name had been mentioned.

"I don't deny that I have some feelings for Miss Sangster, as well you know, but I can only keep telling you that those feelings did not drive me to kill Le Fondre."

"If your father has nothing to do with this crime then why did we find a coat with blood stains on it and shoes with mud on them that appears to be of the same kind as that found around the entrance to Le Fondre's home?" Jake then asked.

"I really don't know, Inspector, though it tells me that one of two things has happened. Either my father was there and he did kill Le Fondre or he wasn't there and someone else is trying to persuade you that he was."

"Would you know of anyone who might want your father to be found guilty of a crime he did not commit?"

"No I do not, Inspector."

"Your father has been a very successful businessman, Mr Ifield and as a result he must have a lot of enemies. Surely there might be one amongst those enemies prepared to go to these lengths?"

"Indeed there might be, Inspector, but just at this moment I could not think of anyone who would be so stupid as to try and destroy my father."

"Things might happen to them you mean?" Jake added.

Ifield smiled. "No, Inspector, things would not happen to them beyond they might find doing business in Aberdeen would be slightly more difficult without the support of my father and his associates. In purely business terms we are very powerful in this city."

Jake thought for a moment. "Is that why Le Fondre came to you in the first place?"

"Yes it is. I think he had already worked it out for himself that Willie Ifield would make a better friend than an enemy. As it turned out Guy Le Fondre would never have made a good friend for anyone; he brought a nastiness to this world that no one would ever want within a friendship."

"Did you know a woman by the name of Mathilde Dupont?" Jake then asked.

Daniel thought for a moment. "No. Should I?"

"She knew your father apparently."

"Maybe so, Inspector, but it is not a name that I recognise. Has she something to do with the case you are building against my father?"

"She might have been the one person to clear your father completely of any suspicion in this crime but unfortunately she, too, is dead."

"Oh, how unfortunate," added Daniel Ifield.

"Slightly more than unfortunate for the poor woman," Jake said and Ifield did acknowledge that his choice of phraseology could have been better.

"When you had your words with Le Fondre at the Business Club on the night he died was the lady friend, who was with him, standing close-by or was she some distance away?"

Ifield thought for a second. "She was standing right next to him."

"So she heard all that was being said?"

"Definitely."

"And she would have seen, for herself, that Le Fondre was clearly showing an interest in Miss Sangster?"

"Oh I think that would have been obvious to anyone," Ifield answered. "Anytime that Le Fondre was in Miss Sangster's company he was always very attentive towards her. Attentive to the point of being a pest, I should say."

"But he only saw her a few times?"

"Three or four at most, I should have thought and always in the company of either myself or my father. We would never have put Miss Sangster in a position where she was alone with the man as there really was no saying what he might have done."

"Very well, Mr Ifield, I think that is all I need for the moment."

Jake left the office but before leaving the building he went across to Miss Sangster.

"Inspector," she said as he paused at her desk.

"Miss Sangster, what was your view of the advances being made towards you by Guy Le Fondre?"

"He was an evil man, Inspector who seemed to get pleasure from making other people uncomfortable when they were around him. I did not give him the pleasure of making me feel uncomfortable on the few occasions that we were in the same room together."

"How about in the car going out to Ellon?" Jake then said. "I believe that Mr Le Fondre was enjoying the fact that your legs were touching."

"That was a particularly difficult time, I will agree, but I just had to grit my teeth and put up with it. After all, the space in the car was limited and there was no way that I could stop our legs from touching."

"You must have felt equally uncomfortable the night Le Fondre had words with Daniel Ifield, seeing as those words were exchanged essentially because of you?" Jake then asked.

"There was general male posturing, Inspector and comments passed that may or may not have been about me. To be honest it seemed more about the two men's hatred for each other rather than any feelings towards me."

"So you were not aware of either Daniel Ifield, or Guy Le Fondre, having feelings towards you?" Jake enquired.

Miss Sangster smiled. "Inspector, I am aware that God blessed me with good looks and that those looks attract men whether, or not, I seek that attraction. I have learned to deal with that in my own way and that usually amounts to me ignoring any man whom I don't like."

"Did you ignore both men?"

Miss Sangster continued to smile. "I most certainly ignored Mr Le Fondre but as for Mr Ifield that is for me to know and for you to ponder forever."

Jake smiled.

"I wish you well in the future, Miss Sangster," Jake then said and set off for the front door.

On his way back to the office Jake went in passed the Daily Journal offices and asked to see Alan MacBride again. They met in the same room as they had done on Jake's last visit.

Jake produced the photograph from his pocket and explained who the man was and why Jake wanted the paper to run a story on him. The fact that he played a part in the Willie Ifield case made it more interesting to MacBride although he knew that he could say that the mystery man might have been connected to the death of Mathilde Dupont he also knew that he could not say that Mathilde Dupont might be connected to Willie Ifield.

"That's a story for another day, "added Jake.

"Thanks for still believing in me," MacBride said.

"Don't worry, Alan, I know that you are not the enemy," Jake concluded and left to head for home.

FOURTEEN

<u>Thursday 15 November: early morning onwards</u>

At a little after eight o'clock in the morning another letter arrived at Sergeant Turnbull's front desk by street urchin post. A dirty-faced young lad, who should probably have been on his way to school, hurried in and handed an envelope to the Sergeant. He then hurried out again before anyone could ask him any questions.

As Jake's name was once more on the envelope, Sergeant Turnbull took it through to the Inspector's office. Jake thanked the Sergeant then opened the envelope. The note inside was written as neatly as the first one and Jake was even more of a mind that he was being communicated with by a person of some education.

You need to speak with either Maisie Strachan, Annie Duff or Nellie Taylor. Willie Ifield arranged for them to go to the farm and make films for Le Fondre and Thane. I'm sure he won't have told you that.

Jake put the note down and then turned his attention to the morning paper in which they had run the story of the mystery man found dead in the Bon Accord Hotel. The photograph didn't look too bad and Jake now hoped that, as requested, someone would come forward and identify the dead man,

Jake then went through to the front desk and asked Turnbull if he recognised the three names quoted in the note.

"They're all prostitutes and they were all rumoured, certainly at one time, to be working for a pimp who was believed to be in the employ of one Willie Ifield. Ifield has always kept himself suitably distant from the seamier side of his business so we've never been able to prove that he had any dealings with prostitution."

"But these women were definitely prostitutes?" asked Jake.

"Oh yes, that's a definite."

"And I already know that Maisie Strachan was certainly at the farm as she's the woman we are trying to find with Wolfgang Schwieger. That means that Willie was lying, yet again, when he said he had nothing to do with the making of the sex films. It does seem as if he is doing himself no favours by constantly lying to me."

"Would you expect anything different from the man?" Turrnbull asked.

"Probably not, "Jake agreed and returned to his office.

He tidied up some paperwork and then put his jacket on. He knew that he would now have to go and speak with Robert Wallace, a job that he was not looking forward to in the slightest. Even though there had been a threat on Mr Wallace's life, Jake still did not feel that it was any part of his job to be trying to tell people how to run their lives. He would, however, inform Wallace of the threat and allow him to make up his own mind once armed with that knowledge.

However, before he went to see Wallace, he decided to firstly go to His Majesty's Theatre and confirm that invites had been sent to various special guests and perhaps also identify who else might have known the names that were to be on the list.

It was a little before half past nine when he arrived at the theatre. The front door was wide open and workmen were coming and going freely. Jake was able to walk in to the building unchallenged and to make his way in to the main auditorium. Eventually a rather angry looking young man came scurrying down the centre aisle towards Jake.

"Might I ask who you are and what you are doing here......?" the young man was saying as he got closer to Jake. However, once he had been able to get a proper look at the 'intruder' he realised that it was the policeman he had spoken to at Lodge Walk.

"Mr Grant, isn't it?" Jake said.

"Yes it is, Inspector and my apologies for not recognising you earlier."

"Not a problem. Could I speak to the manager?" he then said.

"If it is to do with the incidents that have been happening here then I might I be able to help?"

"It may be connected to those other incidents, Mr Grant, but events have taken a rather more sinister turn and it may be that the manager will be the only person to help me. However, should you have knowledge of those special guests who have been invited on opening night then it may well be the case that you can be of some assistance to me?"

"I'm afraid I do not know anything about that, Inspector," Grant responded.

"I rather thought that that might be the case," Jake added.

"It would be best if you spoke to Mr Nelson about that. I'll just go and see if he has time to see you."

"Mr Grant," Jake said quickly," please *tell* Mr Nelson that I *need* to see him and it is not a request that he has the option to decline."

"Oh," Grant replied, rather feebly. "Very well, Inspector, if you would like to follow me."

Minutes later Jake was in Harry Adair Nelson's office. The man himself was looking as dapper as ever with a fresh flower in his button hole and an efficient look to his surroundings.

"I really am very busy, Inspector," Nelson said, waving an arm across the papers lying on his desk.

"As am I, Mr Nelson, so this shouldn't take long," Jake added. "I wanted to ask you some questions about the people who have been invited as special guests for the opening night of this theatre?"

"There have been a few invitations sent out but I would hardly call them special guests as they are no more than people who have done something for the theatre already and I felt it would be a nice gesture to recognise what they have done by way of an invitation rather than have them buying tickets. The Lord Provost and his wife have also been formally invited, of course, but that is mere protocol."

"How many invitations in total were sent out?"

"Fifteen perhaps, certainly no more than that."

"And who else, other than yourself, knew the names of the people being invited?" Jake then asked.

"No one. As I said the list contains only those people who had played some part in the creation of this theatre."

"Did you write a list?"

"No."

"Who posted the invitations?" asked Jake.

"I posted them myself on the way home on Monday evening."

"Was there any time that the envelopes might have been on view?"

Nelson thought for a moment. "They were lying on my desk for the latter part of Monday afternoon and I was not always in my office. I suppose someone could have come in and seen them lying there."

"You do realise that your security is terrible," Jake then said. "I walked all the way in to your auditorium without being challenged by anyone."

"We need to have the doors open for the workmen to come and go," Nelson replied in his defence.

"I appreciate that, Mr Nelson, but those same workmen need to be your eyes and ears when it comes to preventing strangers from entering the building. I believe there have already been a number of incidents?"

"One or two, but nothing very sinister."

"It still shows that someone has been wandering around these premises without anyone noticing. My Constable seems certain that the workmen are not involved so we are looking for someone else."

Nelson looked suitable concerned. "This is not good, Inspector. I have enough to deal with as we head towards opening night without having to concern myself with some unstable person seeking to cause us problems of their making."

"Why did you invite Robert Wallace?" Jake then asked.

Nelson was taken aback by the sudden change of subject. He took a moment before answering.

"Mr Wallace runs the company that installed all the electrics in the theatre. I tried to invite a representative of all the companies who have helped to create this wonderful building."

"So it is possible that someone might have *guessed* that Mr Wallace would be attending on the opening night?" suggested Jake.

"It is possible that someone could have guessed that anyone of standing in the community would be here on opening night because I believe that that will be the case. However, no one could have guessed that I would be *inviting* Mr Wallace, or anyone else, as I only made that decision myself the weekend before I sent the invitations."

Jake knew that it was a strong possibility that it would be general knowledge that anyone who was anyone in Aberdeen would want to be seen at the theatre on opening night. It could have just been an educated guess, but Jake still believed that the threat on Wallace's life had come because the perpetrator of that threat knew, for a fact, that Wallace was going to be there. If that had been the case then the mystery person must have had access to the envelopes on Nelson's desk.

"Thank you, Mr Nelson, you have been very helpful. However, might I suggest that, at least in the lead up to the opening night, you make sure that the security of the building is tightened up?"

Nelson pondered for a moment and then conceded that the police Inspector did have a point.

"Of course, Inspector, I'll get Mr Grant to arrange something immediately."

Jake left the office and made his way down to street level. He took one last look inside the impressive auditorium before exiting on to Rosemount Viaduct. He then made the short journey to Belmont Street where the Aberdeen Electric Company had its offices.

As Jake entered the building he was met by a reception desk manned by a very prim and proper woman who looked to be in her forties. She was only visible from the waist up and wore a white blouse with an ornate brooch pinned to her bosom. Her hair was tied up and she had a pair of spectacles placed at the end of her nose. She was busy writing something in a large ledger that lay on the desk in front of her.

The woman looked up as Jake approached her desk. "Good morning, how may I help you?"

"I would like to see Mr Wallace, please," said Jake, showing the woman his identification.

"If you would like to take a seat, Inspector, I will inform Mr Wallace that you are here."

"Thank you."

The woman stood up and made her way through a short corridor behind her and then disappeared up a stair to her right. Jake sat down and picked up the Daily Journal for that day, which was lying on a small table in front of a row of three chairs.

This time Jake looked beyond the story of the mystery man found in the Bon Accord Hotel and read some of the more general items contained within the paper.

He had managed to read a few pages before the woman returned and informed Jake that Mr Wallace would be down in a moment. She then asked Jake if he would like a cup of tea, or coffee, while he was waiting. Jake accepted the offer of tea and had just received his cup when a tall, handsome man appeared along the corridor. He came over to Jake, his hand already held out in the offer of a handshake.

"Inspector Fraser, how good to meet you, I'm Robert Wallace."

The two men shook hands. Jake noted that Wallace shook his hand with a firm, confident grip. Jake also noted that Wallace's suit was of the best quality and that his rather foppish hairstyle had not come cheap either. For someone who extolled the needs for a political voice for the working man he seemed to live in a world well above that of the working class.

"Thank you for seeing me, Mr Wallace, is there somewhere we could go for a chat?"

"Of course, we can go up to my office. Please follow me."

A few moments later both men were seated in Robert Wallace's office. Wallace had grabbed a cup of tea en route and had even managed to find some biscuits as well.

"My staff look after me well." Wallace said with a smile as he offered Jake a biscuit.

"A sign of a popular boss," Jake added and Wallace nodded his head slightly to acknowledge what he took to be a compliment.

"Now, what can I do for you, Inspector?"

"I believe you have received an invitation to the opening night of His Majesty's Theatre?" Jake began.

Wallace looked surprised that someone else should know that, especially a police officer.

"Indeed I did, Inspector, but why would that be of any interest to the police?"

"Would you have gone to the theatre on opening night even if you hadn't receive a formal invite?"

"Of course I would. I am very proud of the work that all the Aberdeen companies have produced in building the theatre and of course I would have wanted to be a part of the opening night. I believe that this theatre will bring nothing but good to this city."

"Had you been telling friends and acquaintances that you would be going to the theatre?" Jake then asked.

Wallace had a puzzled expression on his face. He could make no sense of these questions but chose to continue to answer them.

"Actually I hadn't mentioned it to anyone beyond my wife of course."

"How would you feel if I were to ask you not to attend that night?" Jake then said.

Wallace laughed out loud. "Now why ever would you be asking me to do that?"

"Someone has seen fit to send a letter to the Chief Constable in which threats have been made to your life. Threats that will apparently be carried out should you attend the opening night of the theatre," Jake explained.

Robert Wallace no longer had an expression of amusement on his face. However, neither did he have one of concern either. He sat back with an expression more of amazement than anything else.

"Are you seriously trying to tell me that someone has threatened to kill me simply because I might choose to go to the theatre?"

"I'm sure the reasons for the threat have nothing whatsoever to do with the theatre, Mr Wallace. I would guess that they have more to do with your politics, which, if I am not mistaken, have made you rather unpopular, in certain quarters, around this city."

Wallace smiled again. "Unpopular would be putting it mildly, Inspector. Just because I do not have the same meaningless liberal views of our local politicians I have been branded as some kind of dangerous anarchist who would bring nothing but revolution to the streets of Aberdeen were I ever to be elected to any political post."

"You do have some rather anti-establishment views, Mr Wallace?" Jake then said.

"Ah, so you are acquaint with my politics, Inspector?" Wallace added.

"Other people have spoken about you. Personally I have never heard you speak but I believe that when you do you have little good to say about our current Member of Parliament."

Wallace laughed out loud again. "My current Member of Parliament has probably forgotten where Aberdeen is considering that his political ambition has taken him to the position of Chief Secretary for Ireland. Considering that he himself is Irish I rather feel he is at home where he is rather than be concerning himself about the people of South Aberdeen."

"But it's not just the person that seems to annoy you, Mr Wallace, it is the man's politics as well," Jake suggested.

"Inspector, this fair city of ours has returned a Liberal to Parliament since the Reform Act of eighteen thirty-two and the current Member for South Aberdeen has been there for the last twenty-one years. My God, the Aberdeen North Member has been there for ten years. It has got to the point where a goldfish would be elected were it to stand under the banner of the Liberal Party. There is no debate in this city when it comes to politics and that basically is all that I seek to introduce. I want people to give some thought to their politics and not to just vote Liberal because that was what their fathers did and their fathers before them."

"Even though it makes you unpopular?" Jake said.

"Inspector my popularity counts for nothing. However, if I can get the good citizens of Aberdeen questioning the values and aspirations of the Liberal Party then maybe, just maybe, I can play some small part in bringing about much needed change."

"An honourable intention, Mr Wallace, but maybe Aberdeen does not seek change?" Jake then suggested.

"I do not believe that enough people *seek* change, Inspector. We are a nation of sheep; we have no natural leaders, only a vast army of people intent on sticking together and clinging to values that have been handed down unchallenged for generations."

"Do you see yourself as a leader, Mr Wallace?"

"Not necessarily, Inspector. As I said, I see myself as a catalyst for debate. I just want people to think about their politics a little more before they vote at the next election. I want politicians elected because they can do some good for their community and not just because they are the only ones who have enough money to stand in the first place."

"I admire anyone for having strong personal views, Mr Wallace, but when those views lead to someone threatening your life doesn't that inform you that many people do not agree with you and that perhaps it is time to slow down on the rate of change that you seek?"

"The rate of change will be dictated by the good people of Aberdeen, Inspector. If they want it then it will happen quickly, however if they are happy with the way that things are then it may take several years before we see any significant change in the politics of this city. I do not need a misguided threat on my life to tell me that many people disagree with my views, Inspector; I see them every time I stand up and speak."

"And you wouldn't consider preventing any attack on your person by staying at home on the opening night of the new theatre?" Jake then suggested.

Wallace laughed again. "Inspector, I have hopes that one day, perhaps in the not too distant future, I will get the opportunity to stand for Parliament. When that day arrives I will be expected to attend many meetings and to explain to those meetings exactly what I can bring to Aberdeen by way of being their Member of Parliament. Of course there will be some who do not like what I am saying; politics should always be about healthy debate between two parties who do not agree on everything. I need to be seen to be strong, Inspector, and I need to be seen to truly believe in re-shaping this wonderful country of ours. I can hardly begin that journey by being seen to take a step back just because someone wishes to silence me."

"But no one would know that you had taken a step back, so it can't hurt your reputation as a prospective Member of Parliament," Jake added.

"Whoever made the threat, Inspector, would know and that is one person too many for my liking," countered Wallace.

"So you definitely won't consider not attending the opening night of His Majesty's Theatre?" Jake then asked one final time.

"No I will not, Inspector. I am not alone in believing that there is a valid alternative to the Liberal views of our current MPs. There are others already flying the flag for socialism; others already arguing that there could be a fairer world for everyone if we could just break through that class structure on which Great Britain stands. The very fact that a Member of Parliament receives no payment immediately creates a situation where only men of means can afford to stand for these positions. I am already being accused of not truly understanding the plight of the working class because I am not, myself, born of working class. However, my reply is quite simple, Inspector; you do not have to be poor to recognise that it is wrong. Every man should have the opportunity to provide for himself and his family and every man should have a meaningful voice at Westminster."

"Very good," Jake then said as he stood up. "I have to say, Mr Wallace that Aberdeen City Police cannot guarantee your safety that night but I wish you well none the less."

Wallace stood up, "Why thank you, Inspector. Look, it may not be of any interest to you but I am due to speak at a meeting of unemployed men on Castle Street later today and then again at the Independent Labour Party meeting in the Public Hall on Leadside Road on Sunday evening. Why don't you come along to one of them and at least get a better understanding of why I am the way I am?"

"What time are you due to speak?"

"Around three this afternoon or eight o'clock on Sunday evening."

"I'll maybe come along."

"Good man," Wallace said with a broad grin.

Jake left the office and went downstairs. He made his way out on to Belmont Street where it was starting to rain yet again. Jake wouldn't have expected miracles with the weather in November but it was still becoming a little wearing to get wet every time he stepped outside the door of a building.

He made his way back to Lodge Walk where he was delighted to be informed that there was a woman waiting for him in the interview room who had come in about the mystery man in the paper. Before Jake went to speak to her he asked Sergeant Turnbull to organise some men who could go out and find Annie Duff or Nellie Taylor. Both women, if possible, were to be brought to Lodge Walk and kept there until Jake could speak to them.

He then went through to the interview room where he found a hard faced woman, who looked to be in her late forties. She was dressed in a black skirt and white blouse and wore a hat pinned to her hair. She was dabbing at her face with a handkerchief and Jake could see at once that she had been crying.

"I'm Inspector Fraser, I believe you wanted to see me?"

"That man in the paper today was my son, Gerald, though I have no idea what he might be doing in the Bon Accord Hotel or why the papers were connecting him to some dead French woman."

The woman dabbed at her face again.

"Can I get you a cup of tea?" Jake then said.

"That would be very nice," the woman replied. "Milk and two sugars."

Jake went out of the room and arranged for a couple of cups of tea to be brought in to the interview room. He then went back and sat down. He took out his notebook and sat ready to take notes.

"What was your son's full name?"

"Gerald Strong."

"And you're full name is what, Mrs Strong?"

"Hilda Strong."

"Address?"

She gave an address in Torry.

"Did your son live with you?"

"Yes he did."

"How old was Gerald?"

"Thirty."

"What did he do for a living?" Jake then asked.

"This and that, Inspector. He did not hold down a proper job, you might say."

Jake immediately thought of all the money that was supposed to have been in his wallet and wondered where that might have come from.

"Was he working at the moment?" asked Jake.

"Not that I know of."

"You never heard him mention a woman by the name of Mathilde Dupont?"

"I never heard him mention a woman of any name, Inspector," Hilda Strong replied. "My son was not in the habit of telling me very much."

"So he could have known Mathilde Dupont?" Jake then said.

"I suppose, though I can't imagine Gerald having anything to do with the French. His father, God rest his soul, never liked the French, he always said they were not to be trusted. Little Gerald was well told by his father never to trust the French."

Jake held back a smile. At that moment the door opened and a Constable came in with the tea. Cups were placed in front of Jake and Hilda Strong before the young officer turned and left the room. Jake gave Mrs Strong a moment to drink some tea before speaking again.

"Perhaps we could move on, Mrs Strong. We have reason to believe that your son not only knew Mathilde Dupont but that he also took the poor woman's life. We also believe that he then committed suicide in a fit of remorse."

"Oh no, my Gerald would never do a thing like that," Hilda Strong said, reaching for her handkerchief again.

"What, not murder someone or not commit suicide?" Jake asked by way of clarification.

"Neither. My Gerald was a good man, Inspector. He was a kind man who would never have considered hurting another human being, let alone killing them. He was also a man whose religious beliefs, though not running as deep as maybe they should, would never have allowed him to take his own life. You won't get to heaven if you take your own life, Inspector."

"Surely committing murder would prevent his entry in to heaven as well?" Jake then suggested.

"Which is why I do not believe he would do such a thing."

To his mother that may have made perfect logic but Jake was sure that Gerald Strong *had* murdered Mathilde Dupont, however, so the only debate that he now needed to have with himself was whether, or not, the suicide was as straightforward as it seemed. After all, there was still the missing prostitute to be accounted for.

Jake took a piece of paper from his pocket. It had been there since the day that Gerald Strong's body had been found in the Bon Accord Hotel. This was the suicide note.

"Mrs Strong, could I ask you to look at this note and tell me if you recognise the handwriting?"

Hilda Strong took the note and read it. She knew at once what it was and the tears sprang to her eyes again.

"If you are asking me if that is my son's handwriting then the answer is no, Inspector."

Jake took the note back and put it in his pocket. A part of him was not surprised to hear that the handwriting was not that of Gerald Strong. It seemed to be further proof that for all the evidence might be trying to say, this was not a suicide.

"Was your son popular with the ladies?" Jake then asked.

"I really don't know, Inspector. He certainly went out a lot but I have no idea where he might have gone or with whom."

"Did your son have any close male friends?"

"He did go drinking with Denis."

"What was Denis's full name, Mrs Strong?" Jake prompted.

"Denis Arthur, he lives with his mother three doors along from us."

"Which number would that be?"

Mrs Strong provided the full address. Jake could see that this was now proving to be a very upsetting experience for Mrs Strong but he now had to ask her something that would probably make her feel even worse.

"I would like someone to formally identify the body of the man we now assume is your son. Would you prefer that I ask Mr Arthur to do it?"

Mrs Strong hid her face behind her handkerchief again and took a little while to respond to the question.

"I identified him from the picture in the paper today, is that not good enough for you?" Mrs Strong then said.

"Unfortunately not, Mrs Strong," replied Jake. "Someone needs to formally identify the body as identifying a photograph would not be accepted in a court of law."

"Very well, Inspector, I think I would like to see my son one more time," Mrs Strong eventually said.

They finished their tea and then Jake led Mrs Strong across to the mortuary where she identified the body presented to her as being that of her son Gerald.

"Thank you for all your help, Mrs Strong and once more my condolences for your loss," Jake then said after leading Mrs Strong back in to the main building and showing her to the front door. He then went back to his office.

It was only an hour later when Jake was informed that both Annie Duff and Nellie Taylor were now in the building. It had not taken long to find both women as they had basically been plying their trade in their known areas. They had both complained bitterly about the loss of earnings that they would suffer as the result of spending time in Lodge Walk. Annie had even lifted her dress and suggested to the young Police Constable who had accosted her first that he might like to supplement her income with a few moments of passion against the nearest wall.

The policeman, though somewhat red-faced and embarrassed, politely declined and was grateful for the arrival of a few more officers. They took Annie to Lodge Walk where they were informed that colleagues had already taken Nellie Taylor there as well.

Jake interviewed both women and was also propositioned by both women. Nellie, in particular, took a shine to the Inspector and even offered him her body at no charge. Jake had thought of how clean and sweet smelling he always found Margaret and then he looked at the woman sitting in front of him with her old clothes and unwashed appearance. He often wondered how any man could have sex with these women, let alone pay good money for the privilege.

Jake also politely declined the offer and continued with the interview. By the time he had spoken to both women he was now better appraised of Willie Ifield's part in the making of the sex films. It was now clear to Jake that Willie not only knew more about the making of the films than he perhaps stated so far but he also had planned to play an active part in the making of the films by supplying the women who were to appear in them.

The possible noose around Willie Ifield's neck tightened considerably. Neither Annie nor Nellie knew anything about Maisie Strachan beyond the fact that they had both heard that Maisie had met a nice man and that she had left Aberdeen. Jake decided that there was little chance of him ever tracing Maisie as it was likely she was out of the country and living somewhere in Germany. However, after what Annie and Nellie had just told him he doubted if he would actually need Maisie's evidence to finally put Willie Ifield away for a long time.

Jake even had more on Daniel Ifield as Nellie said she had met up with Maisie, during Maisie's time out at the farm and she had said that she had heard Wolfgang talking about Daniel Ifield organising some women for their films. Wolfgang had apparently had no idea where these women were coming from but obviously there would have been time to organise things properly as Maisie, Nellie and Annie were supposed to be providing them with at least three months of 'actresses.'

Of course the other fact that came out of Jake's little chat with Annie and Nellie was that Willie Ifield also had more to do with prostitution in Aberdeen than he had ever admitted in the past. It might now be possible to charge Willie with living off immoral earnings as well as murder and the making of the sex films. If Willie didn't hang for murder then, at the very least, he would be in prison for quite a time.

Jake got formal statements signed and thanked Nellie and Annie for their time. He gave both women a few pennies by way of compensation. They were both even more insistent that Jake at least did something to them for the money. Jake was equally insistent that he would do nothing of the kind and showed them both to the front door.

Jake found Mathieson and then arranged for Willie Ifield to be brought to the interview room. It was now just after lunchtime though Jake was yet to have any lunch. Mathieson had fared slightly better having managed to find ten minutes in which to eat a pie and wash it down with a glass of water.

Willie Ifield was offered the chance to contact his solicitor but, on this occasion, he said that it would not be necessary. Jake did organise a cup of tea for everyone feeling that the condemned man deserved something as he listened to the evidence piling up against him.

Once they were all seated Jake began.

"When we last spoke, Mr Ifield, you seemed to be at great pains to tell me that you knew very little about the making of the sex films and that once you were in business with Le Fondre you would have insisted that that all stopped. We've been talking to various people since then and I now have evidence to prove that you not only intended playing a part in the making of the sex films but that you were intent on organising the ladies who would be filmed."

"I don't know who you have been speaking to, Inspector, but I can assure you that that is simply not true," Ifield replied.

Jake could see from Ifield's expression that there was a confidence to the reply, as if he firmly believed that no evidence to the contrary could ever come to light. No doubt he had assumed that he had control over the ladies who worked for him and that it was beyond his belief that any of them would give evidence against him. Jake decided to use the name that was most likely to worry Willie Ifield and least likely to ever cross paths with either him, or his organisation, ever again.

"Mr Ifield, we now know that Maisie Strachan was at the farm for weeks performing in Le Fondre's sordid little pictures. We also know that Maisie was there by way of her paying off a debt to you. That debt was incurred whilst Maisie was prostituting herself for your gain. Do you still say that this is all simply not true?"

Willie Ifield's expression changed almost at once to one of the deepest concern with, perhaps, just a hint of anger. He sat back in his chair and his eyes flicked around the room as if seeking an answer amongst the furnishing. Jake let the silence hang in the air a little longer.

"Is it all lies, Mr Ifield?" Jake then added.

Ifield now looked straight at Jake with an expression of venom and deep hatred. Jake could sense at once that he had his man on the ropes even though he had yet to land the killer punch.

"I never made any financial gain from prostitution in this city," Ifield replied.

"Forgive me for not believing you, Mr Ifield. I may also add that I would doubt if a jury would believe you either. You were clearly connected to these women and the idea that their earnings in no way reached you is quite beyond anyone's comprehension."

Choosing to ignore the subject of prostitution, Willie Ifield turned the interview back to Guy Le Fondre.

"There may have been a short-term arrangement with Le Fondre to help him make his films," Ifield eventually said with much reluctance.

"A short-term arrangement?" Jake repeated with disbelief. "Do you now want me to believe that after Maisie and at least two other women who worked for you were finished with the films being made at the farm that you were then to have nothing further to do with them?"

"Le Fondre was having problems finding women to appear in his films; I was able to help him for a short period of time," insisted Ifield.

"So the fact that your son was in the process of setting up a constant supply of women is another example of something simply not being true, is that the case, Mr Ifield?"

Ifield looked like the trapped man he was. He had no idea how much Fraser now knew though it was becoming abundantly apparent that he knew more than Willie Ifield would have preferred. It seemed clear that the women had been speaking to the police after all. The day might come when they would rue that decision.

"Daniel's only part in this was to do what I told him to do," Ifield said in an emphatic tone. "Beyond that he has had nothing to do with anything involving the making of the sex films and he is not to be involved whilst you continue with this investigation."

"I cannot ignore your son altogether," Jake then added. "He could still have something to do with Le Fondre's death as I still feel sure he had a stronger motive than you."

"But you seem to be saying that / killed Le Fondre, Inspector, so why would you still be considering Daniel as a suspect unless, of course, even you are having trouble in accepting that all the evidence building up against me is actually genuine?"

Jake smiled. "It is possible that you both had a hand in Le Fondre's death. I may still have suspicions regarding your son but, meantime, I am more than happy to accept the evidence that we have against you. It is pretty solid, Mr Ifield and I feel that you should, at the very least, start telling me the truth and stop muddying the waters with the lies you've told up until now."

"Very well, Inspector, I was intending remaining in business with Le Fondre even though sex films would continue to be made and I was to be arranging for 'actresses' to appear in his films. I also admit that some of the women I used were prostitutes but they were not working for me, they simply owed me a debt. I also categorically deny that any of this has anything to do with me killing Le Fondre. I say again, Inspector, what possible motive could I have?"

Jake smiled again. "You have any number of motives, Mr Ifield. Le Fondre was a loose cannon who upset too many people for you to seriously entertain the possibility of being in a partnership with him for any length of time. You knew that the film business could lead to huge profits and the thought of sharing those profits with this young upstart probably riled you to the point where it seemed easier to get rid of him rather than try to buy him out in some way. Then there was the little matter of Miss Sangster. It is not only Daniel who had feelings for her, you also were infatuated by her and would have done anything to protect her honour. Believe me, Mr Ifield, I have no problem in finding a motive for you killing Le Fondre and now that we have evidence connecting you to his business, connecting you to prostitution and connecting you to being outside Le Fondre's home on the night he died, I believe I have more than enough to formally charge you with the murder of Guy Le Fondre as well as the fact that you also seemed to have been living off the earnings of prostitutes."

"I did not kill Guy Le Fondre," insisted Ifield. "I swear to God I did not even know where the man lived so how I was ever going to be standing outside his home is beyond me. I also have not been living off the earnings of prostitutes; good God, man, I don't need to stoop that low to make money."

"We have witnesses who contradict what you are saying, Mr Ifield and we have hard evidence with your coat and shoes that proves you were outside Le Fondre's home. I'll let the jury actually put the rock in your hand."

"Inspector, let us accept for one moment, purely for the sake of argument and in no way asserting that this is the truth, that I had wanted Le Fondre out of the way. Surely I would then have arranged for someone else to take care of that, after all a man of my position in this city would hardly need to get his hands dirty in any way whatsoever. Why would I ever run the risk of being caught by killing Le Fondre myself?"

"A fair point, Mr Ifield," Jake conceded," but the fact is that you may not have had time to organise another way of getting rid of Le Fondre. Perhaps your hatred for the man sparked something in you that demanded instant and personal action. I'm not too concerned with what ultimately went through your mind, I am simply happy for the moment to feel confident that this case is water tight and that you are probably heading for the gallows."

Willie Ifield's face drained of blood and he slumped in his chair. The words he spoke next were barely audible.

"But I am innocent."

Jake then left Mathieson to charge Ifield and then take him back to the cells. Jake also asked Mathieson to get in touch with Porteous and to ask him to come down and speak to his client. A confession might be seen by the judge as a step towards leniency when he considered the sentence he imposed.

Jake then went to the Empress Café for a very late lunch.

***

The South United Church was completely empty apart from one man who continued with what had become his weekly service to God. Unable to get paid employment the man had taken to working for the church, dedicating his time to Jesus Christ and to the wise words of the Bible.

As he worked the man spoke softly to himself. He was talking quietly and even if someone had been there with him it would have been unlikely that they would have heard a word he was saying. His words were in the form of a prayer. He was seeking answers from God to questions that kept passing through his head. He needed to know the road on which he must now travel and only God could provide the answers that he was seeking.

He had not always been so close to God. Before he joined the army he would have laughed at any thought of devoting time and energy to cleaning a church. Before the Boer War, however, he had been a different person.

He had gone off to that foreign land to fight for the Queen against the Boers. He knew nothing of why they were fighting; he was simply a soldier obeying his orders. Those orders had put him literally in the firing line and he now knew that had it not been for God, he would never have survived.

During one long and hard fought confrontation he had been seriously wounded by a Boer bullet. As he had laid amongst the dead and the dying he had had his head smashed by the butt of a Boer rifle. This had been their way of finishing off wounded enemy soldiers who were not to be taken prisoner as providing them with medical attention was not seen as being a Boer problem.

However, he did not die.

He had drifted out and in of consciousness for what seemed like hours. He had tried to call out but no sound would come from his mouth. And then it happened. In a blaze of light above his head he was visited by an angel. Nothing was said, but the mere presence of the angel told him that God was watching over him and that someone would come to save him. Only a few moments after the angel departed he was found by colleagues and taken to a place where he could receive medical help.

As a result he survived.

The bullet had broken bones in his leg and he had lost a lot of blood. Doctors had thought, at first, that he would lose his leg, though somehow they managed to save it. However, he was left with a slight limp that would be with him the rest of his days. More debilitating for him was the fact that the head injury would leave him suffering from occasional blackouts.

The army no longer wanted him, though they softened the blow by providing him with a pension, before telling him he was no longer a soldier and sending him home. That had been at the beginning of 1902.

When he had first returned to Aberdeen he had been willing, although somewhat reluctantly, to accept that he might find it difficult to get employment. At that time he still felt weak from the effects of the bullet and he was still prone to blackouts on a semi-regular basis. He received treatment from a local doctor and occasionally attended the hospital at Woolmanhill so that doctors there could keep an eye on him.

In time he started to get a little better and by 1904 he felt ready to seek employment. He had many skills, which he had learned in the army and he felt sure that at least one of them would convert in to civilian employment. He did not hide the fact that he had been invalided out from the army as he felt sure that local employers would want to honour their returning heroes by offering them jobs whenever possible.

He spent six months looking and in all that time not one employer ever came close to offering him a job. The main problem appeared to be the blackouts. They weren't happening as often, but no one wanted to take the risk that any employee would blackout at their work and in the process put themselves, or their colleagues, in danger.

He came to resent all those people who effectively wrote him off. He came to hate all those employers who did nothing to help him; who could not find it in their hearts to offer him a job of some kind. His hatred soon found another channel.

His local church was the South United Church, which was situated across from the Wallace Statue on Rosemount Viaduct. He had started working there, on one or two days per week, as a means of paying back God for saving him on that distant battlefield. He would do odd jobs around the place and generally enjoy the peace and tranquillity that the building provided.

But there was not always the peace and tranquillity that he sought. To his complete horror they were building a theatre next door to the church. Why would any council agree to something as stupid as that? Why would anyone want to build a place of entertainment next door to a place of worship? The whole idea made no sense to him whatsoever?

And so he had decided to do something about it.

He could accept the Public Library being on the other side of the church. The library was a place of learning; an outlet for the common people to go and learn from books and newspapers, assuming, of course, that they could read. Learning went hand in hand with religion for an open mind was more accepting of the teachings of the Lord. Yes, the library was a good idea.

The same could not be said of a theatre. What possible purpose did a theatre serve? They were places of frivolous humour and often as not, half-naked dancers. They did nothing to promote the word of the Lord; instead they pulled people together and presented them with dubious forms of entertainment. Bad enough when these places were down some dirty, back street but even worse when built directly next door to a church.

The building was too far on to be stopped now so the best he could do was to delay or prevent its opening. He had heard that the opening night was planned for the month of December and that had caused his anger levels to rise ever further. December was the celebration of the birth of Jesus Christ, it was not a month for frivolous entertainment in some gaudy theatre.

There was nothing funny or entertaining about the Lord's birth.

The Lord must be avenged.

For the last ten months he had been visiting the theatre and stealing tools. He had left the dead cat as a sign that he was prepared to escalate his actions. However, everything he had done to date had achieved little. He had not read one line in the paper about his actions at the theatre. No one appeared to be paying any attention to what he was doing.

He had long thought that he needed to do more. He needed to have his actions recognised and he needed some sign that they were going to at least delay the opening until after the Lord's birthday. He needed to increase the level of threat and he needed to do it quickly.

The idea of threatening Robert Wallace had come to him the moment he had seen the envelope lying on that desk in the theatre office. Robert Wallace had been one of those employers who had turned him. Not only had he done that but he was also turning in to a loud-mouthed politician intent on changing the way in which Aberdeen was run. He was a menace to society and he needed to be stopped.

It all made perfect sense to him. He would kill Robert Wallace and in one action he would gain revenge on all those thoughtless employers who had refused him employment and save Aberdeen from the threat of anarchy. He now persuaded himself that this was the reason why God spared him on that battlefield. God had work for him and now he understood fully as to what that work was going to be.

He hadn't decided exactly how he was going to kill Robert Wallace. He had decided, however, that assuming he did not manage to delay the opening night altogether, then he would at least kill Wallace on that evening and forever tarnish the memory. They would not be able to talk about the theatre without having to associate it with the murder of Robert Wallace. Surely that would be enough to keep its doors closed?

He sat down and took his bible from the pocket of his jacket. He began to read some of his favourite passages. This was his way of keeping in touch with the Lord; to sit in the church and read God's word.

He found a piece that seemed to fit the current circumstances to perfection. He read it over and over again:

Vengeance is Mine, and retribution, In due time their foot will slip; For the day of their calamity is near, And the impending things are hastening upon them.

The day of their calamity is most certainly near he thought as he sat back in his seat and looked around the church with some satisfaction. He then bowed his head and offered up a prayer in which he asked God for some clear guidance on what he might do next.

As he prayed he dropped his bible and as he picked it up again it appeared to open at a particular page. The man looked at the page and his eyes were drawn to the line immediately beside where his thumb was lying on the edge of the page.

Abraham stretched out his hand and took the knife to slay his son.

The Lord had spoken to him. He must take up a knife and slay Robert Wallace.

FIFTEEN

Friday 16 November: mid-morning until late evening

Jake went to see Doctor Symon. For once the Doctor was clear of dead bodies. He was writing reports when Jake walked in to the small room that was used as an office.

"I've charged Willie Ifield with the murder of Guy Le Fondre," he said, "but I was reading through your report again and there is something in there that bothers me."

"What might that be?" Doctor Symon asked as Jake sat down opposite him.

"You describe the blow to the side of the head as being likely to have been delivered by a man of at least comparable height to Le Fondre. How did you come to that conclusion?"

Doctor Symon put his pen down and sat back in his chair. "Very simply. It was based on the likely angle of the blow to Le Fondre's head. It did not look to me as if someone had swung the rock upwards, or downwards as might have been the case had his attacker been considerably taller or smaller than him. It's not a definite science, obviously, but as you seek my opinion in these instances that is what you get."

"In which case I might have a problem as Willie Ifield is a good six to seven inches shorter than Le Fondre. Any blow that he delivered to the side of Le Fondre's head would have shown a clear upward motion unless, of course, he had been standing on something?"

"He could have been standing on the doorstep?" suggested Symon.

"Had that been the case then he would have had to have attacked Le Fondre before he had time to open the door and the position of the body and manner of the wounds tells us that that isn't what happened. It would have also meant that, had someone been standing in the doorway then Le Fondre would have seen them as he walked up the path. Even if he had known them and kept on walking, any blow would have been to the front and not the back of his head. Whoever hit Le Fondre had to come at him from behind, which means that they had to be standing on the flat. We have Ifield's muddy shoes, which further seems to prove that he was standing in the garden for at least some of the time. Le Fondre reacted to something, turned around and was struck as he turned. That would mean that it was Le Fondre who was standing on the higher part of the doorway when he was attacked."

"Which means his true killer would have needed to have been *taller* than Le Fondre?" Doctor Symon added.

"Someone, perhaps, like Daniel Ifield?" suggested Jake. "And yet all the evidence points to Willie Ifield, so if he didn't actually deliver the blow why did his coat get covered in blood and why does a pair of his shoes carry the same mud as that around Le Fondre's front door?"

"He could still have been there?" said Symon. "Maybe father and son did it together?"

"Or maybe someone really does want us to believe that it was Willie Ifield who killed Le Fondre even though he didn't." Jake added.

"It may well be the case that someone *is* trying to feed you evidence," Doctor Symon then said.

"Have you found something else?" Jake enquired, moving closer to the Doctor.

"It was the coat that was found in Ifield's shed," Doctor Symon added. "That coat is quite badly soaked in blood and yet I wouldn't have thought that Le Fondre would have bled much until he was lying on the ground. There really would have been no reason for the coat to be any more than perhaps spotted in blood. It looked as if someone had made sure that there was blood on the coat so that you wouldn't possibly miss it."

Jake pondered on that thought for a moment. "We still have those two witnesses who saw a man answering Willie Ifield's description standing outside Le Fondre's house the night he died. They can't have been part of some elaborate plot to have Willie Ifield hanged for a crime he may not have committed. There had to be some truth amongst the evidence that we are gathering."

"So what do you do now?"

Jake thought for a moment. "We continue to go with the evidence, Doctor, until there is new evidence to make us believe otherwise. I have clothing, I have witnesses and I have a catalogue of lies from Willie Ifield himself that I have been systematically able to disprove. Apart from the anomaly of the angle of the blow and now a debate over how much blood should or should not be on the coat, everything else points to the killer being Willie Ifield."

"My views on the possible height of the killer amount to nothing more than personal opinion and may not stand up in a court of law," Doctor Symon then said." To be honest I tend to agree with you, Jake, the evidence does seem to be forming a compelling argument that Willie Ifield is your murderer."

"And yet the anomalies in the evidence seem to raise even more questions than I seem able to answer. Apart from what we have discussed already there is the other, less than small matter of the suicide note found along with Gerald Strong. I now know that it was not written by Gerald and therefore have to assume that someone else wished to tie Gerald to the death of Mathilde Dupont. The implication, as I am sure you will already have gathered, is that Gerald may not have had anything to do with Mathilde Dupont's death beyond providing us with what appears to be another clue towards Willie Ifield's guilt."

"All a bit of a mess then, Jake?" the Doctor then said rather cheerfully.

Jake smiled. "A mess, indeed, Doctor."

"And one that I feel sure you will sort out in time."

"I wish I shared your confidence, Doctor."

Jake then thanked the Doctor once more for his time and then left the building and made his way back across to the main building at Lodge Walk

***

Peter Grant was doing his rounds of the workmen checking that all the jobs that needed to be done before opening night, were being done. He had asked the workmen to be more vigilant in dealing with people who should not be in the building but he had little confidence in them actually helping. They all seemed to be there to simply do a day's work and not to act as part-time security staff in the process.

His tour concluded on the stage. To reach the finishing point he made his way in to the main auditorium and walked down the central aisle. As he began his walk towards the orchestra pit he could see something lying on the stage. There were still workmen working either side if the stage, each one high up on a well-structured piece of scaffolding. No one seemed to notice Peter Grant walking below so he had to assume that no one would have noticed someone else throwing something on to the stage.

Grant made his way up on to the stage and now noticed what seemed to be a body lying on the stage. Fortunately, the closer he got the more he realised that it was nothing more than a dummy, which was dressed in a man's suit. There was a note pinned to the jacket.

Grant unpinned the note and read it. He then took the dummy to a room at the back of the stage before going upstairs to inform Mr Nelson of what he had found and then he put his coat on and set off for Lodge Walk.

***

"A Mr Grant from His Majesty's Theatre, sir," Sergeant Turnbull said as he popped his head around the door of Jake's office.

"Put him in the interview room, please. I'll be with you in a minute."

"Very good, sir."

Jake eventually went through to the interview room and found Grant sitting at the table. There was a piece of paper lying on the top of the table.

"You wanted to see me?" Jake said as he moved over to the other chair and sat down.

"Someone left a dummy on the stage of the theatre and this was attached to it," Grant said handing the paper to Jake.

Jake read it:

This is Robert Wallace as he ought to be seen by the people of Aberdeen – quite dead. One final warning before Mr Wallace dies. Do not open this theatre. Do not insult God in the process. December is for the celebration of the Lord's birth, not the childish entertainment of an atheist audience. This is your final warning - For the day of his calamity is near and the impending things are hastening upon him.

Jake looked up. "This is all very interesting, isn't it?" he said.

"I don't follow," Grant added.

"The note begins with the threat to Mr Wallace and yet it seems to be the opening of the theatre that is upsetting the note-writer more. He seems to see the theatre as being an insult to God rather than Mr Wallace doing anything personally."

"But why would anyone be so averse to the theatre opening?" Grant then asked.

"He's telling you that in his note, Mr Grant. He sees the theatre as insulting God in some way. We are clearly dealing with a mind that has, in some way, mixed everyday surroundings with his fervent religious beliefs."

"But we are committed to opening on the third of December, Inspector and there is no way that we could contemplate even postponing the event."

"I appreciate that, Mr Grant," Jake acknowledged.

"Do you seriously think that someone would actually kill over an issue as petty as the opening of a theatre?" Grant then asked.

"Robert Wallace has already had his life threatened, Mr Grant. It is obvious, therefore, that the writer of this note does not view the opening of the new theatre as being a petty event. Someone clearly sees the theatre as being an affront to God, in some way. I shall need to keep this note and I'd like one of my officers to collect the dummy as well."

"Of course, Inspector, I'll keep it locked in a room until someone calls for it."

"Thank you again, Mr Grant," Jake then concluded and showed Grant to the door.

Jake then went back to his office to give some more thought to who this person might be and why he should be so angry at the theatre opening. After all, there were other theatres in the city so why should this one be any more offensive than the others?

***

The young woman sat in the corner of the café, her dark brown eyes constantly looking towards the door eager for sight of the young man she was expecting to join her. At a little after midday the door opened and the young man came in. He scanned the other occupants of the café until his eyes eventually fell on the smiling face of the young woman.

He made his way across to the table and by the time he got there the woman was on her feet. They kissed briefly and then sat down.

"We shouldn't really be seeing each other in public," the man commented, looking around again as if checking that no one might recognise him.

"I know it's a bit dangerous, but I just had to see you and anyway, there's no one here who knows either of us."

"Perhaps you're right," the young man added and he took hold of the young woman's hand. "I do love you. I haven't stopped thinking about last Sunday."

The woman blushed. "It was nice wasn't it?" she said.

"Meeting behind closed doors is all good and well," the man then said, "but meeting like this could destroy all our plans."

"It's just lunch," the woman added.

The man squeezed her hand. "Indeed it is, so let's order something nice and enjoy the moment."

***

At the very moment that the young man and woman were turning their attention to the menu in the café Johnnie Gordon was sitting in the Business Club enjoying a drink and looking forward to what he hoped would be a very enjoyable lunch. He was enjoying both the drink and his own company when Courtenay Troup came in to the bar with his daughter, Daisy, on his arm. These were the last people that Johnnie would have wanted to meet.

He saw Courtenay say something to Daisy and then they both came over to where Johnnie was sitting.

"Sorry to bother you," Courtenay Troup announced in a tone that clearly indicated he was anything but sorry," but may Daisy and I join you for a moment?"

"If you feel you must," Johnnie replied casting a glance at Daisy who seemed to be looking even more radiant as she stood looking down at him. She smiled; Johnnie did not smile back.

"Thank you," she then said and sat down. Courtenay Troup sat down as well and gestured for a waiter to come across. He ordered three drinks and then sat back in his chair.

"I wanted a final chance to speak to you," Troup then said. "I appreciate that you might believe you have feelings for this young woman, Alice, but I urge you to think again about tying yourself to someone of her class for the rest of your life."

"God, Courtenay, but you are such a snob," Johnnie added.

Courtenay Troup did not look offended by the comment. "I merely recognise that those of us with money and position need to mix with our own kind. Young ladies like Alice are to be applauded for she is intent on improving herself in life and that can only be seen as good. However, for you to feel that you need to invite a woman like that in to your own life, is quite unnecessary. You really should reconsider your own future."

"And why would I do that?" Johnnie then asked.

Courtenay Troup looked at Johnnie with an expression of surprise. The question hardly merited answering as surely the answer would have been obvious to any gentleman. He continued to look at Johnnie for a few seconds and then realised that he was expected to provide an answer.

"As I have already said, you were born of a different class, Johnnie and you would be making a grave mistake if you try to mix with people who are not of that same class."

"You don't believe that the classes can mix?" Johnnie said again, hiding the smirk that he felt should be on his face.

"Absolutely; we are all born to take our place in the natural world. Our place in that world is determined by our birth and those born of different classes already know their place. There is no way that any woman who is not born to be a lady can ever actually *be* a lady."

"You seem to be suggesting that I need a lady in my life, rather than simply a woman?" Johnnie then asked, still finding great humour in the pomposity of Troup's argument.

"I believe that every gentleman reaches a point in his life where the affections of a good wife are necessary to his needs. I further believe that that wife needs to come from the same class as the gentlemen, otherwise how can she understand and meet his needs. "

"And Alice couldn't meet those needs, is that what you are telling me?" Johnnie then said, getting some pleasure out of being as awkward as possible.

Courtenay looked at Daisy with a reddening of his cheeks. Mention of a gentleman's needs in front of his daughter had clearly embarrassed him.

"I'm sure that she could satisfy your more basic needs," he eventually said," but you need a woman from your own class to satisfy all your needs. You need someone to be at your side when you go to formal functions and you need someone to run your home. Only a woman of a certain class can do all that for you."

"Daisy you mean?" Johnnie added, glancing at Daisy in the process.

"Well, yes, Daisy would meet the necessary requirements. My daughter has been brought up to be a good wife to someone and I would like that someone to be you, Johnnie. Good grief, you were friends before so I am sure that you could be friends again and who knows where that friendship might lead."

"I would be delighted to have Daisy as a friend," Johnnie started to say and Daisy's face lit up in a broad smile," as I am sure would Alice, after all she does not have many female friends."

Daisy's smile disappeared and Courtenay Troup's eyes flashed anger.

"That was not what I meant, as well you know," he then said.

Johnnie paused as the waiter delivered their drinks to the table. Once the waiter had left them alone again, Johnnie provided Troup with his response.

"Alice is not a dalliance, Courtenay, but my time with Daisy was. We hardly spent any time together and there was never a moment when I ever felt that I was falling in love with your daughter. On the other hand, the moment my eyes fell on Alice I knew that she was the one for me."

Johnnie now looked at Daisy.

"You are a lovely girl and I am sure you will make someone the perfect wife. However, that someone is not going to be me."

Daisy looked like she was about to cry. Troup did not; his fury rose another notch.

"Alice was a …….." he began to say.

"We all know what Alice was," Johnnie interrupted, "but we also know that she does not live that life anymore and I would ask that you kindly stop referring to her past as if it is going to change the present in some way."

"I did love you Johnnie," Daisy suddenly said. "Did you not have feelings for me?"

Johnnie turned his full attention on Daisy once again. "You may have thought you were in love with me, Daisy, but I doubt if you really know what love is. We were friends, Daisy, nothing more. To be quite frank I don't think love ever came in to our brief relationship, you simply wanted to make your father happy by snaring a husband."

Daisy did start to cry at that point and Courtenay Troup hurried to provide her with a handkerchief.

"Now see what you have done," Troup said.

"What I have done?" replied Johnnie. "You were the one who brought her here and took her to my table. Stop interfering, Courtenay, in your daughter's life and maybe, just maybe, a proper suitor will come over the hill on his white charger."

"I am not interfering in my daughter's life," Courtenay Troup said, his tone still louder than perhaps might have been necessary and one or two eyes were turning in their direction.

Johnnie laughed. "All you ever do is interfere. Daisy cannot breathe without your permission and she lives in fear of ever upsetting you. Her entire life is built around pleasing you as, no doubt, is your wife's as well. For goodness sake, man, take a step back and watch your daughter's life develop without your help. Daisy is a beautiful young woman who will have no problem in attracting suitors. Now you may wish to have an opinion on whom Daisy may finally marry but, please, let her find her own husband with as little input from you as possible."

Courtenay Troup stood up. "Come, Daisy, we are clearly wasting our time here."

Daisy wiped her eyes and stood up. "I'll never forgive you for this," she then said looking down on Johnnie.

"I didn't think I needed your forgiveness, Daisy," Johnnie replied, "but I still wish you well in the life that lies ahead for you."

Courtenay and Daisy Troup stormed out of the bar and Johnnie sat back to think things over. Clearly he needed to send out a proper signal about how he felt about Alice. There seemed only one course of action that would achieve that; he would ask her to marry him.

***

The young couple were finishing the last of their light lunch. They were still holding hands across the table and to anyone else watching them they looked every bit the couple in love.

"How much longer do you think the police will keep asking their questions?" the woman asked.

"Until they feel they have all the answers," the man replied. "As I said at the start of all this, we need to keep calm and let all this police interest pass. Then we will be able to go public on our relationship without, hopefully, incurring further interest from the police."

"Do you think that Inspector Fraser is believing us?" the woman then asked.

"I think he is following the evidence," the man then said, "and that is all we can hope for. He needs to reach the conclusion that we want him to reach and once that is done we will be home and dry. Once our plan comes to fruition we will have even more money to spend than we do at present. Life can only get better, but first we need to get through these difficult times with the police."

"Oh, darling," the woman added," what a life we are going to have together. It will just be us, won't it, there's no one else attracting your affection?"

"Of course not," the man said, squeezing the woman's hand again. "I may need to make Fraser think there are others but as far as you are concerned there is no need to worry about the prospect of other women in my life. I love you and that is all that matters."

The woman smiled and the man attracted the attention of a waitress so that he could get the bill.

The bill was then paid and the man and woman went their separate ways, each leaving the café at a different time. Even as he made his way back to work the young man was looking around, just to make sure that no one was watching him.

***

Margaret was feeling very nervous. The chairs were laid out and the kitchen was ready to supply teas, cakes and biscuits. Around twenty people were expected to attend the meeting at which they would discuss organising ambulance instruction for the seamen. It seemed a good idea and the hope was that the meeting would start to put some meat on the bones of the idea.

Margaret certainly thought it was the right thing to do and that the more medically trained the fishermen could be then the better prepared they would be for any incident that might occur whilst at sea.

By half past seven everyone was at the Institute and seated. Margaret saw to it that everyone got a cup of tea and something to eat and then she sat and took notes while the meeting was run by the Councillor for the harbour area.

The meeting went well and Margaret was in high spirits as everyone left around nine o'clock. Her spirits rose even further when she noticed Jake standing at the front door when she saw the last of her guests out. She invited him in.

"What are you doing here?" she asked.

"I wasn't going to have you walking around this area on your own at this time of night," he replied.

"I'm surprised you even remembered the meeting was on tonight," Margaret then commented.

"I'm a policeman, Margaret, I'm paid to remember little details."

"Well thank you very much," she then added and they kissed.

Jake helped Margaret tidy up then after she had locked all the doors they began walking back along Regent's Quay. Margaret had her arm looped in Jake's and they walked as close that their bodies were passing warmth back and forth. The night was dry but very, very cold.

They went back to Margaret's flat and she put the kettle on. "Would you like a beer as well?" she asked.

"That would be lovely."

Once they were settled on the settee with their drinks Jake continued the conversation they had started earlier about how well the meeting had gone.

"You really care about the welfare of our fishermen, don't you?"

"I care about my job, Jake and that is to run a building where seamen can come for food, comfort and hopefully education. They have a hard life with a poor return financially and if I can help to give them even a little back then that is what I will do."

"So do you think there will be ambulance instruction for the seamen?" Jake then asked.

"It seemed to be generally and quite rightly agreed tonight that they should get instruction of that kind and that we should start it as soon as possible."

"Who will pay for it?" Jake then asked.

"As ever, that is the worrying question because you usually find that no one is prepared to finance something like this, no matter how beneficial everyone agrees it might be."

"I wish you well at any rate, Margaret," added Jake and he raised his beer in a toast to his lovely lady friend.

***

Although it was late Johnnie Gordon wanted to speak to Alice. She had been sewing in the front room when he had returned from the Business Club. He had spent the latter part of the day doing a lot of thinking and he was delighted to find Alice still up and awake when he arrived home.

He told Alice how he felt about her and how happy she made him feel. He told her that he already had Jake's blessing and that he wanted her to make him the happiest man on earth by accepting his proposal of marriage.

It took Johnnie a long time to say all that he wanted to say. It took Alice hardly a second to say yes and throw herself in to his arms. The kissed as passionately as they had ever done before and then sat down to start discussing the details of their wedding, which Johnnie hoped would be as soon as possible.

Alice felt an elation that seemed to fill her entire body. She had come to love Johnnie Gordon a lot and now that she was to be his wife she could hardly contain her excitement. However, unlike the Alice of old, she did not suggest going to bed. She now knew of other ways to thank a man other than offer him her body.

SIXTEEN

Saturday 17 November: late morning until midnight

Jake was at his desk reading the note that had been pinned to the dummy. The dummy itself had been retrieved later on Friday and was now lying in the corner or

Jake's office. There had been little to be gained from the clothes on the dummy and for now, Jake was paying more attention to the note.

The reference to God implied that the desire to keep the theatre closed was driven by religion. *This is your final warning - For the day of his calamity is near and the impending things are hastening upon him* read like something from the Bible, though Jake had no idea in which part of the Bible a quote like that might be found. For some reason this particular theatre was upsetting someone and insulting their religious beliefs. Jake thought about all the other theatres in Aberdeen and wondered how His Majesty's could be perceived as being any different.

After a few seconds Jake suddenly realised something that had been staring him in the face. The new theatre had been built next door to a church. Was that the reason for this person's anger? Did he see the building of a theatre next door to a church as being a direct slight on God? Did the answer lie, therefore, in the church next door to His Majesty's?

Jake was still pondering on those questions when Constable McGill came in to the room. "I was told you were looking for me, sir?"

"Yes, Constable, have a seat." McGill sat down and Jake continued. He told the young officer that he would be taking over the theatre investigation but only because it had now become something more sinister than mere mischief making. Jake asked McGill, however, to continue to work on the case with him.

"How religious are you, Constable?" Jake suddenly asked.

"Not very, sir," the Constable replied. "Why, do I need to be to continue with this case?"

Jake smiled and handed the note to McGill. "No you don't but I fear that whoever wishes ill of His Majesty's Theatre is deeply religious and that those beliefs could lead him to do anything. I think the catalyst for these recent threats is the fact that the theatre has been built next door to a church. Now with that in mind I feel we need to speak to someone connected to that church. Find out who the Minister is and where he lives."

"Do you want to see him today, sir?" McGill then asked.

"As soon as you have an address we'll go and see him," Jake replied. "It probably won't get us anywhere but at least it might be a place to start.

***

Mathieson had been given the job of gathering as much information as he could with regard to Gerald Strong. He had decided to begin with the friend who lived a few doors from where Strong's home had been. He had caught the Torry tram and was now getting off and heading up Victoria Road towards the address that he had been given.

Denis Arthur had opened the door and as soon as Mathieson had identified himself, Arthur had immediately become nervous and had looked both inside the house and then up and down the street, as if making absolutely sure that no one was watching.

He then told Mathieson that he would see him at the end of Sinclair Road and closed the door.

Half an hour later Mathieson found himself standing at the end of Sinclair Road with Denis Arthur. Arthur had lit a cigarette and was looking rather shifty as he pulled the collar of his coat up around his ears and looked around to ensure that no one was seeing him talking to what was obviously a police officer. Mathieson couldn't understand why Arthur was acting so strangely for, as far as he knew, Denis Arthur was not known to the police for any previous activities.

"Do you not like being seen with a police officer?" Mathieson asked.

Arthur sucked on the end of his cigarette and blew a cloud of smoke in to the air. "You just make me nervous, that's all."

"I just have a few questions then I'll be on my way."

"Good. Now, what do you want to ask?" Arthur then said.

"How well did you know Gerald Strong?"

Denis Arthur seemed to relax a little at the mention of Gerald Strong. It gave Mathieson the impression that Arthur was hiding something and yet he had no reason to suspect Denis Arthur of being involved in anything. He quickly concluded that Arthur was just one of those naturally nervous individuals.

"As well as anyone I suppose. We'd been mates since primary school," Denis Arthur replied.

"Were you surprised to read that he had committed suicide?"

"I was more surprised to read that he was connected to the death of some French woman. I can't imagine Gerry killing anyone, he was such a mild-mannered character."

"Did he ever mention the fact he was seeing a French woman?" Mathieson then asked.

"I know he was seeing someone but he never said she was French. Gerry liked to be with the ladies so he never hid the fact that he was working on a relationship with one. He did speak about the fact there was someone in his life but he never told me any more than that."

"Have you ever heard of Mathilde Dupont?"

"Not until I read her name in the paper."

"Did Gerald Strong have any other close friends that you know of?"

Arthur thought for a moment. "No one as close as I was. Gerry liked the ladies but he had few friends really. To be honest I'm sure that a lot of the ladies only existed in his head."

"So there maybe wasn't someone in his life when he died?" Mathieson suggested.

"No, I believe the current lady did exist. Gerry let me smell his scarf one day and it positively reeked of perfume."

"Where would he have gone with a lady friend?"

"I really don't know. There aren't that many options when you only know a girl fleetingly. I suppose he may have called at her home or they may have gone out for a meal."

Mathieson already knew that Gerald Strong had been seen calling on Mathilde Dupont. That being the case it seemed obvious that the woman in his life only existed because he paid for her company. After all he had been in the company of a prostitute the night he had killed himself.

"Was Gerald Strong in the habit of paying for sex?" Mathieson then asked.

"What kind of question is that?" Arthur replied. "I suppose a lot of men pay for sex so no doubt Gerry was no different. This Mathilde Dupont was never a whore was she?"

Arthur sucked on the last of his cigarette and then squashed the stub underfoot. Mathieson did not answer the question though his silence probably did. Mathieson felt that he had possibly asked enough and that he was unlikely to get anything very meaningful from Denis Arthur. However he did try one final avenue.

"What did Gerald Strong do for a living?"

Arthur lit another cigarette. "Gerry made his money in various ways but I never knew any of them. If I asked where he had got a bundle of notes from then he would just tap the side of his nose and tell me not to ask. He seemed to know people who could give him little jobs in return for cash."

"Legal jobs?"

"I'm guessing not always. Some days I would see him with a lot of money in his wallet and then other days he'd be asking me for a loan as he couldn't even afford a packet of cigarettes."

"Did you ever hear Gerald Strong talking about Willie Ifield?" Mathieson then asked.

Arthur shook his head. "I know who Mr Ifield is and I can tell you with some confidence that Gerry never mentioned him, certainly not in my company."

"Very good, Mr Arthur, thank you for your time."

Mathieson made his way back on Victoria Road and waited at the stop for the tram back in to the city centre.

Denis Arthur, however, had other matters on his mind. He hadn't been strictly truthful with the police officer for he now saw an opportunity to make some money for himself. He had seen a whole lot more than he was ever going to tell the police. He had information that other people would not like the police to hear. It was just a matter of how much they would be prepared to maintain his silence.

Arthur was singing to himself as he made his way back to the house. After a spot of lunch he would pay a visit to someone whom he hoped would be generous towards him; after all what he knew could no doubt destroy what must have been carefully made plans.

***

As Mathieson was making his way back in to the city centre Jake and McGill were walking along Westfield Terrace towards the address of the current Minister of the South United Church. The houses were substantial buildings and of the style that Jake would have quite liked himself. Westfield Terrace itself was nice and secluded offering a degree of peace and quiet to its inhabitants.

They reached the desired building and Jake knocked on the door. It was quickly opened by a young maid who looked to be no more than fourteen or fifteen years of age. She confidently showed the police in to a front room and then went to get the Minister.

A few minutes later the Reverend MacKintosh-MacKay walked in to the room. He was a man in his early forties, with short, slightly wavy hair and a full and heavy moustache. He offered a handshake to both officers and then asked what he might do for them.

Jake explained why they were there and the Reverend quickly suggested that it might be better if the police inquiry moved on to the Church Officer.

"My dealings with the church and its congregation are very much on a spiritual level, Inspector. I know the people who attend my church on a level of helping them through problems in their lives or through enhancing their understanding of the power that God holds over us all. When it comes to the more daily routine at the church then I leave that very much up to Mr Shewan. He organises voluntary help for example and might know more about the character of my congregation than I would."

"I believe the person we are seeking, Mr MacKintosh-MacKay, may now have a slightly misshapen view of religion in the sense that he clearly see it as a gross offence to the Lord that anyone would build a theatre next to a church. If that individual is a member of your congregation then there would surely be a strong chance that he would want to talk to you about such matters?"

"This would appear to be a man who has lost his way with the Lord in a very specific manner. Given that he sees the building of the theatre as such a gross insult to God then it could well be the case that he would see me as perhaps being complicit in the act by not doing enough to stop it happening. He may view me as letting him down and if that were the case he would not be speaking to me."

Jake could see that there was some sense in what the Reverend had said and took a note of the address of the Church Officer, Alastair Shewan. Jake then thanked the Reverend for his time and they left.

Alastair Shewan's house was on Skene Street, which meant that Jake and McGill could call in on their way back to Lodge Walk as they were almost passing anyway. The visit was not productive, however, as Mrs Shewan was only able to tell them that her husband was at work. Jake said that they would not bother him there and that they would try to see him during the church service the following day.

***

Jake caught up with Mathieson to find out what he had learned from Denis Arthur. It had not amounted to much. Gerald Strong's part in the investigation still remained unclear. Jake actually achieved little more as the afternoon got underway and he left work around three o'clock to go home and get ready for his night out with Margaret.

***

Denis Arthur had followed Gerry Strong on more than one occasion. Having nothing better to do with his own life he had taken an interest in the fact that Gerry finally seemed to have a woman in his life. Denis was keen to see what she looked like as, at least from the smell of her perfume, it seemed she might be quite high class.

Denis had never been with a woman in his entire life; not even a prostitute. He thought a lot about women and what it might be like to have sexual relations with one but it had never even come close to happening. Denis rarely came in to contact with women and when he did there was never any opportunity for him to engage in conversation that might lead to a relationship.

Denis had seen Gerry with two women recently. He now knew that the woman who lived in Park Street had to be Mathilde Dupont and he also knew that she was a prostitute and presumably Gerry was paying her for her company.

That meant the other woman, the one he had seen coming out of the Bon Accord Hotel on the night Gerry had died, had to be of more interest for the police had not mentioned her. Maybe they didn't know about her and maybe she might want things to stay that way.

He wondered how much she might pay for his silence and also whether he might be able to persuade her to do other things for him by way of payment. He had smiled to himself at the thought of lying between clean sheets with a beautiful woman intent on meeting his every desire. He got quite excited at the thought and he was actually whistling as he left home and set off to where he knew the woman lived.

Denis was distraught to be told by the neighbours that the woman had moved and that they had no idea what her new address might be. He stood outside her old building and lit a cigarette. He thought for a moment and then he remembered the man he had seen with the woman on the night Gerry had died.

Denis made his way to where he knew the man worked and waited outside the building until he came out.

***

It was two hours later when the man he had been waiting for came out of the building. He started to walk along the pavement and Denis followed him on the opposite side of the road.

The man caught the Torry tram back in to the centre of the city and Denis sat two seats behind him. Once they reached Bridge Street they both got off and the man started walking along Union Terrace.

Denis lit another cigarette as he followed a few steps behind. Forty-five minutes later the man was letting himself in to what Denis assumed was his own house. He closed the door and Denis sat on a wall opposite and smoked yet another cigarette.

He gave some thought as to what he might do next. Eventually he decided to cross the road and knock on the door of the house he had just seen the man go in to. He would tell him what he knew and also what he would do with the information if he was not paid handsomely.

He felt sure that this was going to be his ticket to a better life. He threw away the cigarette butt and started to cross the road.

***

Jake collected Margaret at a little after five. They went to the Palace Hotel for High Tea prior to going to the Palace Theatre for an evening's entertainment. The Palace Hotel was very busy and Jake presumed that other people had had much the same idea with regard to having a pre-theatre meal.

Margaret was looking as beautiful as ever. Beneath her coat she wore a purple dress and she had tied her hair up prior to placing a matching hat on her head. Jake had dressed in his Sunday best suit and had also chosen to wear a hat. They looked very good together and exuded an air of happiness as they sat down and prepared to eat some food.

Having completed their meal they then retrieved their coats from the cloakroom and made their way outside in to the cold, damp night. Fortunately the journey round to the theatre was a short one and they were soon leaving their coats at the cloakroom of the theatre before going through to take their seats.

The Palace Theatre was a busy place and Jake felt sure that they would be sitting in yet another full house. The people of Aberdeen liked their entertainment. Theatres were well attended and there seemed no reason why His Majesty's would not be the same when it opened.

The seats filled and the lights dimmed. The evening's entertainment got underway with Spry and Monti coming on stage and telling some jokes. Laughter filled the air and everyone settled down to a good night.

At the interval Jake and Margaret went in to the foyer for a bit of exercise. It was already busy with men standing at the door smoking and women milling around chatting to each other.

"Mr Fraser, how good to see you again," a voice announced from Jake's left.

Jake turned to see Robert Wallace moving towards him.

"Mr Wallace," was all that Jake said as the two men shook hands.

"And your lovely companion is....?" Wallace then said turning his attention to Margaret.

Jake introduced Margaret and Robert Wallace introduced his wife, Dora. Jake noted that it took Wallace longer than may have been appropriate to release Margaret's hand.

"Enjoying the show so far?" Wallace then said.

"It has been highly entertaining," Jake replied.

"Have you decided if you are coming tomorrow night?" Wallace asked.

"I have quite a busy day tomorrow but I will come along if I can," Jake answered.

"Excellent. Well I'll see you then. Lovely to meet you Margaret."

Robert and Dora Wallace made their way off back through the crowd. Margaret turned to Jake.

"However did you come to know Robert Wallace?"

"Through work."

"You do know he has some rather strange views?"

"Politically, perhaps, but he seems an interesting man none the less."

"What is happening tomorrow?" Margaret asked.

"Mr Wallace is speaking at a hall on Leadside Road. He asked me to go along and I think I will."

"I'm not sure that the Chief Constable would be happy to have you in the company of a man who I have heard speaks of anarchy and revolution."

Jake smiled. "As I said my contact with Mr Wallace was work related so I am sure the Chief won't mind if I take a personal interest in what the man has to say."

"How intriguing," Margaret commented as they turned to make their way back in to the theatre.

***

Denis Arthur was making his way through to catch the tram. He was happy. The meeting had gone better than he could ever have hoped. The man seemed worried that Denis knew as much as he did and seemed keen to keep Denis quiet. He had promised a lot of money but had told Denis that he did not have that kind of money at home. He further explained that he could get the money from his work and they arranged to meet the following evening. Denis was happy to give the man a little time to gather the kind of money that he had never imagined he would ever see in his lifetime.

He waited at the stop on Fountainhall Road for the tram and as he did so he lit another cigarette and began to think of all the ways that he might spend his new found fortune. Not surprisingly the first thought that sprang to mind was that he might now be able to afford the company of a pretty woman. Maybe, at long last, Denis Arthur would lose his virginity and he only had to wait twenty-four hours or so for his life to change forever.

***

The second half of the show had an even greater excitement attached to it as each act pulled the audience ever closer to the moment when the great man, Harry Lauder, would walk on stage and entertain them. When the moment arrived there was a roar of approval as he walked out to the centre of the stage and began singing. He had been doing this for nearly two weeks at that theatre and every night it seemed the roar got louder.

His time on stage seemed all too short for the audience. He sang and joked his way to the end when he stood and took his bow. The applause seemed never-ending and the crowd bellowed for more. Eventually a well-dressed man appeared from the wings and made his way across to Harry Lauder who was, by then, dressed as a sailor in preparation for his song "We Parted On The Shore."

Mr Lauder stopped and turned to watch the other man approach. It was clear to the audience that he had no idea what was to come next. The approaching man turned out to be the manager of the theatre and he was carrying a handsome, leather dressing case. He stopped centre stage and urged the audience to sit down and to quieten while he said a few words.

He began to offer his thanks to Harry Lauder for bringing such joy to the city though much of what he said was lost to a neighing sound that seemed to be coming from backstage somewhere. The audience laughed every time the sound was heard and the manager was having trouble concentrating on what he wished to say. Eventually he handed the case over to Harry Lauder who accepted it with a nod of his head. The manager then went offstage a moment before returning with the source of the neighing.

Mr Lauder was also then presented with a shaggy, little pony. In his speech of thanks for both the gifts and the wonderful reception he had received from the audience that had attended every night of the show, Mr Lauder did make it known that he had no idea what he was going to do with the pony. There was even more laughter when he announced that. Having accepted his gifts and then having those gifts either carried or led offstage, Harry Lauder returned to what he knew best; entertaining an audience. By the time he was finished and he and all the other entertainers had taken their last bows the auditorium was in turmoil with more clapping and cheering and a general clamour for just one more encore.

However, it did not come and the audience had nothing more to do than leave in an orderly manner and head for home.

Margaret gripped Jake's arm as they made their way up Bridge Street and onwards along Union Terrace. Margaret was still grinning with joy. She kept thanking Jake for getting the tickets though he did explain, once again, that it had been sheer good fortune.

"What an entertainer," Margaret was still saying as they arrived back at her flat. "I honestly never thought that I would ever get the chance to see him."

"Me neither," added Jake as they took their coats off and Margaret went to put the kettle on. Jake made himself comfortable in the front room and waited for her return. His mind wandered back to Robert Wallace. He seemed such a personable individual and it was hard to imagine how unpopular he had made himself with his rather radical political views.

Politics had not been of any great interest to Jake throughout his life. His father had been a staunch Liberal and Jake assumed that he had had Liberal values instilled in him, though he had never looked at himself as being either formed or driven by any particular political belief. As far as Jake was concerned politics was like religion; if you wanted to get involved then fine but otherwise leave it alone.

Robert Wallace was that most dangerous of political animals, the ones who sought change. Not only did he seek change he sought radical change. He wanted the world of politics thrown up in the air and have the pieces fall in a totally different manner, changing the shape of British politics forever.

Jake thought that it would be very interesting to hear what Wallace had to say the following night. But until then there was the finale to a lovely evening with Margaret and then another day at work to get through.

At that moment Margaret came in to the room with some tea and home baking. For Jake the night just continued to get better and better by the minute.

***

At the very moment that Jake was having a cup of tea poured for him a woman was coming out of the property recently visited by Denis Arthur. She had gone there for some casual sex with her new lover but had come away worried that all their plans could be up in the air because of some misguided friend of Gerald Strong's.

She was content that her lover had dealt with the situation well and now that he had asked her to take care of Mr Arthur, she could begin planning how exactly she would get rid of him. Denis Arthur was to be met outside the Forsyth Hotel on Union Street at seven o'clock on Sunday evening.

The woman now knew that she would turn up for that appointment. She would suggest that she be part of the payment for Arthur's silence. She knew she was beautiful and that no man could resist such an offer.

Once she had him in the hotel room then she would be able to deal with him in much the same way as she had done with Gerald Strong. It really would be that simple. As she made her way back to her house she was smiling. She was not just smiling, she was feeling a happiness inside that she had not felt since the night she had killed Gerald Strong. She was beginning to now realise that killing made her feel happier than anything else that she did in her life.

SEVENTEEN

Sunday 18 November: mid-morning until late

Jake had been very late in leaving Margaret's and had not got a great deal of sleep before having to be up and on his way to work. He had spent a little time at the office before he and McGill made their way up to the church where they were hoping to see Mr Shewan.

They timed their arrival to fit in with the church emptying and it was the Reverend who introduced Jake to Alastair Shewan. Shewan then suggested that they went through to a room at the back of the church where all three men could sit down and be a little more comfortable.

Shewan was a small man with shrew like features including a rather tame looking moustache which, if trying to match the magnificent growth on the Reverend's face, had failed miserably.

Jake explained what had been happening, though he did not provide all the details; after all, Shewan could well have been the man they were after.

"And you think someone at this church would do something like that?" Shewan then asked, with some disbelief, after Jake had finished talking about the attempts to disrupt the work next door.

"It is certainly someone who views the building of the theatre next to a church as some form of sin. I assume, therefore, that it is someone with deep rooted beliefs. Now I am sure many of the congregation at this church would claim to have deep rooted religious beliefs but is there anyone in particular that you can think of who might be of a mind to take things to extremes?"

Shewan thought for a moment. "We have many people who come here who might be offended by the fact that a theatre had been built next door to the church but I honestly cannot think of anyone who would be moved to violence over it."

"Do you have many people who work here during the week?" Jake then asked.

"We have a group of volunteers who help keep the church clean and who greet visitors, should any arrive."

"How large a group?"

"Fifteen to twenty possibly."

"Do they work to any particular pattern?"

Shewan shook his head. "No, they come in when they can. They tend to arrange things amongst themselves as we only have a limited number of keys and they need to pass them on once a shift has been agreed."

"Do they meet formally, maybe on a day such as this?" Jake then enquired.

"Nothing formal I'm afraid, Inspector. We are grateful for the work that they do and the arrangement has worked fine up until now."

"Would you mind giving me a list of the names of your volunteers?"

"I shouldn't think that that will be a problem," Shewan replied. "I will need to write it from memory so I only hope that I remember everyone."

Shewan went off to write his list and Jake went out in to the main area of the church. Everyone else had gone by that time apart from a young couple who were still hovering at the door. Jake got in to conversation with them and they explained that they were waiting to see the Reverend so that they could arrange their wedding ceremony. They looked to be so much in love.

"Do you have a problem with the theatre being built next to the church?" Jake had then asked.

"Not at all," the young man replied.

"What a strange question to ask," added the young woman.

Jake smiled. "Perhaps. I just wondered if putting a source of entertainment next to a source of religious education was such a good idea."

"There must be all kinds of buildings sitting next to churches around the land," the young man then said," and I hardly think anyone gives it a second thought."

I'm trying to find someone who does, thought Jake. He thanked the young couple for their time and wished them well in their life ahead. By the time he returned to the room at the back Alastair Shewan was back with his written list of volunteers. Jake took the list from him and counted the number of names written upon it. There were eighteen; twelve men and six women.

Jake thought it safe to discount the women as there seemed no way that the activities within the theatre had been carried out by a woman. She would have been more easily noticed in that world of males for one thing. That left him with twelve names to follow-up on. However, there was still a very real possibility that the person he was looking for had nothing to do with The South United Church whatsoever, in which case all this work would be a complete waste of time.

***

He had seen the men talking to Shewan and knew at once that they were police officers. They had to be investigating what he had been doing in the theatre; that meant they were getting closer to him. In a sense it made all that he was doing even more exciting. After all, he was doing the work of the Lord and each day he could feel the presence of the Lord within him. The fact he was getting pleasure from doing these things confirmed, in his own mind, that the Lord must have wanted him to continue.

He had gone home after the service and sat at the window with his bible. He had read passages to himself and thought over what he now needed to do by way of killing Robert Wallace. Getting the knife would be the easy part; getting close enough to Wallace might be slightly more difficult.

The more he thought about things the more he realised that he knew very little about Robert Wallace other than where he worked and the fact he had radical political views that were destined to destroy the very fabric of what made Aberdeen the city that it was. In killing Wallace he would not only make a statement with regard to insulting the Lord but he would also rid Aberdeen of a man who could damage the political stability forever.

It still bothered him that the theatre had been built next door to his church. The church had been there first. It had stood on that site, unbothered apart from the building of the library, for over sixty years. He had been a part of that church for the last ten years. Why did anyone need to change that?

His mind then turned to the fact that the police were now asking questions. If they had spoken to Shewan then they probably had the names of the volunteers by now. That being the case they had his name and that would mean the inevitable visit. He took strength from God at that moment and felt a confidence inside. He knew that he could speak to the police; he could answer their questions and yet they would never connect him to the events that had happened in the theatre.

More importantly they could never connect him to Robert Wallace.

***

Denis Arthur got to the hotel early. He waited outside for the man to appear with his money and smoked three cigarettes before he was eventually approached by a woman. She was practically standing beside him before he recognised her as the same woman that had been with Gerald. She looked even more beautiful close-up.

"I believe you have an arrangement with a mutual friend of ours over some money?" the woman asked.

Denis Arthur looked at the woman with a lust that she noticed immediately. "Have you brought the money?" he then said.

The woman held up her bag. "Yes I have and to ensure that you keep your mouth shut I am prepared to spend a little time with you, if you get my meaning?"

Denis Arthur did not need any further explanation for her last comment. He looked down the length of her body and back up again.

"I get your meaning. Where do you want to go?" he then asked.

"Why don't you go in here and book a room. Then you come out and tell me the number of that room. I will give it a few moments and come up and see you. Then we can have some fun."

Denis Arthur was positively salivating at the thought of being able to touch this woman let alone probably make love to her. He hurried inside and walked up to the reception desk. A moment or two later he was back outside telling the woman the number to the room that he had booked. He then went back inside again.

The woman allowed nearly ten minutes to pass before she went in to the hotel and walked up to the reception desk. She booked another room and gave them a fictitious name. She paid for the room in cash and after collecting the key went upstairs.

Once in the room she closed and locked the door. She then went to the bed and laid her bag down. She opened the bag and took out a change of clothing, which amounted to little more than expensive underwear. She then started to remove her clothes.

Fifteen minutes later there was a knock on the door of the room in which Denis Arthur had been sitting smoking and beginning to think that the woman was not coming. He hurried to the door and opened it. The woman was standing in the hall still wearing the hat and coat she had been wearing down in the street.

Denis stepped back and the woman entered. She walked to the far side of the room and then spun to face Denis as he closed the door. By the time he had taken two steps towards her, the woman had taken her hat off and undone the buttons on her coat, letting it slip to the floor. She wore nothing underneath but her underwear. Her breasts showed through a thin chemise and Denis could not wait to cross the remainder of the room and to start enjoying her body.

The woman managed to evade Denis's first rather frantic attempts to grab her and she made her way to the bed and sat down. Denis followed her and started to run his hands over her body. Slowly he then pulled the straps of her chemise down and moved his lips towards her breasts.

Five minutes later Denis Arthur was dead.

The woman had then placed a glass on the floor and then casually put on her coat and hat and left the room, making sure that no one saw her. She went back to the room that she had booked and closed the door. She turned the lock and then went to the bed again where she took off all her clothes and moved over to the wash basin.

Having thoroughly washed herself she then dried off the last of the water and put her clothes back on again. She sat on the bed and looked at her own reflection in the dressing table mirror. Another successful day and another loose end removed.

She felt pleased with herself. She wished that her lover could now come through the door and make love to her with a passion that would set her every nerve-ending tingling. She knew that was not going to happen and that there was nothing further to do other than to wait a little while and then slip out of the hotel whilst again making sure that no one saw her.

***

Jake arrived at the hall on Leadside Road at a little before eight. There were seats laid out for around fifty people but there were only around ten already there when Jake arrived. Robert Wallace was there and hurried over the moment Jake walked through the door.

"So glad that you could come," he said and once more shook Jake's hand.

"Classified as official business," Jake said. "I just thought that the person threatening you might choose to come to your public events. If it's all right with you I'll keep more of an eye on those who turn up than on you."

Wallace laughed. "You just have to listen, Mr Fraser, you don't need to look."

The event got underway a little late and there was still only a few men in the hall. Robert Wallace stood up at the lectern and started to speak.

"Thank you for coming here tonight. I know it takes far more courage than should be the case to come here tonight and listen to someone like me. To listen to someone who does not say the same things as other budding politicians; to listen to someone who has no party line to follow. What I have to say is from the heart. What I have to say is born from an upbringing that did not mean poverty for me but did mean that to survive my father had to work long and hard. My father worked all his life and made enough to allow his family to eat and be clothed. We had a nice house and generally a decent living. It was okay, but it could have been better.

Gentlemen, let us briefly take a look at the men who currently represent this city and then perhaps you can tell me if they are really the right people to be arguing our case at Westminster. James Bryce, Member of Parliament for Aberdeen South, has been an MP for this city since 1885. He was born in Belfast and he is currently the Chief Secretary for Ireland. Do you not detect, gentlemen, a great deal of Irish connection to our illustrious MP but very little interest in anything Scottish, let alone in Aberdeen itself? Here is a man who is using Aberdeen merely as an excuse to be an MP so that he can then continue with what amounts to nothing more than personal ambitions. He cares little for the people of Aberdeen and he cares even less for the future of Aberdeen.

I cannot say much more, gentlemen, but I have been recently led to believe that James Bryce is, in the not too distant future, going to be offered a post that will take him out of the country and lead to a by-election being held in his constituency. This by-election will be required to take place within the next six months if my source is accurate in the information provided to me. I am of a mind, gentlemen, to offer myself for election if and when Mr Bryce moves on. I believe that I can bring a local knowledge to local politics and I believe that I can represent the people of Aberdeen a lot better than some distant Irishman.

I will return to my own ambitions in a moment but let me first turn to Aberdeen North. Here we find Duncan Pirie, an MP in Aberdeen for the last ten years. The man is a soldier, gentlemen, not an MP. The man needs to be on a battlefield but not a political one, he needs a gun in his hand and men around him to follow his every order. He at least is Scottish though he lives and moves in circles that take him well above the needs of the people of Aberdeen. Again, gentlemen, we find that the upper class always want to rule those beneath them.

The upper class really do see themselves as better than everyone else. Not for one moment would they accept that anyone, from a class below them, could possibly take on the role of MP. I am here to prove them wrong. I believe that I can find the money that will allow me to be an MP; that will allow me to take my place at Westminster and to truly speak for the needs of Aberdeen.

Some say that I have dangerous political beliefs and that I advocate revolution. This is not true, gentlemen, for all that I advocate is that every man should be given a fair chance to make a life for himself. It should not be down to how you are born it should simply be a fact of life; we should all be equal.

There is already the beginnings of a new future. There are some good men in both the Social Democratic Federation and the Independent Labour Party, but these men spend more time arguing amongst themselves than actually taking their case to the electorate. I am more inclined to follow the line taken by Keir Hardie and his Labour Party. I see that as being our future; a future in which working men will see only good coming from membership of a Trade Union and where MPs will finally come from working stock themselves.

We need to break away from the constant procession of well-to-do men who see politics as nothing more than a bit of fun. They view it as something to dabble in as they go about their normal lives. They do not view politics as I do, gentlemen. They do not see that the whole future of this country will be shaped by men like me and not aristocrats who appear to have been blessed with more money than sense.

As I said earlier, gentlemen, I believe the time is right for me to put my name forward if there is to be a by-election in this city sometime soon. I hope that if I do I can count on some of you to vote for me and to help me change the political face of Aberdeen forever. Thank you for coming here tonight and a safe journey home to you all."

Robert Wallace came down from the lectern and there was ripple of polite applause from the small number in the hall. Jake had listened to every word but had kept his eyes on the men who were seated around the hall. They, too, seemed intent on hearing what Wallace had to say and it did not look, to Jake, as if any of them were there with malice in their hearts.

Most of the men started to drift out of the hall. Jake made his way to the front where Wallace turned to face him with a smile.

"Well, Inspector, do you still think I'm an anarchist who seeks revolution with every breath of his body?"

"I believe you might be an idealist," Jake commented.

"There is no crime in hoping for a better future for all. I just want to see the working men of this country have more say in the running of the country. We need to take the power away from the rich."

"Now that sounds anarchic," Jake added and Wallace smiled.

"It is more to do with the philosophy of Karl Marx than anything else, Inspector. I do not wish to bring down the monarchy, nor do I wish to do away with the upper classes. I merely want a better distribution of wealth and influence."

"An honourable intention, Mr Wallace but clearly one that has upset at least one individual in Aberdeen. I don't suppose you would reconsider your decision to go to the opening night of the theatre?"

"A valiant try, Inspector, but there is absolutely no chance of me changing my mind. I have always stood by my beliefs and I have no intention of stopping that now. If the individual who had threatened my life really does want to harm me in some way then they will simply wait for another chance should I not attend the theatre."

"I think the threat on your life had more to do with the theatre than it has with you personally, Mr Wallace. I believe this to be a one-off threat and should you not attend the theatre then I am sure that the threat will go away."

Wallace looked intrigued. "You mean someone is using the threat on my life to try and stop the theatre from opening?"

"That may well be the case," agreed Jake, "so you see it would make a difference if you would just stay away on the opening night."

"But the theatre can't postpone the opening," Wallace then said. "Everything has been arranged and there is a performance of a pantomime to be watched. Even if I didn't turn up the theatre would still open and the show would still go on."

"I'm sure you are correct in that assessment, Mr Wallace but the fact still remains that if you turn up on the opening night of the theatre it may well be remembered in history as the night you were killed rather than the night a pantomime started."

Jake shook Wallace's hand again and thanked him for an interesting evening. Just as he turned to go Robert Wallace spoke again.

"Look, Dora and I are having a few friends and acquaintances over to the house next Saturday evening. I would be delighted if you and your lady-friend, Margaret, would grace us with your company?"

"But I hardly know you, Mr Wallace?" Jake said.

"Perhaps not, but I feel that you are someone that I should like to know better. Please say that you will come?"

Jake assumed that Margaret would be happy to go with him so he eventually accepted. Wallace provided both an address and a time for Jake and Margaret to arrive. Jake then left the building and made his way around the corner and up Esslemont Avenue.

EIGHTEEN

Monday 19 November: Morning until mid-evening.

Jake and Sergeant Mathieson were in room twenty of the Forsyth Hotel on Union Street. They were looking down at the clothed body of a man lying at a diagonal across the bed, his arm outstretched in much the same way as Gerald Strong's had been. There was also another glass lying on the floor.

"This is Denis Arthur," Mathieson said as he looked a little closer at the body.

"One suicide in a hotel room I can just about accept," Jake added, "but two is just pushing your luck."

"Do you think this is murder?"

"I really don't know, but you have to admit it seems highly unlikely that Denis Arthur would choose to end it all in exactly the same way as Gerald Strong, particularly as there was no way that he could have known the details of Strong's death. Only one person might know that and that is the mystery woman who was with Strong on the night he died."

Doctor Symon came in to the room at that moment. He gave the body a cursory inspection and then declared the same outcome as that of Gerald Strong.

"Suicide again, Jake."

"Could it be murder, Doctor?" Jake then asked.

"There were no signs of bruising on Gerald Strong, which might have indicated a struggle or the fact that someone held him down whilst the poison was administered. On first glance I can't see any signs of bruising here either. I'd say both men died in the same way."

"I don't disagree that both men died in the same way, Doctor, I'm just finding it hard to believe that both men died by suicide."

"I'll check this glass for sign of any poisons," Doctor Symon then said as he picked the glass up from the floor. "To be honest I'm not at all sure how you would get someone to take poison without them knowing about it."

"In a drink I presume?" suggested Jake.

"Symon smelled the glass. "It looks like there was nothing but water in this glass. Any poison would have been evident to him had he not intended drinking it."

"Maybe," added Jake, showing signs of not believing what the evidence was telling him. "The fact is that this man spoke to Sergeant Mathieson on Saturday morning about his friendship with Gerald Strong. The day after he decides to book in to a hotel and kill himself. It just doesn't make any sense."

Doctor Symon smiled. "I'm not here to help you make sense of everything, Jake, I'm just here to offer my medical opinion based on the evidence presented to me. Within those confines I still say that this is suicide though as to why this young man would choose to end his life is something that you alone will need to identify."

"Thank you, Doctor. We'll get the body to you as quickly as possible so that you can have a proper look at him."

Doctor Symon left the room and Mathieson went away to organise the removal of the body to Lodge Walk. Jake went downstairs to talk to some of the staff of the hotel. He did not learn very much.

Arthur had booked a room and then gone and stood outside the hotel for a while. No one saw him speak to anyone while he was outside. He had then come in to the hotel and gone straight up to his room. No one saw Denis Arthur again until the maid had found his body when she entered the room to clean it that morning.

"Was he alone all the time?" Jake asked of the young man who had been on the reception desk most of Sunday.

"I didn't see him with anyone else."

"Did you see a woman hanging around the outside of the building?"

"I didn't see anyone."

"Did a woman book a room around the same time as Denis Arthur?"

The man from reception thought for a moment. "As a matter of fact a woman did book a room a few minutes after Mr Arthur, but I had no reason to believe that they were connected in any way."

"Maybe they weren't connected. Can you describe this woman?"

"Very pretty. Dark hair."

"Anything more than you can tell me about her?" Jake prompted.

"Not really. I just noticed she was very pretty."

"Is the woman still booked in to the hotel?"

"She had gone by this morning; the room was empty when the maid called around half past eight."

"Did anyone see her leave?" Jake then asked.

"I certainly didn't, but I can't speak for all the staff."

"So she could have left almost as soon as she arrived?" Jake suggested.

"She could have done, but why would anyone book a room and then not stay in it?"

"Why indeed?" Jake replied. "Why do you think Mr Arthur booked a room in your hotel?"

"I really don't know, Inspector."

"Perhaps Mr Arthur had arranged to meet a young lady?" Jake then said.

The reception clerk looked horrified. "Surely not, Inspector. Not on the Sabbath."

"You would be surprised what some people do on the Sabbath," Jake added. "Could I please have the key for the room, which the young woman occupied?"

The clerk took the relevant key off the row of hooks behind him and gave it to Jake. Jake then thanked the clerk for his help and went back up to the room where Mathieson was still waiting for the ambulance to arrive and take the body away.

"Any luck with reception?" Mathieson asked.

"Not a thing," said Jake. "It appears that Denis Arthur arrived himself and came up here himself. However, a woman did book another room a few minutes after Arthur. It could be our mystery woman again?"

"There can't be a woman wandering around Aberdeen forcing men to kill themselves," Mathieson said. "How would she ever get them to do that?"

"If it is the work of this mystery woman then she has managed to get two men to take poison it would appear of their own free will. I agree, Sergeant, that that does seem rather strange to say the least."

The frustration of this case was beginning to show both on Jake's face and also in his tone. He had to be missing something and yet the evidence did not seem to suggest that.

"There is something not right about all this but I just can't think what it is," Jake then said. "Anyway, would you stay here until they take the body away. I'm going to have a look at the room in which, I believe, our mystery woman waited either side of killing Denis Arthur."

Jake made his way to the room and let himself in. The maid had already visited so there was little chance of any clues being left. However, Jake chose to sit on the bed and look around for a few moments. Whoever this woman was she was utterly calm and in complete control when she felt the need to kill. Clearly the act of killing someone did not upset her in any way. Perhaps she even gained some enjoyment from killing another person, or perhaps it was simply a means to an end? These men had been an inconvenience that had to be removed; nothing more.

As he expected, there was nothing to be learned from sitting in the room. The fact that she had booked another room had shown an element of forward planning and the fact that she had managed to leave again without anyone noticing had confirmed her desire not to be seen and therefore, not remembered.

This woman was good at what she did. Jake began to wonder if he would ever catch her. He got up from the bed and walked to the door. With one last look around the room he opened the door and left the room. He locked the door and returned the key to the reception point.

He then left the hotel.

***

Jake caught the Torry tram and went to visit Denis Arthur's mother. He wanted to tell her personally what had happened to her son and he also hoped that he might get the chance to look around the Arthur home. It was highly unlikely that he would find anything of any use but he felt it was at least worth a try.

Mrs Arthur cried briefly on hearing what had happened to her son. She then wiped away her tears and offered Jake a cup of tea, which he accepted. Mrs Arthur reminded him of his own mother with her greying hair tied up in a bun and her countenance being of such a friendly nature. It upset him greatly to be the bearer of such bad news.

When they were once more seated with a cup of tea and a biscuit, Jake started to ask Mrs Arthur some slightly more specific questions about her son.

"Was Denis a close friend to Gerald Strong?"

"Not that close of late. They were very good friends through school but as the years passed after that they started to drift apart a little."

"Did Denis have other friends?"

"Not really, he was always was a boy who liked his own company."

"Any lady friends?" Jake then asked.

"Oh no, my Denis never was one for the ladies. I don't think he had the self-confidence to be around women, after all, apart from me, there were no women in his life."

"Did Denis ever speak about Gerald Strong?"

"He mentioned him at times but then Denis never said much about anything really."

"What did Denis do for work?"

"He did a bit of labouring on the building sites. He wasn't the brightest lad so work had to be at a pretty basic level. He was more brawn than brain, if you understand me?"

Jake nodded. "Would you mind if I had a look in Denis's bedroom, just in case there are any clues as so why he would now choose to take his own life?"

"Not at all, go right ahead."

Jake put his cup down and followed Mrs Arthur through to her son's bedroom. She then turned and left again, leaving Jake to have a look around at his leisure. The room was quite small with very little in it. There were no books or any other form of entertainment. The tops of all the surfaces were polished within an inch of their lives and Jake could only assume that Mrs Arthur was the house-proud one as it seemed inconceivable that a man of Denis's age would care much about keeping any room clean.

Jake looked in some of the drawers and saw neatly folded clothes and everything in its place. He had maybe been wrong about Denis not wanting the room spotless. In the bedside cabinet he found a small book. Jake took it out and opened it. It wasn't exactly a diary but it did seem to include scribbled notes that had presumably been written by Denis.

Jake sat on the edge of the bed and flipped through the book. There were references to Gerald Strong and Jake detected a hint of envy in the writing as Denis referred to Gerald have a lady in his life. It was also obvious from what had been written that Denis had been watching Gerald. He must have followed him on more than one occasion if the notes were to be believed.

Jake thought for a moment. It was even more evident to him now that Denis had known something about Gerald that he had not bothered to tell Sergeant Mathieson. Denis had then probably tried to exhort money from someone, no doubt threatening to go to the police in the process. Rather than give him money someone had either killed him, or arranged for him to be killed.

The fact that Denis had booked the hotel room rather implied that he thought he was in control of the situation. He had arranged to meet someone, but why? Surely if he needed money from them then there was no need to go to a hotel room to either discuss the subject or to exchange money.

Gerald Strong had booked a room because he was with a woman. He obviously thought that in booking the room he would have sex with the woman. After all, wasn't that the main reason why strangers booked hotel rooms? Did that then mean that Denis Arthur was expecting to have sex with someone? In other words had he too arranged to meet a woman?

It certainly made more sense. Maybe he had even been offered sex as part of the pay-off and the woman had insisted that they meet somewhere neutral. If that were the case then Jake now knew that he was looking for a woman who seemed to have the ability to kill men by persuading them to commit suicide.

But how would any woman persuade a man to kill himself? Surely that was just nonsense to imagine that you could kill anyone by persuading them to commit suicide? Suicide is usually borne of depression or from some other catastrophe that visits a life. Neither Gerald Strong nor Denis Arthur appeared to be depressed. Quite the reverse; both men had every reason to be upbeat. Why then would they commit suicide simply because a pretty woman asked them to?

Nothing made sense to Jake and the more he now thought about the two deaths the more he came to the inescapable conclusion that he was missing something. This woman had poisoned both men in some way; but how? It seemed unlikely that the empty glasses had been anything other than a prop placed within a scene for the benefit of the police. If the men hadn't taken the poison in liquid form then how had she got them to take it?

And what about this woman? He had absolutely nothing on her. He had no description and no evidence that she even existed. In the case of the Forsyth Hotel he didn't have a witness who could categorically confirm that any woman had been there with Denis Arthur. It might have been mere coincidence that a woman booked a room a little after Arthur, after all he was never actually seen with anyone.

The only reason that Jake still felt sure that he was seeking the same killer of both Gerald Strong and Denis Arthur was that only the mystery woman knew how Gerald Strong had died and only, therefore, would she know how to kill Denis Arthur in the same way. There was no evidence to support his theory of course.

Jake decided there was nothing more to be gained from remaining in Denis Arthur's room so he took the book and went back to where Mrs Arthur was finishing her tea. He showed her the book and asked if he could keep it at least until he had read it all. Mrs Arthur saw nothing wrong with that and Jake went on his way again.

***

With Willie Ifield in prison awaiting trial, Daniel Ifield was having to do everything regarding the family business as well as now trying to run the Business Club. He had been unwilling to take his father's advice and to employ a manager for the Club. Daniel would have preferred to do things the other way around and to have someone help run the family business. Of course, he knew he couldn't as not all of the family business was suitable for public consumption.

With some regret Daniel had interviewed three young men who worked in the finance area of the family business. He had selected them from what he knew about each of them and the work they produced. From these interviews he had identified James Ross as being the best candidate. This was to be the first day in which Ross would start his new role at the Business Club.

Daniel went with him and both men sat in the office going through the paperwork. James Ross was twenty-three years old, had bright red hair and an almost constant abundance of freckles across his face. He looked as if he could be ten years younger than he was with no sign of facial hair whatsoever. He might have been young but he was highly intelligent and understood what was needed to make a business a success. He was relishing his new role and attacked the paperwork with some delight.

Daniel could see, within the first half an hour that he had selected the right man for the job. James had his jacket off and was furiously making notes as he read through the various items of interest, which Joe Tredwall had left for them.

At the same time as James Ross was coming to grips with his new role, Ben Aspinall was struggling to handle his responsibilities. Aspinall had been pretty much left to get on with things himself. Scott Thane was in prison, as was Henry Davis. Winston MacDonald was nothing short of useless and although he had been given some other names by Thane no one seemed to be of a standard, at least mentally, to be of any help to Aspinall as he tried desperately to keep the flow of money going.

He had visited Thane in prison on two occasions and had been pointed in the direction of some information that might have been of help to him. However, it had not been enough and he was now in a situation where he felt he was doing little more than papering over cracks rather than actually mending them.

Aspinall could have done with a James Ross to help him but he already knew that he would have to plough a single furrow in the days ahead.

***

Jake was back in his office, sitting in his chair and doing nothing more than thinking. He had read through some more of Denis Arthur's notes and it was abundantly clear that he had uncovered something of interest, while he had been following Gerald Strong, but Denis had not seen fit to say what that was. He referred to a man and a woman though, which was certainly of interest to Jake, however these references were not in any meaningful context. If only he had told Sergeant Mathieson what he had known then he would still be alive today.

There was also reference to a woman in Park Street, which Jake now knew was Mathilde Dupont. At least that further confirmed that Gerald Strong at least knew the woman and it was still perfectly possible that he had also killed her, although at the moment there was no motive to support that theory.

So now Jake had the little puzzle of who this man and woman might be. It seemed logical that if these people had some connection to Gerald Strong, who in turn had a connection to Mathilde Dupont, who in turn had a connection to Willie Ifield, then there seemed every chance that this mystery couple had some connection to Guy Le Fondre, or at least to his death.

Loose ends were being done away with and that usually meant one thing; those loose ends knew too much. But what was there to know?

Gerald Strong obviously knew Mathilde Dupont and the police were certainly meant to believe that he had killed her. But had he and if so, why? Denis Arthur knew things that he thought might bring him wealth or at the very least a little fun with a woman who was above his usual standards. Both men were now dead and Jake remained convinced that the same woman had been with both men around the time that they had died.

Then there was the whole business with Willie Ifield. Much as Jake was delighted to have the man finally admit to some of his less acceptable activities, he did not want to have an innocent man found guilty of a murder he had not committed. However, if Willie Ifield had not committed the murder then why was all the evidence apparently pointing in his direction?

Who stood to gain from Willie Ifield's misfortunes? Obviously his son Daniel would be the main benefactor and at least in Jake's estimation, Daniel still had more of a motive for killing Guy Le Fondre. Did that mean, therefore, that Daniel was pulling the strings and trying to have his father found guilty of a crime that *he* had actually committed? Doctor Symon had surmised that the killer ought to be taller than Guy Le Fondre and Daniel certainly fitted that description, which was something his father never would.

Jake then pondered on the fact that Daniel might be his man after all. Were that the case then who was the mystery woman? Surely it could not be the lovely Miss Sangster? There seemed to be some sign of interest on behalf of Daniel but Miss Sangster had always remained cool and detached when talking about him. Was that all an act? The other factor, which meant it was highly unlikely that the mystery woman was Miss Sangster, was the fact that the reception clerk had described the woman who booked a room with them as having dark hair.

If it wasn't Miss Sangster, however, then who else could it be? Jake had never heard Daniel talk of anyone else other than Miss Sangster, but it always seemed as if he was still chasing her and that they were nowhere near having any form of relationship. To be arranging murders then the couple would need to be very close or at least have a shared interest in the outcome.

So who would have a shared interest in the outcome of putting Willie Ifield to the gallows for a crime he did not commit? Jake could think of no one, however he did still have Harriet Cruickshank in his mind with regard to Guy Le Fondre's murder. She most certainly was the main benefactor of that particular crime. She may have benefitted from Guy Le Fondre dying but why then would she play any part in Daniel Ifield having his father hanged? On the other hand, she did at least have dark hair.

As far as Jake was concerned there was no connection whatsoever between Daniel Ifield and Harriet Cruickshank. For the moment, at any rate, his deliberations were getting him nowhere. All that he really had was evidence that said that Willie Ifield killed Guy Le Fondre and unsubstantiated evidence that said that Gerald Strong killed Mathilde Dupont.

There still seemed to be much to do, but for the moment Jake turned his attention back to the theatre and to the person trying so desperately to keep the place closed.

***

Later that afternoon Jake and McGill went back to His Majesty's Theatre. They quickly found Peter Grant and were shown to his little office. Grant was looking flustered and annoyed at having to speak to the police when there were obviously so many other, far more important, matters to be dealt with.

"More problems, Mr Grant?" Jake asked, picking up on the fact that Grant looked red faced and bothered.

"It is nothing but problems at the moment, Inspector," Grant replied. "We are due to open in two weeks' time and we are still far from ready. There is much work to be done to have the building ready for its final inspection and if we don't pass that then we don't open."

"Are these problems being caused by our mystery pest?"

"Not as far as I can see. These are problems that come from any new building. We need to get everything finished off and ready for the public to attend. There really is a hundred and one things still needing to be finished before the third of December."

"But our pest isn't helping?" Jake probed.

"Now that we know that someone has been stealing tools and moving things around we can see that delays have been created by whoever this person is, but it is fair to say, Inspector, that the workmen are doing a pretty good job of delaying things without any help from anyone."

Jake turned to McGill. "And you're still sure that none of the workmen are involved in the criminal activities that have been going on?"

"Pretty sure, sir, they all seemed genuine in their answers when I spoke to them."

"How many people will be here on the opening night, Mr Grant?" Jake then asked.

"We are expecting a full house on the opening night so that would be two thousand and three hundred patrons."

Jake whistled at such a number. "Many of whom will be buying their ticket on the night, I assume?"

"The reserved seats are sold out already but people will need to queue for the unreserved seats. We've had busy theatres before, Inspector, so I am sure we will manage."

"Could you please take us for a tour of the building?" Jake then asked.

Grant still seemed annoyed at having his working day disrupted. "Constable McGill has already been shown around," came the rather grumpy retort.

Jake smiled. "I haven't seen it before, Mr Grant and I really would be obliged if you would let me get a better look at how the building is designed."

"Oh very well," Grant added, standing up from his desk.

They went round the entire building and Jake now felt that he had a completely different understanding of how it might go on opening night. The first thing that struck him was the fact that the audience appeared to be segregated in such a way that those in the cheaper seats were never allowed to come in to contact with the other patrons. They had a separate entrance and a separate bar to attend in the interval. There was a physical partition between them in the main auditorium and it seemed clear to Jake that there was no way that an attacker could get near Robert Wallace inside the theatre unless he was to be moving in the same social circles.

Jake experienced a passing thought concerning Robert Wallace. Here was a man arguing fiercely for the working man and an equality for all and yet here he was accepting an invitation to the theatre that would allow him to keep well away from the working man.

"So it would only be those people who already have tickets who could be in this part of the theatre?" Jake then asked as they paused at a particular spot in the auditorium.

"That would be correct."

"Where would Mr Wallace be seated for the performance?" Jake then asked.

"Mr Nelson's special guests have seats allocated to them in the Dress Circle. They will gather an hour before the performance for drinks in the Dress Circle bar."

"Can we have a look at that area, please?" Jake enquired.

They made their way up to the Dress Circle area. Again it seemed to be difficult for anyone who did not have a ticket or a pass to get up to that level without someone asking them for proof that they should be there. The Dress Circle bar was still not completely finished but it was already an impressive sight. Jake knew that there would be few occasions when he would be back in such a scene of opulence. Jake marvelled at the marble counter on the bar and wondered if such extravagance was really necessary for a theatre.

"Thank you for your time, Mr Grant, I'll let you get back to your work," Jake finally said and Grant departed with a look of relief on his face.

Jake and McGill went to the front door. Jake paused and looked at the various entrances. He tried to picture the opening night with the queues waiting for their tickets to the unreserved area. They would be in first leaving the way free for the carriages to roll up with those better off people aboard.

The only point at which Robert Wallace could really be attacked was here at the door. In other words his assailant had to be outside the building. Jake looked around with the eye of an assassin and did not like what he saw. There were places across the road where a man could wait with a hidden gun. With the crowds that would be milling around the front of the building that same assassin could be in amongst the masses just biding his time to strike. Being that close he could now be using a knife.

Jake had another thought. He turned to McGill.

"Have you checked out all the staff?"

"I have studied all the paperwork regarding the new staff, but as no one has actually started yet, I haven't spoken to anyone as I didn't feel it would help me much."

"The man we seek sees his mission as avenging the Lord. He sees the building of this theatre as being a sin. He could, therefore, have been planning his actions for some time and that might include getting a job here. If he were one of the staff then he would have better access to Robert Wallace on opening night. In fact, if he were one of the staff then he could attack Mr Wallace almost anywhere in the building and make it even more difficult to guarantee Mr Wallace's safety."

"But surely if this man has such a hatred of this building and a burning desire to see it closed, then he would not be applying for a job," McGill added.

"Perhaps not," agreed Jake," but if he saw it as a way of getting closer to Wallace then getting a job here would make perfect sense."

"Forgive me for saying, sir," McGill then said," but surely the threat to Mr Wallace came quite late in this game. The mystery man has been stealing tools and generally indulging in mischief making for some time. By the time we had any inclination that he was now about to indulge in violence against Mr Wallace he would have had no chance of applying for a job here. All the staff would have been employed by then."

Jake thought for a moment. McGill certainly had a point. It did seem unlikely that the person who was now threatening Robert Wallace had always intended to take action of that kind. This was definitely some kind of escalation and probably would have come after all the staff had been employed.

"Just in case there might be a connection between the mystery man and an employee would you bring all your paperwork to me anyway and we'll have one last look through it. Before then, however, would you speak to Mr Grant and find out if he has decided where the staff will be based on opening night. If he has already made that decision then please get the names of those staff who will be working in the Dress Circle and those who will be in the main foyer?"

"I'll see to it at once," McGill said and went off to annoy Mr Grant one more time.

***

Mrs Gladstone brought the early evening meal through and placed it in front of Harriet Cruickshank. Mrs Gladstone was still getting accustomed to the fact that she now had a mistress to work for and not a master. It was something that she was not at all confident that she would ever quite accept, especially given what had had to happen to bring Harriet to the house.

Mrs Gladstone left the room and Harriet began to eat her meal. She felt good to be living the life that she was now living and looked forward to spending Guy Le Fondre's money.

She thought of the new man in her life. She hadn't known him long but she already knew that he was the one for her. Life together would be so good especially as she no longer needed to be the kept woman. Harriet no longer had to do anything for a man if she did not want to. However, when it came to her new lover she wanted to do everything.

He brought her whole body to life with the manner in which he made love to her. He was tender and loving and everything that Guy Le Fondre was not.

There would still be some difficult days ahead before the police investigation in to Guy Le Fondre's death was completely over. Obviously they had charged Willie Ifield and she would have to attend his trial when it came round. She wouldn't be able to say much about Willie Ifield but she would tell the court what a wonderful man Guy Le Fondre had been and how saddened she was to have lost him. She hadn't decided yet if she would squeeze out a tear or not bother.

The meal was excellent; Mrs Gladstone could certainly cook, which was a skill that Harriet had never had much need to master. Once finished Mrs Gladstone took the plate away and Harriet retired to the sitting room.

She sat down and did some sewing. She had an urge to visit her lover again but knew that that might be too dangerous. Her body tingled at the thought of seeing him and of letting him touch her in places that no one else could. She fought the desire and poured herself a drink. Harriet was unsettled. She just wanted everything to be perfect and the quicker that happened the better.

***

He was now back in the house, nursing his bible and rocking gently back and forth in his seat as he recited passages to himself. He had followed Robert Wallace from his work. He had followed him all the way to the front door of his house and had watched as the door had opened and an attractive woman had stepped out to welcome her husband home from work.

She had kissed Robert Wallace, so the man felt he was in order to assume that the woman had been Mrs Wallace. He had committed Mrs Wallace's face to memory and then made his way back home.

He would show Robert Wallace how close he could get to him. He smiled at the thought of what he would do next and then returned his attention to the Bible.

NINETEEN

Tuesday 20 November: most of the day

Jake went to see the Chief Constable to update him on the work he had done regarding Robert Wallace. The Chief appeared to have more to discuss than usual and Jake was in his office for quite a while.

"I presume Mr Wallace is not for changing his mind?" the Chief said after Jake had gone over the basics of what he had done so far.

"There is nothing that you or I could say that would make Mr Wallace stay away from His Majesty's Theatre on the third of December, sir. However, I have had a look around the premises and it seems to me that unless our assailant has access to a ticket already for the opening night then his only chance of attacking Mr Wallace would be outside the building."

The Chief went over to a small cabinet that lay beneath the only window in his office. He opened a drawer and took out a folder, which he brought back to his desk. He opened the folder and started to look through some of the contents.

"Inspector Wilson has been doing some preparatory work for me regarding the security arrangements on the opening night of the theatre. Obviously we do intend to have officers visible at the theatre that night but given the numbers expected to attend I will have a number of officers at my disposal here at Lodge Walk, so if anything happens regarding crowd control at the theatre then we will be ready."

"I plan to have Mr Wallace at the theatre long before the performance starts. He is to have drinks in the Dress Circle bar before the show begins. I have McGill checking, once more, the staff who have been employed to work at the theatre and we will pay particular attention to those who may be working in that Dress Circle Bar. Although we will have Mr Wallace safely inside the theatre I still want a carriage to appear to be delivering him to the door of the theatre. That way if our man is hovering outside the theatre he ought to move forward as he sees Mrs Wallace climb down from the carriage. I have to say, sir, that although we are taking all necessary precautions, I am now of a mind to dismiss any notion of our man planning to attack Mr Wallace *inside* the theatre."

"I tend to agree," said the Chief. "I think we are dealing with someone of unstable mind who is unlikely to be thinking rationally about how he might stop this theatre from opening. This is a person more likely to do something that we couldn't predict."

"As a further precaution, sir, I believe we should have an officer paying close attention to Mr Wallace at all times, whilst he attends the theatre that night. If someone does get close for an attack then we need someone close to deal with it."

"I had thought of that already, Jake and feel that you are the perfect choice for a job like that. You have already made contact with Mr Wallace so he knows you and hopefully would trust you to do a good job on the night. I will speak to Mr Nelson and arrange for you and Margaret to be added to their guest list."

"Margaret?" Jake asked with some surprise.

"I think it would look less intrusive if you were seen to be there with a partner," the Chief explained. "Should our attacker be on the inside then he is less likely to be suspicious of someone who is there with a partner. We police officers tend to be on our own when we are on official duties."

"It could be dangerous, sir?" suggested Jake.

"If Margaret feels that the danger is too great then just let me know and we can arrange for someone else to go with you. However, from what I know of Margaret I feel sure that she would be delighted to go to the theatre with you even if there was an element of police work to be done once you were there."

"Very good, sir, I will speak to her," Jake then said.

The two men went on to discuss a few more items of interest to them both before Jake eventually went back downstairs. He put on his coat and left the building.

Jake did not believe that it would lead anywhere but he decided to visit Her Majesty's Theatre, on Guild Street and talk to the manager there about how his staff were feeling about their theatre having to close to accommodate the opening of His Majesty's Theatre.

Jake had visited Her Majesty's whilst investigating the murder of Mabel Lassiter so he was known there to the staff. It was a short walk from Lodge Walk to the theatre and he was soon being led up to the office of Percy Young, the manager.

"Why, Inspector, I never expected to see you again," Percy said as Jake arrived in his office.

The two men shook hands and Jake sat down. Percy Young's office had not got any bigger since Jake's last visit and there was hardly room to sit back in the chair such was the cramped nature of the furniture. Young himself looked a little more dapper than the last time Jake had seen him with his suit looking new and his balding head almost polished in its appearance.

"I'm investigating a matter concerning His Majesty's Theatre," Jake began," and I wondered how the staff of this establishment had taken to the fact it was being closed down so as not to provide any opposition to His Majesty's Theatre?"

"Have you reason to be suspicious of someone working here?" Young then asked.

"There have been some incidents at the new theatre which appear to have been man made. I am simply trying to identify anyone who might have a motive to bring mischief to the new theatre and wondered if anyone, within your staff, had shown signs of being more upset with what was happening than others?"

Percy Young looked saddened by the Inspector's line of thought. "I really don't think that any of my staff would stoop to criminal acts simply because they were aggrieved at losing their job, Inspector. Anyway, until we bring the final curtain down on our own stage all my staff are still gainfully employed here."

"Perhaps the threat of losing your job can be a strong motive for doing something out of character. Will many of your staff be moving to the new theatre?"

"Quite a few. There have been some who were not chosen to move, however and they have all been told. It would be fair to say that those not going to His Majesty's would be amongst our less successful workers."

"How about yourself, Mr Young?" Jake then asked.

"I am heading for pastures new, Inspector. Mr Robert Arthur, who as owner made the decision to close this theatre, has arranged for me to take up a post at Her Majesty's Theatre in Dundee. I am delighted to have been offered such a post and I am already looking forward to the move. I have visited the site and know that my office at least will be worth having. It is like a mansion compared to this cupboard."

Jake smiled. "So it was Robert Arthur who did not want his two theatres to be in competition with each other?"

"It was. Mr Arthur felt that there was only room for one theatre in Aberdeen producing high quality entertainment. With the money that he has put in to His Majesty's he will take no risks with any profits that they may go on to make.

"Of those staff who are moving to the new theatre, was there any one of them who has been more vociferous than others regarding the opening of the new theatre? Anyone who has expressed religious reasons for opposing the new build?"

"I'm sure that everyone working here is hurting inside at the thought of this theatre closing. It has been here since eighteen seventy-two and we had hoped that it might be here for many years to come. Obviously Mr Arthur has other ideas. As for anyone bringing religion in to this, well I really can't see the connection, Inspector. As far as I am aware there are no deeply religious people amongst my staff. Anyway why would someone working for one theatre see anything wrong with the building of another?"

"You are not situated next to a church, Mr Young," Jake replied and Percy Young's face adopted an expression of understanding.

"Ah, I see. Anyway, I think I am safe to say that I have no one on my pay list who cares enough about God to let it tarnish their views any further on the building of His Majesty's."

"Very well, Mr Young," Jake then said and stood up. He shook hands with Percy Young once more. "I wish you well in Dundee and hopefully, one day, this lovely theatre will be alive again to the sound of a happy audience."

"Thank you, Inspector," added Percy Young as Jake went out the door.

***

Scott Thane appeared in court. He pleaded guilty to making films of a sexual nature but again insisted that he had played no part in the abduction and murder of the women used in those films. His trial was set for the second week in December.

***

Two hours later Bella Davis was in court charged with the murder of George Cathcart. She pleaded not guilty to the charge but her solicitor was prepared to allow his client to plead guilty to manslaughter. The judge heard about Bella being under attack at the time she used the knife on Cathcart. He was also told of the kind of man that George Cathcart was. The judge then said that he did not want to hear anymore and that, in his mind, Bella Davis did what any woman would do at a time like that.

Bella was sentenced to two years in prison, which was the most lenient sentence the judge felt he could set. Bella was taken away crying; her only thought being that of her children and how they would survive for two years without her.

Willie Ifield was also taken in front of the judge who set a trial date of the seventh of January after Willie had pleaded not guilty in the most emphatic tone.

***

Constable McGill had presented Jake with the list of men likely to be working in the Dress Circle area on the opening night. He had felt it unnecessary to mention the women who would be working there. The list consisted of nine men, all of whom were leaving Her Majesty's to go and work at His Majesty's. There were no other names attributed to the Dress Circle as Peter Grant had wanted experienced staff for his well-to-do guests.

Jake looked at the names and then looked at what little information had been provided on them from Peter Grant. There was very little on which to form any opinions. No one stood out as possibly being their mystery man; not that Jake had expected anything different. This was nothing more than clutching at straws and Jake decided to set the list of names aside and only to return to it should further evidence arise.

Feeling that he had done all that he needed to do that day, Jake put on his coat and set off for Margaret's flat. It was after six by the time he got there and Margaret wasn't that long in from work. She was, as usual, delighted to see Jake at her door and she greeted him with a kiss.

"You'll stay for some food," Margaret said, more as a statement than a question.

Jake was happy to oblige as he had very little to eat in his own home. Jake rarely did any shopping and usually bought items as he realised he needed them. For someone who was so well organised at work he had very little by way of a plan for the domestic side to life. His home life was a bit of a shambles and he welcomed these moments in Margaret's company when she brought that element of organisation to his domestic world.

They sat in the kitchen and ate beef and potatoes, which Margaret heated from the day before. They drank water to the meal and chatted almost non-stop. Jake eventually worked the topic of conversation around to the opening night of the theatre. He further explained that he had been asked by the Chief Constable to attend the night by way of being a bodyguard to Robert Wallace. He further stated that the Chief thought it would be better if Jake was there with a partner and he had suggested that Margaret be that partner.

"But it could be very dangerous if this assailant tries to harm Mr Wallace in any way," Jake added quickly.

"We have the chance to be at the opening night of the new theatre in some of the poshest seats available and you want to put me off by saying how dangerous it might be?" Margaret asked with some disbelief in her voice.

"Someone has threatened to kill Robert Wallace, Margaret, which means they could fire guns or anything. I'm not sure that I'd be happy having you that close to danger."

Margaret took Jake's hand. "I trust you to protect me, Jake."

"I cannot guarantee your protection though, Margaret and I would not be able to live with myself should something ever happen to you."

Margaret smiled. "It is my choice, Jake. You have asked me to go to the theatre with you and I have said yes for all the selfish reasons under the sun. I will never get another chance to dress up and sit amongst the people with money in this city. You can't deny me that, Jake Fraser."

Jake softened and they kissed again. "Okay, but you will have to do whatever I say on the night."

"I'll do whatever it takes to just be there," Margaret added.

"Mr Wallace clearly wants to get to know us better," Jake then said, "as he has invited us both to a soiree on Saturday evening at his home. I was rather hoping you would be happy to come with me?"

Margaret smiled again. "Suddenly we have a social life and it is one that we can share together. I can't think of anything more enjoyable than a night out with you so it really doesn't matter where we are going."

"Then I'll let Mr Wallace know that we will be happy to attend on Saturday," Jake then concluded.

As Margaret left to make a cup of tea Jake was already planning how he would get Robert Wallace, his wife and Margaret safely in to His Majesty's Theatre and also praying that there would be no attempt on anyone's life and that it had all been a bluff.

TWENTY

Thursday 22 November: Morning until late afternoon

Jake had lost Wednesday to a sea of paper. He had finished all that was necessary for the Scott Thane trial and had also passed everything that he had on the Willie Ifield case to the courts as well, including his belief that some of the evidence was not necessarily to be believed. If the courts wished to proceed then that would have to be someone else's decision.

 By the end of the day his desk was satisfyingly clear and his workload was basically down to finding the man behind the threats on Robert Wallace's life.

Doctor Symon had put across his reports on both Gerald Strong and Denis Arthur. Both men had died of poisoning and there were no signs on either man of a struggle or of them being held down forcibly. Doctor Symon was still saying that both men had died by their own hand although he did question where the poison might have come from seeing as there were empty glasses in the room but no sign of a bottle or some other means by which the poison was brought in to the room.

The final statement took Jake back to the mystery woman. She had certainly been there when Gerald Strong killed himself so presumably she took away all the evidence as well as the money in Strong's wallet. Was the second death identical in that case? Was the same woman present yet again to take the evidence away? If that were true then what reason would two men possibly have for committing suicide in front of this woman?

In Jake's experience suicide had been a personal act. It had been the last desperate act of someone in deep mental anguish. Neither Gerald Strong nor Denis Arthur had been reported as being mentally disturbed in the days before they had died. Denis had spoken to Sergeant Mathieson on the Saturday morning and had shown no signs of being disturbed by anything. The evidence said suicide but Jake's gut feeling was that there was another hand in these deaths.

Doctor Symon also said in his report on Denis Arthur that there had only been water in the glass found in the room. If Denis Arthur had committed suicide by taking tablets then there ought to have been some sign of them in the stomach contents. There was nothing, which led the Doctor to suggest that Arthur had taken a liquid of some kind only there was no evidence to support that by way of a container for the liquid.

How then had he managed to commit suicide without obvious access to a liquid poison?

Jake felt more and more convinced that the mystery woman was the poisoner and not simply some witness to the event. However, that raised another question. How did she get them to drink the poison without suspicion? Both men would have needed to have trusted the woman implicitly to take a drink from her and not fear for their lives. The fact that they both seemed to be in a room expecting sex might explain why they were so relaxed.

The men are lying on the bed; the woman comes in to the room. She pours a drink for them both only the man's drink is laced with some form of poison. The man dies, the woman clears up and leaves. It made sense but the woman would have needed a bag and would also have needed to be remarkably calm as to clear up a room full of evidence while a man lay dead on the bed.

Jake put on his coat and hurried out of the building. He made his way round to the Forsyth Hotel and was delighted to see the same young man was working on the reception desk. He waited until the young man had dealt with a guest and then moved forward.

"When the woman booked her room just after Denis Arthur, did you happen to notice if she was carrying a bag of some kind?"

The young man thought again. "Yes, she did have quite a big bag with her. I just assumed it was her clothes for the next day."

"Thank you," Jake concluded and went back out in to the street. Yet again the rain was falling in a fine mist and the overhead skies were a dirty grey. Jake went to a nearby café and ordered tea and toast. He sat in the corner and enjoyed the short break. He found himself once more thinking about the mystery woman.

She had been carrying a bag at the Forsyth Hotel but there apparently had been no bag at the Bon Accord Hotel. Maybe the woman at the Forsyth Hotel had just been there for a short rest and had nothing to do with Denis Arthur's death? Jake wondered if he might now be seeing connections where there weren't any, but then he thought back to the similarity of how Denis Arthur and Gerald Strong had died. Only the existence of a woman linked the two deaths beyond the fact they had apparently committed suicide.

Somehow he had to find this woman and hopefully he would do so before she killed again.

***

Henry Davis was not enjoying being in jail. Word had got out pretty fast that he had been a police officer and the other prisoners had not taken kindly to having to share their meagre rations with a dirty copper. The prison warders tried to keep an eye on Davis but he was not always within their line of vision. Any time that he found himself on his own he had usually been jostled and punched.

He knew that it would be another few days before he would be in court. He would just have to grit his teeth and hope that he could see those next few days through. As Jake had been sitting in the café enjoying a short break, Henry Davis was out in the yard of the prison enjoying a few moments of fresh air and stretch of his legs.

He was on his own. No one would ever be seen to be in his company. Henry Davis actually preferred things that way. He was slowly walking round when a man broke from the group of men walking behind him and started to get closer.

Henry Davis turned to face the man and his body immediately took up a defensive posture just in case he would be required to fight. The man approached, a snarl more than a smile appearing on his face. Henry noticed the man put his hand in his pocket just as he drew alongside.

The next action was so swift and so severe that Henry had had no time to react. The man's hand came out of his pocket and swung at Henry Davis in an arc that culminated in his hand sinking into Davis's stomach. Unfortunately for Henry Davis, within the man's hand was now held a knife.

"This is from Mr Aspinall in memory of George Cathcart, you bastard," the man snarled as he sunk the knife once more in to Henry Davis's stomach before stepping back and re-joining the other prisoners. He was trying to wipe the blood off his hand as two prison warders realised something had happened and came hurrying over.

By the time they got to Henry Davis he was dead and Mr Yule was well concealed by the other prisoners. Mr Yule had also long perfected the art of looking innocent when he was, in fact, the guiltiest of them all.

***

Dora Wallace left the house and made her way on to the pavement. She turned left and began to walk along to where she knew she might catch a tram in to the city centre. As she walked along she noticed a man coming towards her. He was a scruffy looking individual and he seemed to be walking straight at her. She moved to one side, but he seemed to move with her.

Much as Dora Wallace tried to prevent their coming together she still managed to bump in to the man. He apologised and hurried on his way. Dora thought it all rather strange but continued on her way.

The man, hurrying off in the other direction, looked down at the small item he had taken from Dora Wallace's coat and smiled.

***

Jake got back to the office and began working his way through the list of men who he now needed to contact with regard to the South United Church. Jake had twelve men listed on the paper lying before him. He drew a line under the first four and then another line under the next four. He allocated the first group to Constable McGill, the second group he would take himself and the third group would be given to Sergeant Mathieson. With the three of them conducting the interviews Jake felt certain that they could see everyone within a day.

Jake found McGill and Mathieson gave them their list of names and their orders to get the interviews done within twenty-four hours and to report back if they found anything even remotely suspicious.

Jake then left the office again and went to check out the addresses provided by Mr Shewan, along with the names.

The first two he visited were not going to be in until later. Both men were at work and did not usually get home until nearer six. Jake said that he would call back later. His third visit proved a lot more successful.

Almost as soon as he knocked on the door it was opened. A thick-set man, with dark hair that was turning slightly grey and a mouth that seemed filled with decaying teeth asked who Jake might be.

Jake identified himself. "Might you be Mr Ogston?"

"That's me; but what have I done to require a visit from the police?"

"I'm sure you haven't done anything, Mr Ogston," Jake replied, "but I was hoping you might be able to help with a current inquiry concerning the church that you attend."

"You'd better come in then," added Albie Ogston as he stepped back to let Jake enter the house. Ogston then led Jake through to a room at the back of the house. Jake got the impression that there were a number of rooms in the house but that Albie Ogston probably only used a few of them.

"What exactly is all this about?" Ogston then asked reaching for a cigarette that lay on the mantelpiece. He lit it with a match and then dragged on the end, pulling smoke in to his lungs before exhaling a cloud towards the ceiling.

"Just a few questions with regard to an investigation that is currently taking place concerning incidents that have happened at His Majesty's Theatre."

"I thought you said something about my church?" Ogston then said.

"I did. It may be the case that the incidents that have happened in the theatre are, in some way, connected to the church," Jake explained.

"Incidents, what kind of incidents?" Albie asked.

"Silly little things really," Jake replied," but annoying to the workmen and management of the theatre none the less. May I sit down?"

"Of course," said Albie. Both men sat down and Jake cast an eye round the room. It was very untidy and looked as if it had not had a good clean in a long time. There was signs of a meal having been eaten at the table recently but little attempt had been made to clear up the mess. Albie Ogston himself was equally untidy.

Jake took his notebook from his pocket and flipped it open. He looked down at one of the pages as he spoke. "Before we continue can I just clarify that I am speaking to Mr *Albie* Ogston?"

"Yes, that's me."

"And I believe you are a member of the congregation at the South United Church?"

"That is correct; but what has that got to do with anything?"

"If you would just bear with me, Mr Ogston. I have been told that you help with the cleaning of the church and that you also carry out other small jobs around the premises as and when they arise. Is that correct?"

"I try to be helpful when I can," Albie replied. He was still looking at Jake with some suspicion, no doubt still trying to make sense of Jake's questions.

"Are you in employment at the moment?" Jake then asked.

"No, I can't work. I was wounded during the Boer War and just live off my small army pension."

"Oh, I'm sorry to hear that," added Jake. "How often do you work at the church?"

"As you said, I do jobs for them as and when they arise. Some weeks I'm there nearly every day and other weeks I'm not there at all."

"Do you usually work alone when you are there?" Jake then enquired.

"The Minister is there sometimes, but often as not I am on my own. I never feel like I'm on my own though, you always feel that the Lord is with you when you work in a church."

"I'm sure you do," Jake agreed with a weak smile. "What are your thoughts on having a theatre being built next door to the church?"

Albie Ogston sat back in his chair and seemed to be giving the question a lot of thought. He finally began to speak.

"I hadn't really thought about it before, but now that you ask I suppose I'm quite pleased to see another theatre being provided for the entertainment of the people of Aberdeen."

"And the fact the theatre is opening in December doesn't bother you either?"

"It has to open sometime," Albie said and smiled at what he obviously thought was a whimsical retort.

"Will you be going to see the pantomime?" Jake then asked.

"Oh, no, I've never been a fan of such childish entertainment."

"What did you do in the army, Mr Ogston?"

"I was a corporal, Inspector and I fought in many a battle for Queen and country."

"May I enquire as to how you were wounded in the Boer War?"

"I was shot in the leg and clubbed to the head, Inspector. I have suffered from severe headaches ever since and occasionally I blackout altogether. The doctors tell me that it would be dangerous for me to take a job as I might pass out at any moment."

"In the times that you have been working at the church have you ever seen anyone hanging around the outside of the theatre in a rather suspicious manner?"

Ogston though for a moment yet again. Each question was actually getting more thought than was necessary and Jake began to wonder if Albie Ogston's head injury might not be a whole lot worse than he was saying, or perhaps even knew himself.

"I really don't think that I have, Inspector. There was a woman came in to the church the other week. She was acting very strangely but I believe that that had more to do with her trying to get away from her abusive husband. I really don't think she would have wished any ill on the new theatre. Why do you believe that incidents at the theatre might be connected to the church?"

"It's just a line of enquiry, sir, nothing more than that," Jake replied. He then paused for a moment. Part of him wanted to ask a few more questions but the other part was telling him that it was unlikely that Mr Ogston would tell him anything very helpful. Although Albie Ogston sounded as if he was being helpful he wasn't really saying much at all. Jake cast an eye around the room once more and then decided that he would draw a halt to his questions for the moment.

Jake stood up. "Well, thank you very much for your time Mr Ogston, but I believe that is all I need for the moment."

Ogston now stood up and started to make his way to the front door. As Jake followed he took one last look around the room. There was a crucifix on the wall and a bible lying on the table. However that proved nothing other than Albie Ogston seemed to be an extremely religious man.

What Jake still didn't know, was whether or not, Albie Ogston could also become a killer.

***

When Jake got back to Lodge Walk he was told about what had happened to Henry Davis.

"Damn!" Jake had shouted and slammed his fist off the table. "Have they got someone for it?"

Sergeant Turnbull had the details. "No one claims to have seen who did it and it is highly unlikely that anyone is going to talk now. We should have realised, sir, that a dirty copper would be a target inside prison. We maybe should have done more to protect him."

"Damn right more should have been done to protect him!" Jake snapped. "However, that ought to have been the work of the prison staff, Sergeant. They should have been more aware of the danger that Henry Davis was in. Find someone to go out and notify his parents. I will go and see Bella, it's only right and proper that I should be the one to tell her what has happened to her husband.

***

Somehow Bella Davis still managed to look beautiful even in prison garb and with her hair desperately needing a wash. She sat opposite Jake and the tears welled in her eyes as he told her what had happened to her husband. Jake felt like crying himself. Henry Davis had let his police colleagues down badly but he had not deserved to die for it.

Once he had made sure that Bella was calm again Jake left the prison and made his way back to Lodge Walk. Just before he had left the prison he had arranged for the prison staff to show extra vigilance around Bella Davis just in case retribution was planned on her as well. Jake did not believe that anyone would harm Bella, but he did not want to take the risk.

On his return to Lodge Walk he was informed that Sandy Wilson had been given the task of finding Henry Davis's murderer, though with any crime committed behind bars the chance of him achieving his goal was remote to say the least. No one spoke to the police at times like that and no one ever saw anything. The fact that Henry Davis had been a police officer would only amplify the silence.

Jake sat at his desk and gave some further thought to the Willie Ifield case. He was still greatly bothered by the ease with which the evidence was being presented to him and the more he thought about the specifics of the evidence he had received, the more something began to niggle at the back of his mind. He sat back in his chair and let the embryo of an idea formulate inside his brain. As the thought process matured everything began to fall in to place and suddenly Jake felt certain that he now knew where he had to go with the enquiry in to Guy Le Fondre's death.

He had finally thought of an explanation that covered everything that had happened. It was possibly the only explanation that did make sense of it all. However, to prove his new theory he needed proof and he could think of only one way that he might get that proof.

Jake put his jacket and coat on and left the office.

***

It was just after lunchtime when Jake walked in to the Banks of Ythan public house that lay on the corner of Lodge Walk and Queen Street. The place was as busy as ever with a host of flat-capped men enjoying a pint and a pie for their lunch. Jake looked around and finally saw the person he had come to speak with.

Sitting in the corner, hunched over the morning paper and guarding a pint of beer as if his very life depended upon it was Stinky, Jake's number one informer. Stinky kept Jake informed of anything he heard on the street, though he had been pretty quiet of late.

Stinky looked up as Jake approached.

"Have you gone deaf these days or is there just nothing on the street worth hearing?" Jake said as he sat down opposite Stinky. He was a man who lived up to his nickname and he was usually to be found with space around him.

"Very quiet, Mr Fraser, very quiet indeed."

"You'll have heard that Willie Ifield is in custody?" Jake then said.

"Now I had heard that," Stinky replied," but I didn't feel the need to tell you that as I assumed you knew."

Jake smiled. "I want you to do something for me," he then said.

"Would it be worth another pint to me if I were agree to help?" Stinky then suggested.

Jake took some coins from his pocket and placed them on the table. "It will be worth quite a lot to you if you bring me the information that I'm hoping you will. Meanwhile you can buy yourself another drink once I've gone, though don't go getting drunk and forgetting that we had this conversation."

Stinky looked suitably offended. "Mr Fraser, where money is involved my memory remains sharp no matter how much I might choose to drink in any one session."

"Then listen to what I have to say and act on it immediately."

Jake then proceeded to tell Stinky that he wanted him to get one or two associates and to organise themselves so as to be able to follow someone on a twenty-four hour basis. Jake provided the name of the person and the work and home addresses. He only wanted Stinky to get back to him if there was evidence that the person they were following had met someone of significance. Jake then suggested someone who, if seen, would most certainly be deemed significant. Stinky committed all that he had been told to memory for he had never learned to either read nor write, so there would be little to be gained by someone writing anything down for him.

"If you bring me good news on this, Stinky, then you will be paid well, I can assure you of that."

"Very good, Mr Fraser, I'll just have the one more and then I'll get on to this right away."

"Make sure it is just the one," Jake added as sternly as he could. He then stood up and made his way out of the pub. By the time he had closed the door behind him Stinky was already at the bar. While he stood watching his next pint being poured he began to give some thought as to whom he would ask to work with him as they set about following the person named by Inspector Fraser.

***

The man left his place of work at a little before six o'clock. He started to walk along the pavement, turning his collar up to the cold. He felt happy with how life was going and content that the plan he had formed with his lover was going so well.

However, unknown to this man there was someone a few paces behind who was paying close attention to anything that might happen. Had he known that he was being followed then he might have acted slightly differently over the coming few days.

As it is, he didn't.

TWENTY-ONE

Friday 23 November: Morning to early afternoon

Jake, McGill and Sergeant Mathieson met in Jake's room at a little after ten in the morning. They each had a cup of tea and McGill asked permission to eat a sandwich as he hadn't had anything to eat since arising that morning at six. Although frowned upon by the Chief, Jake was happy to allow the Constable to eat in his office.

"Okay, gentlemen, how did the interviews with the Church helpers go?"

Mathieson spoke first. "Nothing much, sir. Three of the four I interviewed don't do very much for the church at all and it seemed to me that the little they did do was done purely to then allow them to brag about it. It was all about being seen to be helping the church rather than actually *doing* very much."

"And the fourth?" Jake prompted.

Mathieson referred to his notes. "Yes, that was Angus McCallum. He lived with his mother and seemed a bit strange for a man who is in his thirties."

"Define strange?" Jake then asked.

"A loner. He gave me the impression that if he hadn't had God with him then he would have nothing. However, he didn't strike me as a person who would be motivated to do anything more supportive of the church than turn up and clean it now and again. He also seemed pretty genuine when he said he had no idea who Robert Wallace was."

"Okay. How about you Constable?" Jake then asked McGill, who was frantically chewing on his last mouthful of bread before answering.

"Pretty much the same, sir. I had three who seemed clear of any suspicion and then there was Michael Hamilton who left me wondering if he might be our man. He spends a lot of time at the church and he did seem rather agitated by the fact a pantomime was to be performed around the time of the birth of Jesus. However, he then went on to say that he would still like to attend on opening night so that he could see for himself how the theatre looks, seeing as he had read about how magnificent it was."

"Unlikely to be our man then," Jake added, "which leaves us with the one interview that I had that seemed a little strange. Albie Ogston was wounded in the Boer War and has had a severe head injury ever since. He gets headaches and blacks out regularly, so he can't do anything by way of conventional work. Because of that he tends to do a lot of work at the church. He lives alone and could do with a good wash though, of course, that in itself does not make him guilty of anything. He didn't say anything that seemed particularly out of the ordinary and yet there was just something about him that started to get me a little suspicious that he might not have been telling me everything. It's really no more than intuition but he may be one to watch."

"The problem with some people who are deeply religious is that they tend to come across as being a bit weird, so it makes it all the more difficult to identify the potential criminal from the individual who just likes reading the Bible," observed Mathieson.

"Which doesn't leave us with much," McGill added, rather downheartedly.

"I've been thinking, sir," Mathieson then said, "why has our man chosen Robert Wallace to threaten? I mean if he really wanted to make a statement then why not threaten the Provost, or even the Chief Constable as they are both going to be there as well. I know that Robert Wallace irritates a lot of people with his political views but, generally speaking, he really is a bit of a nobody around town."

Jake pondered on that for a moment. "When you put it that way, Sergeant, it does seem rather strange. I just assumed that our man saw the list of invites and probably thought that Wallace was the best known of that small number."

"But our man surely wants to make a statement and even if he killed Robert Wallace I doubt if it would have the same impact on the city as if he had killed the Provost or someone else of some standing. After all, sir, there will be a lot of important people there on the night; far more important than Robert Wallace is ever likely to be."

"Then he chose Wallace for another reason," Jake said, more by way of thinking aloud.

"I think this is all personal, sir," Mathieson then added. "I think it is a personal insult to this man that they have built a theatre next door to a church and I think Wallace has personally upset in some way and that is why he has chosen him as his target that night."

"A personal vendetta. You may well have hit the nail firmly on the head, Sergeant, well done. Unfortunately it still does not make it any clearer to us as to who our man might be. However, if it is personal then perhaps Mr Wallace can help us more than he realises."

***

A small boy entered the building where Robert Wallace had his offices and made his way up to the reception desk. He didn't actually know that it was a reception desk but he had noticed a very pretty young woman and had made a direct line to speak to her. As things turned out the little boy did not actually say very much but he did hand over a small box and said that it was for Mr Wallace.

The boy then left the building and the young woman made her way up to Mr Wallace's office where she told him the story of the charming little boy and then left the box on Wallace's desk.

Robert Wallace thanked the young woman and she left. He then sat for a few moments and looked down at the box. He wondered what it might be and why had it been delivered by a little boy and not the postman? A part of him now wanted to open the box, whilst the other part was unsure as to whether, or not, he really wanted to know what might be inside.

Eventually he picked the box up and shook it. Something inside rattled. He paused for a few seconds longer and then decided to open it. He tore open the rough paper that had been wrapped around the box and then flipped open the lid. Wallace recognised the contents immediately. It was a small brooch that he had bought, some time ago, for his wife.

Also inside the box was a note. Wallace read through the badly written message. The spelling was terrible but the meaning came through loud and clear. He folded up the note and put it back inside the box. He then closed the lid and stood up.

He put his jacket and coat on and then left the office. He told the young woman on the reception desk that he would be back soon and then made his way out of the building.

***

Albie Ogston was in the church. He always felt at peace when he was in the church. It was the only place where he felt truly settled, where he never felt alone. His thoughts turned to Robert Wallace. How he wished he had been able to see the expression on the man's face when he opened that box.

Albie then started to think about how it would feel as he pushed a knife in to Robert Wallace and watched the life drain out of him. Hopefully it would not have to come to that; if only they would announce that the theatre was no longer going to open in December. He could just about come to terms with a theatre being next door to the church as long as there were no shows on at Christmas and Easter. Surely twice a year they could acknowledge that the Lord took precedent over idle entertainment.

The door of the church opened and two young women came in. They were talking quietly to each other and one of them smiled at Albie as they passed on their way to the front. Albie thought that they were both very pretty and he smiled back. He watched them continue to the front and bow their heads towards the figure of Jesus.

Albie thought again about how lonely his life was and that it was highly unlikely that that would ever change. There would never be a woman in his life. There never had been a woman in his life beyond a couple of whores he had met whilst in the army. There was no love offered to Albie Ogston except, of course, from the Lord.

The two women said a short prayer and then turned to leave. Albie watched them pass, deciding that the one on the right had been the prettier of the two. He wondered what it would be like to step out with a pretty woman on his arm. What it would be like to have sexual relations with a woman who actually cared for him and was not just spreading her legs for a few pennies.

Albie then remembered where he was and banished all thoughts of women from his mind as quickly as he could.

***

Robert Wallace walked through the front door of Lodge Walk and strode up to the front counter, behind which stood Sergeant Turnbull looking as efficient as ever. Wallace asked to see Jake Fraser and five minutes later both men were sitting in the main interview room. Robert Wallace took the box from his pocket and placed it on the table in front of Jake.

"This was delivered to my office this morning by a small boy. Inside the box is a small brooch, which my wife usually wears on her coat and a note. I will wait until you have read the note before saying anything further."

Jake opened the box and took out the folded piece of paper. He opened it out and read through the message. It was clear that the message had been written by someone of limited education but, as with Wallace, Jake understood the meaning at once.

Wallace began to speak again.

"As the note says, Inspector, the brooch confirms that the man who has been threatening me was close enough to my wife so as to have been able to steal it from her coat without her knowing. Although he does not actually say so, he is implying that were he to be of a mind to do so, he could harm my wife as easily as he could harm me."

"And he further stresses," Jake then added," that the theatre must not open in December. It's interesting that he now appears to be accepting the theatre being there as long as it remains closed over Christmas and Easter."

"Which, of course, we all know isn't going to happen," Wallace added. "Pantomime season is one of the most profitable times of the year for any theatre."

"Indeed it is," agreed Jake, reading note again. After a few seconds pause for thought, Jake then looked up at Wallace. "Does this change your mind about going to the theatre on opening night?"

Wallace smiled. "Not at all, Inspector. It may make me change my mind about taking Dora with me, but it will most certainly not prevent me from attending. As I keep saying, I have never run away from a battle in all my life and I have no intention of starting now."

"Don't worry, Mr Wallace, I have no intention of trying to persuade you to do otherwise. However, before you go, perhaps you can help me with a name that has cropped up in our enquiries. Have you ever met a man by the name of Albie Ogston?"

Wallace thought for a little while. "Not that I can recall. It is possible, however, that this man Ogston may have applied for a job with me or I may have met him in some business capacity without his name actually registering with me. I will get my staff to check back through our paperwork and see if his name pops up anywhere."

"Thank you, Mr Wallace."

The two men stood up and shook hands again.

"Thank you, Inspector. I assume you will still be coming to my house tomorrow night?"

"Of course. Margaret and I are looking forward to it."

"Excellent. By the way, Inspector, you have yourself a fine woman in Margaret. I would, if I were you, work very hard at keeping her happy, you do not want to lose her to another man."

Jake smiled. "I have no intention of losing Margaret to another man."

"That's what I wanted to hear," Wallace added with a grin. "See you tomorrow then."

TWENTY-TWO

Saturday 24 November: Evening only

Jake had had a relatively quiet couple of days at work. He had heard nothing from Stinky nor had anything further happened at His Majesty's Theatre. He had been able to finish relatively early and make his way home to wash and change for his night out with Margaret at Robert Wallace's house.

Jake had met with Margaret at her home. She looked stunning. Her dress was a dark blue colour with a low bodice that showed off her cleavage. Her waist looked thinner than ever, beneath which the dress billowed out in a sea of material. Her hair was tied up and her eyes were sparkling with delight as they got ready to leave.

Jake felt so proud to have a woman like Margaret in his life and he remembered what Robert Wallace had said the previous day as they went downstairs and stopped a carriage on Union Terrace. Jake told the driver of their destination and the horse started clip-clopping along the cobbled streets.

Half an hour later they were standing at the door to Robert Wallace's home. Again this was not the sign of a working class man nor, it would further be assumed, of a man with any idea of what it might be like to be working class. The house was large and stood alone amongst many other large houses. Clearly Robert Wallace had done very well for himself out of his electrical business.

The door was opened by a young and rather plain looking girl dressed in an ill-fitting maid's outfit. She seemed nervous but took Jake and Margaret's coats and then showed them through to the main room where the gathering was being held. As Jake and Margaret entered the room all eyes turned in their direction and Jake could tell at once that all male eyes were drawn to Margaret in an instant.

Robert Wallace broke free from a small group of men to whom he had been talking. By the time he reached Jake and Margaret he had been joined by his wife, Dora.

"Jake, I am so pleased you could come. And the lovely Margaret," he added, taking Margaret's hand and kissing the back of it. Wallace then shook Jake's hand and pulled him a little closer. "I haven't told anyone what you do for a living. I thought that I would leave it up to you as to whether, or not, you wanted to be drawn in to police matters at a function such as this."

"Thank you," Jake said.

"Now," Wallace then added in a louder voice as the two men separated again, "what would you both like to drink?"

Glasses of wine were requested and provided and Robert Wallace quickly introduced Jake and Margaret to one or two chosen guests. Jake was simply introduced as a 'friend' though most eyes were really on Margaret.

After the initial burst of interest had passed Margaret was taken to one side by Dora and Jake found himself talking to Robert Wallace and three other men. The other men all owned companies who had provided the work for the new theatre and all four men were going to be at the opening night with their wives. Jake glanced across and noticed that it was probably those wives whom Margaret was now talking with.

"I've told these other gentlemen, Jake, so it seems only fair that I tell you," Wallace then said. "I'm afraid there has been a threat made on my life, if I attend the opening night of the theatre. Now, as I know that you will be there with me, I thought I should give you the same chance to change your mind, should you feel that I might be making things a little too dangerous for your liking?"

Jake almost smiled at the manner in which Wallace had brought him in to the confidence of this small group of men. It obviously allowed them to talk about the event without knowing the true part that Jake would be playing.

"Why would anyone threaten your life?" Jake asked, with as much surprise as his limited acting skills would allow.

"I have no idea," Wallace said. "Perhaps this misguided person believes that I am a threat to their Liberal values."

"There could be other reasons," Jake then added rather casually.

Wallace paused and then turned to face Jake. "What other reasons could there be?"

"Work related, perhaps?" suggested Jake.

"I can't imagine that there is anyone in Aberdeen who would wish me dead because of any business motive."

"Perhaps we can discuss this later?" Jake then asked.

Wallace smiled. "Why not."

"Anyway, whatever the reason, you should surely be thinking about not going," Jake then said. "You cannot put your life in danger for the sake of a night at the pantomime."

"We've tried," added one of the other men, "but he won't listen."

Wallace gave Jake a look of amusement. He had expected the Inspector to have at least one last try to persuade him to change his mind. Jake had not let him down.

"Jake, you know what kind of man I am. Would you honestly expect me to capitulate to threats of this type? I wish to be a politician and being a politician involves saying things and making decisions that are almost guaranteed to make you unpopular. You have to be seen to be strong in mind if nothing else."

"As am I, Robert, "Jake then said. "I have already invited Margaret to attend the opening night with me and we do not intend to miss it for the world. I assume Dora will still be going with you?"

"Actually she is," Wallace replied with another smile. "I obviously gave her the same opportunity to drop out as I have done with all of you, but she is a loving and loyal wife who feels she should be seen nowhere other than at her husband's side. Although not actually married yet, I am sure that Margaret will feel the same way about you Jake."

Wallace was grinning broadly. He was enjoying poking fun at Jake and as he did so he glanced in the direction of Margaret. "It will be nice to see you on opening night, Jake, but I am even more delighted to know that Margaret will be there as well. You are a very lucky man, Jake."

Jake looked across at Margaret, who caught his eyes and smiled. "Oh I know that, Robert, I know that only too well."

To Jake's surprise they were then all taken through to one of the back rooms in the house and asked to take a seat at a large table that had been set as if to feed royalty.

Jake was able to sit with Margaret and found Dora sitting on his other side. Robert Wallace sat opposite, in the middle of the row of people and holding court with gusto. Jake watched Wallace closely. The man was an extrovert who clearly liked to be the centre of attraction. That in itself seemed to make him perfectly suitable for politics. He was also very funny. He passed comments about people and events that had the whole room full of laughter and Jake could see that for all the newspaper talk of this man being a danger to the political structure of the city, he was still, never the less, very popular with his friends and acquaintances.

After the meal the men went in to another of the back rooms for cigars and brandy and the ladies returned to the front room. Jake would have preferred to be with Margaret but felt obliged to follow the men.

"So, tell me Jake, what are your politics?" one of the other men asked.

"I don't believe that I have any," Jake replied.

"And that is why he makes such a good friend," Wallace added quickly, putting an arm around Jake's shoulder. "Here I am stirring up all kinds of nonsense throughout the city of Aberdeen and all the time I have Jake nearby to keep a calm head and to also keep reminding me not to go too far. I need to get debate going in this city but I do not need to alienate everyone as there would be no one left to vote for me if I did."

"So you will stand for Parliament one day?" another of the men asked.

"I heard something of great interest the other day," Robert Wallace then said, dragging on the end of his cigar and exhaling a heavy cloud of smoke. "It appears that James Bryce, the anonymous Member of Parliament for South Aberdeen, is soon to be offered a new job, one that will take him to the United States of America."

"Wherever did you hear such nonsense?" someone asked through the ever increasing cloud of smoke.

"I have my contacts," Wallace said. "The man will be off to America and we will be left to have a by-election. I am thinking of putting my name forward for that by-election and taking my chances with the voters of South Aberdeen."

A couple of the men laughed openly. "Come on, Robert, you won't stand a chance of being elected in South Aberdeen," one of them said. "Your brand of politics will never go down well with people who have money. You need to be speaking for the poorer areas of the city and might have a slightly better chance in the North."

"I like a challenge," Wallace announced rather grandly and he finished his brandy.

"But whatever would take Bryce to America?" someone else then asked.

"The offer of a job that he won't be able to refuse," was all that Wallace would say. "Come on gentlemen that has to be good news. Aberdeen will have a chance, a lot earlier than anyone could have imagined, to strike a blow against Liberalism."

"Come on, Robert," another voice said," even if Aberdeen is to have a by-election you cannot seriously believe that you would have any chance of winning enough votes to take you to Parliament. You live in a house like this and yet you claim to be the voice of the working class. No one is going to believe you."

Wallace crossed the room and poured himself another brandy. He offered the bottle to his guests and most of them accepted a re-fill. Jake declined, choosing to make his first glass last as long as might be necessary.

"As I have already explained to my good friend, Jake, you do not have to be poor to understand the plight of the poor. However, you do have to be rich to be a Member of Parliament seeing as no one sees it fit to give MPs payment of any kind. I run a business, which employs a lot of staff and I gain knowledge from the people who work for me regarding their lifestyle and the things they complain about. I want to help these people have a better life and I don't just mean by paying them more. I also firmly believe that women should be allowed to vote as well as men. The quicker the fair sex has a say in British politics the better it will be for all of us."

There were loud guffaws of disbelief around the room. Some of the men in the room looked as if the very idea would be the end of the world. Jake smiled to himself and wished that Margaret had been there to provide a feminine view.

"Good Lord, Robert, you cannot be serious," one voice said rather loudly. "Whatever would women know about politics?"

"More then you obviously know," Robert Wallace countered. "Why should political decisions be left in the domain of the male of the species? Why shouldn't women have a say in the future of this country every bit as much as the men? Both sexes must live together so why should only one be able to shape that world in which we live?"

"But women voting," said another with total disbelief.

"These damned suffragettes should be locked up and the key thrown away," was the opinion voiced by another.

Robert Wallace simply smiled. "That would seem to be the view of Mr Bryce as well, however, it may not happen in our life time, gentlemen, but the day will come when you will all have to swallow that misplaced male arrogance and accept that women will have their say. Women have their opinions already; we see them getting on to school boards and other formal bodies so it can only be a matter of time before their interest in politics begins to influence their right to vote. Mark my words, gentlemen, you will either have to swim with the tide of change or drown in your own prejudices."

Robert Wallace gained little support from the room but he still smiled broadly at the fact that he had managed to get some healthy debate going. With the cigar and brandies finished the men made their way back to the front room where all the women were sitting in a circle chatting politely.

Jake made his way across to Margaret who stood up and took his arm. "I thought I'd lost you," she said with a warm smile.

"You'll never do that," answered Jake as they both accepted the offer of another glass of wine.

The conversation returned to more mundane topics for another hour before Jake announced that it was time that he and Margaret left. Robert Wallace escorted them to the door and waited while they put their coats on. He then shook Jake's hand and kissed Margaret's hand again.

"Thank you both for coming. Margaret, I look forward to meeting you again at the opening of the theatre and Jake I will, no doubt, see you before then as you continue to try and identify the idiot who is threatening me."

"I had been hoping to discuss the matter further, tonight," Jake added, "but time seems to have run away from us. Would it be in order for me to visit you at your place of work on Monday?"

"It would be better if you did see me at work," Wallace responded. "I have some staff checking the paperwork for that fellow you mentioned yesterday so perhaps they will have found something by the time I see you next."

"Perhaps. In that case I shall see you sometime on Monday, all being well," Jake concluded.

There was a carriage waiting for them outside. Jake and Margaret climbed inside and the carriage set off.

"What a lovely evening," Margaret said. "I quite like Robert Wallace."

"He's very charming, isn't he?"

"Without being overpowering," added Margaret.

"He seems to think he will get a chance to stand for Parliament at a by-election soon to be held in Aberdeen."

"Well I would certainly vote for him," Margaret added with some conviction.

"Then you will be pleased to know that Robert champions the need for women to get the vote," Jake said.

Margaret smiled. "I like the man even more."

"Why would you vote for him?" Jake then enquired.

Margaret thought for a moment. "He just strikes me as the kind of man who would get things done. He obviously deeply believes in his politics and he also seems to revel in stirring things up. I think we need a man like that to be our Member for Parliament rather than these rather stuffy gentlemen who are only in politics to meet their own ambitions and not to really represent their constituents."

"Robert is so right, isn't he?" Jake then said.

Margaret looked a little confused. "What do you mean?"

"If all women are as perceptive as you, Margaret, then the quicker you all have the vote the better."

Margaret took a hold of Jake's hand. "Thank you for saying that, now give me a kiss."

***

Stinky had been outside the house for half an hour. He was cold and he was getting wet but he was driven on by the thought of how much alcohol he would be able to buy with the money he received from Inspector Fraser. Stinky knew that he would get a decent amount of money from the Inspector because he now knew he had something to tell him. Something that the Inspector would welcome and something that the Inspector would definitely be able to use.

Stinky had been outside two houses that evening. The first had belonged to the person whom Jake had wanted followed. Stinky's mate had followed the man back to his house and Stinky had taken over around eight in the evening. Nothing of any consequence had happened in the time they had been following this man and Stinky had been starting to think that he wouldn't get the chance to earn much at all from Inspector Fraser.

At ten minutes passed eight all that had changed.

A woman had appeared from a street just along from where Stinky had been standing. He was lighting a cigarette and he noticed the woman crossing the road and walking down on the other side of the street. To Stinky's surprise the woman then walked up the short path towards the door of the house he was watching. She knocked and waited. The door opened and as she went in through the door she kissed the man full on the lips. The door then closed.

The woman had not come out again until two hours later. Stinky had decided to follow her and to his amazement and complete joy she went back to a house that also had a part to play in the case on which Inspector Fraser was currently working.

Stinky had just proved that there was a link between two people who should not have been linked. Inspector Fraser would be delighted to receive this information and Stinky would be delighted to receive a handsome payment in return.

As he lit another cigarette and started to make his way home, Stinky felt that at long last the world had been kind to him. He had a smile on his face as he walked home and he could not wait for Monday morning to arrive so that he could collect his reward.

TWENTY-THREE

Monday 26 November: Mid-morning until mid-afternoon

Sergeant Turnbull informed Jake that the rather smelly gentleman who sometimes provided Jake with information was sitting in the interview room. The look on Turnbull's face was the usual expression of disgust when he ever spoke about Stinky.

Jake went through to the interview with two cups of tea, one of which he placed in front of Stinky. Jake sat down and took a sip from his own cup.

"I presume you have something for me," he then said.

Stinky sat forward, his hands cupped around his tea. "I most certainly do, Mr Fraser."

There was a silence in the room, which annoyed Jake as he was keen to hear what Stinky had uncovered.

"Well, what is it?" Jake said with some impatience.

"We followed the gentleman as requested and not very much happened until the weekend. I was waiting outside his house when a young woman called to see him. She was in the house, with him, for over two hours. Anyway, when she came out I decided to follow her. She didn't go far but I was still surprised to see what house she eventually went in to. You'll never guess who the young woman was, Mr Fraser?"

"Harriet Cruickshank," Jake said.

Stinky looked crestfallen. "How did you know that?"

"Because it was the only woman it could be."

"Then why did you ask me to follow Daniel Ifield?" Stinky then said.

"I had a feeling they were working together but I had no proof. You have confirmed that they know each other and if her time spent in his house is anything to go by, they know each other rather well. That being the case the two people who always stood to gain the most from Willie Ifield being convicted of Guy Le Fondre's murder were actively involved in some kind of plan together. I can only assume that they, therefore, are behind the deaths of at least three people. Thank you, Stinky, you have been a great help to me," Jake then concluded as he took some money from his pocket.

He gave the money to Stinky and asked him to ensure that his friends received their cut of the money. He had a feeling, however, that those other associates were unlikely to see any part of the payment as it would inevitably end up being poured down Stinky's throat.

Jake wasted no time in organising a team of officers to go to King's Gate and to accompany Harriet Cruickshank down to Lodge Walk. She was to be placed in the first interview room. Jake, himself, went with Mathieson and McGill to Daniel Ifield's place of work where he was taken from his office and led out to the carriage. Miss Sangster was told to close up the building and to take a couple of days off. She still had a look of complete shock on her face as the four men marched out of the building.

Less than an hour after Stinky had called at the police office, Daniel Ifield and Harriet Cruickshank were sitting in separate interview rooms with a Police Constable for a guard. Jake decided to leave them both to stew a little in their own juice before he went to speak to them.

First he went up to see the Chief Constable and to explain what he was doing. The Chief listened to everything Jake had to say and then sat forward in his chair.

"So why did you finally decide to have Daniel Ifield followed?"

"This has always been a case where it was apparent that someone wanted to steer us in the direction of a particular solution. We have been getting helpful hints along the way through the anonymous letters and everything we were told led us to believe that Willie Ifield was our killer. The problem with those helpful hints, however, was that the evidence did not back up what we were being told. However, things were then further complicated by the fact that Ifield was lying to us about his involvement in the sex films and a few other matters as well. His lies seemed to imply guilt of some kind on his part, so it was always just possible that he might actually be our killer. The biggest problem always was, however, that no matter which way you looked at this case it always seemed to come back to the only two people who really stood to gain from Guy Le Fondre being murdered and Willie Ifield being convicted of that crime."

"In terms of motive it always came back to Harriet Cruickshank and Daniel Ifield?" the Chief suggested.

"Exactly. It seemed the more someone tried to send us in a different direction the more we continued to be pulled back towards the most obvious of suspects. There just wasn't anyone else who gained from what had happened and if there was no gain there seemed to be no reason, whatsoever, for not only the murder but then the rather crude attempt to make us think that Willie Ifield was the murderer."

"You still haven't explained why you have only now decided to have Daniel followed?" the Chief added.

"If I am honest, sir, out of a sense of desperation." The Chief smiled and Jake continued. "I remained convinced that Daniel and Harriet were in this together but they had been very careful about ever being seen together and there was no obvious reason for linking them. I eventually decided to have Daniel followed in the hope that he might lead us to Harriet. As it turned out she was the one who came to him. Once I knew that they were connected then I obviously had more reason to believe that they were definitely behind the murder of Le Fondre and everything else that has happened since."

"Did you not think that Daniel Ifield was romantically interested in Miss Sangster, who worked for his father?"

"I still believe that Daniel had feelings for Miss Sangster but I doubt if those feelings were ever going to be reciprocated. On the other hand, Harriet Cruickshank would have done anything to get her hands on Guy Le Fondre's money without having to wait until she was old. I suspect she has known for a little while that she had a very healthy place in Le Fondre's will and so she set about finding someone daft enough to get involved with her. Daniel Ifield would have been easily persuaded as even his father thinks Daniel places all his lady friends on a pedestal. He seems to worship every woman who shows even a passing interest in him. How then must he have felt when Harriet offered him her body as well as her mind?"

"So you now believe that Daniel Ifield killed Guy Le Fondre?" the Chief then asked.

"To be honest, sir, I'm still not entirely sure whether it was Daniel Ifield or whether Harriet merely convinced Gerald Strong that he should do it. I believe that Harriet Cruickshank had enough control over Gerald that he would have done almost anything for her. I think he definitely killed Mathilde Dupont and it is therefore quite possible that he killed Le Fondre as well. Whether, or not, Daniel Ifield killed Le

Fondre he most certainly was the one to provide the items of clothing from his father's house that were meant to ensure his guilt. That alone confirms his part in the planning of this crime."

The Chief still looked slightly puzzled. "But what about the witnesses who saw someone fitting Willie Ifield's description on the night Le Fondre died, surely neither Daniel nor Gerald Strong look anything like Willie Ifield?"

Jake paused for a moment. "That is the one area where I don't have an explanation, other than the witnesses must have been forced in some way in to lying to us. Daniel and Harriet would have known that the coat and shoes alone might not have meant much as anyone could have been wearing them that night, but in arranging for us to be given a description of the mystery man they were pretty much sealing Willie's fate."

"And how did Harriet get those men to take the poison?" was the Chief's next question.

"Shared a glass of something with them, perhaps?" Jake suggested. "Whatever she did she had time to clear up before she left the room."

"So what now?"

"Now I interview them both separately and see how quickly it will be before one of them starts to tell me anything that is remotely close to the truth," Jake said.

"Good luck," the Chief concluded and Jake stood up and left the office.

Jake then returned to his own office to collect the items he needed before he spoke to either Daniel or Harriet. He then met up with Mathieson and told him his thoughts on the case and what he thought he might get from interviewing the two suspects. They then made their way along the corridor to the interview room in which they had placed Daniel Ifield. Jake asked the young Constable, who had been keeping an eye on Ifield to wait outside and then he and Mathieson sat down.

As soon as they were seated Daniel started protesting about the manner in which he had been treated and also requesting a solicitor if anyone was going to start making accusations. Jake let him calm down again before starting to speak.

"I'll no longer be charging your father with the murder of Guy Le Fondre," Jake began. "In fact, there is every chance that I will be releasing your father from custody tomorrow morning, though of course there will be other, lesser, charges still to be brought at some later stage."

Daniel Ifield sat for a few seconds before responding.

"That's excellent news, Inspector, but surely you didn't have to take me down here to tell me that?"

Jake smiled. "Oh that wasn't the reason I wanted you here. I wanted the chance to have a chat with you, Mr Ifield, about Guy Le Fondre."

"I thought we had said all that we needed to say on that subject."

"I thought we had as well," added Jake," but then some more evidence came in to our possession, which has led to the need for me to speak to you again."

Jake studied Ifield's face for any sign of emotion or concern. He didn't seem to be too worried so far.

"Evidence concerning me?" Ifield then asked with some surprise in his tone, his eyes glancing at Mathieson before returning to Jake.

"In a manner of speaking, yes it is evidence that concerns you. Would you mind telling me if you are currently in a relationship with anyone?"

"I fail to see what my private life would have to do with you, Inspector, so, yes, I do mind answering that question."

"It is a perfectly innocent question, Mr Ifield and I really would appreciate you answering it," Jake insisted.

Ifield sat in thoughtful silence before eventually responding. "Very well, Inspector, I will answer your question. No, I am not in a relationship with anyone at the moment."

"But you would like to be in a relationship with Miss Sangster?" Jake then suggested.

Ifield smiled. "I'm sure that there are many men who would like to be in a relationship with Miss Sangster and, yes, I would place myself on that list. However, there seems little chance of anything developing in the foreseeable future."

Jake shuffled some papers and glanced down at a particular page, as if it contained some valuable piece of information. He then looked up.

"Mr Ifield, do you know a woman by the name of Harriet Cruickshank?"

Ifield's expression changed fleetingly, but it was enough to tell Jake that he had struck a nerve ending with the introduction of that name. Ifield again took a little while to think before eventually answering.

"I don't think so."

"The name means nothing to you?" Jake prompted.

"No, I really don't think that it does."

"I know for a fact that you have met with Harriet Cruickshank," Jake then said.

Ifield looked a little more concerned on hearing that but he still insisted that he did not know anyone of that name. Jake explained that she had been the young woman with Guy Le Fondre on the night that the two men had exchanged words in the Business Club.

"I didn't realise that that was her name," Ifield then said, noticeably relaxing.

Jake paused for a moment longer. "So the woman who spent around two hours in your house on Saturday night was not Harriet Cruickshank?" Jake then asked.

Ifield's expression changed again. His body tightened again. This time that tell-tale look of concern crossed his face and didn't entirely depart. His eyes again flicked to Mathieson and then dropped to the table.

"I'm not exactly sure of what you mean by asking me about this Harriet Cruickshank?" he then eventually said.

"We know that a woman spent two hours in your home on Saturday night. We also know that when that woman left your house she went back to her own home. That home, Mr Ifield, used to be occupied by Guy Le Fondre, which means that it had to be Harriet Cruickshank, seeing as she is the new occupant of that property. Now, I ask you again, do you know Harriet Cruickshank?"

Ifield looked as if he wanted to run. His muscles had tightened and a thin line of sweat had appeared on his brow. His eyes kept looking towards the door as if he was gauging his chances of escape. It would have been a pointless gesture as he knew that beyond that door were enough police officers to catch him long before he made it to the front door.

"Very well, Inspector, I do know Harriet."

"Intimately?" Jake then asked.

"That is none of your business," Ifield snapped.

"In a murder enquiry, Mr Ifield, everything becomes my business. Now will you please just answer the question?"

Ifield paused again for a moment. There seemed little reason to lie now as it was quite obvious that someone had seen Harriet leaving his home. He had always told her how dangerous it had been for them to meet. If only she had waited as he had originally suggested. He sighed and then answered the question.

"Yes intimately."

"How long have you known her?"

"She came to see me about a month ago."

"*She* came to *you*?"

"Yes. She somehow knew my address and called at my home. She said that she knew I was going in to business with Guy Le Fondre and wanted to warn me in terms of what kind of man he was. We chatted that night and found that there was an immediate connection between us. We met on quite a few occasions after that."

"And eventually you started making love on the occasions that you met?" Jake then asked.

"Harriet told me that she never made love with Le Fondre as he found the sex act a sordid affair. She said that she needed a real man in her life and wanted me to be that person. I have to say that I was infatuated by her and have enjoyed our times together."

"So when did you start talking about murder?"

Ifield looked up at Jake with an intensity in his expression that might have been intimidating to someone other than Jake Fraser.

"What do you mean, we've never talked about murder."

Jake let that answer hang in the air for a moment. "You never discussed murdering Guy Le Fondre and trying to persuade the police to believe the killer was your father?"

"No."

"So the fact all that happened was just by chance?" Jake added.

"Guy Le Fondre's death had nothing to do with either myself or Harriet. We were just lovers, Inspector, nothing more."

"And very good actors as well," Jake then added.

Ifield looked somewhat surprised. "You're talking in riddles again, Inspector."

"Not at all. You have both managed to hide the fact that you knew each other from everyone. You even managed to be in each other's company the night that Le Fondre was killed without anyone suspecting that you were a couple already. You even kept up the pretence of having feelings for Miss Sangster."

"Oh that wasn't pretending, Inspector, I do have feelings for Miss Sangster but I am wise enough to know that those feelings would never have been reciprocated. With Harriet it is different; she takes the lead."

"I'm sure she does," Jake added. He then sat back in his chair and allowed a few seconds of silence to remain in the room. He then sat forward again and asked another question.

"Do you know a man by the name of Gerald Strong?"

Again Ifield appeared to give the question some thought before answering.

"Not that I can recall."

"How about Denis Arthur?"

"No. Who are these men?" Ifield then enquired.

"They are men whom Harriet Cruickshank murdered, Mr Ifield," Jake then said in as chilling a tone as he could muster. "I also believe that Harriet Cruickshank used the offer of sex to control Gerald Strong, as well as you, so you weren't the only real man she was looking for in her life."

"You've lost me now, Inspector," Ifield insisted.

"You did know that Harriet was a prostitute when she first came to see you?" Jake then asked.

"Harriet *used* to be a prostitute, Inspector. She is not one anymore."

"She may not take money for her actions anymore, Mr Ifield, but using sex to manipulate men in to doing what she wants is still prostitution in my book. Are you still intent on telling me that you have no idea who Gerald Strong and Denis Arthur are?"

Ifield sat for a little while and said nothing. Eventually he felt obliged to say something as it was becoming apparent that Inspector Fraser had no intention of speaking again until he had received some response to his question.

"I do not know these men, Inspector and any talk of Harriet being a killer must be your idea of some kind of sick joke."

"Oh, it is no joke, Mr Ifield. Harriet Cruickshank poisoned both Gerald Strong and Denis Arthur. Now I know that Gerald Strong also knew Mathilde Dupont who was the woman who could have provided your father with his much needed alibi. Still just coincidence that the perceived murderer of Mathilde Dupont then ends up dead himself almost immediately?"

"Did I not hear that he had committed suicide?" Ifield then said.

"It may have been made to look like suicide, Mr Ifield, but there was no *evidence* of suicide. No bottle containing the poison and in Denis Arthur's case no evidence of poison having been in the glass that had been conveniently left lying on the floor. Two men poisoned and yet no sign of poison anywhere. However, there is evidence of a woman being present at both deaths. It could only, therefore, be that woman who cleaned up after both deaths. Now why should she do something like that if she, herself, had nothing to hide?"

"I have no idea," Ifield said, though he was looking more concerned now than he had been at the start of the interview.

"But let me go back a few pages in the story, Mr Ifield," Jake then continued. "Ever since Guy Le Fondre was killed we have been presented with a variety of convenient items of evidence, all pointing, it would seem, towards your father being the murderer. We had the two witnesses giving us your father's description; we had the blood-stained coat and muddy shoes and we had the anonymous letters informing us of the sex films and the farm. Not only did that evidence get Scott Thane out of the way but it further seemed to point the finger even more positively at your father. If we simply accepted all that evidence then, surely, there could be no doubt that Willie Ifield was the murderer and if we convicted Willie Ifield and he went to the gallows then what was left behind? With both Guy Le Fondre and Willie Ifield dead there really were only two people who might find reason to celebrate; those people were you and Harriet Cruickshank."

"This is all nonsense," Ifield insisted.

"The one and only inescapable fact in this whole contrived mess, Mr Ifield, is that you and Harriet Cruickshank are the sole benefactors at the end of the line. In terms of motive there is no greater incentive to murder than the fact a large pot of gold sits waiting at the end of the rainbow. No one else really gained anything by the death of Guy Le Fondre and certainly no one else, other than yourself, would have gained from Willie Ifield being hanged. However you look at this case it always keeps coming back to the same two people."

"Just because we are the benefactors does not, in itself, make us killers," Ifield reasoned.

"That may well be true," Jake conceded, "but you see there were other holes in the evidence being provided to us that rather spoiled the story of Willie Ifield being the killer of Guy Le Fondre. For one thing the blood-stained coat was too blood-stained."

"Whatever do you mean by that?"

"The blow to Guy Le Fondre's head bled severely as he lay on the ground, particularly as there was a second blow once he had fallen. There is no way that blood would have carried to the coat whilst he was still standing. The other and possibly bigger hole in the notion that Willie Ifield killed Guy Le Fondre was the angle at which the first blow was delivered. For possibly the one and only time in your father's life he will welcome the fact that he is so short. The person who delivered that first blow to Guy Le Fondre's head was much, much taller than your father."

"And you now think that killer was me?" Ifield asked.

"If truth be known, Mr Ifield, I have *always* thought it was you. Had it not been for the constant smokescreen that you and your lover was putting up around us we would have been having this little chat a long, long time ago. I give you credit for causing as much confusion as you did. You obviously knew yourself that you would be the number one suspect and you did a good job of diverting our attention. The problem was your father's lack of height; there was absolutely nothing you could do about that."

"So someone else killed Guy Le Fondre that does not mean that someone else has to be me."

"No one else had such easy access to your father's coat and shoes. No one else could have provided us with the evidence about the sex films and the farm. No one else was having a relationship with the only other benefactor in this whole sorry tale. You had motive and you had opportunity, Mr Ifield and for the moment, I will leave it at that. I will get Sergeant Mathieson here to bring you a cup of tea and I suggest that you think long and hard, as you drink it, about what you are going to say to me when I return to the room in a little while."

Mathieson then went for the tea and was also told to sit with Ifield but to say nothing, even if Ifield asked him a direct question. Any suggestion of Nigel Porteous being called was to be knocked back at once. Until he got his confession, Jake was not of a mind to let anyone near Daniel Ifield.

Jake left the room and went to the front desk. He instructed Sergeant Turnbull to find some men who could go and find Stanley Zanre. He would probably be in his shop in Rosemount. They were to bring him back to Lodge Walk and to keep him in one of the spare offices. Someone was to remain with him at all times. Jake then hurried over to the mortuary where he was given a photograph of Gerald Strong by Doctor Symon.

Jake put the photograph in his inside, jacket pocket and then went to speak to Harriet Cruickshank.

***

As Jake was leaving the first interview room Inspector Sandy Wilson was sitting down in a small, stuffy room at the prison in the company of a prison guard and Donald Yule.

Sandy had quickly come to the decision that only Donald Yule could have any link to Henry Davis. They had both worked for George Cathcart and it made sense that associates of Cathcart would not have taken kindly to knowing that their friend had been murdered by a police officer.

Sandy had also found out that Donald Yule was in the vicinity of Henry Davis at the time of the attack, though most of the guards were of the opinion that it was out of character for Yule to be so violent. Sandy Wilson was more inclined to believe that Donald Yule would have done anything asked of him as long as his wife and family were looked after.

In other words, as ever, money speaks louder than anything else.

Sandy had organised better protection for Bella Davis, just in case the need for retribution continued onwards to her. He hoped that the death of Henry Davis would be seen as payment enough for the death of George Cathcart and that poor Bella would now be left to serve her sentence and then get back to a life with her children.

In the meantime, Sandy had to try and identify who it was who had killed Henry Davis and the best possible starting point just had to be Donald Yule.

Yule sat with a sneer on his face. He looked to be an angry man but a man who had long forgotten why he was angry. He had lived a life of obeying orders and dishing out violence for so long that he no longer knew what a normal life might have offered. He had spent so much time in prison that another term achieved nothing had rehabilitation been the aim of his sentence. To Donald Yule a spell in prison was just one of those occupational hazards that had to be overcome.

"I am Inspector Wilson of Aberdeen City Police," Sandy began and the sneer on Yule's face grew even more fearsome.

"Good for you," Yule said.

Sandy smiled. "Did you know a man by the name of Henry Davis?"

"He was the copper who worked for Mr Cathcart," Yule replied.

"And did you know he was killed in this prison the other day?"

"I had heard."

"You only heard about it, you weren't actually there?" Sandy then asked.

"I might have been nearby," Yule then conceded.

"You were seen approaching Mr Davis just before he was killed," Sandy then said. It wasn't actually true, in the sense that no one had formally admitted to seeing anything, but Sandy still felt it might be the way to get Yule to admit to what he did.

"No one saw me," Yule said and then looked away. Yet again the organ inside his head had let him down badly. Yet again Donald Yule's ignorance and total inability to think on his feet had led to him saying something that pretty much incriminated him before he need go any further.

"So no one saw you doing something that you say you never did?" Sandy then said and Donald Yule looked even more vacant as he tried to mentally digest that last statement. Sandy continued. "You broke free from a group of prisoners, stuck the knife into Henry Davis and then hurried back to once more be concealed by that same group of prisoners. There is no doubt that it was you, Mr Yule, the only doubt is over how you managed to get a knife in the first place. I didn't think you would have found anything in the prison so that meant it had to be brought in from the outside. As far as the prison records indicate the only person who has visited you, whilst you've been in this prison has been your wife. Oh and I did talk to one guard who remembers Henry Davis speaking to you at one time. That seems to be a further indication that you knew Mr Davis a lot better than him just being someone else who worked for George Cathcart."

"You keep my wife out of this," Yule then said, the sneer softening in the process.

"I will gladly keep your wife out of all of this, Mr Yule, if you simply tell me the truth about what happened with Henry Davis."

Yule considered his position for a moment. It was clearly not good. However, he was prepared to do anything to keep his wife from being visited by the police. The last thing he wanted was for her to find out exactly what he had been doing by way of employment. It was enough, for the moment, that Aspinall had ensured a steady flow of money towards his family, no matter what might now happen to him.

He started to talk and by the time he had finished Sandy Wilson had solved the murder of Henry Davis. Yule said nothing about Aspinall, for the moment. He would say more if he ever needed to, but for the moment it was sufficient for him to take the blame for Henry Davis's death. Yule also said nothing more about the knife for if he had he would have had to mention Aspinall. It had been Aspinall who had arranged for one of the guards to be bribed in to taking the knife to Yule.

Yule went back to his cell, now knowing that he was destined to be there for a very long time. There was also a strong chance that he might hang for his crime, in which case he would never mention Aspinall's name. Yule needed to know that his wife would never want for anything once he was gone. He actually thought she could be better off without him, after all, what had he ever really done for her apart from father their children?

He had never been much of a husband or a father. Maybe the best he could do for them was to die and leave behind a regular payment that would ensure his family had a better life than he could ever have provided. At least he would die knowing that he had finally done some good for his family, even if it had meant him having to murder another human being to achieve that.

Sandy Wilson went back to Lodge Walk happy in the fact that he had solved the murder of Henry Davis. Donald Yule sat in his cell happy in the fact that he had just set his family up for life.

***

Harriet Cruickshank looked relaxed and unbothered by the fact that she had been sitting in a police interview room for the best part of an hour. Constable McGill was sitting across from her and nothing had been said in the whole time that they had sat there.

Jake entered the room and sat down beside McGill. Harriet Cruickshank's eyes had followed Jake all the way from the door until he sat down opposite her. There was almost a smile playing around her lips as if she was finding this whole experience mildly amusing. She sat there, looking pretty as a picture and exuding the air of someone who was in complete control of their surroundings.

Jake decided to get straight to the point.

"How long have you and Daniel Ifield been lovers?"

Harriet did not flinch in the slightest as she answered.

"A month perhaps."

"Why did you decide to take Daniel Ifield in to your life?"

"Is that what I have done, Inspector?" replied Harriet and the smile grew even more prominent on her pretty face.

"You do not see your relationship as being permanent?"

"I really don't know. We like being with each other and Daniel is a good lover. He brings me to life when we are in bed together; not every man I have been with has managed to do that."

"When did you decide to discuss murder, Miss Cruickshank?" Jake then asked.

"Why would we want to do that, Inspector? Our time together was precious. I was getting no sexual satisfaction from Guy so I needed to find it elsewhere. Daniel filled that void, if I can put it that way."

"When did you know that Guy Le Fondre was intent on leaving you his entire fortune?"

"When that nice lawyer read out the will in his office," Harriet replied with another sweet smile.

"I'm afraid that just isn't true, Miss Cruickshank. I know that Scott Thane told you before then but I'm also pretty sure that you knew even before Scott Thane came to see you. Did Le Fondre tell you one night while you were washing him?"

"All right, Scott Thane did come and tell me but that was the first I knew about the contents of Guy's will."

Jake did not believe her but, for the moment, he had no proof to the contrary. He now realised, however, that this woman was very cold and calculating in how she approached things and it would not be easy to break her down. He thought for a moment on how best to proceed and then decided to play his half-truth and see what reaction he got.

"The day you went to the Bon Accord Hotel with Gerald Strong you were seen by the reception clerk. I'm sure that when we have an identity parade he will pick you from the line and that will clarify, once and for all, that you are connected to the death of Gerald Strong as well as one or two others that have occurred in this city over the last two weeks."

Harriet was fairly sure that she had not been seen at the Bon Accord Hotel, although she did not know that for certain. However, what she did know for certain was that the man at the Forsyth Hotel would most definitely remember her so she did not want the police involving him if she could help it. She decided to confess the fact that she knew Gerald Strong and hope that that would divert the Inspector's interest away from the Forsyth Hotel and what may have happened there.

"I openly admit that I knew Gerald, Inspector and I openly admit that I did go to the Bon Accord Hotel with him. However, the poor man was distraught at the fact he had apparently killed some French woman and he insisted that I left him alone. Had I known he was going to kill himself I would, of course, have remained with him."

"How did he kill himself, Miss Cruickshank?" Jake then asked.

"I believe he poisoned himself."

"But how did he manage to poison himself?" Jake pressed.

"I wouldn't know, Inspector. As I have already said, I had left the room before he did whatever he did."

"So let me get this clear in my mind, Miss Cruickshank, you would like me to believe that you went to a hotel room with Gerald Strong, presumably to have sex, but he decided that he no longer wanted to do anything so he asked you to leave?"

"That is exactly what happened, Inspector."

"And then he committed suicide?" Jake added.

"That would appear to be the case, yes."

"How would you imagine Gerald Strong took the poison that killed him?" Jake then asked.

"I presume he drank something," Harriet suggested.

"And had he drank something then we would have to assume that the poison he drank, or at the very least the bottle he transported it in, would still have been in the room with him. We searched the hotel thoroughly, Miss Cruickshank and we didn't find anything. Now, would you be able to help us out and explain why there was no bottle?"

Harriet Cruickshank no longer looked quite so confident. She took a little while to compose herself enough so as to answer the question.

"I really don't know, Inspector. Now you come to mention it I didn't see him carrying anything when we went to the room."

"And if you were the only other person to enter that room, Miss Cruickshank, then it surely follows that if there had been a bottle of some kind then only you could have removed it and that would confirm that you were actually still there at the time Gerald took the poison."

"But I wasn't," Harriet insisted. "Someone else must have gone in to the room after I left."

"Oh, I see," Jake then announced as if he had just thought of something helpful. "Now I get it. Gerald had actually arranged to meet two women at the hotel that day and he only wanted you to leave so that the other woman could enter his room and help him kill himself. Now that makes perfect sense," he concluded, his tone full of heavy sarcasm.

Harriet could now see for herself how stupid the notion was. She could also see that she had rather talked herself in to trouble and she was no longer sure how she might manage to talk herself back out of it again. She had prepared a few answers to give the police but suddenly none of them appeared to be very helpful to her at the moment.

"Very well, Inspector, I was in the room when poor Gerald took the poison. He did not want any evidence left behind so he asked me to take the bottle away with me."

"So now we are to believe that Gerald asked you to go to the room, not to have sex, but to help him commit suicide?"

The sarcasm was every bit as heavy.

"Gerald was distraught, Inspector. He had murdered some woman and he no longer wanted to live with the thought of what he had done."

"So why ask you?" Jake then asked.

"Gerald and I had known each other since before I met Daniel. I got the impression that he didn't know anyone else to ask."

"And was Denis Arthur also glad to have your company as he killed himself?" Jake added.

"I don't know anyone called Denis Arthur," Harriet eventually replied but there had been that tell-tale hesitation again and Jake had picked up on it.

"It just seems strange that a woman books in to the Forsyth Hotel not moments after Denis Arthur. Then Denis apparently commits suicide but just like Gerald there is no evidence of where the poison came from. We find no bottles, no needles and in Denis's case, no note. Having said that, the note left by Gerald Strong didn't really say much and anyway, I now have witnesses who can testify that the note was not written by Gerald but, no doubt, by his killer. That is the evidence, I am afraid, Miss

Cruickshank; we have a note that was not written by the victim and we have a man who died by ingesting poison but left no trace of where that poison may have come from. In short, we have a hotel room that is just too tidy. In fact, if we include Denis Arthur then we have *two* hotel rooms that were just too tidy. Two men poisoned and in both cases no evidence of poison being in the room. The only known connection between the two deaths was the presence of a mystery woman at both scenes. As you have admitted to being with Gerald Strong then I have to assume that you were also with Denis Arthur, but I still have to ask myself why?"

"As I have said, Inspector, I did know Gerald but I have no idea who this Denis Arthur is," Harriet added.

"Forgive me if I say that I simply don't believe you, Miss Cruickshank. I believe you were present at the deaths of both men and I believe that their deaths were required as part of the plan you had hatched with Daniel Ifield."

"Daniel has nothing to do with Gerald or anyone else," Harriet added very quickly.

"Not directly, perhaps, but they both had their part to play in this little charade that you and Daniel have created for us all."

Harriet smiled. She looked even more beautiful as she did so and Jake found it very difficult to continue to believe that this young woman could be the cold-blooded killer that she was.

"This really is all in your mind, Inspector. I may have known Gerald and I may have known Daniel but, beyond that, there is no connection to anything else and certainly not to anything to do with Guy Le Fondre's murder."

"Hear me out, Miss Cruickshank," Jake then said. "When you went to see Daniel Ifield it may well have been little more than a warning visit; after all, only you really knew what kind of man Guy Le Fondre was. However, I believe that you and Daniel found that there was an instant, mutual attraction. You wanted to see each other again and you wanted intimacy. You were lost in this world with Guy Le Fondre in which sex could not exist and yet you had lived a life built around the sexual act. You had needs; you had feelings and you soon realised that Daniel Ifield could meet both of those. Then you both realised that with Willie Ifield out of the way, as well as Le Fondre, life would be even better for both of you. Daniel has always lived in the shadow of his father and has always, no doubt, felt he has been held back by the need to have his father's approval before he could do anything in his own life. I am sure, for example, that his father would never have approved of his son taking up with a whore such as yourself."

Jake had deliberately chosen to call Harriet a whore as it sounded much more offensive than calling her a prostitute. He wanted to get under her skin; he wanted to ruffle those pretty feathers and get her to drop the act of being this sweet, young woman who would never dream of harming anyone.

A brief sign of anger flashed in Harriet Cruickshank's eyes before passing and being replaced by that half smile on her lips again. It was as if she had realised that Jake was just baiting her and that she was not going to rise to his taunts.

"I really don't know what Willie Ifield would have made of me, however the fact he kept his own little *whore*, rather implies that he would have been somewhat two-faced to pass judgement on anything that Daniel may have done."

The word *whore* was stressed more than seemed necessary, as if in throwing the word back at Jake she was in some way defending herself. Jake decided to move on.

"You were not prepared to wait for nature to take its course and allow you to inherit Guy Le Fondre's money; instead you wanted him dead now so that you could start living the kind of life that you had always dreamed of. You turned to Daniel Ifield and Gerald Strong for help, using your body as a means of controlling both men. However, once you thought things through a little further it suddenly seemed more sensible to you and Daniel that life would be even better with his father out of the way. And so you hatched your devious, little plan."

Harriet's smile was even broader. "You are a great story-teller, Inspector. Have you ever considered writing a book, I do believe you would be rather good at it."

Jake smiled back. "I only wish it had been no more than a good story. Had that been the case then Mathilde Dupont, Gerald Strong and Denis Arthur would all still be alive. As it is, they are all dead and for no other reason than to play some bit-part in your horrendous little creation."

"This is still all in your mind, Inspector," insisted Harriet.

"And that is where we will leave it for the moment," Jake then said and he stood up to leave.

"Am I free to go then?" Harriet asked.

"You will never be free to go, Miss Cruickshank, but at least for the moment you are free to keep on sitting there. Constable McGill, please keep an eye on her."

"May I at least have a cigarette?" Harriet then asked.

Jake turned to McGill. "Constable, please find Miss Cruickshank a cigarette and bring her a cup of tea at the same time."

"Yes, sir," said McGill who then hurried out the door. Jake arranged for one of the uniformed constables, still waiting in the hall, to come in to the room and keep an eye on Harriet Cruickshank. Jake then went on his way.

TWENTY-FOUR

Monday 26 November: late afternoon in to early evening

It had taken longer than ought to have been the case to find Stanley Zanre. He had not been at his place of work and he had not been at home, as he had told his assistant at work that he would be. His wife had an idea that he might be visiting a friend and she provided an address.

The friend did not know where Stanley was either but after a few more questions and some veiled threats of further police action if he didn't tell them the truth, he eventually confessed to the fact that Stanley had a weekly assignation with a young prostitute called Bertha. They would probably be found in room twenty-one of the Royal Hotel.

The police officers then visited the hotel and found a naked Stanley sitting on the bed with an equally naked Bertha looking very pleased with whatever had just happened between them. Whilst the two police officers waited outside the door, Stanley paid Bertha her usual fee and then got dressed.

It was late afternoon, therefore, before Stanley Zanre finally arrived at Lodge Walk. Jake was a little tired waiting and took Stanley in to his office, where he sat him down and started to apply a little pressure.

"Mr Zanre, I now know that you lied to the police about seeing a man outside Guy Le Fondre's house on the night he was killed. I would now like you to tell me why you lied?"

Zanre looked flushed. He was still recovering from being caught in the hotel room with Bertha and still wondering how best he would explain it all to his wife, should she ever find out. Basically he was now beyond wanting to lie anymore.

"A man came to see me at my place of work," he said. "He threatened to harm my family if I did not cooperate. I felt I had no other option, Inspector, you have to believe me."

Jake took the photograph of Gerald Strong from his jacket pocket and showed it to Zanre.

"Is this the man who threatened you?"

Zanre studied the photograph for a moment and then shook his head. "No, I have never seen that man before."

"So because of these threats to your family the story you told us was complete fabrication?"

"The man told me exactly what I was to say to any police officer who came asking questions. I have a wife and two daughters, Inspector; I could not take the risk with their safety otherwise I would have told you earlier of my lies."

"Very well, Mr Zanre, I would like you to do something for me....." Jake said and then went on to outline what he had in mind.

***

Ten minutes later and Jake was back in the interview room with Daniel Ifield. It had been nearly three hours since he had left Ifield in the room and the young man was now looking rather annoyed at the manner of his treatment. He further insisted that he should see his solicitor immediately and that he would be complaining, in the strongest terms, to the Chief Constable about the way he had been treated since arriving at the police office.

"I've been speaking to Harriet Cruickshank," Jake then said, ignoring any comments that Ifield might have been making about treatment or solicitors. Ifield was suddenly quiet. He looked at Jake, then at Mathieson, then back to Jake.

"Is Harriet here as well?"

"Of course she is, Mr Ifield. After all, you are both in this together so you both have to be charged together."

"Charged?" Ifield repeated with some outrage in his tone. "How can you charge me with something I haven't done?"

Jake ignored the question. "Harriet said some very interesting things. She has acknowledged that she knew Gerald Strong and of course we know that Gerald probably killed Mathilde Dupont whom, as I am sure you know even though you said you didn't, was your father's alibi for him not committing murder at Guy Le Fondre's house. We can now also put Harriet in the hotel room with Gerald Strong when he killed himself and we can also be fairly certain that Harriet was also present when Denis Arthur killed himself. I'm sure you'll know Denis as he was the man who tried to blackmail one or other of you over what he had seen on one of the occasions that he had followed Gerald Strong. I'm guessing that he saw both of you and that was the secret you could ill-afford for him to make public. It seems, therefore, that all the murders in this sordid little case have been committed by other people and that you might be the only one who can legitimately claim to be blame-free, at least in terms of murder. Now, that being the case, there is a strong chance that you won't hang, which is more than can be said for Miss Cruickshank. If you were also to cooperate with me at this moment, Mr Ifield, then I feel sure that the judge would also take that in to account when it came to sentencing you."

At that moment there was a knock at the door and a Constable came in with three mugs of tea. He walked to the table and placed the tea on the table. He then turned and walked out again. Daniel Ifield had barely looked up, but the Constable was paying much more attention.

"Are you ready to start telling me the truth now?" Jake then asked as the door closed again.

"I have nothing to say, Inspector."

"Okay, Mr Ifield, have it your way for the moment."

Jake then stood up and left the room. Stanley Zanre, still dressed in the police uniform, was standing out in the corridor.

"Well, Mr Zanre?"

"That was definitely the man who threatened me, Inspector."

"And you are willing to say that in a court of law, Mr Zanre?"

"I most certainly am."

"Excellent," added Jake who then asked a Constable to take Mr Zanre back to the room where his own clothes were lying. Jake then went back in to the room with Daniel Ifield.

Ifield looked up with an expression of growing concern. It seemed every time that the Inspector went out of the room he came back with something else to make Ifield worry that little bit more. He watched as Jake Fraser crossed the room and sat down opposite. He did not like the smile that was playing on the Inspector's face.

"Mr Ifield, I said earlier that you did not seem to be involved in the murders of Mathilde Dupont, Gerald Strong and Denis Arthur, however I never actually got around to talking about the murder of Guy Le Fondre. Now that is where you come in to this little scenario. There was no one else to batter Le Fondre to death and anyway you were the one with your father's coat and shoes, weren't you?"

Ifield looked very concerned now. He was still intent on bluffing his way through.

"I did not kill Guy Le Fondre," he insisted.

"But you really are the only one with any motive, Mr Ifield. You see that motive had nothing whatsoever to do with Mr Le Fondre. That was simply another smokescreen, wasn't it? No, Mr Le Fondre had to die so that Harriet could inherit the money *now* and Willie Ifield had to hang so that you could inherit the business *now*. As with so many crimes it was all about greed, mixed in perhaps with a little bit of misplaced love. You and Harriet wanted it all and you wanted it now; you personally were fed up of having to do everything that your father wanted. You wanted to be free of your father so that you could start living your life the way you wanted to. What better way to get rid of your father other than have him convicted of Guy Le Fondre's murder. That way, no one would ever have suspected that you had had a hand in his demise."

Ifield forced a smile. "This is all nonsense, Inspector."

"Do you know a man by the name of Stanley Zanre?" Jake then asked.

"No," came the almost instant reply, but the expression on Ifield's face did not match the answer. The name had clearly meant something to him and that nervous twitch around the eyes led Jake to believe that Ifield was close to breaking.

"Now that's very strange, Mr Ifield, as Stanley Zanre most certainly knows you. In fact, Mr Zanre is quite happy to state in a court of law that you threatened him and his family if he did not lie to the police about seeing a man, resembling your father, hanging around outside Le Fondre's house. Am I in any way improving your memory by informing you of that fact?"

Ifield's expression changed again and this time he now looked like a man who was running out of ideas. It had always been the main risk to involve Zanre and young Maurice but it had been a risk worth taken to divert attention away from themselves.

"Okay, so I do know who Stanley Zanre is," Ifield eventually admitted.

"So, what do we have so far," Jake then said with a satisfied smile. "Harriet Cruickshank is definitely your lover. Harriet Cruickshank was definitely with Gerald

Strong when he died and almost definitely with Denis Arthur. Gerald Strong definitely killed Mathilde Dupont but I'm guessing that was on the instructions of Harriet. You had to have Mathilde Dupont out of the way as you knew she would be your father's alibi. You definitely threatened Stanley Zanre and his family and somehow either you, or Harriet, managed to persuade young Maurice Leith to lie as well. After all one witness might not have been enough. With two people saying that they saw someone there was a far greater chance of the story being believed. The evidence shows that the blow to Le Fondre's head was delivered by someone taller and that brings you back in to the equation, Mr Ifield. Add to that the fact that you could get your father's coat and shoes more easily than anyone else and we really do seem to have quite a case building against you, don't we?"

Ifield was clearly thinking over the position he was in. Jake was still not convinced that he was going to get a full confession just quite yet, so he decided to leave Ifield to ponder on things for a while and go back to see Harriet Cruickshank.

Jake sat down opposite Harriet and smiled broadly. "We have all that we need from Daniel Ifield, Miss Cruickshank, to get you convicted of the double murder of Gerald Strong and Denis Arthur and conspiracy to murder Guy Le Fondre. I also suspect that you were the one who persuaded young Maurice to lie to the police and also the one who persuaded Gerald Strong to get to know Mathilde Dupont and to then kill her."

Harriet Cruickshank remained cool. Her expression did not change and that annoying smile continued to play around her rouged lips.

"You have nothing on me, Inspector and there is no way that Daniel Ifield could have told you anything incriminating as there is simply nothing to tell."

"Stanley Zanre has now told us that Daniel threatened his family if he did not lie to the police. I can't imagine you threatened Maurice but somehow you managed to persuade him to help you."

Harriet had an image of Maurice touching her breasts and looking at her with an expression of triumph. No, she had not really had to persuade young Maurice to do anything. In return for his reward he would have done anything for her; poor misguided child.

"Who is Maurice?" Harriet then said.

Jake chose to ignore her question. "So Stanley Zanre now confirms that Daniel forced him to lie to the police and that there never was a man, matching Willie Ifield's description standing outside Guy Le Fondre's house on the night he died. I suppose, had Mr Zanre been at his window that night, he was more likely to have seen Daniel standing outside his gate for that was who really turned up that night to kill Guy Le Fondre. The only real motive for him being there was greed, though not personal greed at that time for he was killing to release your inheritance."

Harriet Cruickshank's expression changed to one of shock. "My God, Inspector, are you telling me that it was Daniel Ifield who killed Guy? I know they didn't like each other but I never thought he would stoop to murder."

Jake smiled. "You really are very good, Miss Cruickshank. There still seems to be a small piece of you that thinks it can talk its way out of the situation you now find yourself in. Once the man from the Bon Accord Hotel confirms it was who he saw with Gerald Strong on the day that Gerald died then you'll find it very difficult to explain why all the jigsaw pieces of this case will fall so neatly in to place. You see we know that Denis Arthur was in the habit of following Gerald and was therefore very likely to have seen both you and Daniel at some point of that day. Denis tries to blackmail you and you decide that he has to die as well. I'm sure that the reception clerk at the Forsyth Hotel will also be able to identify you as the woman who booked a room only moments after Denis Arthur. Why else would you have been there if not to kill Arthur?"

Jake did not wait for a reply.

"So you see, we can connect you to both these men and as you were present when they died you obviously know more than you have said. Add to that the fact that we know Daniel Ifield's part in all this as well and I think even you will have to agree that neither you, nor Daniel, are going anywhere other than to jail to await trial, Miss Cruickshank."

The confidence in Harriet's expression waned a little. Like Daniel Ifield she was beginning to realise the sheer swathe of circumstantial evidence was beginning to overwhelm her. There was still a chance that the reception clerks at both hotels would be able to identify her and once it was proved that she was there it became almost impossible to offer any other reason other than she was there with Gerald and Denis.

She also didn't know exactly how much Daniel might have said. She had always thought him to be quite weak; happy to go along with the plan but always threatening to buckle at any moment. She had even thought at one time of killing Daniel as well but, of course, that wouldn't have achieved anything. The more that Harriet thought things over the bleaker it looked for her.

Harriet let out a huge sigh and then started to talk again.

"Very well, Inspector, I did kill Gerald Strong and Denis Arthur and I was working with Daniel Ifield in the murder of Guy Le Fondre. It was actually only meant to be Guy who died but then I soon realised that my control over Gerald would end the moment he knew that I really wanted Daniel in my life. Gerald was like that faithful puppy dog who will trot by your side through thick and thin. He was infatuated with me and would have done anything that I asked. However, once he had murdered Mathilde his services were no longer necessary. I arranged to meet him at the Bon Accord Hotel so that he could be paid both with money and with sex. He did not live long enough to really enjoy the sex."

Jake noted that Harriet Cruickshank had become even colder as she talked. It was as if she was now talking about someone other than herself. As she spoke she continued to look straight in to Jake's eyes as if she was getting some form of pleasure out of now being able to tell her story.

"Did you take the money from Gerald Strong's wallet?" Jake then asked.

"I took *my* money from his wallet, Inspector. I had paid him always knowing that he would never live to enjoy any of it."

"And you took the poison away with you as well?"

"I did. With Gerald dead I assumed that would be the end of it. However, that annoying little shit, Denis Arthur, turned up at Daniel's house and started to threaten all kinds of things if we didn't pay him rather a lot of money. Daniel and I agreed that I should go to the Forsyth Hotel where I offered Arthur sex as well as money if he booked a room. Once we were in the room he didn't last much longer than Gerald."

"I need to ask you, Miss Cruickshank, how did you manage to get both men to take the poison?"

Harriet Cruickshank smiled again. "Very easily."

Jake grew annoyed at her reluctance to explain her actions fully, so he pressed her again.

"Miss Cruickshank, will you please tell me how you managed to persuade both men to take the poison?"

"Quite simply, Inspector, neither Gerald, nor Denis Arthur, were aware that they were taking poison. You wondered how I had managed to persuade young Maurice to lie to the police, well that was in almost the same way as I got Gerald and Arthur to take the poison."

Jake did not understand and he said as much. Harriet then leaned forward and pointed down at her breasts.

"I used these," she said with a broadening smile.

Jake was still confused. "You will have to explain more fully, Miss Cruickshank," he then said.

Harriet smiled again and sat back in her seat. "The male of the species is so easily pleased, Inspector. For the opportunity to touch my breasts young Maurice was prepared to sell his soul to the devil. Gerald and Denis were more interested in kissing and licking my breasts so it was simply a matter of putting the poison where I knew they would go, if you now get my meaning."

Jake now fully understood how Gerald Strong and Denis Arthur had been killed and he had to admit, that in all his years as a police officer, he had never heard of a woman's breasts being used a murder weapon. Before saying anything further Jake made a note to himself to have a word with Maurice at the earliest opportunity.

"And all this came about because you wanted Le Fondre's money now?" Jake then enquired.

"Why wait, I thought. Anyway, once I started talking to Daniel the whole plan rather fell into place quite quickly. It seemed only right that he should get some financial reward out of it as well, especially as that father of his has always been a bit of a tyrant."

"Well he'll be a free tyrant now, Miss Cruickshank, which is more than can be said for yourself. Constable McGill, would you please present all the charges to Miss Cruickshank and arrange to have her complete and sign a formal statement."

Jake then left the room and went back to speak with Daniel Ifield. Once he had been informed that Harriet had confessed there seemed little point in Daniel Ifield lying any longer. He, too, was soon sitting writing a full confession and Jake returned to his office feeling more than satisfied that yet another case had been solved and yet another two people were more than likely going to find themselves having a liaison with the hangman.

As he sat in his office he checked the time. It was too late to go and see Robert Wallace now. That would have to wait for another day. Jake then put his coat on and set off for home.

TWENTY-FIVE

Thursday 29 November: the afternoon

The last few days had not brought much in the way of helpful information for Jake. He had gone to see Robert Wallace on Tuesday but at that time no one had been able to find anything to connect Albie Ogston to Robert Wallace. Two of his staff were still working their way through cabinets of paper trying to find an application or some other evidence that Albie Ogston had once been in contact with Robert Wallace.

Wallace, meantime, felt happier due to the fact there had been no further contact made with Dora and he was content to view that as an unfortunate one-off. He was grateful that Dora had not been aware of the brooch being taken from her coat and he had been able to return it without her knowledge.

Jake had decided not to say any more to Wallace about Albie Ogston but to wait until something, hopefully, turned up in the files. The two men had spent time, however, discussing how well Saturday evening had gone. Jake informed Wallace that, had she had the vote, Margaret would have been at the ballot box supporting Robert Wallace.

Wallace grinned even wider. "Didn't I always say that Margaret was a highly intelligent woman, Mr Fraser?"

Jake had smiled. "Margaret is many things, Mr Wallace," he had added.

"Indeed she is," Wallace had agreed and they had continued to chat generally over a cup of coffee, which had been brought to the office by another, attractive young woman. It seemed to Jake that Robert Wallace liked having pretty women around him, though he at no time had ever given any indication of inappropriate behaviour towards any of them.

On the Wednesday Willie Ifield had been in to Lodge Walk thanking Jake for all that he had done, even though it had led to his own son being found guilty of murder.

Jake got the impression that Willie might even look at his business with new eyes now that he had spent some time behind bars. It had clearly been an experience that he had not enjoyed.

Willie had also faced the wrath of his wife with regard to the time he had spent with Mathilde Dupont. Ada had not minded the fact that her husband was seeing a prostitute, after all their own physical relationship had ended some time ago, but she had minded the fact he had kept that information from her. Her wrath had resulted in Willie buying her a ring of considerable expense, which had meant that Ada had got something out of the whole experience after all.

Jake sat back in his chair. He felt satisfied that he had solved a lot of issues over the last three months and there were a large number of people behind bars as a result of his efforts. He just had one more puzzle to solve and then he hoped his working life would settle down at least until he got through Christmas.

He was just returning to his paperwork again when the door opened and Sergeant Turnbull walked in to the room.

"A lady and a gentleman at the door to see you, sir," he said.

"Did they give you a name?" Jake asked.

"They said you would know them, sir," Turnbull added and Jake could now only think of one couple who might be wanting to see him.

He hurried through to the front room where Johnnie and Alice were waiting. They were grinning broadly and Alice was holding up her left hand in a rather flamboyant manner. As Jake drew nearer he could now clearly see the shining ring that informed him that they were finally and formally engaged.

He drew Alice in to his arms and embraced her closely. "Congratulations, I hope you will be very happy," he said and as he released Alice from their embrace he now shook Johnnie's hand.

"We've just this minute bought the ring and we knew that you would have to be the first person to see it," Johnnie said.

Alice held her hand up again and Jake inspected the ring once more. "It's lovely, as are you," he added looking into Alice's sparkling eyes. Jake could not remember Alice ever looking quite as happy as she was now and from the expression on Johnnie's face he knew that he should have no fears about Alice being treated properly. They were a couple clearly very much in love.

"So when is the wedding going to be?" Jake then asked.

"Early next year but the exact date won't be known until we can get somewhere booked for the reception," Johnnie replied. "I assume you will get time off all right?"

"Nothing will prevent me from giving Alice away," Jake replied and Alice threw her arms around his neck again and planted a kiss on his lips.

"I am always at my happiest when I am in the company of the two men I love the most in the whole world," Alice said.

"Anyway, you must have lots to do," Johnnie then said, "so we will be on our way."

Jake felt an immense internal elation having just met Johnnie and Alice and bathed in their joy for a while. He sat at his desk and realised that he was still smiling. He then wondered if it might be possible for him and Margaret to experience such elation, or was that not a thought he ought to be having only two months after meeting her. Then again, how long did it take to realise you were in love with someone. Johnnie had known Alice for less time and everything had turned out well for them.

Jake eventually removed all thoughts of love and happiness from his mind and returned his thoughts to the work lying on his desk. He had only been working for a few moments when he suddenly sat back in his chair. He suddenly remembered that he was due Alan MacBride a story. It wasn't the story he thought he'd be bringing to the journalist, but at least it still concerned one member of the Ifield family.

Jake hastily scribbled down some notes, put on his jacket and set off for the offices of the Daily Journal.

***

Peter Grant was a worried man. Time was running out and the theatre was still not ready for the opening. He was walking round with the men from the Council and he could tell by their expressions that they were far from happy. Even Peter could see that there were a number of jobs still needing to be completed before everything would be in order.

If these men from the Council had also known that there was a madman intent on doing almost anything to keep the place closed then the chances of them giving the theatre a thumbs up for opening would have been practically nil. As it was they could only see the problems that lay in front of them and that was more than enough for the moment.

They left Peter with some very glum expressions still on their faces and Peter had to pass that rather sad news on to the manager. Mr Nelson was less than impressed and went to see the foreman personally. Some very strong words passed between the two men and Alf Douglas was left in no doubt whatsoever of the trouble that would come his way were the theatre not to be ready on time.

Mr Nelson got back to his office just in time to meet the Chief Constable, who had taken it upon himself to visit the theatre and get a feel for the problems his men might have in keeping the place safe and secure on opening night.

Mr Nelson practically bowed in the presence of the Chief Constable. He offered him a seat and apologised for not being there to meet him personally when he had arrived at the front door.

"I could hardly have expected you to meet me, Mr Nelson," the Chief Constable had said, "when you did not even know that I was coming."

"What might I do for you, Chief Constable?"

"It is more what I can do for you, Mr Nelson. We have reason to believe that someone will try to harm one of your guests on Monday night and I need to ensure that that does not happen. To that end I would like to have a number of men present at the theatre so I would like you to explain our presence as simply being here to ensure crowd control. As it is I will have men checking out the building before anyone enters and I will also have some men mingling amongst the audience. I presume everything is in order for Monday?"

Nelson became a little flustered at that point and eventually admitted that all was not as well as he would have hoped. However, he felt confident that everything would be in order and he hoped that the large presence of police officers would not upset the audience too much.

The Chief Constable then asked for a tour of the building and Mr Nelson was only too happy to do that himself.

***

Jake received a message that Robert Wallace wanted to see him. Twenty minutes later he was being shown into Wallace's office one more time. The two men shook hands and then sat down.

Wallace had some papers in front of him, which he shuffled as he began to speak.

"I believe we may have finally found the connection between Albie Ogston and myself," he said. "Albie Ogston tried to get a job with us just after we got the contract to work on the new theatre. That would have been over two years ago now. He came to see me and was honest enough to say that he had been wounded fighting in the Boer War and that he sometimes took blackouts. I told him that I could not take the risk of having someone working with electrical equipment if that someone was likely to pass out at any moment. That would be a danger to the person himself let alone anyone else who may have been nearby. I remember he almost pleaded for a job; he even suggested doing something else for me if the electrical job was too dangerous. I really had nothing else to offer him even though he seemed to think that his country owed him something after all that he had done in the army. It was purely a business decision, I had never meant to offend the man."

"Of course it was the correct decision and only someone, like Albie Ogston, would have been offended. He seems to have a rather warped view of life and to him you now seem to be the Devil incarnate. I have to say that his motive for wanting to harm you is far stronger now than it was when we thought it might be political. I don't mean to upset you but it never seemed right that someone as low down the political chain should attract such violent attention."

"Better that I had upset him on a working matter, you mean?" asked Wallace, feeling his pride had been slightly dented.

"Preventing him from earning an income is quite a strong motive compared to you just not being Liberal enough," Jake added. "That mixed with Albie's deeply religious beliefs seems to have created a bit of a monster."

"But at least it's a monster you can now cage."

"It's a monster we can hopefully help, Mr Wallace. Albie is ill and needs medical attention rather than locking up."

Wallace looked suitably chastised. "Of course you are quite right, Inspector."

"May I take some of these papers?" Jake then asked.

"Of course. Use whatever you want."

Jake put some papers in his pocket and then left the office. He went back to Lodge Walk where he collected McGill. They both then went to Albie's house but there was no one there.

"Where might he be, sir?" McGill said.

"I don't know where he is just now," replied Jake," but I do know where he will be on Monday night."

And with that Jake organised for a Constable to remain outside Albie's house, in case he returned, before he went back to the office to get on with some other business.

TWENTY-SIX

Friday 30 November: the afternoon and early evening

The month of November drew to a close with Jake having the quietest time in his working life that he had had for some time. At long last the endless procession of death in the city appeared to have ended and he had the deep satisfaction in knowing that he had played a major part in bringing a peace back to the city.

All that remained was the threat to Robert Wallace and the need to find Albie Ogston who now seemed intent on spoiling the opening night of His Majesty's Theatre. Unfortunately the final act on that particular investigation would probably have to wait until the opening night itself when Ogston would have to show his face in whatever attempt he made on Robert Wallace's life.

Before any of that could happen, however, Jake went to see Cedric Hay, who had been in touch to tell Jake that they had found a possible solution to the problem of who actually owned the Esslemont Avenue property.

Cedric Hay welcomed Jake in to his office. Already seated in the room was another gentleman who now stood up as Jake entered.

"This is Brian Talbot, of Talbot and French. Brian has been working with me on this rather unusual problem and we believe that we may have come up with an answer that keeps everyone happy. Please, have a seat," Hay said.

Talbot shook Jake's hand then they all sat down. Hay then took some papers from the drawer of his desk and sat forward with some purpose.

"As this firm has the authority to act on all legal matters concerning Esslemont Avenue we have taken the decision to buy the property from the estate of the late Tom Anderson. That money can then be returned to the Treasury where it rightfully belongs. We will then lease the property to yourself, Inspector Fraser, although should the day ever arise where you feel you have the money to buy the property then, of course, we would be amenable to that. I believe you own a property in the Guestrow so, perhaps, we might sell that for you and then do a deal of some kind on Esslemont Avenue?"

"I wouldn't get enough from the sale of the Guestrow property to allow me to buy Esslemont Avenue," Jake then commented.

"As I said, Inspector, we may be able to come to an arrangement."

"And all this is in order?" Jake then asked with some suspicion.

"Absolutely," added Mr Talbot. "As Cedric says, everyone is more than happy with the outcome."

"In that case," Jake then said, "I authorise you to sell my property on the Guestrow and once we see what I get for that we can sit down and discuss how best I might acquire Esslemont Avenue."

"I should tell you," Cedric Hay then said, "that we have said nothing to Mrs Thomson about any of this. We felt that it would be kinder not to tell her what her husband had been doing."

"I totally agree," added Jake. "There is no need for Mary to know any more than she does already. My thanks, gentlemen, for your help in this matter."

Jake stood up and turned to leave the room. "We will be in touch with regard to the Guestrow," Hay said.

***

Jake had gone to see Margaret in the evening. She wanted to show him the dress she had bought for Monday evening. She was aware of how the other ladies would look on the night and she did not want to be outdone.

She insisted on putting the dress on and when she walked in to the room Jake nearly fell over, such was the effect that Margaret had upon him. The dress was of the deepest blue, flaring out from the waist in a sea of material. The bodice had a white design on it and the low neck did everything for her cleavage that might have been possible.

Margaret looked absolutely beautiful and Jake's breath was almost taken away.

"Do you like it?" Margaret asked, her eyes twinkling in accompaniment to the smile that had spread across her face.

"Margaret," Jake said in reply, "you look beautiful. I am so proud to be the man who will be seen at your side."

"Oh don't be so soft," Margaret then said and hurried over to give Jake a kiss.

It was quite evident that both Jake and Margaret were now looking forward to the opening night of the theatre more than ever.

TWENTY_SEVEN

Sunday 02 December: afternoon to evening

The theatre was a feast of activity with the cast taking the chance of their only rehearsal, filling the stage and an army of police officers checking the rest of the building for an assassin possibly concealing himself within the property.

It had been very much a last minute decision by the Council to provide the theatre with the necessary clearance to open its doors on the designated date. The workmen had pulled out all the stops in a successful attempt at getting all the jobs completed on time so that when the Council men made their last visit everything was ready.

Jake was on duty and spent some of his time watching the activities on the stage. It never ceased to amaze him how actors and actresses managed to remember their lines, especially when there seemed to be so many for this particular production. The conductor worked with the orchestra to iron out some last minute problems and generally the auditorium and backstage were a mass of activity.

The Chief Constable had also turned up to supervise the search and to make sure that men were left at the end to mount guard until the production actually started.

The theatre was looking amazing and even Jake felt a pride in having such a prestigious building in the city of Aberdeen. However, as the afternoon went on he did start to worry slightly at the length of the pantomime. The show appeared to go on forever and Jake felt sure that they were to be in for a late night on Monday.

Jake also spent some time at the main entrance planning how he was to take Robert Wallace in to the theatre without attracting the attention of his assassin. Obviously it would be a night in which there would be an endless procession of carriages pulling up at the main door and then there would be the few moments while the occupants climbed down and entered the building. The ladies would want to pause long enough to let the gathered crowd see how wonderfully they were dressed.

It would be a night when every lady was out to ensure that her dress was the best. Jake knew that they were all wasting their time; Margaret would put them all to shame.

As he stood in the main foyer he began to formulate a plan that ought to ensure the safety of Robert Wallace and hopefully everyone else. It was important to Aberdeen that the opening night went off without a hitch and that there was never to be any reports of anything other than the performance and how much that performance was enjoyed by the audience.

***

Albie Ogston had arranged to stay with a friend for the last few days leading up to the third of December. The friend had been told that there was dampness in Albie's property and that he had had to get out for a few days. The friend did not need to know that Albie was keeping away from the police.

Albie had taken a large kitchen knife from home with him. It was wrapped in an old towel and lay at the bottom of the bag he had also taken with him to his friend's house. He felt sure that the knife would make a perfect weapon with which to attack Robert Wallace. The more Albie thought about Wallace the more he looked forward to ending the man's life.

How dare he play God with men's lives. There was only one God and he cared for *all* his people, especially those who could no longer care for themselves. Albie had gone to Wallace willing to do any work that might be offered and yet he was sent away without a second thought.

He had taken a bullet for his country; what had Robert Wallace ever done? It would have seemed more satisfying to Albie if he had been able to put a bullet in Robert Wallace come Monday evening, but he had been unable to find a gun from anywhere. That being the case he would have to make do with a knife. That obviously meant getting closer but so be it; Albie was more than ready to carry out his threat.

Albie sat on his bed and read through his bible. He felt the power of God all around him and he was even more convinced that what he was about to do was the right and proper thing and definitely what God wanted.

Albie also could not wait for Monday evening to come round.

TWENTY-EIGHT

Monday 03 December 1906 – The opening night of His Majesty's Theatre

A large crowd had gathered across the road from the theatre by the time the first carriages started to pull up at a little before seven o'clock. The early doors tickets had already been sold and they were inside eagerly awaiting the show. Those looking for their seats in the balcony had already begun the endless climb to the top of the building. Here was where the usherettes had to change before making their way back to the front of house to be allocated their job for the night.

Just short of the final flight of stairs to the balcony a wooden door was closed across the stair so that only one person at a time could pass through. Here tickets were checked or sold and those lucky enough to gain entry were allowed through. Their destination was the rows of benches that seemed precariously positioned on a slope that made each individual think they were about to slide down on to the stage.

Usherettes in the balcony were provided with wooden poles. These were used to get people to move along the benches so that more people could sit at the end. The people in the rows behind had their knees pushing in to those sitting in front of them and all around a layer of smoke hung in the air.

At the front door the carriages were bringing those people who could afford better tickets. The ladies in their finest dresses of many colours were of particular interest to the watching masses. As each carriage arrived and each new feminine arrival started the short walk to the main entrance of the theatre it was as if they were all competing to outdo each other in the finery of their dresses. Each one that little bit more colourful or just that little bit more décolletage in the bodice.

As this scenario unfolded Jake was at the front door, watching everything that was happening. He smiled to himself as each woman passed for within his own mind there was no contest as to who looked the best that night. Jake had taken Margaret across earlier and she was already safely inside the theatre. The way she was looking there was simply no competition, at least in Jake's eyes.

The Chief Constable was also there. He had brought a number of officers with him and many of them were already in a line on the other side of the street, ensuring that no one stepped out of line in their excitement at being part of such a major event in the city.

Jake surveyed all the faces. He was the only one who knew what Albie Ogston looked like and therefore, the only one who could respond to seeing him. It was nearly twenty past seven and Jake knew that the carriage after the one sitting in front of him would be bringing Robert Wallace and his wife, Dora, to the front door. If Ogston was to try anything then it would be within the next few moments.

The Chief went off to check that all the arrangements for the internal security of the building were going to plan and Jake started to move forward as the next carriage approached. As the horse stopped at the entrance to the theatre Jake saw movement out of the corner of his eye. He turned to have a better look and could see the figure of a man hovering at the pillars in front of the church next door. Although he couldn't get a clear view of who it might be his instinct told him that this had to be Albie Ogston. Jake started running towards the mystery man.

Seeing Jake coming towards him caused the man to turn around and head back towards the front door of the church. By the time Jake got there the man was already inside the church. Jake paused for a second before opening the door and stepping inside.

Jake passed through the entrance area and in to the church where he was surprised to find that the lights were on. He stood at the back of the church and looked around for any sign of the man he assumed was Albie Ogston.

"Come on, Albie," Jake shouted," you might as well come out, it's all over."

Nothing happened. Jake began walking down the central aisle all the time looking from right to left in case Albie was hiding somewhere. He reached the front and stood looking back at the main area of the church. Suddenly and apparently from nowhere, a man raced from the shadows and launched himself at Jake as if he were possessed.

Somehow Jake managed to grab the man's wrist as they fell backwards together, which was just as well for Jake as in the man's right hand he held a long and very lethal knife. The two men lay on the ground, Jake on the floor and Albie Ogston on top of him. Their faces were within touching distance of each other as Jake grappled to get the knife out of Albie's grip.

Jake managed to roll over and take Albie with him. The knife moved ever closer to his face as they now fought for supremacy. Jake was surprised by Albie's strength, but then he was a younger man who had been in the army. A walk to work was the extent of Jake's idea of exercise and he had never seen any need to build up muscle power. After all he was only a policeman.

Jake eventually gripped and shook Albie's wrist enough to cause the knife to break free and clatter across the floor. Albie swung a blow at Jake and caught him on the side of his head, stunning him momentarily. Albie pushed Jake away and started to crawl across the floor towards the knife.

Jake got up and and hurried after Albie even though his head was still stinging from the blow. Jake grabbed Albie and pushed him over on to his back. Jake also managed, as he did so, to strike a blow on Albie's face, which seemed to hurt Jake more than it did Albie. Jake had never been one for fighting and he was rapidly finding out that he was not very good at it.

Albie hit back but from his lying position he had been unable to get much purchase and the fist that landed on Jake's jaw had little power to it. Jake resorted to more basic tactics by slamming his forehead on to Albie's nose. There was a crunch and blood started to flow immediately. Albie, however, seemed to gain strength from this and he brought his knee up and pushed Jake away.

Albie stood up and made his way towards the knife once more. Jake caught him again and spun him round. Jake swung another punch, which missed and in doing so made himself an easier target for what was to come. Albie landed two punches, both of which arrived with venom and almost made Jake lose consciousness as he fell to the floor.

Jake could only watch as Albie picked the knife up and started walking back towards him. Jake tried to move but his body just would not respond to what his brain was telling it. His jaw ached and his head felt fuzzy. Albie now stood over him.

"I wasn't doing any of this for me, you know," Albie said. "I was doing it all for God and his son, Jesus Christ, who died to save us all. You only had to close the theatre and God would have been happy. You only had to show some respect, nothing more."

"It's what's called progress, Albie," Jake said as he again tried to move.

"Insulting the name of the Lord can never be progress," Albie then said and as he did so the door of the church burst open and Sergeant Mathieson and three police officers came rushing in.

"Don't do anything silly," Mathieson shouted as he started to walk up the aisle.

"Listen to him," Jake added in softer tones.

Albie looked down at Jake and then up at the officers walking towards him. He paused for a moment and then started walking towards Mathieson, holding out his hands as he did so to show that he was not intent on using the knife. His actions caused Mathieson and the other police officers to relax their guard momentarily.

That was all Albie needed. Suddenly he pushed in to Mathieson and knocked him aside. He rushed the other officers and once again succeeded through the element of surprise, in forcing his way through. One of the officers nearly stopped Albie's progress, but another swinging punch sent him reeling and Albie burst through the door and out in to the night air.

Mathieson got to his feet first, just as Jake was making his way, rather gingerly, down the aisle.

"Get after him, Sergeant!" Jake called out and Mathieson turned and headed out the door.

Mathieson raced down the steps of the church and looked to his left and then his right. He was just in time to see Albie disappear round the corner at the end of the library building. With a deep breath Mathieson gave chase.

Albie did not find running easy and he was nowhere near as fit as Mathieson. Albie's war wound had left him with a slight limp, which became even more pronounced when he tried to run, resulting in him almost dragging his leg rather than placing any weight upon it.

The gap between them quickly began to reduce. Albie continually looked back and to his horror he could see the police officer getting closer. He turned away again and tried to inject more speed in to his hobbling version of running. Not only was there little difference in his speed but his breathing was starting to get heavier and he knew that he would not be able to keep this up for much longer.

Mathieson, on the other hand, always felt that he could catch Albie. He was younger and fitter and did not have a Boer bullet wound in his leg. He could see that the gap was reducing to such a level that if he stretched out his arms he could almost catch his man.

Albie spun around and faced Mathieson once again. He still held the knife in his hand and Mathieson held back a little so as not to put himself in any further danger. Albie waved the knife around in a threatening manner and a young couple, out taking the air, were horrified to see what was happening when they came upon the scene.

"Put the knife down, there's nowhere for you to go now," Mathieson said, whilst waving to the young couple to be on their way.

Albie looked beyond Sergeant Mathieson and could see other police officers rapidly heading in his direction. He looked around, trying to find another escape route, but there wasn't one. He knew that he could turn and continue running but then he also knew that the police officers would soon catch up with him again.

Albie was gripped by a fit of panic. He had nowhere to go and yet he did not want to be caught either. He could feel the pressure mount in his head as he desperately sought a solution to his predicament. He was still trying to come up with a decent escape route when suddenly everything went black.

Mathieson watched helplessly as Albie Ogston suddenly crumpled to the ground, his head cracking off the pavement as he landed. Albie's skull split at once and blood poured on to the ground around him. Mathieson rushed forward to offer some kind of medical assistance.

Another of the police officers then arrived on the scene and Mathieson told him to go and find a doctor. Mathieson was pretty sure there was one in Golden Square and it was to there that he directed the Constable. He was still trying to comfort Albie when Jake finally caught up with the action.

"How is he?" Jake asked as he knelt down beside Mathieson.

"Not good, sir," the Sergeant replied. "He just passed out on me."

"He was prone to blackouts," Jake added as he looked down on Albie's ashen face.

A moment or two passed before Albie's eyes flickered open. "I hope the Lord has prepared a room for me," he said in little more than a whisper. He then let out one last long breath and died.

Jake looked up at one of the police officers. "Get something with which to cover the body," he said.

The Constable waved down a horse and cart and managed to find a blanket, which would normally have kept the horse warm, suitable for covering Albie's body. The other Constable then began moving a small crowd, which had gathered almost from nowhere, back from where Jake and Mathieson were attending to the dead body.

"Are you okay now, sir?" Mathieson then said to Jake.

"I'm fine, Sergeant. Why did you take so long to join me in the church?"

"I didn't see you go in there, sir," Mathieson replied, "I was still in the carriage with Mrs Wallace."

It had been Jake's rather simple plan to have Robert Wallace and Margaret safely in the theatre long before anyone else arrived. Dora Wallace had agreed to travel with Mathieson so that she could get out of the carriage first and in doing so give Albie Ogston the impression that her husband was to follow.

As it turned out Albie had never been anywhere near to Robert Wallace. Jake now knew that Albie never really had a plan. God had obviously not told him everything. At least now the poor man might be closer to God; a place which Jake thought he deserved even if his devotion had become slightly warped in the last few months of his life.

"Arrange for the body to be taken to the mortuary and then find this seat," Jake then said to Mathieson and as he did so he produced a ticket from his pocket.

Mathieson looked down at the ticket for opening night and a smile spread across his face.

"I never expected this, sir."

"I know you didn't, Sergeant, but seeing as you got all dressed up we thought it only right that you should at least attend the event. I'll see you as soon as you can get inside the theatre."

Jake made his way back to the theatre where there seemed to be an endless procession of people making their way towards their seats. It was just short of half passed seven and the production was about to begin.

Waiting in the Dress Circle bar was Margaret, along with Robert and Dora Wallace. They all seemed delighted to see Jake, although it was obvious by his dusty clothing and marked face that all had not gone well for him over the last few moments.

"Are you okay?" Margaret asked Jake, with some concern on her face.

"I am absolutely perfect," Jake replied, accepting Margaret's kiss of concern, "and looking forward to the evening's entertainment."

"Did you get him?" Robert Wallace then asked.

"Suffice to say that he is now out of harm's way," Jake replied. "Now, we'd better get to our seats."

They all then went to their seats in the Dress Circle.

There was no formal opening ceremony. As the time ticked around to half past seven the curtain rose and the show began. The pantomime was *Red Riding Hood* and it was to have the audience in their seats for a total of four hours. Mathieson had been able to join them after the first half an hour.

During the interval Robert, Dora, Jake, Margaret and Mathieson went to the bar and Wallace bought everyone a drink. They agreed that the first half of the show had been colourful and thoroughly entertaining, if not a trifle long perhaps.

"My goodness," Wallace announced after everyone had been given their drink," I thought that I could keep an audience in their seats for a long time, but this pantomime is set to surpass even myself."

They all laughed.

"It is good though," added Margaret.

"But we're only at the halfway point, Margaret," Wallace added. "That means another two hours before we can ever breathe fresh air again or see the birds flying in the sky."

"Oh Robert," said Dora, giving her husband a playful push.

As it turned out Robert Wallace was incorrect in his assessment that it would be a further two hours before they would get out of the theatre. He had not allowed for the fact that Mr Robert Arthur, owner of the theatre, would wish to stand up at the end of the show and make a speech.

The second half of the show did have its highlight, at least in the opinion of Jake and Margaret. As part of the pantomime there was a conjurer whose main trick was to get a watch from a member of the audience, place it in a bag and have that bag hoisted to the ceiling of the building. He would then clap his hands and the bag would be returned to the stage quite empty. There would be a brief moment when the member of the audience would be left to think that their watch had gone forever before the conjuror would eventually produce the watch from his pocket.

However, on the opening night there had been no watch forthcoming from the audience so a member of the orchestra finally saw fit to fill the gap by offering his gold watch. The watch was duly bagged and the bag disappeared. The conjuror then, for reasons never explained, became side-tracked and did not complete the trick.

The show continued and a few moments later, during a quieter passage, the audience could hear the man in the orchestra asking for his watch back. At first the man was ignored but he became more and more insistent that his watch be returned. Mr Nelson, the theatre manager, even went to the front and tried to remonstrate with the man but it now became quite clear that member of the orchestra or not, he was slightly worse the wear for drink.

Mr Nelson felt he could do no more than have the man removed from his place in the orchestra. The audience were left to assume that the man got his watch back but of course they were never treated to the end of the trick.

It was after midnight when the audience finally began to leave the theatre. Robert Wallace thanked Jake one more time for all that he had done and then he and Dora climbed aboard their carriage and set off in to the dark. Sergeant Mathieson bade Jake and Margaret a very goodnight and then set off along Schoolhill.

Late though it was Jake and Margaret went across to Margaret's and had a cup of tea. They talked about the show and laughed at some of the moments that had been particularly funny. They both agreed that the show needed to be shortened for four hours was just a little too much.

They had also gone on to discuss what they do on Christmas Day and how much they were enjoying each other's company.

After the tea and before Jake felt he should leave, he and Margaret had kissed and talked some more about how their relationship was developing. Margaret had held Jake's hand and looked deep in to his eyes.

"I want our relationship to be more complete and I don't want to wait forever for that to happen," she had said.

"I'm glad that you want our relationship to perhaps move on to another level for there is something that I want to ask you Margaret," Jake then said.

And he asked his question.

==

==

HISTORICAL FOOTNOTE

James Bryce became the British Ambassador to the United States in February, 1907. The resulting by-election, in Aberdeen South, led to George Esslemont being elected. He was also a Liberal candidate.

MPs were first paid an annual salary in 1911. They were paid £400.

Aberdeen's politics were turned upside down by the effects of the First World War. In the 1918 election Aberdeen South returned a Coalition Conservative MP and Aberdeen North returned the first of what would be many Labour MPs. From 1918 to the present day there was to be only fourteen years in which Aberdeen North did not return a Labour MP.

It should be noted that the 1918 General Election, which was held in the December of that year, was the first in which all men were allowed to vote and it also allowed women, aged 30 and over, to vote for the first time.

==